Did You See Melody?

Did You See Melody?

Sophie Hannah

W F HOWES LTD

This large print edition published in 2017 by
W F Howes Ltd
Unit 5, St George's House, Rearsby Business Park,
Gaddesby Lane, Rearsby, Leicester LE7 4YH

1 3 5 7 9 10 8 6 4 2

First published in the United Kingdom in 2017
by Hodder & Stoughton

A CIP catalogue record for this book is available
from the British Library

ISBN 978 1 51008 987 7

Typeset by Palimpsest Book Production Limited,
Falkirk, Stirlingshire

Printed and bound by
T J International in the UK
Printforce Nederland b.v. in the Netherlands

For Lucy Hale, who has supported
and encouraged me from the very beginning

For the longest time, I thought my sister Emory was the lucky one. Sometimes I still feel that way. She died before they could kill her. No life at all is better than a life spent waiting to die.

The hardest thing is when the Kind Smiles promise I'll survive – not just another day or week, but until I'm an adult, maybe even until I'm old. If that's true . . . but it can't already be true if it hasn't happened yet. If it does in the future, I'll have to stop envying the sister I never met and start feeling guilty because I made it and she didn't.

I've got this far, but that means nothing. I can't allow myself to hope. Which I guess means I shouldn't believe the Kind Smiles.

Once the tiniest doubt creeps in, you start to wonder about everything.

When I'm alone, I whisper over and over, 'My name is Melody Chapa, my name is Melody Chapa.' It makes me feel worse – as if the girl trying to convince me must have a different name – though there's no one there but me.

PART I

9 OCTOBER 2017

If I could turn and run, I would. Run back home, however long it took. Six months, probably – and I'd need to be able to sprint across the Atlantic Ocean. My legs twitch with the urge to race back to Patrick, Jess and Olly and pretend none of this ever happened.

Not that anything has really happened yet. So far all I've done is fly and land.

I'm standing outside a café called Lola Coffee in the arrivals hall at Phoenix Sky Harbor airport in Arizona, waiting for the hire-car man. All around me are people in dark suits, brightly coloured T-shirts with underarm sweat stains, crumpled linen dresses, checked shorts with bulging pockets. I spot the man who had the seat across the aisle from me on the second of my two flights. He snored most of the way from Chicago, where I changed planes, to Phoenix, oblivious to the flight attendants tactfully lifting his belly to check his seatbelt was fastened.

One by one, the other passengers stride confidently out of the airport, or else they linger to hug loved ones who have come to meet them. They all sound relieved and happy as they say, 'Let's go home' in a dozen different ways.

No one's saying it to me. As an experiment, I whisper the words to myself. They sound like a threat.

Breathe. Stop thinking crazy thoughts. Be patient. Count away the panic. 1, 2, 3, 4 . . .

The hire-car man is thirty-five minutes late. I try to persuade myself this might be a good thing. It means I'm off the hook. I can decide not to wait any longer and I won't be letting him down. If I want to book myself on the next flight back to Heathrow, I'm in the perfect place. There's nothing stopping me apart from a decision I made.

The right decision. Just because it's hard doesn't make it wrong.

Where the hell is he? He promised he'd be here. I've paid for the car already. It's 10.05 p.m. Arizona time and just gone six in the morning in England. I've missed a night's sleep, which probably explains why I can feel myself swaying from side to side in my attempt to stand still. Driving on the wrong side of the road for the first time in my life is going to be fun. Assuming I ever get something to drive.

I don't want to think that I've ruined everything before I've got anywhere or achieved anything, but it's a conclusion I have to keep batting away as I wait and wait and still no one appears. I should have hired a car the way most people do, from one of the companies at Phoenix airport, but they were all so expensive and I'd spent bone-chilling amounts of money on this, whatever it is I'm doing, already. So I opted instead for the suspiciously good-value internet advert with the cheesy typeface: 'The best cars, dirt cheap, delivered to wherever you are!'

I pull my phone out of my bag and stare at it. Should I switch it out of flight-safe mode so that I can text the hire-car man?

No. Out of the question. I wouldn't have the will-power to ignore all the texts from Patrick and Jess, Jess especially. She and I are the proficient communicators of the family. She, more than Patrick, would know how to craft a message that would leave me no choice but to reply. Olly won't have sent a text. He'll assume there's nothing he can do, that Patrick and Jess will be saying all that needs to be said.

For some reason it's the thought of Olly doing nothing that fills my eyes with tears. *Mum's gone. Oh, well. She might come back. I'll wait and see, I suppose.*

I throw my phone back in my bag, hands shaking.

Maybe I should go for a walk to calm myself down. There's a corridor of shops branching off from the main arrivals hall. I can see a bookshop called Hudson and something called Canyon News. I can't imagine summoning the concentration required to read but I might feel differently in a few days, once I've had time to adjust to the idea that I've done the one thing, the only thing, that I would never do.

I should buy a book. Definitely. To read by the pool at the resort. Pools plural – there are several, according to the website. Also, if I want the hire-car man to turn up, I ought to walk away. As soon I move from this spot, he will appear – isn't that the way life works? I'll walk four paces and turn round and there he'll be, holding up a sign with my name on it.

Either that or there are no secret rules governing our interactions with other people, and we'll miss each other. He'll leave and I'll end up taking a cab to the resort, but only after I've wasted another hour waiting for a man who's been and gone.

I sigh and look at my phone again. Surely I could go out of flight mode for the twenty seconds it would take to ring him? If I did that, and didn't allow myself to look at how many texts were waiting for me . . .

Impossible. Once I knew for certain that I had messages, I'd have to read them.

With my thumb, I press the 'Pictures' icon on my phone's screen and scroll through my photos until I find my favourite one of Jess and Olly. They're sitting on the old tractor in the garden of the Greyhound pub, looking so perfectly like themselves. Olly's mouth is open and his arms are in the air, mid-gesture. He's trying to explain to me how best to hit-marker a trick shot. As I took the photo, I said, 'How to what a *what*?'

Jess is sitting in front of Olly: straight-backed, chin tilted upwards. She's grinning at my bewilderment from her position of superiority, as someone who speaks fluent Olly. Seconds after I took the photo, he sighed and slid off the tractor with a resigned, 'Never mind, Mum. You wouldn't understand.' Jess said, 'Of course she wouldn't. Not everyone is a member of the sniping community. In a *game*, Mum – not in real life,' she added, seeing my worried expression. 'Olly's not really a sniper.'

I press my eyes shut. No way for any tears to squeeze out, however hard they try.

Get a grip, Cara.

My own stupid fault for looking at family photos. Jess and Olly will be fine at home with Patrick. Am I seriously going to spend the next fortnight mooning over their pictures as if I'm not going to see them for years? It's only two weeks. Two short insignificant weeks. I'll be back home before we all know it.

I should put my phone away and not think about it again. Instead, I swipe right with my finger until I'm staring – for the three-hundredth time since I set off – at the last photo I took before leaving home. It's an aerial view of the note I left on the kitchen table.

My family won't know that the version they read was my fourth attempt. I tried to explain too much the first three times. In the end, hating everything I'd written, I decided to keep it short and simple. 'Dear Patrick, Jess and Olly, I've gone away for a while. I didn't tell you before I left because I was scared you'd try and stop me. I need time alone to sort a few things out in my head. Please don't be angry. I'll be back on Tuesday, 24 October. I love you all very much. Cara/Mum xxx'

It's comforting to see it again in black and white: the date I'll be home. That's why I keep looking, I think. Thank goodness I took this photo before I set out for Heathrow. I nearly didn't bother. Without concrete evidence in the form of a picture, I would by now have convinced myself I'd written something terrible that I didn't mean and could never take back. *Dear Patrick, Jess and Olly, You have finally succeeded in driving me away. It will serve you right if you never see me again . . .*

Behind me, I hear a chair leg scrape against a hard surface. I turn and watch a man lower himself into a seat at one of the café's tables. He's young – early to mid-twenties – with dark hair and a wispy beard, baggy terracotta-coloured jeans with turn-ups, sandals with running-shoe soles, and a grey T-shirt that says 'Rock the Hole' next to a picture of a hole on a golf course with a flag protruding from it. On the table in front of him there's a sign with my name on it, though he's spelled my surname wrong: Burroughs instead of Burrows. He's staring straight ahead, avoiding eye contact with me as if the two of us are nothing to do with each other.

For a second, I wonder why he hasn't worked out that the only other person anywhere near Lola

10

Coffee must be the woman he's supposed to be meeting there. Then I get it: his brief doesn't include working anything out. All he's paid to do is turn up at the airport with the car I've hired and a sign with something resembling my name on it. Both of those things he's done; why should he try harder?

Patrick, my husband – whose official title should be 'Patron Saint of the Can't Be Arsed to Do Any More Than the Bare Minimum' – would defend Mr Rock the Hole for sure, using a version of his famous-in-our-family cutlery-divider defence. Shortly after we got married, I tactfully pointed out to him that he might in future return clean forks to the fork section of the cutlery drawer, knives to the knife section, spoons to the spoon area, and so on, instead of throwing them all in haphazardly and letting them land wherever. He sighed and said, 'Cara, I put away a *lot* of cutlery. Mostly things end up where they're supposed to, but if something falls into the wrong bit, I'm not going to *dig it out and move it to a different section.*' He said it as if doing this would be anyone's definition of insanity. Approximately twelve years later, his perfectionist daughter got sick of reaching into the cutlery drawer for a yoghurt spoon and pulling out a steak knife instead, and gave him a savaging he still hasn't forgotten. Ever since, our forks, knives and spoons have known their places.

I blink back new tears – no more thoughts of home allowed, not tonight – and introduce myself to Rock the Hole, who neither apologises for his lateness nor offers to help carry my luggage.

It's warm outside, verging on hot. I remember from the website that my hire car is supposed to have something called 'climate control', which I'm hoping means air conditioning. It must be the same thing. I know next to nothing about cars, apart from the absolute basics of how to drive them.

The air here smells nothing like the way it does at home. I wonder if this is a specific Arizona smell. Does New York smell different, and Chicago? I've never been to America before so I have no way of knowing.

The car is a Range Rover, black and glossy with three parallel silver stripes on each side. It looks and smells brand new. We sit in the front – me in the driver's seat and Rock the Hole next to me – to do the paperwork. His handwriting is a bit like Patrick's: incomplete circles for 'o's, 'a's and 'e's, like broken links in a chain. I wonder how surprised he'd be if I smiled knowingly and said, 'I can imagine what your cutlery drawer looks like.'

Having covered the basics of how the car works, he starts to describe, in a bored drawl, its unnecessary features: eight different colour options for the interior lighting; retractable sun-roof; memory buttons numbered M1 to M4, so that four driver-seat positions can be stored.

Hasn't he noticed I'm alone? The car might be ready and able to remember four people, but it'll have to make do with only one. It's a shame – Olly would love these lights that are orange one minute and bright green the next.

You can still go home. You can step out of the car, and . . .

'I need you to do me a favour,' I say to Rock before I have a chance to change my mind. Pulling my phone out of my bag, I hand it to him and say, 'Keep this for me. Give it back when I drop the car off in two weeks. I'll pay you an extra hundred dollars – fifty now, fifty when I get my phone back.'

'Okay.' He shrugs, not even a tiny bit curious.

Now that he's agreed, I'm not sure I want to do it. How many decisions made and immediately regretted can a woman be expected to stand by in one week?

Rock holds out his hand. I throw my phone at it harder than I need to. *Take that, doubts.*

It's the only way. If I have it with me, I'll crack in a few hours, or a few days, and read all the texts that are waiting for me. I won't be strong enough to resist the pleas for me to come home. 'Thank you,' I mumble.

'Fifty bucks, lady.' Rock holds out his hand again.

I give him the money, wishing I'd offered an extra ten dollars for the right to say, 'You will look after it properly, won't you?' I didn't, so I keep my mouth shut. I'm going to have to trust him, or stop caring about what happens to my phone – one or the other.

13

Finally he says, 'Okay, you're all done.' He gets out of the car and slams the passenger door shut without saying goodbye.

I've never felt more alone in my life. Or more awake. A fizzing mix of fear and excitement, combined with the underlying exhaustion, makes me feel dizzy and nauseous. I open my bag, pull out the driving directions I printed last night and unfold them. 'Ready to go,' I say to nobody.

This is truly happening. I, Cara Burrows from Hertford, England, am on my way to the five-star Swallowtail Resort and Spa in the foothills of Camelback Mountain, Arizona. Without my family's knowledge or permission. To most people, I would look like a woman setting off on the holiday of a lifetime, not one escaping from an unbearable situation.

If Patrick and the children are angry when I next see them, if they scream and shout at me, I'll survive. So will they.

That's why I'm here. It's the only reason. I need us to survive. All of us.

It's ten past midnight by the time I arrive at the resort. The SatNav on my hire car is broken, it turns out – and I had to pull over twice to memorise the next stage of my directions. At one point, I took a wrong turn, thinking, 'This is probably going to be wrong. I bet it's wrong.' It was twenty minutes before I could safely turn round and get back on track, and then I promptly got lost again and ended up driving God knows where for another forty minutes. A journey that should have taken me half an hour took nearly two hours.

Now, finally, I'm here, and I hardly dare breathe. I can no longer tell myself I'm on my way somewhere. This is it. I've arrived. Whatever's supposed to happen at the Swallowtail Resort and Spa – the magic, indefinable thing that will make all my problems go away – could and should and, please God, *will* start happening now.

Soon. Not right now as in immediately this second. Setting unrealistic goals is only going to make me feel worse, and I'm pretty sure no life-changing revelation has ever happened in a car park.

I pull into a space, throw open the door, twist my body round so that my legs are outside the car, and look out at the night. Now that I'm here and the adrenaline rush of handling a strange car on the wrong side of the road in an unknown country has drained away, the tiredness I managed to keep at bay while driving takes hold of me, weighing me down, making patches of my skin ache.

The night sparkles with so many stars it looks staged, like a set in a theatre. I never see any at home. Never have time to look. I stare at the dark outline of what I assume is Camelback Mountain. 'I can't see you yet, but I know you're beautiful,' I whisper, and start to cry.

Cut it out right now, Cara. Get to your room, and

15

then you can do it all: cry, get something to eat, have a relaxing bath, sleep, wish you hadn't given your phone to a rude stranger . . .

Getting to my room might be more of a challenge than I anticipated. The scale of the car park suggests the Swallowtail resort might be the size of a small town. It could be bigger than Hertford, come to think of it. As well as a sign saying 'Main Hotel Building/Reception', I've already seen several suggesting there are lots of different residential areas here: 'Copper Star Villas', 'Monarch Suites', 'Swallowtail Village', 'The Residence', 'Camelback Casitas'.

The sign I saw for reception was quite a way back. I close my eyes, thinking of the effort it will take to wheel my suitcases back to that point – and God alone knows how long a walk it will be from there to my room. I'm not sure I can do it – not tonight at least. I could fall asleep here quite happily, with the car door open to the warm night. Maybe one of the M1 to M4 driver-seat-position buttons contains the memory of how to stretch out flat, like a bed.

The sound of an engine makes me sit up straight. Is it another guest arriving? The noise moves nearer, then stops. No, it wasn't a car. The wrong pitch, and not loud enough. A lawnmower, maybe – one of those big ones you sit on and drive around if you've got a big field to trim. But at this time of night?

I hear footsteps coming closer. A man's voice says, 'Ma'am? I'll bet you're the lady I've been waiting for: Mrs Cara Burrows from Hertford, England. Last guest of the night. Am I right?'

The sound of his voice makes me feel so much better. It's the opposite of Rock the Hole's indifferent drone. I think it might be the most reassuring voice I've ever heard. Disembodied, in the dark, it makes me smile before I've seen the face it's attached to.

'Yes, I'm Cara Burrows. Sorry, I'm later than I said I'd be.'

'No need whatsoever to apologise, ma'am. I'm just real glad you're here now. Welcome to Arizona, and to the Swallowtail Resort and Spa. You're gonna have a beautiful stay with us, I can promise you that. All our guests do!'

Of course they do. When you're paying that much . . . I push away the thought I've managed to avoid so far: how much all this is going to cost. A third of the savings it's taken Patrick and me fifteen years to build up. Oh, God. It's worse when I think of it like this, worse than the specific sum of money. So irresponsible: a whole third.

I could have chosen somewhere less luxurious to stay and at least five times cheaper, could have booked a week instead of a fortnight. Could have, should have . . .

I didn't, though. This is what I did. This was my choice. The best place I could find, money no object.

I wouldn't have thought it was possible to feel proud and ashamed at the same time, but it is.

17

Guilt and defiant pride have been battling it out inside me since I made the booking.

I economised around the edges, not only by choosing a dodgy-looking car-hire firm, but also on the flights – one change in both directions, saving nearly seven hundred pounds – and I regretted it. If I'd had any self-respect I'd have spared myself the three pointless hours at Chicago's O'Hare airport.

I hear a click. Torchlight turns the night yellow. The man with the best voice in the world leans down and smiles at me. He's fifty-odd, bald, and wearing a blazer with a 'Swallowtail Resort and Spa' badge on it, and five gold stars. Beneath this is another badge that says, 'Diggy'. The skin of his face is craggy-looking in places and pouchy in others, as if it was designed to include distinct hard and soft zones.

'Pleasure to meet you, ma'am. I'm Diggy – that's what everyone calls me. Now, much as I'd be happy to show you round tonight, it's pretty dark, and I'm guessing you're tired and maybe you'd rather leave it till tomorrow? So why don't we get you to reception? I've got a club car here – drive you right there. No need to walk at Swallowtail if you'd rather get a ride! Tomorrow, once you're rested, give the concierge's desk a call, tell them you're ready for Diggy's tour. I'll come pick you up from wherever you're staying, and show you everything you need to see. How does that sound? The Diggy-mobile will be at your service!'

'Brilliant. Thank you.'

I watch, amazed, as he picks up my luggage as if it's weightless and slings it into the back of a sort of golf buggy. It has silver wheels, white leather seats, open sides, and a kind of cream canvas awning on the top. I climb aboard. Diggy switches off his torch and leaps into the driver's seat, saying, 'All aboard the Diggy-mobile!'

I haven't got a watch or my phone so I don't know how long it takes us to trundle along to reception, but it's between five and ten minutes – out of the car park and along a series of winding roads, with little golden-white globes of light behind cobbled borders on both sides to point the way in the dark. We pass low houses – some facing us straight on, some turned to the side – with curved edges, terraces, balconies, neat front gardens behind low walls. I catch a glimpse of moonlight reflected in water, lean out of the club car and see a small square swimming pool behind one of the villas. All kinds of shrubbery sprouts haphazardly at the side of each curvy street. I wasn't expecting it; I've always thought of Arizona as dry and desert-like. As we pass a cluster of tennis courts on the right, a rotating sprayer shoots a refreshing mist into the club car from the left: a haze of water dust that lands on my face. Sprinklers: that's what makes all this lush greenery possible.

There are cacti too, lots of them – some that look like eruptions of spikes, in large pots; others, twice my height or more, protruding from flat gravelled-over areas, as if they've grown out of the stone. These tall ones stand in clusters. Some have arms that look raised, as if they're waving. Diggy points this out to me at the very moment that I'm thinking it. 'They look like they're saying hello and welcome, don't they? You know how long it takes one of those arms to start growing? Seventy to a hundred years. Seventy minimum.'

We pass a fountain and some wide steps, a row of high palm trees with fairy lights wound around their trunks all the way to the top, glowing pale pink and pale blue. Lower down, I can see the corner of an illuminated rectangle of vivid turquoise that must be one of the resort pools. A few metres further on, when I turn and look the other way, I see two tall cast-iron lamp-posts topped by large shallow bowls that have been set alight. Actual fire is rising from them: orange flames rising to a point, making a glowing triangle on each side of . . . what? It looks like some sort of entrance.

'Wow,' I murmur.

'Yeah, that's our maze,' says Diggy. 'Make sure to get lost in it while you're here – it's one of Swallowtail's most popular features. You only get the flames at night, though. Which doesn't make it any easier to find your way out than in the daytime, I gotta warn you.'

Eventually the club car stops outside a building that's much bigger than any of the individual houses we've passed. Its façade is a half-circle, with two long arm-like wings branching out from it.

20

'Here we are, ma'am,' says Diggy. 'I'll introduce you to Riyonna. She'll take real good care of you.'

He strolls towards the building with my cases. Watching him, it dawns on me that I need to walk too. My limbs have been asleep and soon start to ache from the shock of having to move again after bobbing along in the club car. I wish the resort had the indoor equivalent, taking guests all the way to their rooms.

I follow Diggy into a spacious lobby area that's all red marble with thin white and black veins in it. I might see it differently in the morning, but tonight it makes me think of the inside of a body. There are tall pot plants positioned in every corner – more like little trees – with rubbery dark green leaves and sturdy brown trunks. They look too alert for the way I feel.

Behind the wooden reception desk there's a wide-shouldered black woman, about my age, with a big smile and the kind of braids that I'm pretty sure are called 'cornrow'. Like Diggy, she has the Swallowtail badge on her jacket, and one that says, 'Riyonna Briggs'. She seems genuinely delighted to see me, and I hope she doesn't say anything too kind or solicitous. I'd burst into tears if she did.

I smile weakly as I hand over my passport and credit card. Each movement is difficult; every impression a blur. I knock something on the desk with my elbow, and it hurts. Looking down, I see it's a tiny bronze Buddha statue, sitting cross-legged beside some kind of weird, messy plant. Is it a cactus? It doesn't look hard-edged or prickly enough; it looks as if someone's cooked a load of green beans and then tipped them haphazardly into a yellow ceramic pot.

The Buddha, facing straight ahead as if determined to ignore the weird bean-cactus, has a pile of ivory-coloured Swallowtail resort business cards balanced on the upturned palms of his hands as if to say, 'Spend your money here and all the wisdom will be yours.' It's clever marketing, I suppose, but it makes me shudder. Or perhaps it's the exhaustion that's doing that.

Riyonna's eyes are full of curiosity, and for a moment I'm afraid she's going to lean forward and say, 'So what's wrong with you? Life falling apart? Run away from home?'

How do most guests behave who arrive in the middle of the night? I can't imagine they're full of beans and eager to chat.

Luckily, Riyonna keeps it businesslike. I try to look as if I'm listening as she tells me about WiFi codes and breakfast times. I don't need to know. Sleep is the only thing I care about. *Tell me about sleep.*

Diggy takes his leave, after repeating his promise to show me around tomorrow.

No. The day after. Please. I can't promise to wake up in time for tomorrow.

Riyonna folds a piece of cardboard in half and inserts a plastic key card into the slit. I was wrong – she's not my age. More like ten years older: late forties. There are lines around her eyes that she's tried very hard to cover with make-up.

I nod automatically at everything she says, not really listening, and start slightly as she moves out from behind the reception desk, holding my room key in her hand. She's short – shorter than I imagined her to be, even in her high stiletto heels. Strange. Sitting down, she looked taller; it must have been because of her broad shoulders.

'I . . . you don't need to come with me. Really. Thanks,' I manage to say.

'Are you sure? Your room's right here in the main hotel building, so it's not far. We like to check guests are happy with their rooms.'

'I'll be fine. Thanks.' I hope I'm not being rude. I can't bear the thought of having to make polite conversation for a second longer. If she tags along in spite of my protests, I'm going to lie down on the red marble floor and cry.

She laughs and nods. 'I hear ya! No problem. You go get yourself some rest.' She hands me the key and I grab it. *Nearly there.*

I start to walk towards where the lifts ought to be – where I'd have put them if I'd designed the building.

'I'll have someone bring up your bags immediately,' Riyonna calls after me.

That's not soon enough. The last thing I want once I'm in my room is someone knocking at the door. I'd completely forgotten about my suitcases. 'No, it's okay,' I say. 'I'll take them up myself.'

'Absolutely fine,' says Riyonna. 'Whatever you want. Oh – elevators are that way.' She points in a direction that would not have occurred to me. Clearly Swallowtail's architect and I would never agree on anything.

The number on my paper key wallet begins with a '3', which I suppose means my room's on the third floor. As the lift doors slide closed, I groan with relief. *Nearly there now. So so close.* I feel numb, and therefore better. I'm too tired to think, worry, regret, miss my family.

I get out at level 3 and struggle to interpret the signs on the wall, though they can't be complicated – I'm just in the wrong condition to be staring at lots of numbers that begin with 3, and arrows pointing all over the place. It takes me five seconds longer than it should to work out that my room is right beside the lift: a sharp left turn around a corner and I'm there.

I touch the key card against the pad on the door and a green light flashes. I let myself in and wheel my cases into the room, swearing under my breath as I bang them against the door frame. It's dark, but I can see I'm in a rectangular space, about six feet by twelve, that widens out at the end. In the light that floods into the room from the corridor, I see what look like the bottom ends of two double beds.

My fingers scrabble for a light switch. Instead, they find a small box-like structure attached to the wall. I know from family holidays in Greek and

Spanish hotels that this is the slot where I need to insert my key card if I want the lights to work. I try to put it in and find I can't. Opening the door wider for more light, I see why: there's already a card in the slot. The person who had the room before me must have left it in, and whoever made up the room didn't notice. I pull out the card, drop it on the floor and replace it with mine. No lights come on.

The door next to the key-card slot has to be the bathroom, opposite the fitted wardrobes, minibar and safe. I open it and walk in, feeling a sudden urgent need to splash cold water on my face. The door to the third-floor corridor clunks shut, and it's suddenly pitch black in here. Fumbling again for a light switch, I find nothing on the smooth, cool bathroom walls.

Feels like more marble. Probably red with white and black veins.

I reach around to grope outside in the hallway – there must be a switch somewhere, surely – and find one eventually, lower than I expected it to be.

Light, at last. I was right: I'm in the bathroom.

Not right, says a voice in my head as my heart starts to pound. Something is wrong in here . . .

The room is full of somebody's possessions: a green and black one-piece swimming costume hanging from a hook on the wall – petite-woman-sized, or teenage girl maybe; a pair of men's swimming trunks draped over the door of the glass shower cubicle; lots of thin metal hair grips; two

25

toothbrushes; two deodorants; one of those old-fashioned rubber swimming caps in a pale pinky-beige colour; shaving foam, a packet of disposable razors.

Shit. Shit shit shit shit shit. Someone's here, in the room. They must be – asleep in the beds I saw. No one would leave this many of their possessions behind.

The key card that was in the slot when I walked in . . .

I hear a girl's voice say, 'I spilled Coke on Poggy. And Doodle Dandy.'

She sounds young and upset. And terrifyingly close.

Because she is.

Looks like I'm not the only one who's not at my best in the middle of the night. Riyonna the receptionist screwed up. This room's already occupied – by someone who, in less than twenty seconds, will find me in their bathroom.

What the hell do I do?

Stay calm, Cara. Think fast.

There's no chance of me escaping undetected, not now that someone's awake in there. All my luggage is in the hallway. No way I could get it all out quick enough.

The next voice I hear is a man's. 'Coke? What?' He sounds disorientated, as if he's been dragged from a deep sleep. 'You shouldn't be drinking Coke in the middle of the night, honey. You brushed your teeth already.'

'I wasn't drinking it.' The girl sounds upset. Unjustly accused. 'I knocked it over by accident. It was on the table, left over from dinner. I was going to the bathroom to see who's in there.'

'No one's in there.'

'Yes, they are. I heard someone moving around.'

Oh, shit. Here it comes. Why am I still standing here, silent and frozen, as if I might be able to wish myself elsewhere? I should have declared my presence at once, soon as I heard the girl speak.

The man says, 'The light's on in there. Did you switch it on?'

'No!' The girl sounds as if she's crying. 'There's someone in there, I know it.'

'Honey, there really isn't. Sssh. Stay where you are, okay? I'll go check it out.'

'But I spilled Coke on Poggy,' the girl whines. 'Look at him!'

'Poggy's gonna be fine. Listen to me: Poggy will clean up and look as good as new, I promise. The Coke'll wash out. And there's no one in our bathroom. It was probably water pipes you heard – but let me go have a look anyway, just so we're sure.'

I shut my eyes and wait. This is going to be unbearably awful. I'm stuck in a nightmare. Please let me wake up. What if he hits me?

'What the hell are these . . .?' His voice is so close. He must be right outside the bathroom door, staring at my two suitcases.

What's wrong with me? How can I let this carry on for a second longer? I have to say something now, before he pushes open the door and sees me. The worst thing I can do is look as if I'm trying to get away with it, hoping not to be found.

'The cases are mine. I'm . . . I'm in your bathroom,' I call out with my eyes squeezed tightly shut. My voice is unsteady and hoarse. 'I'm a woman, on my own, as freaked out as you are, I swear. This is a mistake, and I'll leave immediately. I've just got off a plane from England and driven through the night, I'm exhausted, and this isn't my fault. The receptionist sent me to the wrong room, so . . . please don't be angry with me. My name's Cara Burrows. I'm from Hertford in England and I'm completely harmless.'

When I open my eyes, a man and a girl are standing in the hall outside the bathroom, staring in at me, their mouths open. They look as shaken as I feel. Neither of them lunges at me with a raised fist or a weapon. That's something to be grateful for.

The man's big with a hairy chest, muscly arms and a bit of a belly hanging over the top of his white boxer shorts. Dark hair, bad haircut: ever so slightly too long at the sides and too short on top. I'm surprised by the girl, who looks about thirteen, maybe a bit older. She could easily be in Jess's year at school or the year above. From what I heard when I couldn't see her, I'd have guessed she was no older than seven or eight. What kind of thirteen-year-old cries because she's spilled some Coke?

She's wearing a long, pale green nightdress with white embroidery around the V-neck. Her face is a pale, thin, tear-streaked oval; her hair dark, long, straight, parted crookedly in the centre. With one hand she gently rubs the top of her head near her hairline. In the other she's clutching a pink knitted cuddly toy. I can see what might be a Coke stain: a brown-ish patch on one side. So this is Poggy. He's confusing to look at, but I can see how he got his name. He has the head of a dog attached to the body of a pig. Home-made, I decide – and not in a good way. Whoever knitted him probably kidded themselves that they were creating a pig in every particular, but there's no way that isn't the face and head of a worryingly pink Staffordshire bull terrier.

'You were given the key to *this room*?' The man sounds as if he's weighing up whether or not to believe me. '*Our* room?'

'Yes. How would I have got in, otherwise? I'm so, so sorry. Let me get my cases out of your room and I'll leave you in peace.'

I move towards the bathroom door. He steps forward to block me. 'Who did you say you were again?'

'Cara Burrows.' Wife, mother. Normal, non-threatening sane person.

'Mind showing me some ID?'

'ID? Um . . . no, I don't mind.'

I root around in my bag, pull out my passport and hand it to him. The girl has taken a step back, out into the hall. She's still rubbing that patch on her head. Did she bang it on her way out of bed? Or is it some kind of nervous tic.

'Okay, Cara Burrows. Can I take a look in your bag?'

'My bag? Why?' This is getting a bit ridiculous. And he pronounced my name wrong: *Carrah*. Didn't even try to say it the way he heard me say it.

'You turn up in my room in the middle of the night? I'm taking no chances.'

I hand him the bag. 'You're being paranoid. I've told you what happened: a mix-up at reception. If I was going to do anything scary, wouldn't I have done it by now? I just want to get the hell out of here, get a room that doesn't have anyone in it, and go to sleep.'

He turns and says to the girl, 'You go back to bed, honey. Get some rest. Everything's fine – there's nothing to worry about.'

She does as she's told without a word.

Why does he talk to her as if she's five years old? Because it's night-time and she was scared of the intruder, or does he talk to her the same way over breakfast? If I spoke to Jess like that, she'd say, 'Will I *hell* go back to bed!', list all the ways in which I was handling the stranger-in-the-bathroom situation badly, then proceed to deal with it far better herself.

I don't like this man. He's poking around in my bag as if we're at an airport and he's head of security. 'Where's your cell?' he asks.

'Pardon?'

'Your cell phone. Don't tell me you don't own one. Everyone has a phone.'

I shake my head. *Unbelievable.* 'Yes, I have a phone. I gave it to the guy from the car-hire firm and asked him – paid him a hundred dollars, actually – to look after it for me until I give the car back.'

'Why did you do that?'

Tears start to prickle at the back of my eyes. 'Because I didn't want to have it with me. Because I have messages waiting to ambush me the minute I turn it on, and I don't want to read them, and I knew I would if I had my phone within easy reach. And none of this is any of your business!'

The man hands me back my bag and holds up both his hands in a gesture of surrender. 'I'm sorry,' he says. 'Come on, though, right? You can't blame me for being careful in the circumstances.'

'Probably not,' I mutter, pushing past him to get to my luggage and the escape route.

Now that he's satisfied I'm not a secret agent intent on slitting his throat, he's all charm and compassion. 'Here, let me hold the door for you. Or – better idea – you get the door. I'll take your cases to the elevator.'

'No, thanks. I can manage.' In spite of my best efforts, a tear has escaped and is snaking its way down my face. I knock the door frame again – hard, twice – as I pull my cases out into the corridor.

The man looks alarmed. 'Hey, don't cry. No harm done, right?'

'Good night. Sorry again.'

'Listen, Cara . . .'

'What?' I didn't say he could call me by my first name. Can't he leave me alone? I'm out of his room. So are all my cases. All he has to do is shut the door, so why doesn't he?

'Are you sure you're okay? You don't seem it. Are you in some kind of trouble? I couldn't help seeing the ultrasound photo.' He nods at my handbag. 'If you need help . . .'

Shit. How could I have forgotten the photo? Now he knows something about me that even my closest friends don't know.

'I need sleep and to be left alone,' I tell him. 'That's all.'

'Tomorrow, get your cell phone back from the rental-car guy. Read those messages. It's better to know, right?'

Great. Unsolicited advice from a hairy-chested, half-naked stranger in a hotel corridor.

I stare at him in disbelief. 'Did you not hear me say *I need to be left alone*?'

He shrugs. 'All right, well . . . g'night.'

Hallelujah. Never in my life have I been so pleased to see a door close.

I take the lift down to the ground floor, marked 'L' for lobby. Riyonna's tilted her chair back and put her feet up on the desk. She leaps up when I appear, surprised to see me.

'There's someone in the room you gave me. Father and daughter.'

32

'Ex*cuse* me?' Her eyes widen. She leans forward.

'The room you sent me to – I'm afraid I left the key up there, but I've got . . .' I hand her the folded cardboard wallet with the room number written on it. 'It's someone else's room. It's occupied. Go up and look if you don't believe me. I walked in on a man and his daughter, who were fast asleep. I woke them up.'

Riyonna is already tapping frantically on her keyboard, her eyes darting around as if she's trying to look closely at every part of the screen at once. Her fingernails are long, carefully shaped, and painted a pale eau-de-nil colour. 'Oh, my goodness,' she murmurs after a few seconds. 'I am *so, so* sorry. I . . . that was . . . Oh, my word.' She hits herself on the forehead, hard, with the heel of her hand. 'What is *wrong* with me? I have *never* done that before. I can't believe I did it!'

'It doesn't matter.' I'm not interested in making her feel better. 'Can I have a key to a different room, please? I'm really tired. I just want to—'

'*Room?*' She sounds horrified. 'Oh, you're not just getting a *room* – not any more. Mrs Burrows, I feel so sick about putting you through this horrible experience. I really hope nothing . . . you know, *happened*?'

Is she asking me if the man in the already-occupied room sexually assaulted me? As if that's the only way my experience could have been awful? I glare at the little bronze Buddha, who needn't look quite so smug about everything. I consider flicking him hard with my finger, but manage to resist the urge.

Riyonna turns back to her computer screen. 'I'm upgrading you, for no extra charge and with our compliments, to one of our Camelback Casitas. I took a call ten minutes ago from a couple who are supposed to be here already and can't make it after all, sooo . . . you'll have your own private infinity pool on the terrace, and the very best views of Camelback Mountain that Swallowtail can offer. The Praying Monk too. Please accept this, and my heartfelt apologies, as compensation for the terrible shock you must have had.'

I should be grateful and excited, but Riyonna started to look tearful halfway through her little speech, and all I can think is that if she starts to cry, that will be my limit. I'll walk out of here and go and find the nearest cheap B&B – anywhere that can keep track of how many rooms they have and who's in them at any given time.

'Thank you,' I manage to say. 'That's very kind of you.' What did she mean about a praying monk? I don't want anyone in my casita apart from me, however devout they might be. She can't have meant an actual person.

It is kind of her, though. Very. She didn't have to upgrade me quite so substantially. When I wake up – late this afternoon, hopefully – I'm sure I'll be thrilled, and think Riyonna Briggs is the best receptionist ever.

'Not. At. All,' she says. 'I've put you in number 21.

Let me ring for a club car – you can't walk, it's too far.'

Please let the driver not be Diggy. Let it be someone blank-faced and bland who doesn't speak any English.

'I'd take you myself but I. Am. *Shaking*,' says Riyonna. 'I can't believe I did that! I am just. So. *Sorry*. I can't bear to think what might have *happened* to you!'

Her 'might have' grates on my worn nerves – as if what did happen wasn't bad enough. Is she afraid I'll report her to the resort manager? Do I look that mean? I can't assure her I have no intention of trying to get her fired without sounding as if I'm saying I could if I wanted to.

At this point, I'm not certain any of my thoughts make sense. Might as well pack in thinking for the night.

My club car driver is not quite as mute as I would like him to be, but he's considerably less talkative than Diggy and Riyonna. As we chug along the resort's winding side-lit roads, I'm braced for something to go wrong – a flat tyre, a hailstorm, an ambush – but mercifully, I arrive at my casita a few minutes later without any problems. It's spacious and cool and, even better, there's no one in it. I check every room and find no hidden families stashed anywhere.

I lock the door, put the chain across and pull off items of clothing as I stumble to the nearest bedroom. I have time to say, 'Thank God' to nobody in particular before I black out.

The Kind Smiles believe that Emory died so that I could live. Or something like that. I don't remember the words they used, but I remember thinking it sounded like Jesus, who died for all our sins.

Is that what Emory did for me? I said I didn't think it could be, because she didn't do it deliberately. She didn't choose death, and nobody chose it for her. She died for no reason, without knowing I would ever be born.

The Kind Smiles smiled and said yes, of course, I was right about that. They tried to explain that they'd meant it only as a kind of metaphor. But what they did truly believe was that sometimes, although no one causes a thing to happen with their actions, Fate has a plan, and maybe Fate was and still is determined that I should survive.

I'm supposed to find this idea comforting, but I don't. If Fate is so powerful, why did He make it so that only one of us could live? Couldn't He have shuffled things around so that Emory could have a chance too? It doesn't seem fair.

'Well, you must be the favorite child,' the Kind Smiles said. 'The universe's favorite.

Destiny's favorite.' It became their special name for me: Favorite Child. I've always hated it. It feels disloyal to Emory. She's my sister and always will be.

The Kind Smiles don't care about Emory, only about me, and they think I like it that way. They think it makes up for the way my parents felt about us. They tell me I'm special all the time, and beautiful and kind and good.

I don't want to be special, or anybody's favorite. I want to be an ordinary girl with a sister, part of an ordinary family.

10 OCTOBER 2017

I wake up too hot, with the sun blasting my face through the window. Didn't I shut the curtains last night? Obviously not.

What time is it? With my eyes still closed, I reach out and start patting the first surface I touch, to find my phone. It's a few seconds before I remember that I gave it to Rock the Hole. Damn. That was a stupid thing to do.

I sit up, blinking, and look around. Green leaves press against the window, all along its length to about halfway up. I'm in the biggest bed I've ever seen. Five people could lie in it side by side, no problem. There's a quilt that's slid off onto the floor – shiny red and gold hexagons stitched together to make a honeycomb pattern – and red and gold silk cushions in and on the bed, on the floor, on the high-backed armchair in the corner of the room.

To my left there's a tiled fireplace and, opposite the bed, a television set four times the size of mine at home, with shutters. They're open, and the screen has a blue box on it displaying a message for me: 'Welcome, Mrs Cara Burrows. The management and staff of Swallowtail Resort and Spa wish you a delightful stay. Please contact us if there is anything further we can do to ensure that your time with us is as special as you deserve.'

I ran away from home without telling my family. What I deserve is . . . hm, let's see . . . an alarming encounter with a boundary-violating man, a weird girl and a woolly dog-pig hybrid in the middle of the night.

The bottom right-hand corner of the TV shows the time: 13:10. I've slept for twelve hours, and feel like myself again, which may or may not be a good thing. No longer smothered by fatigue, my mind starts to race.

Giving up my phone was crazy – a serious mistake. What time is it in England? Eight hours later, so ten past nine in the evening. Patrick, Jess and Olly are about to spend their second night without me. How are they all feeling? What are they thinking and saying? I could know the answers to these questions if only I hadn't given my phone to a random stranger. I left a note so they wouldn't worry, but what if they're worried anyway? Really, seriously, desperately worried – like I would be if Patrick did what I've done.

Jess might never forgive me. Olly and Patrick don't remember every tiny slight the way she does. She hoards grievances. Her ex-best friend Nuala was cut off for watching the final episode of *Pretty Little Liars* without Jess after promising not to, and hasn't been seen at our house since.

What I've done is so much worse. I'm the world's worst mother. The man with the hairy chest could see it as clearly as he saw my suitcases in his hotel room. That's why he gave me unasked-for advice, because he could see it was an emergency, that I was about to ruin my whole life.

I take a deep breath. *Start again.*

If all I do in Arizona is make myself suffer, I'll have wasted a hell of a lot of money.

That's not going to happen. I won't let it. I've got these two weeks that I went to the trouble of stealing from my real life, and I'm damn well going to make them count. In a good way.

Yesterday I didn't feel strong enough to receive messages from my family. Today, after my twelve-hour sleep, I do. If they scream at me to come home immediately, I'll calmly explain that I'm not ready yet and that I'll be home on Tuesday, 24 October. It would be nice to talk to them, though, and reassure them as far as I can. It would make what I'm doing feel less extreme.

And I don't need to contact Rock the Hole and get my mobile. I can ring home from a landline. There's a phone on my bedside table.

It occurs to me that the resort must have a business centre. I'd rather email than ring, I think – the first time, at least, until I've been assured that a phone call won't lead to a barrage of accusations.

I'll make contact after breakfast. Or lunch, I suppose I should call it. Eating comes first. I'm so hungry, I feel hollow. There's a room-service menu standing up on the desk beneath the TV, drawing attention to itself, but I'd rather go out and see a bit of the resort. The website said there were five restaurants. I might as well try one.

I shower, dress, brush my teeth and pull what I need for today out of a suitcase: faded blue one-piece swimsuit, sunglasses, green kaftan, pink flip-flops. Unpacking can wait.

It seems wrong to go out without first exploring this amazing little house that I've got all to myself. Was the embarrassment and irritation of last night worth it, for this upgrade? Definitely not. Not today. Though I'm pretty sure if I ask myself the same question in two days' time, my answer will be different.

Last night I only checked for unwelcome roommates, and took in almost nothing else about the casita. I didn't notice the wicker basket in the shape of a flower, piled high with fruit and tied up in a pink satin bow, or the bottles of still and sparkling water like blown glass sculptures – curving cylinders that look as if they've been artfully twisted in the middle. I didn't see the little cream-coloured box, also tied with pink ribbon, with four chocolates nestling in a bed of pink satin inside.

This place is unbelievable.

The TV embedded in the lounge wall is even bigger than the one in my bedroom. There's a sliding door that takes up most of the back wall of the living and kitchen area. Through the glass, I catch a glimpse of a tantalising turquoise rectangle. My own pool. Jess can't know about this. Ever. If she found out I had my own swimming pool at a resort I went to without her . . . No, it doesn't bear thinking about.

I slide open the door and step out onto the tiled terrace. Outside is a surprise after the quiet of inside. The hum of birds and other creatures is strong and hypnotic. I could stay here listening to it all day if I wasn't starving. Maybe a quick dip in the pool . . . but no, I want to see my other swimming choices first. This is five-star-resort maths: dividing your days between the number of beautiful pools available. It's hard to see how any could be more stunning than this one. It's an infinity pool with two blue sides that look rough, as if they'd scratch your palms if you rubbed your hands over them, and two shiny black sides that look smoother than any surface I've seen before. *The rough with the smooth*: I can almost hear the architect thinking those words.

The infinity edge of the pool offers what has to be the best possible view of Camelback Mountain. I can't imagine a better one. I spot a section of rock jutting out near to the top that looks as if it could be a person slightly bent down, as if bowing to the mountain's summit, and say, 'Hah!' quietly as I realise this must be the Praying Monk that Riyonna mentioned. How can it not be?

I go back inside and close the door. At the centre

of a long coffee table of dark polished wood there's a leather folder, the front of which is embossed with Swallowtail's logo: a capital S composed entirely of tiny butterflies. I'm too hungry to look at everything properly now, but I pull out a couple of information sheets, fold them and put them in my bag. I can read them over lunch.

The casita's second bedroom is almost identical to the one I slept in last night, except the colour scheme is blue and silver, not red and gold. The effect is less dazzling, more calming. I sit down on the edge of the bed. A corner of the little terrace pool is visible through the window, which probably explains the choice of blue for the décor in here.

I could divide my nights between the two rooms – more resort maths – but even as I have the idea, I know I won't do it. I already think of the red and gold room as mine. Patrick, if I told him this, would say this is my whole problem – that I grow attached to things too quickly.

I don't like the idea of this beautiful blue and silver bedroom going to waste for two weeks, so I make a decision: this is where I'll do my thinking. Every day I'll spend at least an hour in here, sitting on this bed, or maybe lying on it, actively focusing on my situation and working out what I want to do about it. The rest of the time – when I'm out and about in the resort or when I'm in my red and gold bedroom – I won't feel obliged to think about my predicament at all.

Having made this resolution, I feel happier and

lighter. I go and get my handbag from the lounge area, open it, pull out my scan photo and take it back to the blue room. My twelve-weeks-pregnant photos of Jess and Olly were grainy and hard to decipher, but this one is much clearer. If I had to guess, I'd say this one's a boy, and – though no one who hasn't seen the photo would believe it – he looks as if he's raising one eyebrow.

I know that's impossible. He's the size of a passion fruit, and months away from having eyebrows. Or is twelve weeks a small lemon? I can't remember. Only women who are pregnant for the first time obsess about which fruit most closely resembles their growing child at each gestational stage.

I hold the photo in both hands for a few seconds, then put it down on the bed.

My third baby. I am in Arizona, on holiday with my third child. The idea makes me smile.

That's enough blue-room thinking for now. I pick up the scan photo and return to the lounge, where I notice straight away that something is different. There it is: today's mail – a white square on the floor by the casita's main door. It definitely wasn't there before. I feel a spurt of anxiety in case it's a letter explaining that I can't stay here – Riyonna wasn't authorised to be so generous on the resort's behalf – or, even worse, a note from Hairy Chest Man, who has somehow found out where I ended up.

Thankfully it's neither. It's a printed note on a

square card that has Swallowtail's embossed logo in the top left corner: 'If you would like fresh orange juice delivered to your casita each morning, please press the button by the side of the door so that the light comes on. No need to wake up early! We will leave your juice in a cool-box outside your door. Thank you!'

What button? I look and see that there are three. One has a picture of a maid holding a vacuum cleaner, and another has the same picture with a big red line through it. The third has a picture of a glass with a straw in it. I press it, and it lights up with an orange glow.

Wow.

I put the scan picture back in the safe pocket of my bag, zip it up, check I've zipped it securely, and head out into the hot afternoon.

Swallowtail's main restaurant is called Glorita's and has as many tables outside as in. I've picked one on the terrace that has an amazing view of Camelback Mountain. A large white parasol protects me from the glare of the sun. I'm about to start looking through the options when a black-haired young man with flawless olive skin appears by my side. 'Good afternoon, ma'am. I'm Felipe, and I'm going to be taking care of you today.' He smiles and holds out his hand. I have no choice but to tell him my name, though I wish I didn't have to. Lovely though he seems, I only want him to bring me some food, not become a lifelong friend.

Ugh, I know what this is. It's my Englishness. It's going to embarrass me for as long as I'm in Arizona. At home I'm considered normal – no one in Hertfordshire wants to get pally with the person who delivers their lunch – but the minute I set foot in a friendly country like America, I'm uptight and stand-offish.

To compensate for my cultural deficiency, I smile at Felipe till my jaw aches and tell him I'm nearly thirteen weeks pregnant. It's his fault for asking if there's anything I don't eat. 'Oh, how *adorable*,' he says. He waves at my stomach. 'Hello, Cara's baby! Welcome to Arizona!'

Tears prick the backs of my eyes. The idea that, after me, the person happiest about my pregnancy is a complete stranger who can't really care either way – who is nice by default, because it's his job – makes me so angry, I want to yank the red cloth off my table and send all the cutlery flying.

Thank goodness for sunglasses. Maybe the guests at all the other tables are also crying behind their dark lenses.

Felipe has views about what I ought to eat and drink, and he sounds as if he knows what he's talking about. On his advice, I order Swallowtail's signature blueberry and oat smoothie, and a casserole of butternut squash, chorizo and sweet creamed 'grits', whatever they might be.

While I wait for both to arrive, I look at what I brought with me from the folder in my casita. The two sheets of paper I picked out at random turn out to be a map of the resort and a list of activities available. There's enough here to keep anyone busy for three months at least: guided hikes, canyon jeep tours, an 'Art for Beginners' intensive two-week course, tennis lessons, guided meditation, stargazing, vinyasa yoga, Native American flute workshops, a 'Vortexes and the Sacred' seminar, an Ayurvedic medicine course . . .

The list goes on, in tiny print, filling up both sides of the page. There's a new-age theme to a lot of the options. I'm pretty sure, now I come to think of it, that I read something on the website about Arizona, and Swallowtail in particular, being some kind of spiritual . . . hub. Or something that meant hub – that's not the word they used. Normally any whiff of that sort of thing would have put me off. Instead, I found myself thinking that maybe this was somewhere that could lift the spirits – even of those of us who wince at the word 'sacred' and want nothing to do with vortexes.

At a table on the other side of the terrace, a blonde middle-aged woman wearing a white lacy kaftan, black shorts and high-heeled black sandals says to her companion, 'The best choice – *absolutely* the best, always – is a gay man.' The teenage girl she's with hisses, 'Ssssh! Can you not *shut up*? What is *wrong* with you?'

Must be a mother and daughter. American. I smile as the mother shakes out her long, loose, platinum blonde hair and says in an even louder voice, 'I could shut up if I wanted to. I don't want to.'

Hah. Take that, teenage tyrant.

I wonder why the girl isn't at school. Maybe she's eighteen or older, and just young-looking for her age.

Or the opposite. Maybe she's an ancient-looking two years old, and cries when she spills fizzy drinks on her cuddly toys . . .

Were they father and daughter, the man and girl in the hotel room? I assumed so, but I didn't hear her call him 'Dad'.

Felipe's food and drink recommendations are not entirely successful. The smoothie is the most delicious thing I've ever tasted, but I don't much like the sweet creamed grits. Luckily, I'm hungry enough not to care.

Felipe looks crushed when I reject his next piece of advice, which is to order the Signature Chocolate Trio. It's apparently a life-changing dessert, and Felipe tries to suggest that my baby might benefit from having it even if I wouldn't, but I stand firm, promising to have it after dinner one night instead. Eventually he concedes defeat and brings me the bill to sign.

I'm desperate to see the swimming pool, but as soon as I see it, I'll want to leap in, and I should probably digest my lunch first. While I do, I can tackle the least fun item on today's agenda: sending a message home.

The idea makes me swallow hard. A message means a reply.

Coward.

What if I've done something irreversible and lost my family forever? I thought this as I booked my plane tickets and made my reservation at Swallowtail, and the voice in my head insisted, *You have no choice. You have to get away from them.*

Having done what I've done, I have no right to miss Patrick, Jess and Olly, and no right to feel guilty – that's just a way of kidding myself that I'm a better person than I am. And I have a duty to make contact now, whether I want to or not.

I leave Glorita's and follow a sign to reception. Nothing looks familiar. I pass a fenced-off yard that's clearly the resort's club car depot. Peering through the slats of a white-painted fence that's meant to block the area from the guests' view, I see a group of men and hear them talking and laughing: the drivers, waiting to be summoned to transport those who would rather not walk.

Am I lost? Should I ask one of them to drive me? The resort map in my bag proves useless – or rather, I'm useless at interpreting it – but I want to walk even if I end up taking a longer route, so I pick a random direction and keep going.

Reception ought to be over here somewhere . . .

I cheer quietly to myself when my navigational instincts are proved right. There it is: the main hotel building's semi-circular façade. Riyonna waves frantically as I walk into the red marble lobby, apparently made ecstatic by my arrival. Her fingernails have changed colour overnight: from eau-de-nil green to pale lilac. I hope she's not about to leap out from behind the desk and hug me. Thankfully she's dealing with another guest, so I have some degree of protection. An elderly woman is busy giving her a hard time.

No free upgrade to a casita for you, angry old lady.

'Are you listening to me, Riyonna? Well, then don't look over there! I'm right in front of you.'

'I'm sorry, Mrs McNair. I was—'

'I was *right*. And now I've been *proved* right, I wanna know what you're gonna do about it.'

The woman must be in her eighties. She's wearing a blue shirt, maroon corduroy trousers, brown sandals over tights the colour of burned toffee, and a hat that's nothing more than a white visor attached to a strap that goes round her head, with a buckle fastening at the back. She's white, at least in theory, with hair dyed the exact colour of an aubergine and a tan the same shade and texture as my brown Laura Ashley sofa at home.

I must buy some sunscreen: factor 50. There's no way they won't sell it here. Opposite the reception desk is a shop. Through its open door I can see woven rugs, turquoise and reddish-brown earthenware pots, silver jewellery featuring bright gemstones, wooden painted flutes, inflatable floating things for children to use in the pool. Sun protection cream must be in there somewhere.

The strident old woman's neck and arms are lean and sinewy. They look as if more than the usual number of muscles have been stuffed into them. As she berates Riyonna, gesturing wildly,

50

the muscles twist and ripple beneath the chapped, creased surface of her skin. She needs at least a bottle of moisturiser rubbing into her. Maybe that's why she's come to Swallowtail. There might be a signature massage at the spa that offers de-leatherisation.

'Mrs McNair—' Riyonna tries again.

'No one believed me!' The old woman throws up her arms. 'Least of all you! I said it was definitely her. Definitely Melody! Did anyone listen? No. No one ever does. You all think I'm loony-tunes.'

'I absolutely do not think that, ma'am.'

'Yeah, you do. I don't care. I know what I see, and I know what's true. And last night I saw her *running*. Melody, running. Long dark hair flying out behind her. How come she can run all of a sudden? Can my cousin Isaac *run*? Let me tell ya, he can't even *walk*!'

'Your . . . your cousin Isaac?'

The confusion on Riyonna's face suggests that Mrs McNair has introduced a new character. Melody is the subject of the conversation, whoever she is; what does Cousin Isaac have to do with it?

'So, now that we know for sure, are you gonna call the police?' Mrs McNair demands. 'Tell 'em I saw Melody running away in the middle of the night? Tell 'em she had that *creature* with her? She was with her boyfriend! You don't think he's her boyfriend? How do *you* know? He could be anyone! Are you going to call the police? I've been right every time. Every. Single. Time.'

'Every time? Do you mean like last year? Is that what you mean?' Riyonna speaks to her gently. I sense that she's choosing each word with great care.

'Ye–es.' Mrs McNair sounds unsure now. Then she makes up her mind. 'Yes! Last year, and the year before, and the other years. All the times I've seen her.'

'But Mrs McNair, you see a different child every time,' says Riyonna patiently. 'They can't all be Melody, can they?'

'They are!'

'Do you remember the year you said a boy was Melody?'

I quite like the name. *Melody Burrows.* For a girl, obviously. Mrs McNair might believe in calling boys Melody but I don't. That kind of thing may work in spiritual Arizona but it wouldn't go down well in Hertfordshire.

'I don't care!' Mrs McNair snaps at Riyonna. 'People can alter their appearances. There's no doubt in my mind. I saw her with that creature – which means I have proof now! So! I'm going to do something about it.'

It sounds as if there might be a tragic story of some sort associated with the old lady's delusion. If I wait to speak to Riyonna, I'm bound to end up hearing all about it, and I don't want to. I can't listen to any stories about bad things happening to children.

I sigh and look around for someone else to ask about the business centre.

The shop. Whoever's in charge there will know, and I can buy some sun cream. As I walk away from reception, I hear Mrs McNair say, 'So are you gonna call the police? Tell me if you're not and I'll call 'em myself. I'll tell 'em I saw Melody last night, no doubt about it.'

The woman behind the counter in the shop, instead of directing me to the business centre, rushes off into a back room with a promise to find somebody called Mason. The way she said his name gave the impression that if she were only able to produce him, he would solve all my problems and possibly those of the world at large if he had any time left over.

I wait to be disappointed, and am pleasantly surprised when she returns with a tall, fair, bespectacled young man who hands me an iPad mini in a red leather case, its front embossed with Swallowtail's logo, and tells me I can keep it for the duration of my stay. 'You're all hooked up already – full and fast internet access whenever you want it. No need to put in any codes or anything.'

Like the girl on the terrace at lunch, Mason looks as if he could be anything from sixteen to twenty-five. 'Also?' he says. 'It'll give you directions for getting around the resort. If you . . .' He holds out his hand, and I pass the iPad back to him. 'If you go here, see, you can put in an address anywhere at Swallowtail, and it'll tell you which way to walk. If you want to switch off spoken directions, you press here – then you'll just get the on-screen directions. There's no need to walk – you can always send for a club car, wherever you are, and all in-resort transportation is entirely free of charge – but some of our guests do like to walk, for the exercise or to see the beautiful scenery.'

'Yeah, that's me,' I tell him. 'So, if I type in "Pool" it'll take me to the pool? That's where I want to go next.'

'Oh! No need to type in anything at all.' Mason sounds shocked, as if I've suggested I might try to climb to the top of Camelback Mountain in my flip-flops. 'Wherever you want to go in the resort, click here and you'll get the drop-down menu. See? All the swimming pools are listed.'

'Ah, right. Yes.'

'Let me do it for you this first time. Which pool is it you want? The spa pool is adults only, which means no under-sixteens. Or you could go to the lap pool, or The Pond – that's our eco-pool with a completely natural cleaning system, no chemicals added. Or the family pool?'

'Oh. Um . . .'

'Have you tried out any of our pools so far?' Mason asks, inspecting me closely.

'No, not yet. I arrived late last night and I've mostly been asleep since then.'

'Good to know,' he says. I scour his face for an indication that he was being sarcastic, but he seems sincere. 'In that case, I'm going to recommend you start at the family pool. It's the biggest one with the best views, and there's a fantastic poolside bar and restaurant if you find yourself in need of refreshments. If I say so myself, there are no better cocktails to be had in all of America.'

He has to be joking. Weirdly, he doesn't seem to be.

'There's an at-seat service, so no need to get up if you're relaxing. Just press the button on the side of your sun-lounger and a waiter'll come take your order. The pool is L-shaped, and both bars of the L are eighty feet long.'

I nod. I've seen the photo on the website. I'm keen to see the real thing, if only Mason would stop describing it to me.

'There's also a hot tub with a cold plunge pool next to it. Drinks can be served to the hot tub – again, you just press a button. Towels are provided free of charge. Does all of that sound good?'

I'm tempted to roll my eyes and say tersely, 'It'll do, I suppose.'

'Wonderful. Great,' I say instead. 'The family pool it is.'

'And you want to walk there?'

'Yes.'

'Do you want the voice on or off?'

'Voice?'

'For your directions,' Mason clarifies.

'Oh, right. Off, please.'

'Okay. Here you go.' He hands me the iPad mini with a smile, and says, 'You have yourself a wonderful day, ma'am.'

⋆ ⋆ ⋆

The iPad tells me to walk back through the lobby on my way out of the main building. It doesn't trust me to work out even that obvious first stage for myself. There's no sign of Riyonna or Mrs McNair at reception. I can imagine how glad at least one of them was when that conversation finally ended – unless they moved it elsewhere, out of the way of impressionable guests.

I walk for about ten minutes, turning whenever I'm told to turn, and finally arrive at the shimmering turquoise 'L' that's so much more stunning in reality than it looked in the pictures. There are a few people in the pool, and many more sitting on sun-loungers around it, most of them under white parasols, with blue, green or pink drinks beside them on wooden tables. Every glass I can see is a different shape.

There are at least fifty free sun-loungers for me to choose between. Near the bar seems a good idea. I can't drink alcohol, but a place like this has got to have a mocktail menu, which is a tempting enough prospect. I can live without booze for Child Number 3's sake, but no doctor has ever said pregnant women must also be deprived of glacé cherries and colourful paper umbrellas – my second and third favourite cocktail ingredients.

The mother and daughter from the terrace at Glorita's are sitting as close to the bar as it's possible to sit, which means I'm going to have to sit a bit further away. With all the loungers that are available, I need to leave a minimum of four empty ones between us if I don't want to risk encroaching on their space. To be on the safe side, I leave five and move towards the sixth. From the corner of my eye, I see something coming towards me. It looks like a pile of white towelling with legs. The legs are wearing white shorts, and there are white tennis shoes on the feet.

A man's voice says, 'Ma'am, may I give you a towel, a robe and slippers?'

'Oh, thank you.' I wait while he lays it all out neatly on my lounger. Though I'd give him full marks for effort, I don't like his arrangement and will move it all once he's gone.

'And may I put up the parasol for you, or would you rather be in the sun?'

'No, thanks. I mean, yes, please – the parasol up would be great. Thanks.'

His work done, he tells me to have 'a super-great day'. As he strolls away, I mutter under my breath, 'Don't tell me what kind of day to have.'

Maybe I should have picked a resort in a different country, where everyone's a bit grumpier – somewhere cold and underprivileged.

As promised, there's a button on the side of my lounger with a picture on it of a waiter holding a tray. Much as I'd like a drink, I can't face pressing it. I've had enough conversations for today. I spot a cold water and ice machine on the other side of the pool, with a stack of plastic cups next to it. That's one problem solved. What's the other machine, the white one the size of a large suitcase with a nozzle on the side? It turns out to be a sun-cream dispenser – which reminds me that I forgot to buy any in the shop.

I've never seen that before: factor 30 on tap. Then again, I normally go on holiday to rural Wales or Scotland, to hotels that offer to lend you wellington boots and umbrellas. I rub more cream into my skin than I would normally. The Arizona sun seems a bit more serious than anything I've encountered before.

On my way back to my lounger with a glass of water, I prepare to look away in order to avoid eye contact with the mother and daughter. I feel better when I see that they're as committed as I am to mutual non-acknowledgement. Both are immersed in their books. The mother's is called *Jane Doe January*. The daughter is reading *The Waves* by Virginia Woolf. Older than she looks, definitely; either that or she's unusually highbrow for her age. If Jess were here, she'd be reading something by or about a Kardashian.

I sit down, open the iPad and wonder how to email Patrick when the only email account I have is the one he and I share. If we need to contact each other when we're apart, we always text.

Is there any reason why I shouldn't be able to send an email to and from the same account? Probably not.

Deciding what I want to say to Patrick is harder than I thought it would be. *I love you. I'm sorry.*

I'm angry. I miss you. I feel as if something I've always believed in has turned out to be a shoddy forgery.

I'm definitely not putting that in my email.

'Dear Patrick,' I begin. 'My phone is out of action at the moment (long story), so if you've sent me texts since I left, I haven't seen them. I don't know if, by now, you've worked out why I felt I had to escape for a bit. I don't know if you're angry or hurt or confused. All three, probably. Anyway, I'm truly sorry for whatever problems I've caused for you, Jess and Olly. I hope you know that I didn't do this on a whim, and that I wouldn't have done it if I'd felt I had a choice.

'I'm missing you all like crazy, and looking forward to seeing you again. When I get back, I hope we can talk about everything and sort things out. Please, for now, can you just email me and let me know that you and the kids are okay and coping, and that all is fine at home?

'Lots of love, C xxx

'PS. I'm writing to the kids separately, but you can show them this too if you want.'

I read what I've written. It strikes the right sort of tone, I think. Calm, considerate . . .

Too considerate. It mentions Patrick's hurt and anger, but not mine.

Because you're leading by example. Your email acknowledges his pain. Now let's see if his reply acknowledges yours.

I can't decide if that's a pathetic excuse. I'm not

a representative of the Good Behaviour Exam Board. Why should Patrick take any notice of my feelings when I pretend not to notice them myself?

I go back to the message and, after 'All three, probably' I add, 'I know that I'm angry and hurt – very – but I'm not at all confused. I know what I want, and I know what I'm going to do.'

No, that sounds too combative. I change it to 'I know I want this baby.'

I press send and see that I guessed right: a Hotmail address can send messages to itself, no problem at all. Great. That's that done.

Next, Jess and Olly. They both have email accounts, but they never look at them. All their online communication with their friends happens in other places – Snapchat, Instagram. I know nothing about Snapchat, but I have an Instagram account. I set it up because the kids wanted me to see their photos. Olly's are mostly of his Xbox, computer equipment and skateboards. Each time Patrick buys him a new monitor or headset, he posts a picture of it and it gets 'liked' by all the boys in his class at school, at least four of whom are in Olly's gaming gang, or whatever it's called. ('It's not called *that*, Mum,' Jess would say. 'You're such a dinosaur.')

I know Olly's friends as Fraser, Richard, Louis and Barney, but for gaming purposes they're Illusion Fire, Illusion Sleepwalk, Illusion Stack and Illusion Shadow. Olly is Illusion Blaze.

Jess loves taking odd-angled photos of street scenes

and buildings. 'All my friends just post selfies of their ridiculous pouty faces,' she told me, shaking her head in disgust. 'They look like fish that have been frozen with a stun-gun.'

Unlike Olly who likes his friends in an uncomplicated way, Jess has strong views about hers that aren't always complimentary. Petra is wet and boring, and Hazel's a snidey cow but always disguises her cruel comments as humour, though no one notices this apart from Jess; she calls Jess fat all the time as a joke, even though Jess is skinny, and Hazel is fat, but Jess is kind enough never to point this out. Esther pretends to have life-threatening food allergies but that's a lie, and her parents hate each other so much, they can't be in the same county.

When I see Jess with these girls they always seem to be having the best time ever – hugging each other, giggling, listing the flaws of the smelly, sexist boys with bad breath who read books about elves, and the other girls who aren't in their group: their terrible taste in Netflix dramas, their badly behaved dogs, their gold-digger mothers. I haven't heard any dissent or bitching within Jess's little gang, only complete agreement on every topic, as if the four of them have one mind.

I once presented this to Jess as evidence that she might like her friends more than she claims to. She rolled her eyes and said, 'Mum. I have *no choice* about who I spend time with. I'm stuck at school all day long with these *randoms*. I have to fit in, or I'd have no social life.'

All Jess's Instagram photos, without exception, have been 'liked' by Hazel, Petra and Esther. I'm sure she has reciprocated. I've been forbidden from 'liking' anything posted by either of my children. Jess tried to be reasonable when she imposed this restriction: 'We'd Like *your* photos, Mum, if you ever posted any. But for us it'd be embarrassing to have you Liking our stuff. All our friends would see it.'

My stomach turns over when I see that neither Jess nor Olly has posted anything at all on Instagram since I left for Arizona. Why not? Are they too upset?

A panicky feeling starts to well up inside me. I take deep breaths to drive it away.

'Sod it,' I mutter as I decide to break the rule and 'like' Jess's most recently posted picture – a bay window behind iron railings. I add a comment: 'Love you very much, darling. See you on Tuesday 24 Oct. I'm fine. There's nothing to worry about. All my love, Mum xxxxx'. On Olly's Instagram, I do the same: 'like' the picture he's posted of a box with 'El Gato' on it, and add a message that's nearly identical to the one I sent Jess.

I hear a boy's voice yell, 'Marco!' Looking up, I see that it came from the pool. A girl yells 'Polo!' apparently in response. They're part of a group of five or six who are circling each other in the water. Soon others have joined in and are shouting too.

'Marco!'
'Polo!'

'Marco!'

'Polo!'

The loudest shouter by far is a girl of about ten with the thickest plaits I've ever seen sticking out from the side of her head – bright blue bobbles at the top and bottom on both sides, creating a strange plait-sausage effect.

I hear the girl who's trying to read Virginia Woolf say to her mother, 'Can we move to the spa pool? I can't listen to this. It's torture. Why are people such morons? *Mother!* Are you listening to me?'

No reply. Then a distracted, 'No, I'm not moving.'

'Marco!'

'Polo!'

It must be a game of some kind – though, watching the aimless circling and giggling that's going on in the pool, it's hard to fathom what the rules might be.

'Marco!'

'Why can't we move?'

'Polo!'

'You don't think the spa pool will have morons?' the mother replies eventually. 'Why not? Morons are everywhere.'

'The spa pool doesn't allow children under sixteen.'

'So the morons will be older there, is all.'

'They're less likely to scream, "Marco Polo!" all day long.'

'This pool has better views and a cocktail bar. The spa's all rainwater and fresh-air smoothies. I hate that shit. Don't worry, I have an idea. I need a cocktail first, then I'll deal with those people.'

'Oh, you'll deal with them?' The daughter laughs. 'Right. Cannot wait to see that. You think you're such a badass, and you're so *not*.'

'You'll see,' her mother says with quiet confidence.

If this woman found herself unexpectedly pregnant and wanted to keep the baby, I bet she'd obliterate all opposition within seconds.

I wait, expecting to hear her getting up off her lounger and clacking off in her high-heeled sandals in search of a cocktail. Then I realise: she'll simply have pressed a button. Sure enough, a few seconds later I hear footsteps and a man asking what he can bring her. She orders a Swallowtail Showboat, whatever that is. Her daughter orders Earl Grey tea with lemon.

'Marco!'

'Polo!'

'Marco!'

'Polo!'

'So what's your plan?' asks the girl. 'Drowning them? Like, why aren't they at *school*?'

'Why aren't you?'

'That's easy: because I have a mother who cares more about her vacations than my education.'

'I'm going to need your help,' says Badass Mom.

'With what? With *them*? No. No way.'

'Pick a random name.'

'What?'

'Go on. Someone from that book you're reading.'

'Ugh, Mother, seriously. Quit it. Let's just move to the spa pool when you've had your drink.'

'Okay, I'll pick: Harvey Specter.'

'Who's that?'

'The guy in *Suits*. We get in the pool, get right up close to those bastards. Then I yell "Harvey" at the top of my lungs, and you yell "Specter". Then we do it again, and again. I guarantee we won't hear another peep out of the Marco Polos.'

I hear movement: footsteps, and a scratching sound, like fingernails on material. Is the daughter about to walk away in disgust? Or is it the waiter arriving with Badass Mom's cocktail? I can't turn and look without risking being drawn into something.

'*Suits*? That is so lame. I don't know how you can watch that brain-rot shit. Every single episode, someone says, "Just do your goddamn job and win the goddamn case," while the elevator doors slide shut in front of them.'

'I can do it on my own if you're too shy – yell "Harvey" *and* "Specter".'

Suddenly I hear a different voice, much closer, say, 'It was her. Nobody believes me. Never do, never will. But it was her.'

Oh no. Please, no.

'It was Melody. Sure as I'm born.'

I turn. Mrs McNair has taken a lounger that's set a little back from mine and to the right. Quickly, I look away. Too late. 'Hey you!' she calls out.

Pretend you're invisible. Pretend she's invisible.

'Lady in front!'

There's no way out. I turn back to her with a fixed smile. 'Yes?'

'I don't suppose you'd believe me either. No, I shouldn't tell you. There's something wrong with you. What is it? What's the matter?'

'I'm fine,' I say, keeping my smile firmly in place. Actually, I'm suddenly much too hot, even in the shade.

'No. You're in bad shape. I can feel it. There's no connection.' Mrs McNair points at me, then to her chest, then back to me. 'I can't feel a connection to you at all. None.'

Could that be because you're a complete stranger?

Don't people say that you always think of the perfect comeback when it's too late? Not me. I normally think of it in plenty of time to use it, and I always decide not to. I'm such a wimp – sadass, not badass.

'I know what it is.' The old lady peers at me. 'It's your energy. It's not right. You have a very hollow energy.'

'Mrs Icy Dead People's picked her next hapless victim,' says Badass Mom to her daughter.

Mrs Icy What? My brain plays it back and I realise what she must have said. It's her nickname for Mrs McNair, evidently: Mrs I-See-Dead-People, a reference to the Bruce Willis movie *The Sixth Sense*. Does that mean . . .?

Is Melody dead? That would explain why Mrs

McNair expressed surprise at seeing her running. Her cousin Isaac – who can't walk, let alone run – is very likely dead too.

How long have all these people been at Swallowtail? Badass Mom seems to know all about Mrs McNair and her peculiar ways.

I've switched to the daughter's side: with 'Marco!' and 'Polo!' still being shrieked at full volume, it's way past time to relocate to the spa pool. I start to get up.

'Wait,' says Mrs McNair. 'I know what you need. I have a friend in Oak Creek. Up Sedona way. She does soul retrieval. She can get you your soul back. It's Native American, the technique she uses. Visualisation. She's the best. She's the one you should go see. And give her a testimonial for her website when you're done. You don't have to. Only if you want to. But why wouldn't you want to? What harm would it do?'

She waves her hand dismissively as if she's given up on me already. 'People used to *care*. They gave back. No one gives back any more. You try to help people . . .' She shakes her head. 'It was her. Melody. It was dark, and I couldn't see the top of her head, but it was her.'

Without saying a word in response, I walk away as fast as I can. I hear Badass Mom say, 'Damn. We lost our buffer. Crazy just got closer.'

It's only when I'm closing the gate to the pool area that I remember I've left the iPad mini behind.

Great. Just perfect. How could I be so stupid?

Perhaps it has something to do with my hollow energy or lack of soul. That must be it.

Shit, shit, shit. Where's the Fetch-the-thing-I-forgot-and-spare-me-another-encounter-with-Mrs-McNair button for me to press?

I steel myself and walk back to where I was sitting. Mrs McNair's eyes are closed. She opens them as I approach, looks up at me with a smile and says, 'Hello, dear!' as if this is the first time we've encountered one another.

'It's goodbye, actually,' I say as I pick up the iPad.

Did I just – not hugely, but sort of, a little bit – stick up for myself for the first time in my life instead of running away?

As well as, not instead of. Now I'm running away.

For my sixth birthday, my parents gave me a photo of Emory. It was in a little heart-shaped gold frame. They said they thought I was finally old enough to see her, and to have my own special picture of her. It was kind of a shock. Until then I'd only imagined her face, never seen it.

In the photo, Emory was dead. I knew that without asking. She looked dead, and there's no way anyone could have gotten a photo of her lying on flower-patterned material, or any sort of photo of her at all, while she was alive – apart from an ultra-sound, I suppose.

I unwrapped my birthday present before I knew what it was. My mother and father were smiling and had tears in their eyes, so I thought it was going to be something truly great. When I saw what it was, I couldn't speak. I wanted to scream and throw it across the room, but my parents were beaming at me, expecting me to be thrilled. 'Isn't your sister just so beautiful?' my mother asked me. 'Yes,' I said. If I'd given any other answer, she wouldn't have spoken a single word to me for at least two weeks.

I allowed a few tears to leak out. I could get away with it, I figured, if I made my parents believe I was thinking what they were thinking. 'She should be here now,' I said, quoting Mom's most overused phrase. 'Yes, she should,' my mother agreed, also crying. 'Well, you have a photo of her now to put on your nightstand. That way you can see her beautiful face every day.'

I thought I was going to faint. I didn't want to sleep in the same room as a photo of a dead girl even if she was my sister, but there was nothing I could do about it.

It turned out that my parents had dozens of pictures of Emory. As soon as they'd given me my birthday present, there was a big change in household policy. It was as if they'd been holding back all those years, having judged that I was too young to see images of my dead sister, but now that they'd given me one as a gift there was no need to hide anything, so out they all came. My parents' bedroom, our family room, dining room, den – all were suddenly full of photos of Emory in gold frames of different sizes. The flowery thing that Emory was lying on in my birthday present picture was in most of the others, but not all of them. There were a few where she was lying on some kind of shimmery silver material that looked as if it could have been a fancy bedspread.

At the same time, some pictures of me appeared, propped up against books on shelves in the house, unframed – not dozens, but two or three. No photos of me had ever been put up on display before; hardly any had been taken. At the time, I believed my parents must have realized that I might feel left out if I saw my sister on every surface and me on none, and so tried to compensate me by displaying a few dog-eared snaps. I remember thinking, 'How can they imagine that this will make me feel better? Are they stupid? Do they think I haven't noticed that there are thirty of Emory and only three of me? Do they think I can't see that they've spent money on frames for hers and not for mine?'

I don't think I'd ever have worked out the truth on my own. Yes, I was young and naïve aged six, and I'm less so now, but still . . . I wouldn't have figured it out because it's too horrible. My mind would never have produced the suspicion that any parent could or would do that. And yet, when the Kind Smiles told me, it made sense: my parents were not trying to make me feel better. Their aim was the opposite.

If they'd put up some pictures of Emory and none of me, I'd probably have thought nothing of it. There were no photos of my parents on any shelves. We weren't that kind of family. I think I'd have assumed that pictures of Emory were different because she was gone and we needed to remember her. By putting out photos of me as well – far fewer, and all unframed – my mother and father were trying to send me the message, in case I'd failed to notice, that they loved my dead sister more than me.

I don't think the Kind Smiles understand that every time they call me Favorite Child, it reminds me of how much I wasn't, for my mother and father. It makes me think of all the sad things.

10 OCTOBER 2017

I'm halfway to the spa building, courtesy of my silent electronic guide, when I hear a gasp behind me. I turn and see Riyonna hurrying towards me across the grass, darting left and right to avoid the water sprinklers.

It's the first time I've seen anyone at Swallowtail on the grass. The few people I've seen so far who appear willing to use their own legs have all stuck rigidly to the little streets and paved pathways. The grass is so smooth and radiant all over the resort – a stunning green carpet laid out like landscape art. I assumed there was an unwritten rule that no one was allowed to sully it with their shoes, but maybe that doesn't apply to resort staff.

'Mrs Burrows!' Riyonna catches me up and stands by my side, panting. 'How *are* you today? Did you sleep well? Do you *love* your casita? Pretty great view, huh?'

'I'm fine, thank you. I slept brilliantly and the casita is out of this world. Really fantastic. Thanks so much for the upgrade.'

'You're so welcome. And I'm so sorry about

before – I could see you waiting to talk to me, but that particular guest is a little demanding, as you probably saw. Anyway, I hope you reached out to another member of the Swallowtail team and got the help you needed?'

'Yes, I did, thanks.'

'Awesome! And now – let me guess – you're on your way to our beautiful spa?'

I nod.

'In that case, I'm gonna recommend my favourite treatment. It is, sincerely, divine. Like, from *heaven*. I'm telling you, hand on heart, you have to try it while you're here: the Cactus Needle Full Body Massage.' Riyonna laughs at my expression. 'Don't let the name put you off. Also great is the Sound Bath Body Immersion.'

'I can see I'll be spoilt for choice!' I say cheerily. It sounds fake to me, but it seems to be the easiest way to talk to a happy American. Anything less upbeat and Riyonna might frown and ask if I'm planning to kill myself later tonight. 'Can I just ask . . .' I begin tentatively.

'Yes, of course. How can I help you?'

'The lady at reception before. Is she okay?'

'Mrs McNair? Sure.' Riyonna waves her hand, a brushing-aside gesture. 'She's fine, bless her heart. Comes every year. One of our more, um, imaginative guests, that's for sure!'

'She sat next to me by the pool a few minutes ago and . . . said a few strange things.'

'Well, I hope she didn't disturb you too much.

But really, she's nothing to worry about. She wouldn't hurt a fly.'

'This girl she keeps talking about, Melody . . .?' I hope that's all I need to say. Completing my question would make me sound too nosey. *What's the story there?*

'I know,' says Riyonna. 'She's a little obsessed.'

'Is Melody dead?'

Her eyes widen in surprise. She tilts her head and shakes her index finger in the air. 'You are one smart lady, Mrs Burrows. Yes, I'm afraid poor little Melody passed on years ago. Doesn't stop Mrs McNair seeing her everywhere. She says it's just here, but I don't believe that, personally. I think she sees Melodys *eee*verywhere she goes. She spends two weeks of every year at Swallowtail, and each time, within hours of arriving, she's fixated on some girl she thinks is Melody. Once it was even a boy! It's sad for her, y'know? Not much else in her life, I guess. Oh! Excuse me.'

Riyonna's looking past me, over my right shoulder. I turn and see two men walking towards us. One is dark-skinned, short and stocky with black curly hair. The other's tall, thin and fair. They're both wearing suits, white shirts and ties.

Riyonna's lost interest in me. She tells me to have a great day, as if she's barely aware of who she's talking to and what she's saying, and runs towards the men.

Odd. A little rude, too. Still, at least now I don't

have to hear a tragic story about Mrs McNair's dead child or grandchild.

I'm about to set off for the spa when I hear the word 'detective'. A man said it. Was it one of the men talking to Riyonna?

It must have been. There's no one else around, and the voice sounded as if it came from that direction. I look back and see the tall blond man slipping something into his pocket. What was it? I just missed it.

Was it a detective's badge? His police ID?

I suppose it's possible – likely, even – that I'm leaping to all the wrong conclusions. Maybe he said 'defective'. *My orange juice this morning was quite defective. It tasted of bananas, not oranges.*

But I heard Mrs McNair say she'd call the police herself if no one else would. That must be what's happened.

Riyonna ran towards them as if she was expecting them, though. I saw it with my own eyes. So she must have known they were coming. Why wouldn't she call them and tell them not to bother – to ignore crazy Mrs McNair?

Is this a regular part of Mrs McNair's annual stay at Swallowtail? Is there so little crime in Arizona that detectives are willing to take a day off from real work once a year to humour an old lady?

Highly unlikely. Far more plausible is that either I heard wrong and no one said 'detective', or else the police are here about something quite different.

Since there's no way of solving the mystery for

the time being, I decide I might as well go and get to grips with the spa's treatment menu. I'm pretty sure I want to avoid cactus needles, but there must be a relaxing aromatherapy massage for pregnant people. I probably won't ask my masseur if she knows anything about Mrs McNair and Melody, or why there are two detectives at the resort.

Almost definitely not.

Nothing has happened, I tell myself firmly. *Nothing. There is no mystery.*

Then why did Riyonna look anxious when she saw the two men? Why did she run to them, to stop them getting any closer to where I was standing?

The answer must be: for a reason. I don't know the reason, but that doesn't mean it doesn't exist. Why should I know anything? I've been here less than twenty-four hours. A jewellery theft from a casita, a smashed car window . . . It could be any one of a thousand things. Riyonna would want to conceal any and all problems from me because I'm a guest. Stands to reason.

There's nothing to worry about – nothing I didn't bring with me, anyway. I need to get a grip before I end up as loopy as Mrs McNair.

The spa proves almost impossible to find, even with the help of a bossy iPad. The trouble is the resort junctions: there are places where 'Turn left' might in theory mean taking any one of three paths, all of which could be said to be on the left depending on your definition.

After a series of wrong turns and doublings-back, I finally arrive. The building that houses the spa is much more attractive than the main hotel. It's a large rectangle with curved edges, made of dark, glossy metal of a deep green-ish grey colour. Stripes of mirror, reflecting the green of the trees all around, alternate with long, thin windows that reveal other trees inside the building bordering a dark, shimmering rectangle with a moving surface. It takes me a few seconds to work out what this is: a pool with black, glittery tiles.

Wow.

Inside the spa is equally stunning. Three members of staff stand behind the reception desk, all wearing the same tunic-and-trousers uniform: white with a pale green Swallowtail logo. I was hoping to explore on my own, but I don't have the energy to insist on it, so I let a young woman called Sujata show me around. We start off in the ladies' changing rooms, where there are robes, slippers, towels, lotions, hair products. Sujata tries to tell me about each item, but I can hardly hear her on account of the large screen embedded in the wall. An advertisement for something called Dolbrynol is blaring out. It's some kind of medicine, I think. The ad seems to go on forever.

Sujata points out what look like two solid silver cylinders in the corner, both with nozzles. One is for boiling water, the other for warm water. Around these, other things are laid out so beautifully, it could almost be a religious shrine: elaborately patterned china cups and saucers, dozens of different kinds of teabags in tiny pastel-coloured paper envelopes, raisins, dried apricots . . . and probably other things too, but by now I'm too fascinated by the TV to pay attention to what Sujata's showing me.

The Dolbrynol advert has ended and the next one, for something called GlucoFlush, is behaving in exactly the same bizarre way: listing the negative side effects of the product in the loud, pedantic tone of a worst-case-scenario-obsessed neurotic: 'GlucoFlush may cause cardiac arrest, leukemia, athlete's foot, blindness or halitosis. Do not take GlucoFlush if you are pregnant, asthmatic, diabetic, a talented violin player or keen on tennis. Side effects include loss of teeth, hair, sense of humour, car keys and virginity. Ask your doctor before taking GlucoFlush if you don't want to die, shrink, turn to green slime, swell up like a balloon, lose all your friends and family, or vomit forever.'

I'm exaggerating, but only slightly. I wait for the doom-mongering voice to perk up at the end and say, 'Apart from that, it's a really great product!' but no; like the advert before it, this one offers no happy ending.

How on earth do Americans ever manage to buy anything if this is the way their advertising works? I wonder if it's only medical stuff that needs to be advertised in this way, or if it works the same way for movies and cars. *The new Jaguar Blah-Blah may cause hideous death involving petrol fires and twisted metal. Do not drive the Jaguar Blah-Blah if you like having feet, ears or a small intestine.*

'Sorry?' I say, suddenly aware that I haven't been listening at all. 'What did you ask me?'

'You'll need to take off your shoes for the rest of the tour, and put on your spa slippers,' says Sujata.

I leave my flip-flops in a locker. For the four-digit code I need to lock it, I choose my baby's American due date – American only in the sense that they put the month before the day.

'Ready?' asks Sujata.

We leave the perplexing TV behind and go through to the spa proper. The smell is the first thing I notice: it's sort of watery, but green leaves are also involved, and some kind of rich spice. It's gorgeous. I'd wear it as a perfume. To say that the facilities are extensive is a ludicrous understatement. There's an orange steam room, a rose steam room, two hammams, three saunas ranging from very hot to only a little bit hot, a bar and café area, twenty treatment rooms, the glittery black indoor pool, a beautiful blue outdoor pool with sun-loungers and parasols around it, a hot tub with bubbles and one without, a freezing cold square plunge pool, a warm hydrotherapy pool, and – perhaps my favourite thing of all – a sort of network of outdoor Jacuzzis.

'We call it the Hot Tub Circle,' says Sujata. 'You access it through the hydrotherapy pool, so no need to get out of the water and lose any heat. Just go on through – see the hanging beads in the corner? Walk through there and you'll find yourself outside, still in the water up to roughly your waist. Go straight ahead for six feet or so and you'll find yourself at the entrance to the circle. There's a current that'll pull you all the way round. If you imagine the shape of a ring donut? You can swim if you like, with help from the current, or just float and let it carry you round. As you go, you'll see that off the circle, to the left and right, there are Jacuzzi areas of varying sizes. Some are ideal for one person alone, others can seat four or five. There's a big one that takes twelve. In the Jacuzzi areas there's no current, so that's where you can stop for a rest if you want, for as long as you need. No two Jacuzzis are the same. They all have jets in different places, so you can try a few, see which you like best. Some have lots of high-pressure jets for a really intense full body massage. Others are quite mild, like sitting in a bubble bath with a very faint movement to the bubbles. Anyway – you be sure to try them all!'

I nod. This is unbelievable. I've been for the odd spa day in the UK – a Christmas present from Patrick, a hen weekend – but I've never seen anything like this before.

'Oh, and before I let you go and relax, I must show you my favourite thing of all – the crystal grotto.' Sujata leads me along a tree-lined, glass-sided corridor. We come to a rough-textured semi-circular wall sticking out of a smooth, flat one. In the sticky-out part, there's an open arch-topped doorway. I look inside and see what looks like a cave with a dark red floor. Sujata slips off her white slippers and walks in. I do the same.

We're in a perfectly round room with a dome-shaped top. There are soft yellow wall lights at regular intervals, and about two dozen large mauve and pink crystals in metal brackets, also attached to the walls. I don't know what I'm standing on: some kind of terracotta-coloured powdery stuff. It's warm, as if heated from below. On the ground are more pink and mauve crystals – smaller ones in circles, free-standing heaps, metal bowls. There's a stone bench running all the way around the circular wall, for people who want to sit down.

Close to the entrance of the grotto there's a tall silver table – like a lectern but with a flat top – on which sits a large dimpled silver pot and, next to it, a notepad and a few pencils. 'The crystal grotto is for leaving your worries behind,' says Sujata. 'It's amazing. It really works. Here's what you do: tear off a sheet of paper from the pad and write down something you're worried about – anything that's been preying on your mind, maybe a grudge you've been hanging on to or some old pain or trauma. Then sit in the grotto, holding the paper in your hand. Sit with your eyes closed and breathe deeply, reflecting on whatever it is you've written down. After about ten minutes, or however long feels right to you, stand up and say, 'I choose not to carry this worry or pain into my future,' and put the piece of paper in the silver bowl before you leave. I guarantee: that worry will be *gone*, and it won't ever come back.'

'Mm-hm,' I say diplomatically. I like this little round room – I can imagine lying down on whatever this powdery stuff is and having a long, deep sleep – but you'd have to be an idiot to write down details of your personal problems and leave them in a pot for other guests to read.

After the crystal grotto, Sujata leaves me to my own devices. I have a quick look round the spa shop – healing crystals, dream catchers, soap, body lotion, books about the sacred properties and ancient wisdom of Camelback Mountain – before heading for the outdoor pool.

Damn. Badass Mom and Highbrow Daughter are here, reading their books on sun-loungers. I wonder if that means the attempt to silence the Marco-Polo shouters was unsuccessful. I studiously avoid catching their eye and they reciprocate. Good. I feared they might be tempted to try and engage me in a bitching session about poor old Mrs McNair, but they evidently want nothing to do with me, which is a relief. If they keep ignoring me like this, I'll soon be able to see them around the resort and not think, 'Oh, shit.' I hope they don't think I'm following them around.

The layout here is much more regular and symmetrical than at the family pool: a rectangle of royal blue – somehow more satisfying to look at than the traditional turquoise – in a white-walled courtyard with one potted tree in each corner and four rows of sun-loungers parallel both to the walls and to the four sides of the pool.

Little tables next to the loungers have folded maps of the spa on them, as well as piles of menus: food, drinks, spa treatments that include everything from a Chakra Realignment Revitaliser to an Aromatherapy Aura-Enhancing Foot Massage. A young white woman wearing a name badge that says 'Kimbali' appears with towels for me and takes my order of a Virgin Colada.

Kimbali? Is that a misspelling of Kimberley, I wonder, and by whom – the spa-badge maker or the girl's parents? Maybe her mother's called Kim and she was conceived in Bali. Still, that's no excuse. With one hand on my stomach, I whisper to my baby, 'I swear I will not give you a stupid name.'

I'm about to lie back on my lounger and close my eyes when a man walks out of the spa building, scans the terrace as if looking for someone, runs his fingers through his hair as if he knows people are watching, then goes back inside. It's the taller of the two men I saw Riyonna talking to – the blond good-looking one, made considerably less attractive by his air of seeming pleased with himself for no apparent reason.

One of the detectives.

Why's he here? Who was he looking for? Mrs McNair?

Without stopping to ask myself what on earth I think I'm doing, I get up off my lounger and walk into the spa building, in pursuit. It takes me a while to find him – I can't move fast on these smooth tiled floors in my white slippers – but eventually

I see him ahead of me, talking to a white-uniformed spa employee, the only male member of staff I've seen here so far. He lowers his voice when he sees me approaching, but not before I hear him say '. . . see Melody'.

That name again.

I'm going to have to walk past the two men in order to look natural. I slow my pace, hoping to hear some of their conversation, but it's no use. The detective spotted me straight away and is saying things he's decided it's okay for me to hear: 'Thanks for your help' and 'Worth a try, whatever the odds'.

I smile as innocently as I can as I pass them. They stand shoulder to shoulder, smiling back.

Poor odds of what? Who the hell is this Melody person? A while ago I decided she must be someone Mrs McNair had lost, but if there's a detective involved . . .

That's what he is. I no longer doubt it.

I don't know how I got here, but I'm at the entrance to the crystal grotto again. There's no one in there, so I walk in, sit down and try to think.

Was there something criminal about Melody's death? Was she murdered?

Riyonna said with total certainty that she was dead – so why would the police follow up on a possible sighting, especially when the woman claiming to have seen her has made the same claim every year, about a different child each time?

Maybe if I write my questions on a piece of

paper and put them in the silver pot, some answers will pop out.

Yeah, right.

I stand up, walk over to the pot and stick my hand in to see if there's anything inside. The neck is only just wide enough.

It's almost empty but not quite. My fingers touch a few folded papers.

No, Cara. Bad and wrong. Plus, someone could turn up at any moment and catch you.

I start arguing with my conscience – about the practicalities, not the ethics. *It'll only take a few seconds to pull them out. Once they're in my hand and I'm sitting back on the bench, no one who came in would know I got them from the pot. They'd assume they were mine.*

I'm going to risk it.

For a few minutes, I forget all about the detectives, Mrs McNair and Melody as I read what Swallowtail guests have chosen to write and put in the silver pot. There are six folded bits of paper in total. One says simply, 'Loan/debt'. Another says, 'I have to give a speech to more than a hundred people next week and I'm terrified. Hate public speaking.' The third says, 'Be a better husband, be a better dad'. I shake my head and tut. Sujata said nothing about putting resolutions in the silver pot; it's supposed to be anxiety, grudges, trauma and pain. Whoever he is, the inadequate husband and father has bent the grotto rules.

The fourth one is more interesting, and in a

child's writing: 'Do Mom and Dad love me? Why do they love Emory more?'

Oh, dear. My family isn't the only one with problems, clearly.

I blink at the endless, dull detail of the next paper I unfold. It says, 'Vanessa told me I would NOT be needed on 23rd. She said there would be no role for me and so she was sorry but I would have to find another opportunity. So I arranged to do something that day, and now I have commitments, and suddenly she decides she DOES want me involved after all because she's realised it won't work without my input, but she's too chickenshit to tell me face to face, so she had Paul do her dirty work and ask me on her behalf. And now I have to either say yes and she gets away with treating me that way, and I have to let other people down, or I say no and miss out on an opportunity I wanted that'd be really beneficial.'

How tedious. Whatever's happening on the 23rd, I'm sure it's something I'd hate to have to take part in.

I unfold the sixth and last piece of paper, hoping for something more entertaining, and see my own name.

I make an undignified noise and drop the paper. It falls to the floor.

No. Must be a mistake.

My heart has started to pound hard.

That can't be what I saw. I must have imagined it. People imagine all kinds of things – like the time

I had the most vivid memory of putting Olly's lunchbox in his school bag, and the secretary rang and said Olly had no lunch and could I bring it in, and when I looked it was still in the fridge.

I slide off the bench and sink down to my knees on the red powder floor. Hardly daring to look, I force myself to reach for the paper again.

It was no hallucination. The words I read are still there. In forward-slanting handwriting, someone has written, 'Cara Burrows – is she safe?'

'Okay. Okay,' I say to myself out loud, in my regular voice and at a normal volume. 'Just because some freak has written about me in the crystal grotto, that doesn't mean I need to panic.'

I feel an urgent need to take control of the situation. Grabbing a pencil from the table, I write, beneath the slanty handwriting, 'I don't feel particularly safe after reading this. Who are you and what the hell do you mean? Yours, Cara Burrows.'

I refold all six papers and put them back in the pot before leaving. Once outside the grotto, I inhale deeply as if I've been underground, deprived of air.

I'm never going back in there. Not even walking past the entrance. Never again.

I'm going back every hour on the hour, to see what else people have written about me.

One of those statements will probably turn out to be true. I just don't know which one yet.

I start marching towards reception, then stop when I work out that there's no way I can report what I've seen. I had no business snooping in the pot. It would be too humiliating to admit that I did. I could say I found the piece of paper on the floor, I suppose, but what good would it do? The spa staff would have no way of knowing who wrote it. Even if they did, there's not much they could do. People are allowed to write what they want in the grotto, and there's nothing menacing or unpleasant about 'Cara Burrows – is she safe?' On the contrary, it sounds as if someone's concerned for my welfare.

Who? Why?

Stay calm. Think for a second. Who at Swallowtail knows your name?

Diggy. Riyonna. Maybe some other members of staff, but no one else. Or . . .

Yes, someone else. Two other people.

The man and girl from the room I barged into the night I arrived. I told them my name. And the man seemed concerned about me. He asked me if I was in trouble and needed help. Of course – that must be it. It must be him. He's been in the crystal grotto some time today, and he wanted to put something in the silver pot, just for the sake of doing what you're supposed to do in there. He couldn't think of any big anxiety in his life at the moment. Then he remembered the semi-hysterical woman who'd invaded his hotel room the night before, how close to the edge she'd seemed . . .

In his place, I wouldn't have said 'safe', but that's a minor quibble. I'd have written, 'Cara Burrows

– is she okay?' Perhaps he thought no one could work themselves up into such a state unless they were being pursued by a psychopath.

Having thought it through, I feel better. I walk around inside the spa for a while, hoping to catch another glimpse of the detective or the man he was talking to. There's no sign of either of them, so I go back out to the pool. My first swim at Swallowtail is long overdue.

I love swimming. At home I go three times a week without fail, while the kids are at school, to a health club that used to be lovely and is now a little shabby around the edges.

The spa pool at Swallowtail is a very different proposition. Every aspect of it is perfect, from the temperature and texture of the water to the beautiful blue tiles to the stunning views. Whichever direction you're swimming in, there's something amazing to look at. Above the white walls of the courtyard you can see beautiful trees, Camelback Mountain, other hills with cacti climbing their sides, purple and grey mountains in the distance.

As I swim, I have an idea. I'm going to take some photos on the iPad Mason lent me and post them on Instagram, like I might if I were on a normal holiday, so that Jess and Olly can see I'm having a good time and there's nothing to worry about. Obviously I can't take a picture of Camelback Mountain or anything that would identify where I am. I don't trust Patrick not to come out here and try to make me feel guilty, and that would ruin everything. And I can't take pictures of the pool – that would send Jess wild with envy – but there are plenty of other things to photograph.

The sun's so strong, I'm dry almost as soon as I get out of the water. I take the iPad and walk around the pool terrace looking for Instagram fodder. A tree in a pot – that'll do nicely. Two drinks on a table, one green with a grainy texture and little black bits in it, and one pink – perfect. Both glasses are full. The couple the drinks belong to are both asleep; obviously the effort of ordering proved too much for them.

I return to my lounger, sit down with the iPad and log in to Instagram. I wish I'd thought of a better name for myself. I chose 'Docendo79', which is half of my old school motto, *Docendo Discimus*, plus my birth year.

Jess and Olly laughed when they saw I'd called myself that. They accused me of being *'such* a nerd'. I told them that's exactly what I was at school, and proud of it. 'Nerd' in their language means 'clever person who works hard and cares more about books than about nail varnish or computer games'. I was always top of my class at school, got a first at university, was offered the job of my dreams a week after I graduated, did it quite happily until Jess came along and I decided I wanted to be as wholehearted and focused about starting a family as I'd always been about work.

I was happy as a non-working mother and wife. I never looked back, never once regretted my decision.

Not until I got pregnant a third time and everything changed . . .

You're not supposed to be thinking about that now. You're supposed to be posting photos.

Neither Olly nor Jess has left me any kind of message, but . . . come to think of it, I don't know if it's possible to send private messages on Instagram. I've never done anything on it apart from look at my children's posts. Maybe all you can do is leave comments underneath photos.

That makes it even more urgent for me to get my photos up. Once I have, Jess and Olly can write whatever they want to say to me as comments attached to my pictures. I write stupid captions to go with the images: 'pretty tree!' and 'exotic smoothies!' How long will I have to wait before one of my children replies?

Neither of them has posted anything since I last looked, but I didn't expect them to. It's night-time in England; they'll be asleep.

I log out of Instagram and into Hotmail. Patrick hasn't opened the email I sent him. It's still showing as an unread message in the inbox of the account we share. He's probably asleep now too. He and I have always had body clocks in opposition to one another. He bounces out of bed every morning at 5.30 or 6, eager to start the day, but can't keep his eyes open later than 10 in the evening. I feel as if something terrible has happened to me if I have to wake up before 8 a.m., but I can easily stay up till 1 or 2 in the morning if I need to. It worked really well when the kids were little and barely slept: I did the night shifts and Patrick took over at 4 a.m., having gone to bed at 8.30 or 9 the night before, allowing me to sleep till 9 when he had to set off for work. Each of us was convinced we had the better deal.

Why isn't Patrick willing to go to bed at 8.30 and wake up at 4 for this baby? He's done it twice before – would it truly be so unbearable for him to have to do it a third time?

I sigh, log out of the email account and close my eyes. I wish, wish, wish I had my phone with me. It makes me sick to think of it lying somewhere in Rock the Hole's office or apartment, with messages from my family on it that I'm desperate to read. How could I have been so reckless and stupid?

That's what Patrick said, word for word, when I told him I was pregnant. He'd wanted to go out and buy condoms. I was the one who said, 'I can't believe it'll matter, just this once. It's not even close to the middle of my cycle.'

Stop.

I can't let myself think about any of this now. I'll wait till I'm back at my casita in the blue and silver bedroom, my thinking room.

When I open my eyes, Badass Mom is staring at me. *Shit.* I must have sighed too loud. I look down at my iPad and tap buttons randomly to avoid meeting her eye. The Google home page appears on the screen. What can I search for? There must be something I want or need to know.

There's only one thing I'm curious about at the moment. I type 'Melody dead police McNair' into the search box. This is going to be a colossal waste of time, but it'll keep me busy until Badass Mom has lost interest in me.

I tap return.

Wait a second . . .

I stare at the first page of results, unable to believe what's in front of me. Words and names blur as I blink repeatedly, trying to focus. There's a surname: Chapa. Melody Chapa. And the word 'murder'. It's everywhere. *Murder, murder, murder . . .*

No. This can't be the same Melody. This Melody is famous.

Scrolling through, I see, in the first line of text under one of the search result headings, another familiar name . . .

The world tilts, then freezes.

Oh, fuck. Oh, God. What is this? What have I found?

The churning in the pit of my stomach tells me I'm better off not knowing, that it's safer to run away. Except I've already done that, and this is what I seem to have run into.

I don't have to look. I could switch off the iPad and forget about it.

Taking a deep breath, I scroll up to the top of the search results and open a blog called 'Melody Chapa: the Full Story'.

★　★　★

94

There's too much here to read quickly. It's divided into sections with headings like 'Trial Evidence', 'Attorneys and Jury', 'Opening Statements and Witness Testimony', 'Verdict and Sentence', 'Media Coverage'. The first section, longer on its own than any blog I've ever read, is called 'The Murder of Melody Chapa: an overview'. That's just the first part of twelve, and . . . bloody hell, even the overview is divided into three parts. The whole thing goes on forever. Breathing too fast, I start at the top, then give up halfway through the first paragraph.

I can't concentrate. I can't read this now, not properly. A quick scroll through the whole entry gives me a few of the basics – enough to know that now is not the time to sit and read quietly for hours. I have to do something. Urgently.

I try to stand up and fall back down on my lounger. Badass Mom and Highbrow Daughter both look up at me. Can they tell I'm in a state? It'll give them something to bitch about later.

Before I go anywhere, I need to work out what I'm going to say. What do I know? What are the basic facts? I try to make a list:

1. Melody Chapa is dead, according to the internet. She was murdered when she was seven years old.
2. Her parents are in prison for her murder.
3. Melody Chapa can't be dead, because I saw her.

I saw her.

She was the girl with Hairy Chest Man, in the hotel room I should never have walked into. I know this because of the toy, Poggy. That was the other familiar name I saw in the search results. Now, after skimming this blog for only a few minutes, I know that Melody Chapa owned a beloved cuddly toy called Poggy. It looked a bit like a pig and a bit like a dog, and so Melody's parents, while she was still a baby, had given it the name Poggy.

The same parents who'd murdered their only child seven years later.

Wait – didn't I see something about them having another daughter?

I scroll up and down frantically, not certain I saw it at all. My eyes land on random sequences of words that blur when I try to focus on them. The sun isn't helping; I should go back to my casita.

Wait, here it is. Annette and Naldo Chapa had another baby that . . .

I cover my mouth with my hand. *Oh, Jesus. Oh, my God.*

Melody Chapa's parents had another daughter, before Melody. Her name was Emory.

Do Mom and Dad love me? Why do they love Emory more?

The piece of paper I pulled out of the silver pot in the crystal grotto. Did Melody Chapa write those words – the same Melody Chapa who's been dead since 2010?

How common a name is Emory in America?

No. This is crazy. It was her. If it was Poggy, it was Melody. I heard Mrs McNair say to Riyonna, 'She had that creature with her.' Did she mean Poggy? I assumed she meant a person because she said something about a boyfriend straight after.

And the girl I met was rubbing her head. I'm sure I saw . . .

I scroll through the blog again. The text flies up and down. Yes. Her head – there it is. Mrs McNair mentioned that too: *It was dark, and I couldn't see the top of her head, but it was her.*

Either I'm as insane as she is, or Melody Chapa is still alive.

I gather my things together and force myself to walk at a normal pace to the spa reception, breathing slowly and deeply. Too much adrenaline's bound to be bad for the baby. The man in white who was talking to the detective is behind the desk. He smiles at me. 'I hope you're having a superlative day, ma'am,' he says. 'Is there something I can do for you?'

'Yes. The detective – the one you were talking to before. Is he still here?'

'Oh!' He's surprised that I know. 'I, uh . . . No. He set off back to the hotel in a club car around five minutes ago. If you like I can reach out to them and—'

'Can you call me a club car, as soon as possible, please? Same destination. I need to speak to him urgently.'

'Coming right up, ma'am.' I can't see his hands

beneath the counter, but I imagine the relevant button is being pressed. Less than a minute later, my driver and car arrive.

All the way back to the hotel, I stare hard at every building, tree, bench and balcony I pass, hoping to catch a glimpse of Melody with Poggy in her hand. When I don't see her, I wonder – for no reason apart from a fear that I'm too late – if she's dead now even if she wasn't last night.

For God's sake, Cara. If she's lasted a whole seven years since she was supposed to have been murdered, why would she suddenly die now?

I gasp as the answer hits me: because of me. I might have ruined everything by seeing her, seeing Poggy, hearing her say the name . . .

'You okay back there, missy?' asks my driver.

Missy?

'Yes, thanks. Fine.'

I'm getting carried away. It makes sense, though. If Melody was here at Swallowtail, then she was here secretly. A girl who's supposed to be dead wouldn't openly parade herself around a holiday resort – it would be too risky.

And she ran away in the middle of the night after you saw her with Poggy because to stay suddenly became too risky. Her cover was blown.

'*Cara Burrows – is she safe?*'

Hairy Chest Man must have written that. Except . . . if he and Melody left Swallowtail in the middle of the night when the crystal grotto and spa were closed, how is that possible?

98

At the main reception desk I'm offered help by a man with a receding hairline and a thin straight line of moustache. He looks about my age and is wearing a badge that says 'Dane Williamson, Resort Manager'. More senior than Riyonna, then. Good. He'll do.

'There were two detectives here before, about a possible sighting of Melody Chapa,' I say as if all this is normal. 'Are they still here?'

'I . . . ah . . . I think you must be mistaken, ma'am.' His smile is ferocious.

'I'm not. I met them before, with Riyonna, then I saw one of them again at the spa just now. A guest called Mrs McNair—'

'Yes, yes, I see.' He shushes me with his hands. 'Why don't we go through to my office where we can talk in private?'

'First I need to talk to the detectives.'

'They left five minutes ago. But I'll do my very best to—'

'I'm happy to talk to you, but first you need to call the police and tell them to come back. Ring them now. They can't have got far.'

'Please,' Williamson says, gesturing towards a closed door behind reception. I assume it's his office.

'Please what?' I'm not moving until he does as I ask. 'Are you going to ring the police? It's not only Mrs McNair. I saw Melody Chapa too. Is that how you pronounce it – Chapper? She was here at Swallowtail, last night.'

Williamson's smile falls a little lower on his face. 'If you know who Melody Chapa is – was – then you know it's impossible that anyone saw her here last night. Right?' He pronounces it Chah-pah.

'I know why it ought to be impossible. I also know what I saw.' I explain that I was sent by mistake to a room that was already occupied. To protect Riyonna – because Dane Williamson strikes me as a man who might enjoy firing better people than himself – I say 'a receptionist' made a mistake, and don't name her. I tell him about Mrs McNair and what I overheard her say earlier, including the part about her having 'that creature' with her.

'The girl I met in the hotel room had Melody's favourite toy with her – Poggy. Part pig, part dog. I saw it with my own eyes, and I heard her refer to it as Poggy. Also, Melody had a sister – sort of, an already-dead sister – called Emory.' I tell Williamson about the piece of paper I pulled out of the silver pot in the crystal grotto.

'Oh, my.' He seems more shocked by this than by my sighting of a murdered girl. 'Ma'am, the crystal grotto is a place for guests to privately—'

'Oh, for God's sake! Yes, I violated the privacy of other guests – but they chose to leave personal details lying around in a public place. I'm sorry. I shouldn't have done it, okay? The point is, the detectives can look and see for themselves what Melody wrote: not only a reference to Emory, but to a sibling called Emory. She doesn't say explicitly that Emory's her sister, but it's pretty clear. I mean, come *on*.'

Williamson upgrades his smile. 'If it'll make you feel better, I'll be sure to pass on the information you've given me.'

'Good. Thank you. So . . . what should I do?'

'No need for you to do anything, ma'am – just carry on going about your regular business.'

'Where's Riyonna? Can I speak to her?'

'As I say, there's no need for you to worry about anything. I'll take care of it. You make sure to enjoy the rest of your vacation.' He smiles again and gives me a wave, then disappears into the back office, closing the door behind him.

'Notice he didn't ask your name, room number, cell number,' a woman's voice says. 'He has no intention of ringing any detectives.'

I turn. It's Badass Mom. There's no sign of her daughter.

'You heard all that?'

'Most of it. By the way – the pot in the grotto? Don't worry about it. I snooped too – who could resist? Boy, are people dull! Right? When I looked there was one that said "Loan" – just the one word. Whoever wrote that must be a real raconteur, huh?'

'You mean "Loan/debt"?'

'Yeah, that's right.' She grins. 'You saw it too, huh?'

'When did you look? How many were in there?'

'First day here. So that'd be . . . four days ago. There were only two, both as boring as each

101

other: "Loan/debt" and then one about . . . ugh, I can't even remember. Someone had invited someone, or not invited someone, and there was a date . . .'

'Was it Vanessa, who made Paul do her dirty work?'

'I honestly couldn't tell you.' Badass Mom peers at me as if I'm a peculiar specimen. 'Why do you care?'

'Was a specific date mentioned – the 23rd?'

'Yeah, that's the one. It was so achingly boring, I nearly passed out.

'You're sure there were no others in the pot, just the two?'

'Oh, yeah. I scraped those sides, baby.' She laughs. 'The one you told that pompous creep about, with Emory in it? No sign of that, so it must have been more recent.'

'Was there one that said "Cara Burrows – is she safe?"'

'There was *not*.' Badass Mom gives me a sharp look. 'I'd have *loved* to find that one. Sounds juicy. Who's Cara Burrows, and why might she not be safe?'

'Because last night she walked into the wrong hotel room and saw a dead girl – one who was supposedly murdered seven years ago.' It's weird, talking so freely to this woman whose eye I've been studiously avoiding all day.

'Cara Burrows is me,' I tell her.

Melody Chapa – The Full Story

An Overview

The Murder of Melody Chapa:
Part 1 – Melody Disappears
(all ages given are as per March 2, 2010)

Before she went missing on March 2, 2010, Melody Grace Chapa (2003–2010) – who has been dubbed 'America's most famous murder victim' by some media commentators – was an ordinary seven-year-old girl living in Philadelphia, PA, with her parents Annette Connolly Chapa (39) and Naldo Enrique Chapa (38). At the time, Annette ran a marketing company, and Naldo was an actuarial analyst at the Reliance Standard Life Insurance Company in Philadelphia. Melody was their second daughter. In February 2002, Annette lost a baby at twenty-four weeks' gestation. The baby, who died *in utero* after the placenta broke down, was named Emory Laurel Chapa. She was buried at Saint Mark's Episcopal Church in Center City, Philadelphia, on March 18, 2002.

When Annette Chapa arrived at Hoade Godley Elementary School on the afternoon of March 2, 2010 to pick up Melody, she was told by teachers that Melody had not been seen at all that day. She had never arrived in the morning, and the woman who normally dropped her off, Kristie Reville, had phoned the school office to say that Melody would not be in because she had been vomiting. When asked however, Kristie Reville denied making this call and claimed she had dropped Melody at school as usual and had watched her walk into the building. The school secretary could not confirm that it was Kristie who called her, she later said, only that the woman identified herself as Kristie Reville.

No one seemed to have any idea where Melody was. The last time she had been seen for certain was at seven thirty on the morning of March 2, 2010, when, according to both women, Annette Chapa had dropped her off with Kristie Reville to be taken to school. At ten o'clock the following morning, Melody Chapa was declared officially missing.

Kristie Luanne Reville (40) and her husband Jeff Reville (42) were the next-door neighbors of Annette and Naldo Chapa. With no children of their own, they were said to be 'like another set of parents to Melody'. Jeff Reville was an art teacher at Barbara Duchenne Center City High School and Kristie Reville was an aspiring artist with no paid employment apart from babysitting Melody occasionally, which she did when Annette and Naldo Chapa were busy with work and needed her help, usually during school vacation periods, or for school drop-offs and pick-ups. Kristie and Jeff also used to look after Melody for free on a regular basis. She was in the habit of staying at their house one night each weekend so that Annette and Naldo Chapa could have some time alone together as a couple.

The local area was extensively searched by police and by teams of volunteers. At first no trace of Melody was found. Detectives were initially suspicious of Kristie and Jeff Reville. No parents or teachers who had been at the school gates or in the playground the day Melody disappeared had any memory of seeing either Melody or Kristie that particular morning, and police started to wonder if Kristie was lying about having stood in the playground and watched Melody walk safely into the building.

At the police's suggestion, Naldo and Annette Chapa appeared on the *Jessica Sabisky Show* on March 5, 2010, where they were supposed to make a heartfelt appeal to whoever might have taken Melody. Annette stuck to the script given to her by detectives, saying that she had already lost one precious child – Emory – and could not bear to lose another. She was later accused by media and online commentators of sounding wooden and unemotional and reciting words she had memorized in advance. Naldo Chapa did not use the agreed wording of his pre-prepared statement: 'Please, whoever has our darling Melody, bring her home safely.' Instead, he broke down and controversially said, 'I'm going to hunt down whoever's killed my daughter and kill them with my bare hands.' Annette Chapa followed this by saying, 'Whoever you are, if you're the person who's done this, we will ask for the death penalty to be taken off the table if you admit you murdered our daughter and tell us where her body is.'

This live-on-air appeal attracted a considerable amount of publicity and attention, most of it negative. News feeds had been created on multiple networks, and many online chat groups devoted to discussing the latest in the Melody Chapa case sprang up at around this time. Annette Chapa was thought by many to be too detached, and her husband too vindictive. Shock was expressed about the obvious assumption by the Chapas that their daughter was already dead when there was no evidence to suggest that she was.

Some who saw the appeal were more sympathetic. Celebrity psychotherapist Ingrid Allwood said that to reach for the worst-case scenario and assume it's true is a common defense mechanism in traumatic situations. On March 9, 2010, Allwood defended this position on the popular NBC show *Justice With Bonnie*, claiming that many people would not allow themselves to hope, for fear of potential disappointment. She said, 'The Chapas might superstitiously believe that by assuming the worst has happened, they're encouraging Fate to prove them wrong.'

The host of *Justice With Bonnie*, legal commentator Bonnie Juno, did her best to demolish Allwood's arguments, stating that, as a former prosecutor she had met hundreds of victims of serious crime and it was highly unusual – and therefore suspicious – for parents of a missing child, especially one that had gone missing so recently, to have apparently no hope of getting their daughter back alive.

On that episode of *Justice With Bonnie*, Juno strongly implied that she believed Annette and Naldo Chapa had murdered their daughter. She received widespread condemnation for this, and was accused of having no evidence to support her theory. At that stage, no one else had pointed the finger at Melody's parents, probably because the media was full of all the evidence that was stacking up to implicate Kristie Reville.

Kristie was in the habit of picking up her husband Jeff after work on any weekday afternoon that she was not picking up Melody from school. On March 2, 2010, Annette was due to pick up her daughter and so Kristie went to pick up her husband, who doesn't drive.

A colleague of Jeff Reville, Nate Appleyard (56), happened to see Jeff and Kristie in their car, a Toyota Camry, in the parking lot of Barbara Duchenne School that afternoon. He remembered something he needed to tell Jeff and hurried over to the car. He later told police that Kristie had been visibly upset and gasped with shock when she saw him. Clearly, he said, she had not expected that she and Jeff would be disturbed inside their car. Her eyes were puffy and red and she had obviously been crying. 'I asked her if she was okay,' Appleyard told detectives, 'but she was trying not to look at me. She was fiddling with buttons on the side of her seat, maybe trying to adjust it. I don't know what made me look down to where her hand was, between the seat and the door, but I saw she had blood on her lower arm, just above her wrist: a streak of blood. Then I wondered if she was pushing her arm down between the seat and the driver door to try and hide the blood.'

Appleyard told police that he wondered if he should ask Kristie Reville if she needed help, and almost did, but both she and Jeff were avoiding eye contact and in the end he decided not to embarrass them. As he was taking his leave of them, he noticed something on the floor of the car beyond Kristie's feet: a child's white, lace-topped sock with bloodstains visible on it. Later, interviewed on *Justice With Bonnie*, Appleyard said, 'Kristie seemed to see the blood-soaked sock the same time I did. It was lying about three inches in front of her foot. Soon as I saw it I thought, "Woah, something ain't right here." I opened my mouth to ask, but before I could get the words out, she'd slid her seat all the way forward and the sock wasn't visible any more. I'll tell you one thing for nothing: whatever Kristie knew that day, whatever she'd done, whatever she was trying to hide, Jeff knew it too. He was acting peculiar – they both were. I started to ask about the sock, but they drove away while I was talking. I'll be honest. I thought, "There's two people with something to hide."'

By the time police searched Kristie Reville's Toyota Camry, there was no bloodstained sock inside it, but forensic testing found Melody's blood in the car, despite clear attempts to scrub it clean. Jeff Reville had an alibi – he had already set out for work when Annette Chapa brought Melody to his house and left her with Kristie, and he was with people at work for the whole of that day.

Kristie Reville at first offered no alibi. She insisted she was innocent of harming Melody and knew nothing of the child's whereabouts. When asked how she had spent March 2, 2010 between dropping Melody at school at 8.15 a.m. and picking up Jeff from work at 4.30 p.m., Kristie claimed she had 'gone for a long walk'. She was unable to produce any witnesses who could verify her activities that day.

On March 7, 2010, a local gas-station owner came forward to say that the Revilles had stopped at his gas station on March 2, the day Melody disappeared, and that Kristie had had blood on her hand and arm. She'd used his bathroom to wash it off, he told detectives; when she came out of the bathroom, her arm and hand were clean. This was enough for the police, who took Jeff and Kristie Reville into custody.

The area around the gas station had not yet been searched but now it was, and a bag was found in a wild, overgrown patch of grass nearby. This turned out to be Melody's school bag, and contained her pencil case, books and the remains of a packed lunch in an airtight plastic container. To the detectives' surprise, the bag did not contain Melody's cherished soft toy, Poggy, that she took to school with her every day and hid in her bag so as not to appear babyish to her friends. Neither the toy nor Melody's body was ever found.

The bag was stained both inside and out with blood that DNA testing revealed to be Melody's. It contained one bloodstained white lace-topped sock that Annette and Naldo Chapa later identified as Melody's and that Nate Appleyard confirmed looked identical to the one he'd seen in Kristie's car.

Socks, of course, come in pairs – and one interesting feature of this story is that, in ninety-nine out of a hundred cases, there might have been no way of being sure that the bloodstained sock Nate Appleyard saw in Kristie Reville's car was the same one that later showed up in Melody's school bag. However, both Annette Chapa and Kristie Reville separately told detectives that it had proved impossible to find Melody a matching pair of socks that morning, and so, for the first time in her life, Melody set off to school wearing only one sock with a border of lace around the top of it. The other sock she wore that day was white and ribbed, with no lace. Hence, detectives were able to conclude that the sock that had shown up in the school bag was very likely to be the same one Nate Appleyard had seen in Kristie Reville's car.

There were also strands of Melody's hair in her school bag, and lots of dead blowflies and larvae from the same species – one that's known as the coffin fly on account of it regularly being found in close proximity to corpses. Tests on the strands of Melody's hair revealed that she had been subject to arsenic poisoning for a period of at least three months.

On May 22, 2010, the day the case was put before a grand jury to see whether Kristie Reville should stand trial for murder, Bonnie Juno interviewed Annette and Naldo Chapa live on *Justice With Bonnie.* Melody's parents won over many Americans by insisting that Jeff and Kristie Reville could not possibly have abducted or hurt their daughter. Most people by this point believed that Kristie Reville had murdered Melody and hidden her body, and that Jeff was covering for her. Nevertheless, the Chapas' determination to believe in the goodness of their trusted neighbors and friends endeared them to the nation. Bonnie Juno told the Chapas that she understood only too well why they believed the Revilles to be innocent, strongly implying again that they themselves were guilty. Annette Chapa broke down, and she and her husband walked off the set, ending the interview prematurely.

Bonnie Juno, by now as unpopular as Kristie

Reville, was attacked extensively across all media platforms. Juno is six feet tall and sturdily built, and she was accused by legal commentator Mark Johnston of being 'a rancid, vindictive transvestite-drag-act bitch' – an insult for which Johnston later publicly apologized. Juno's former husband, renowned defense attorney Raoul Juno, gave an interview to his ex-wife's professional rival, HLN's Nancy Grace, in which he went into detail about the problems that had ended their marriage and revealed much that was embarrassing to Juno. Her attempt to sue him for his revelations was unsuccessful, and on June 18, 2010, she was arrested for causing a disturbance of the peace outside Raoul Juno's home. After this incident, Bonnie Juno was absent from her own show for two months. When she returned on August 21, it was to announce that she would soon have the privilege of interviewing, live on *Justice With Bonnie*, a guest whose testimony would change everything in the Melody Chapa case.

10 OCTOBER 2017

'**I** just don't get it.' I look up from the iPad. 'This all happened – the bit I've read so far – before anyone declared Melody officially dead. How can this Bonnie woman suggest Melody's parents are murderers on live TV and get away with it?'

I'm at Swallowtail's Mountain View Cocktail Bar with Tarin and Zellie Fry, sitting at a table on the terrace. It's going to be a while before I can think of them as anything but Badass Mom and Highbrow Daughter. Tarin is the mother. Zellie is short for Giselia. As we sat down, Tarin told me, 'You can say what you like in front of Zellie. Don't think of her as any kind of child. She'd seen every episode of *Dexter* by the time she was thirteen.'

She's sixteen now and should be at school but isn't because, according to her mother: 'What's the point? No one in that sorry-ass establishment teaches her anything worth missing a vacation for. She'll learn more reading on her own. Her father disapproves, so I left him at home. If you're married to a whiner, you've gotta come down hard, soon as he starts to complain.'

'Like you wouldn't have found some excuse to leave him at home anyway,' Zellie muttered.

'Welcome to American justice,' Tarin says now with a grin. She seems to be enjoying the situation, and my bewilderment in particular, as if it's all precisely what she'd hoped for as an accompaniment to her holiday.

'You mean this is all normal and . . . allowed?' I take a sip of my latest mocktail – a blue one this time, with some purple towards the bottom – and wonder if I'll end up having dinner with these two strangers. I want and need to talk to someone about everything that's happened, but a whole meal together feels like a big commitment to people I don't know.

'NFA – normal for America.' Tarin chuckles.

'How can it be normal?' I say. 'If anything goes to trial, the jury'll be massively biased, having heard all this on a . . . daily justice show, or whatever it is.'

'Oh, it goes to trial – just not the trial anyone was expecting,' says Tarin. 'You know it's Melody's parents who are in jail for murder, not Kristie Reville?'

'Yeah. And from what I've read so far, that makes no sense.'

'You need to read the rest. We Yanks were lucky: we got the story spread out over *years* by the time the trial came around. Bonnie Juno was obsessed that whole time. She kept finding new people to interview – anyone who'd ever met Naldo Chapa

114

at a conference, anyone who'd ever sold Annette Chapa a sandwich – she'd have them on the show and ask for their decades-old *impressions*, as if that was going to tell anyone anything. You weren't lying, huh? None of this reached you over in England?'

'Nothing. I'd never heard of Melody Chapa until today.'

'Lucky you.'

I don't feel lucky. What am I supposed to do if the resort manager won't take me seriously? Should I ring the local police myself? How? I don't know the names of the two detectives who were here, and I've no reason to think anyone would listen to me any more than they listened to Mrs McNair. Why should they? As the internet reminds me every time I check, Melody Chapa is dead.

'The bloodstained sock . . .' At this rate I'll soon be as obsessed as Bonnie Juno. 'I mean, everything Nate Appleyard said on *Justice With Bonnie* about what he saw in Kristie Reville's car . . . it's like the whole trial – evidence, arguments – is happening on TV instead of in court.'

'You're right.' Tarin nods. 'Whole system's fucked. It's not justice, it's a farce. Google "Melody Chapa justice farce" – you'll find a hundred long analyses of how twisted it all got.'

'So there's really no rule over here about not publicly saying anything that might bias jurors?'

'Nope. Appalling, right? I'm telling you, you'd be horrified.'

'I am.'

'We've got it all in the good ol' US of A: jurors signing up to sell their stories before the trial's even started and facing no sanctions whatsoever, bereaved family members banned from courtrooms because the psycho that sliced up their loved one managed to convince a judge that he finds their presence in court *traumatic*. Yeah, right. More like: the jury's less likely to convict if they can't see his victim's sobbing family members. And don't get me started on the doctoring of crime scenes.'

'Tell us how to get you stopped,' says Zellie.

Tarin, in full flow, ignores her. 'You won't believe this, Cara. Sometimes juries are taken on tours of the crime scene, so they can get a real feel for things. Great idea, huh? Except wouldn't you think the court'd impose some kind of obligation for the crime scene to be kept as it was immediately after the crime was committed? Wouldn't you think a defence attorney'd face a fine – or, better still, contempt charges – if he had all the blood and brain matter cleaned away so the place was spotless, and hung framed photos of the wife and kids his sicko client killed all the way up the stairs, as if they'd been there all along – as if the killer ever gave enough of a shit about them to bother?'

'The longest rhetorical question in the world,' Zellie murmurs. She picks up her mother's glass and takes a sip of Campari and soda, giving me a look that clearly says, 'Say one word and you're dead.' Tarin doesn't notice. It's turning into a beautiful night; I can already see a sprinkling of stars. Camelback Mountain looks stunning: a black outline against a deep blue sky.

I scroll down on the iPad, scanning the text for the words I'm looking for. 'I can't find the bit I saw before, about Melody's head. The girl I met last night didn't stop rubbing the top of her head. I wondered about it at the time.'

'That's right. Melody had a mark in front of her hairline.' Tarin points to her own head. 'Here, right?'

I nod. Exactly where the girl rubbed, same spot.

'It's a big, dark brown circle, like an oversized freckle – about as big as a quarter. Americans know it intimately. Bonnie Juno had photos of it on her show for months, enlarged, zoomed in . . . It came up in court at the Chapas' trial. Melody had cradle cap as a baby. You're not supposed to pick it off, though it's tempting – like picking at a scab. Everyone warns you: scraping off cradle cap can lead to infection and/or scarring for life. Annette Chapa admitted in court that she'd picked off a large globule from Melody's head – she couldn't resist. Course, that gave the rabid Bonnie Juno an opportunity to do a whole show around "What kind of *terrible, abusive* mother would do such a thing against official medical advice?" Do me a favour!' Tarin snorts. 'I did all kinds of stuff I wasn't supposed to do when Zellie was a baby. Once I gave her a jar of anchovy paste instead of baby food – I was so goddamned bored of that stinky mush you're supposed to give them. She was sick *everywhere*.'

117

Zellie reaches for the Campari again. This time Tarin notices and slaps her hand away. 'Cut that out!' Turning to me, she says, 'Annette Chapa didn't heed the warnings. She picked off the cradle cap and it left a brown spot. As Melody's head increased in size, so did the spot. That doesn't make Annette Chapa a murderer.'

'So how did she and her husband end up in prison for killing Melody?'

Tarin nods at the iPad. 'Read on. I'm guessing you haven't got to the part about Mallory Tondini?'

'No.'

'Well, you will.'

'The girl I saw must have been Melody. Why else would she do that rubbing thing? She didn't know I'd never heard of Melody Chapa. She was scared I'd see the brown mark on her head and recognise her.'

Zellie makes a dismissive noise. 'You're talking as if she isn't dead. She's dead.'

'How do you know?' Tarin asks.

'What, you actually believe this crap?' Zellie turns to me. 'I'm not accusing you of lying, okay? But come *on*. Melody Chapa's long dead. Any girl can have a weird fixation and name her soft toy Poggy and rub her head for, like, a wide variety of possible reasons.'

'They never found her body,' says Tarin. 'Plus, they found her bag with Poggy not in it.'

'Yes, and that means the body and the toy could be literally anywhere. The school bag they found had Melody's hair in it, and tests showed arsenic poisoning. And there were flies in the bag – the kind that only bother to turn up if someone's *dead.*'

'I know.' Tarin is unperturbed. 'Still no body, though.'

'Mother, a court decided she was dead.' Zellie rolls her eyes. 'Her parents are in prison, never to come out. It's so typical of you to think you know better.'

'Is your job something to do with the law?' I ask Tarin.

'Ha! Go on, Mother, tell Cara what you do. District Attorney, is it? Supreme Court judge? Oh, wait, no, it's neither of those two things.'

Tarin's grinning. I have the impression Zellie has said this or similar to her before. 'I'm a florist. Got my own shop in Lawrence, Kansas. So fucking what, right? Doesn't stop me thinking.'

'It's only fair you know this, Cara. My mother is totally biased. She wants you to have seen Melody Chapa, and she wants Melody to be not dead. You know why? Because then Bonnie Juno'd look like the biggest moron that ever lived, and she *hates* Bonnie Juno.'

'That is true,' Tarin confirms. 'All civilised Americans hate Juno. She's a hypocrite, or an idiot, or both. Probably both. When she was a prosecutor, *every*one was guilty. Especially the people she prosecuted – they were the guiltiest of all, naturally. Then she switches careers and becomes a legal commentator on TV, and suddenly everyone's being callously and cynically framed according to her. The cops are always wrong, the prosecutors always wrong, defendants always innocent. It's like something happened to turn Juno against her former profession and push her into the arms of the other side, the *darker* side. Melody Chapa disappears and Kristie Reville looks guilty as hell, and the cops think she's responsible? Juno makes a point of declaring her blameless. No one suspects the parents? Oh, wait, someone does! Bonnie Juno does, mainly because the police don't. She'd say anything to be contrary. I swear to God, if the cops had pointed the finger at Melody's parents from the start, Juno would have protested their innocence like her own life depended on it. Narcissism – that's what it is. She's a narcissist. Those accused of crimes are guilty or innocent to suit the needs of her ego at any given time.'

'If Melody's parents are in jail for her murder, that might mean . . .' I don't finish the sentence.

'That Bonnie Juno got it right this time?' Tarin makes a derisory hissing noise. 'Cara, you're the one who *saw Melody*. Here, at Swallowtail. Alive. Or rather – keeping an open mind – you saw a girl who might be Melody. I suppose it's possible the girl you saw was someone else with a toy called Poggy – a tribute to Melody's Poggy – and it's possible this girl happened to have an itchy head last night. Or – better idea! – her *thing*, her schtick, is pretending she's Melody. Maybe she was worried you'd see *no* brown mark on her head and break the spell by yelling, "Wait a second – you're not Melody!"' Tarin laughs, sticks her arm up in the air and yells, 'Another Campari and soda over here.'

The nearest waiter hurries away to do her bidding.

'Don't bother asking if we want anything,' says Zellie.

'I think you saw her,' Tarin tells me, paying no attention to her daughter. 'Real her, and real Poggy. Mrs McNair seems pretty nuts – so when I heard her blabbering on about seeing Melody Chapa, I paid no attention. But you? You're sane.'

'How can you tell?' asks Zellie.

They both stare at me.

'Easy,' says Tarin. 'Crazy people – as in, deluded – make shit up. They're imaginative. Cara, when you mentioned the girl saying she'd spilled Coke on Poggy and Doodle Dandy, I'll admit that I thought, "Here we go! Doodle Dandy – that's a red-flag crazy alert, this woman's invented a new character toy for a dead girl." Then I realised: you're not that imaginative, are you? Don't take that as an insult. Not everyone has to be imaginative.'

'What do you mean? I mentioned Doodle Dandy because she did – the girl.'

'Right. That's my point. I believe you. I don't think you've got the imagination to dream up a new toy and name it.'

I can't help bristling at this. 'Actually, I've named plenty of toys. When my children—'

'Please!' Tarin waves my words away. 'You named stuffed toys you had to name, because your babies were too young to do it themselves. I bet you called the white ones "Snowy" and the black ones . . .' She stops and frowns. 'Shit, my mind's gone blank. What's black?'

'Nelson Mandela,' says Zellie in a bored drawl. 'Maybe he's not really dead either. I swear I saw him in our bathtub this morning.'

'My point is, Cara, if you were making up a bunch of crap, you wouldn't need to give Melody any other toy but Poggy. He's all you'd need for a convincing Melody encounter. I don't think you'd make up a second cuddly thing. If you did, being British, I don't think you'd call it Doodle Dandy, which is an abbreviation of Yankee Doodle Dandy.'

I'm getting tired of hearing about myself from this woman who knows nothing about me. I want to have dinner alone. Not that I'm at all hungry.

'When Mrs McNair was being an asshole before, by the pool, you moved. An imaginative person would have found a way to make *her* move. And you're here on your own. Why? You're not here for business.'

'How do you know?'

'You don't move briskly enough. You seem kind of lost and unfocused, and you're not with friends or family. If I had to guess . . .'

'You don't, though,' Zellie advises. 'You could mind your own business for the first time ever.'

'. . . I'd say you have a problem of some kind and you don't know how to solve it. Which proves you're unimaginative. There must *be* a way to deal

122

with it. If I knew the problem, I'd give you the solution. Not that I'm prying. But, yeah . . .' Tarin nods at me as the waiter puts a full Campari and soda down on the table in front of her. 'I believe you saw and heard what you say you saw and heard. Which means – maybe, probably – that for once Mrs McNair's right: Melody and her male chaperone ran away last night.'

'Because of me. Because, since I barged in on them, they think I'm a threat. They weren't packed or anything. They were asleep, with their stuff all over the bathroom: razors, a swimming cap, hair clips. Nothing I saw indicated that they were planning to go anywhere last night.'

I sit forward in my chair. 'The room! We can find out who's supposed to be in that room, or the police can, if we call them – what name it's booked in, whether anyone's in it. Shit!'

'What?' Tarin grabs my arm. 'Have you remembered something else?'

'The opposite. I can't remember what number room it was. It was on the third floor, but beyond that—'

'Don't worry about that. There'll be a record on the system.' She stands up and throws the rest of her drink down her throat, spilling some down her neck in the process.

'Mother!' Zellie protests. 'Manners.'

Tarin snaps her fingers. 'Club car!' she calls over her shoulder. Then, to pacify Zellie, 'If you *please*.'

123

Melody Chapa – The Full Story

An Overview

The Murder of Melody Chapa:
Part 2 – A Surprise Alibi

The media vilification of Bonnie Juno continued for the two months that she was away from her show. Also during this time – unknown to the public – one of the officers involved in the Melody Chapa case was starting to have grave doubts about Kristie and Jeff Reville's guilt. Detective Larry Beadman had been contacted by a man named Victor Soutar who described himself as a massage therapist. Soutar claimed that Kristie Reville had spent the whole day with him on March 2, 2010. She arrived at his apartment at nine that morning, he said, which would have given her just enough time to get there in the heavy morning traffic if she'd dropped Melody at school at the usual time, and she stayed until three thirty in the afternoon: the exact time at which she would have needed to leave in order to pick up her husband after work at four thirty.

Soutar told Larry Beadman he had thought twice about coming forward, hence the delay. He had been following the case in the news as most of the country had, and he had taken Kristie Reville's failure to produce him as an alibi to mean that she would rather risk a murder conviction than have the truth come out. Soutar said that personally he couldn't see why she would be so ashamed of the truth, but if she was, that was her business. Asked why, in that case, he had come forward, Soutar replied, 'I don't know. I guess it's not just about Kristie. It's about the little girl too. Whoever killed her could get away with it. I don't want that on my conscience.'

Soutar turned out to be no ordinary massage therapist. He was 'a charmer' with impeccable manners and presentation, and he specialized in erotic massage specifically for women with fertility problems. Kristie Reville had responded to an ad he'd posted on Craigslist.

When Detective Beadman looked closely at Soutar's operation, he soon discovered him to be 'a fraud with a lot of extremely gullible clients'. These included Kristie Reville, who had said nothing to her husband about her regular sessions with Soutar at his apartment. She subsequently admitted, 'Deep down, I knew the line Vic was spinning me was pure fantasy, but I didn't want to admit it to myself because I needed to believe something might work, and Jeff and I had tried everything else. We were so desperate for a baby – Jeff too, though I think I was probably worse than him. I'd have done anything, paid any money, even for something I didn't really believe in.'

With this news, the media erupted all over

again. If Kristie was so desperate for a child, said some, then surely this gave her a powerful motive for murdering Melody, who could never be her own? Others argued the opposite: Melody was the closest thing Kristie Reville had to a child of her own; it would therefore make no sense for Kristie to murder her. Either way, Kristie Reville suddenly had an alibi for March 2, 2010. No one could think of any reason for Victor Soutar to lie, especially since his exposure as a charlatan who faked success stories and references from women who didn't exist put an end to what for him had been a lucrative business. Kristie Reville confirmed his account of her day and admitted she'd lied because she was afraid of her husband finding out. She was not sure, she said, that Jeff wouldn't regard her 'treatment' from Soutar as a form of sexual infidelity as well as a betrayal on account of the secrecy involved.

Soutar confirmed that Kristie Reville had left his apartment in tears on March 2, 2010, after a long heart-to-heart. 'A fortnight before I saw her that day, she'd turned forty. I think she saw it as a milestone. If she wasn't pregnant by the age of forty, maybe she never would be. Women's fertility declines fast after forty, they say. Kristie asked me if there was anything I could do beyond what I was already doing for her, and she said if there wasn't then maybe she'd stop coming to me.'

Soutar persuaded her to agree to at least one more session, but he was unable to lift her spirits.

This perhaps explained why Jeff Reville's colleague, Nate Appleyard, saw her with red, puffy eyes that day.

Asked about any blood on Kristie's arm and hand, Soutar said he was certain there had been no blood on Kristie's arm when she left his apartment.

Asked if she had confided in anybody at all about her fertility massage treatments from Victor Soutar, Kristie Reville at first said no, but Larry Beadman did not believe her. He pressed her on this point, but she maintained her silence. The answer, surprisingly, came from Soutar. When the police asked him the same question, he told them Kristie had mentioned to him that she'd confided in one close friend: Annette Chapa. Annette confirmed this, and finally Kristie admitted that she had told Annette but no one else. To explain her lies, she later said in an interview with Bonnie Juno, 'It sounds crazy, but I just felt it was bad enough me not telling Jeff. If I admitted to telling anyone else, it'd make me keeping it from Jeff sound so much worse. I had no job of my own – not a real job. Most of what I paid Vic, Jeff earned that money.'

Shortly after the story of Kristie's alibi from Victor Soutar broke, a school parent, Shannon Pidd, came forward. She remembered having seen Kristie Reville's Toyota Camry in the school parking lot, with Kristie and Melody inside it. Interviewed later by Bonnie Juno, Pidd broke down in tears and admitted she had not 'suddenly remembered' this – she had remembered from the start, but had been reluctant to contradict the general view that Kristie and Melody had not been there that day.

When Juno yelled at her, 'What were you thinking? How could you withhold such important evidence?', Pidd agreed her behavior was reprehensible but said, 'I guess I just assumed I'd remembered wrong. If everyone else was sure they weren't there, I figured I might have had the days mixed up.'

Crucially, Pidd did not see Kristie or Melody get out of the car that morning. Both were still in it when Pidd and her son left the parking lot and headed toward the school building. Asked by detectives if she'd been able to gauge the mood of either Kristie or Melody, Pidd said, 'Kristie was on her phone, and Melody looked as if she was just sitting there waiting – pretty bored, really.'

Bonnie Juno, when she returned to the air after two months away, was eager to talk about the white bloodstained sock seen by Nate Appleyard in Kristie Reville's car and later found in Melody's school bag in the grass behind the gas station. Juno had a question and she wanted an answer: if Kristie hadn't abducted and killed Melody (and Juno believed she hadn't) how did that bloodstained sock end up in Kristie's car?

On *Justice With Bonnie* on August 24, 2010 Juno said, 'There's only one way it could have

128

gotten into that car: if Annette Chapa put it there in a deliberate attempt to frame Kristie Reville for Melody's murder. Think about it: Kristie had confided in nobody but Annette Chapa about her sessions with Victor Soutar. No one in the whole world knew Kristie's car would be parked outside his apartment that day – apart from Annette Chapa.' Juno and Lexi Waldman, the Chapas' lawyer, had a heated argument on Juno's show in which Waldman accused Juno of being 'the only one desperate to frame innocent people in the entire vicinity of this case'.

By now Bonnie Juno was more unpopular than ever, but it was clear she had no intention of backing down from her stated position. The interviewee she had promised, whose testimony would convince the world of Annette and Naldo Chapa's guilt, did not materialize as quickly as Juno had implied, and several people – including guests on her own show – accused her of being a fraud and a liar. Meanwhile, Juno berated Detective Larry Beadman for the failure of the police to do a thorough search of Annette and Naldo Chapa's property and their two cars. Beadman told her, live on *Justice With Bonnie*, that she didn't know what she was talking about, and provided the two dates on which the Chapa home had been searched.

Juno argued these searches did not count, for a different reason in each case. The first search of the family property took place the day after

Melody disappeared, when detectives had hopes of finding her safe and sound, so it was as much a search for a child who was still alive as for evidence of a murder. The second search was carried out once Kristie Reville was already under heavy suspicion, therefore the detectives searching the Chapa home were unlikely to have been particularly thorough, given that their suspicions at that stage were focused elsewhere.

Detective Beadman called Juno's theories 'laughably weak' and accused her of inventing a story that suited her need to persecute and vilify others, and trying to force it to fit the facts. He made it clear that there were no plans to search the Chapa home a third time. By this point he and his team were treating the case as a suspected murder. He said, 'Even if Annette and Naldo Chapa are guilty of murdering their daughter – and I personally believe it's a monstrous insult to innocent, twice-bereaved parents to suggest they are – anyone with a functioning brain who'd killed a child in March would have used the five months since then to remove any incriminating evidence. I don't believe Naldo and Annette Chapa are stupid any more than I believe they're killers. If Kristie and Jeff Reville are innocent, that does not mean the Chapas are guilty.'

Ingrid Allwood put forward an interesting theory at around this time. In discussion with Mark Johnston on CNN, Allwood said, 'Whatever he claims, I believe Detective Beadman and his colleagues would by now have searched the Chapa home again if it weren't for the aggressive approach adopted by Bonnie Juno. For a smart woman, she's acting real dumb, if you want my true opinion. By upbraiding the cops for what they aren't doing, when for all she knows they might have been just about to do it, she's antagonizing them quite needlessly. Last time Larry Beadman went on her show, there was utter loathing in his eyes. I think there's a real danger that his determination to reject anything that comes from Juno could lead to vital aspects of this case being overlooked.' When asked what these vital elements might be, Allwood replied that it was not her place to speculate. Asked if she, like Bonnie Juno, suspected the Chapas of murdering their daughter, she said, 'I'm happier keeping my suspicions to myself when I can't prove anything either way. I'd also like to remind people that Melody Chapa's body has not been found. We still don't know for certain that this poor little missing girl is dead.'

The police were slow to drop the charges against Kristie and Jeff Reville – something Bonnie Juno took them to task for on numerous occasions. And then an episode of *Justice With Bonnie* changed everything.

10 OCTOBER 2017

I can feel Tarin's impatience as Riyonna stares at the computer screen in front of her, shaking her head every few seconds. Zellie, by her side, is listless. She doesn't want to be here with her mother and me, pursuing this stupid Melody business. There's no doubt in her mind that the whole thing's a giant waste of time.

Tarin's frustration is more purposeful. She taps the little bronze Buddha on the top of its head, like a drumbeat, as if that might make something happen quickly. It's killing her that all she can see is the back of the monitor. What's Riyonna looking at that's making her eyes widen like that? I want to know too, but apparently not as much as Tarin does. She'll march round to the staff side of the desk if Riyonna doesn't tell us something soon.

I don't like the way she's made herself the driving force in all of this. She was the one who told Riyonna the full story, more succinctly than I could have. I feel as if she's intruded on something that's mine, which makes no sense given that I'd never heard of Melody Chapa until today.

'I sincerely apologise,' says Riyonna, blinking

furiously, bereft once again thanks to me. 'I'm so dreadfully sorry, really I am. This whole mess is my fault. I sent Mrs Burrows to the wrong room, and now I can't remember the number, and I can't find the information you need on our system. Maybe someone else could, someone who knew how to look for data that's been deleted, but from what I can see, it's just . . . not here.' She shakes her head again, as if she can't understand it. 'It should be . . .' Her voice tails off.

'Wait, what do you mean?' asks Tarin. 'Are you saying the system ought to have a record of the mistake you made, but someone's erased it?'

Riyonna looks stricken.

'She can't tell you that without being unprofessional,' Zellie says.

'Oh, screw unprofessional,' says Tarin. Now she's playing with the green-bean plant in the yellow pot. Any second now she's going to rip off an entire bean with her sharp nails. 'No, I mean screw *professional*. I want to know what's going on here. What kind of freaky resort is this? Murdered girls apparently wandering around, people with cancer who'd be better off in hospital, crazy octogenarians staggering around like zombies . . .'

'So sensitive, Mother.' Zellie turns away in disgust. 'So you're a doctor now, who knows what medical treatment people need? If you say one more thing about Hayley, I swear . . . Can't sick people go on vacation? And old people, for that matter?'

'Why, yes, they can – at the Five-Star Resort of the Zombies, where the brain-dead play Marco Polo in the pool until you want to kill yourself, and where an automatic side dish of guacamole comes with every freakin' meal, unsolicited. Even steak.' Tarin leans in and puts her face right in front of Riyonna's. 'Are you going to tell us what's going on, or what?'

Riyonna has started to cry. I'm fairly sure that wouldn't have happened if I'd been able to deal with this on my own, without Tarin in tow.

'What?' Tarin asks Zellie. 'I didn't swear. I said "freakin'".'

'I'm going to be real honest with you, Mrs Fry,' Riyonna says shakily. 'I don't know what's going on any more than you do, and it's scaring me a little.' She wipes her eyes. 'The system wouldn't record anything as a mistake – it wouldn't flag up any sort of error – but it does keep a record of all the check-ins and check-outs dating back several months. What ought to be here is the information that Mrs Burrows was checked in to that room and then, very soon after, checked out of it. If that were here, I could find the room number – but it's not here, and I can't think why not.'

'Could be the system's not working properly,' I say. 'That might also explain why the room appeared as available when it wasn't.'

'Maybe I should say . . .' Riyonna begins hesitantly. 'I couldn't tell you the room number even if I found it. That kind of information's confidential.'

'Even though I *went* to the room? I could easily have remembered the number.'

'But you didn't, and . . . well, as you unfortunately discovered, it's another guest's room.' She shrugs apologetically.

'Typical bullshit,' says Tarin briskly. 'Why bother looking for the number if you had no intention of telling us what it was? Are you sure you didn't delete whatever record ought to be on the system to make like your screw-up never happened?'

'Yes, ma'am,' says Riyonna tearfully.

'If she'd deleted it, why would she tell you it ought to be here and isn't?' says Zellie.

'This is getting us nowhere.' Tarin slaps the palms of her hands on the countertop. She turns to me. 'You said it was on the third floor. How sure are you?'

'Completely.'

'Let's go, then. Once you get up there, you might remember. Something might jog your memory.'

I open my mouth, then close it again.

'What?' Tarin leans in to peer at me. 'What is it?'

Of course. I can find the room easily, even without knowing the number. I feel stupid for taking so long to think of it, and at risk of being added to Tarin's list of brain-dead and otherwise flawed specimens littering the resort with their presence.

'I know what I did when I got out of the lift – how I walked. I was in the lift on the left, not the right – there are two side by side. I came out and turned immediately left. Not just left as in I veered left, but left and back, to kind of behind where the lift was. And it was a dead end, I remember that. The end of the corridor. I couldn't have walked past the room to other rooms.'

'Let's go,' says Tarin. To Riyonna she says, 'Once we have the room number, we'll be back to find out who's in there.'

'Mrs Fry, I'm afraid there's no way I can share confidential information about—'

'Just make sure no more information gets wiped before then. And get those detectives back here.'

'Many people have access to the hotel's network.' Riyonna sounds panicked. 'I'm not the only one. But . . . I can't understand what's going on, I really can't!'

This is awful. I should be thinking about my own children, not Melody Chapa. My own new baby – not a dead American girl.

I don't belong here. All of this . . . it's someone else's nightmare, not mine.

'Mrs Burrows, are you okay?' Riyonna's kind voice breaks into my silent panic.

'I . . . yes, I'm fine.' Or rather, I'm English, so that's how I'm always going to answer that question.

Tarin jabs me with her elbow. 'Come on,' she says. 'Third floor.'

Zellie sighs as she trails after us towards the lifts. As we step inside the first one that comes, Tarin sighs and says, 'This is going to be disappointing.'

'Why?' I ask. Doesn't she trust my memory? I can hardly blame her, if so. I'm terrified that we'll get up there and I won't have a clue. The blue light moves from the '1' to the '2' above the lift doors.

'You didn't notice anything, down there in the lobby, before we got on the elevator?' Tarin asks me.

'Like what?'

'Yeah, like what, Mother? Let's hear more of your genius observations, please.'

Tarin smirks. 'You'll see,' she says. 'Both of you.'

Automatically, without thinking – that's the best way to do it. The doors open and I step out, pretending to myself that I'm alone, praying Tarin will keep quiet while I get my bearings.

It's late, you're exhausted, you've just driven from the airport . . .

This is easy. I remember. I stood here, looked at the numbers and arrows painted on the walls, realised I had to turn left, round the corner, behind . . .

Shit. Not so easy after all.

'What is it?' Tarin pounces.

Out of the lift, turn left around the corner – that part is right. Definitely right. And the dead end: also correct. There's a problem, though. There are two doors in front of me, not one. Rooms 324 and 325.

'Aren't you going to—'

'Hush, Zellie. I'm not saying a word. Not yet. Cara? Which room was it? Which of the two?'

'I don't know. I . . . I don't remember there being two doors. I only remember one.'

'Maybe some ghostly guests have been adding

137

on new rooms as well as erasing information from the computers,' says Zellie.

'Obviously not,' I say. It comes out flatter and harder than I intended. 'Obviously both these rooms were here last night, but I didn't notice the second. I saw only what I needed to see: the door I needed to open to find the bed I was going to sleep in – or so I hoped. And I can't remember which door that was. I'm sorry.'

'You'll be even sorrier in a second,' says Tarin. 'Come here.' She beckons me back towards the lifts. When I get to where she's standing, she says, 'Okay. What do you see?'

Tell her you're not prepared to play games.

'The lifts. A corridor. A grey carpet. A framed picture of the Grand Canyon on the wall.'

'Okay, stop. How many elevators do you see? Or "lifts", as you Brits call them?'

What's wrong with her? Isn't it obvious how many? 'Two.'

'*Two?*' Tarin squeals. 'Seriously?'

'I'm looking at two. You asked me what I could see. I know there are others behind me.'

'Winner, winner, chicken dinner!' Tarin claps her hands together. She grabs hold of me and whirls me round. 'And what do you see now? How many elevators?'

Oh, God. I can't believe I've been so stupid.

'Two elevators this side, two that side,' says Tarin. 'You remember getting out of the elevator and turning immediately sharp left into a corridor with a dead end – but look, there's a dead end over there too. Rooms 322 and 323 – exactly the same, a mirror image. You remember you were in the elevator on the left, not the right, but there's a left and a right on *both* sides. You could have come out of the one on the left on *either* side, turned left round the corner and found yourself in a dead end looking at two doors. I'm guessing from the look on your face that you don't remember which side you got in?'

I shake my head.

'After you pressed the button, while you were waiting for the elevator to come, what could you see?' Tarin persists.

'I don't remember. Lift doors, I suppose.' I want to lie down on the floor and cry. How do I get away from these people, from this situation?

'Yeah, but in the lobby they're mirrored on the outside, right? All fancy schmancy. Looking one way, you'd have seen the doors to the Sunset Grill restaurant reflected. Looking the other way you'd see the little fake shop – you know the one I mean?'

'Fake shop?'

'Wow, Cara. Do you not notice *anything*? Big glass bulge in the wall, with gold shoes and diamond-studded handbags inside it? There's a poncho in there that I wanted to try on and no one could get inside the goddamn glass case for me. There's supposed to be a key, but could I find a single member of resort staff who knew where it was?'

'Poor dear Mama,' says Zellie. 'It must be so hard to be you.'

'Well, I'm sorry, but what the hell is the point of having a glass bubble stuck to the wall with merchandise inside it that you want people to buy, and then when they want to look at it, you can't find the key?'

'I don't remember seeing anything reflected in the lift doors,' I say. 'I was knackered. I was barely looking, barely aware.'

'Well, we've narrowed it down to four rooms, I guess. That's better than nothing.' Tarin squeezes my arm. It hurts. 'And Zellie and I can help out. We can get it down to three.'

'How?'

Tarin walks over to the door of room 325, pulls a key card out of her shorts pocket and holds it against the metal pad. A green light flashes and the door opens. 'The room you went to wasn't this one,' she says. 'This one's ours – mine and Zellie's.'

No. I refuse to believe it. Something's not right.

Tarin's holding the door open, waiting for me to come in. Zellie's already inside, kicking off her sandals.

'Are you coming in or what?' says Tarin. 'We'll ring reception and get the names from Riyonna – the guests in the other three rooms – then order room service. Aren't you starving? I could eat a fucking horse. With guaca-fucking-mole, obviously – no chance of the horse arriving without, not at this resort. We can eat on the balcony, there's plenty of room. Cara?'

'325 is your room?'

'Well . . . yeah? I mean, that's why I'm in it. Problem?'

'Why didn't you tell me?'

Tarin's mouth flattens into a line. 'Tell you what? Tell you when? I *have* told you. I just did.'

'When I said I remembered the room Riyonna sent me to was on the third floor. Why didn't you say then that your room's on the third floor?'

'It's irrelevant. Why would I mention it? There must be fifty rooms on this floor. I didn't know we weren't easily going to be able to get the number of the room you got sent to, and I didn't know you'd end up narrowing it down to four rooms that included mine. Satisfied?' Tarin's hand is on her hip now. My doubts are delaying her dinner.

I don't know if I'm satisfied. I'd like a chance to think without her watching my every move.

'Of course,' I say. If I play nice, it'll be easier to get away. 'Listen, I'm going to go back to my casita. I'm not especially hungry and I need to do a few things, so . . .'

'What things? Don't you want to know who's in the other three rooms?'

'Yes, but I really just need—'

Tarin's burst of laughter cuts me off. 'You *really just need* to learn to speak your mind. You don't wanna have dinner with Zel and me? Fine. I don't care. If you suspect me of hiding Melody Chapa in my hotel room because it's one of the four in your line-up, go right ahead. I'm not offended. I think it's hilarious!'

'I just want to be on my own for a bit, that's all.' Why do I sound as if I'm pleading with her?

'Okay. Well, I'm going to find out who's in those other three rooms, and if the police are on their way. I want to know what the hell's going on. Don't you?'

Behind her, Zellie appears, with her strawberry-blonde hair up in a bun on top of her head. She glances at me, makes sure I register her not-impressed look, then opens a door behind Tarin. It juts out into the narrow entrance corridor, blocking my view of the room. I hear the sound of a tap running and smell vanilla.

'I don't think you and I can find out very much,' I tell Tarin. She's right: I should be more straight-forward instead of always trying to smooth things over. 'We've got no authority to ask questions. If there's anything dodgy going on, the police will sort it out. Yes, like you I want to know what's going on. Of course I do – this is the most bizarre thing that's ever happened to me. I'm as intrigued as you are, but I don't think we're going to get the answer today.'

Tarin's biting the inside of her lip. 'You know what? I'm not sure the Arizona police are the guys we need right now. They've already been and gone – no surprise there. Melody Chapa was murdered in Philadelphia – what the hell does that have to

142

posted. That must mean she stayed up late – later than I'd have allowed. It's 7.30 p.m. in Arizona, so eight hours later in England: 3.30 a.m. She left her comment at what would have been midnight her time.

Beneath my photo of the two colourful cocktails, she's written, 'Yeah looks great thanx for not taking me with you. Dad and Olly have been driving me mad. Olly's an infuriating little squit!! Why did you go off without telling us?! WTF is going on? Are you and Dad breaking up? You better not! Dad is incaperble of doing proper parenting, btw. Me and Olly are at Granny's. It's too hot, none of the windows open and there are radios talking shiznit in every room. She leaves them on all the time!! Come back!!!!!xxxxxx'

Olly and I, not me and Olly. Incapable, not incaperble.

I start to cry, missing home, happy that Jess sounds like Jess. She's okay. They're okay. Everything will be fine, somehow.

On her Instagram, Jess has posted a photo of a closed window with paint peeling off its frame. I recognise Patrick's mother's house. Olly always sleeps in the attic room and Jess in the main guest bedroom. I leave a comment beneath the picture: 'I will come back, soon – on Tues 24 Oct. Dying to see you, darling. Lots of love to you and Olly xxxxx. And no, Dad and I are not breaking up, I promise.'

Can I promise that? Too late. The comment's up.

Patrick wouldn't leave me and the kids. No

matter what. Not even if I make him have one more child than he wants.

Are you sure about that?

Tarin's words come back to me: *I'd say you have a problem of some kind and you don't know how to solve it. Which proves you're unimaginative. There must be a way to deal with it. If I knew the problem, I'd give you the solution.*

Please God spare me Tarin Fry's prescription for how to improve my life.

I flop in my scented bath for an hour, looking at the list of activities on offer at Swallowtail. If there were a workshop on decision-making, I'd consider signing up – 'What to Do in Impossible Situations' or something like that.

My chicken Caesar salad arrives with an unasked-for bowl of guacamole, which makes me think about Tarin again. I wish I hadn't made it so obvious that I suspected her of deliberately deceiving me. Thinking about it rationally, she's right: there was no reason for her to say, 'Wait! Third floor? That's where my room is!' when I first mentioned it.

I don't honestly believe Tarin and Zellie are hiding anything – anything, in this case, being an officially dead girl whose parents are in prison for her murder. The idea's laughable. Embarrassing. I'm going to have to find Tarin at some point and apologise. In my desperation to extricate myself from her overbearing clutches, I overreacted.

Finishing my food, I push my plate aside. I wish

146

I could push my thoughts away as easily, stop them circling back to Melody Chapa.

She must be dead. There was a whole trial, huge amounts of money spent, no doubt, on prosecuting, defending, appealing. It was all over the media for years. The whole of America can't be under the illusion that this girl is dead if she isn't. It's impossible. That ought to be my starting point. Or even better, not mine – someone else's. Ownership is the last thing I want – this is nothing to do with me.

I want to find out the end of the story, though. Who was the surprise guest on Bonnie Juno's show, the one who changed everything and caused suspicion to shift from the Revilles to Annette and Naldo Chapa?

I reach for the iPad and type the names 'Bonnie Juno' and 'Melody Chapa' into the search box together. Some of the first results that come up are YouTube clips. The top one, as well as the most recent, is dated 2014 and has the tagline: 'Bonnie Juno talks Melody Chapa on the *Ken Hayun Show*: the Bloody Sock Controversy.'

I click on the white arrow and the clip starts to play.

BONNIE JUNO INTERVIEWED BY KEN HAYUN, CNN, JUNE 23, 2014

KH: My next guest needs no introduction. Welcome, Bonnie Juno. Thank you for being with us today.

BJ: Always a pleasure, Ken. Thanks for having me on the show.

KH: I didn't expect a 'yes' from you, Bonnie. I'll be frank: I thought you'd said all you had to say about Annette and Naldo Chapa—

BJ: I thought so too, Ken, now that justice has been done and those two evil monsters are behind bars where they belong. But certain other people – people determined to bury their heads in the sand – keep putting misinformation out there like it's going out of style, and I can't let that go unchallenged, for poor little Melody's sake, for the sake of her memory.

KH: Well, I guess I can underst—

BJ: Even with her murderers behind bars, injustices can still be perpetrated against her, and that's what I believe is happening here. This latest outpouring of trash from Ingrid Allwood – I refuse to call her 'Doctor', she doesn't deserve the title – is the perfect example of—

KH: Bonnie, I'm glad you raised Dr Allwood's recent opinion piece. We did invite Dr Allwood to join us here tonight. Unfortunately she declined our invitation.

BJ: Yeah, I just bet she did!

KH: For those of you at home who missed it, we're talking about Dr Ingrid Allwood's article in the *New York Times*—

BJ: It's not an article, Ken, it's a piece of worthless trash. Just 'cause it's made out of words doesn't make it any better than trash. It's an insult to poor little Melody is all it is. I swore to myself I'd always defend her interests to the best of my ability and that's why I'm here today. What Allwood's doing, it's all lies – dangerous lies designed to attract sympathy for Annette and Naldo Chapa. Hey! I've got news for the American public: some people in prison are actually guilty, whatever you enjoy watching on your TVs. All these shows about the system framing innocent people – they're twisting people's minds! A little girl is dead, the right people are locked up, and I'm determined to keep it that way.

KH: Bonnie, you clearly feel passionately about this—

BJ: Damn straight.

KH: Sure, but can we talk about a specific point raised by Dr Allwood in the *New York*

Times – Melody Chapa's sock, with the blood on it? She says—

BJ: No, Ken – sorry to cut you off, but you're already wrong, I'm afraid. Allwood doesn't say anything at all. That's the problem! She has no conclusions or even theories to offer. She doesn't seem to think the Chapas are guilty of murder, but neither will she admit to suspecting Kristie and Jeff Reville. Who does she think did it, then? Santa Claus? She asks plenty, and answers nothing – that in itself is highly misleading. Just leaves those questions hanging there. It's a rhetorical trick, and most people are too dumb to see it. She's trying to make everyone think the answer, if only we knew it, would surely point to Annette and Naldo Chapa's innocence.

KH: Wait – let me drill down a little here. No, please – I really want you to address this key point that Dr Allwood made. To do that, we're going to need a recap of the uncontested facts. Nate Appleyard saw the sock with blood on it – a child's white sock – inside Kristie Reville's car on the day that Melody went missing. But when detectives searched the car, the sock wasn't there. Some time later – forgive me, I can't recall the exact length of time, but it was some weeks, I think

– a bag was found that turned out to be Melody's school bag. Am I right so far?

BJ: Entirely correct.

KH: Okay. Inside Melody's school bag, the sock was found. Stained with blood that turned out to be Melody's. Nate Appleyard was asked by detectives if this was the same sock he'd seen in Kristie Reville's car and he positively identified it: same stains in the same places – no question about it.

BJ: Yeah.

KH: And so Dr Allwood raised the question, and I must admit it seems a valid one to me . . . let's say Annette and Naldo Chapa wanted to frame the Revilles—

BJ: That's exactly what they wanted. They set the whole thing up and it nearly worked. Poor Kristie Reville who'd always been a good neighbor to them, taken care of their little girl while Annette was busy with work. Annette and Naldo Chapa were prepared not only to kill their poor sweet daughter in cold blood, but also to frame an innocent couple who'd never done them any harm. That's why I call them the embodiment of evil, and I'll stand by those words till the day I die. They make my skin crawl.

KH: So let's imagine for a second that you're the Chapas, you've murdered your daughter and you want to frame Kristie Reville. You somehow manage to get Melody's bloodstained sock inside Kristie's car – that's quite a coup, right? Kristie Reville told detectives categorically that she *always* locked her car, that she never forgot – she was very security-conscious, especially when she visited her masseur Victor Soutar, who lived in a down-at-heel neighborhood—

BJ: Look, Ken, I believe Kristie thinks she's telling the truth there. I believe she thinks her memory's 100 per cent accurate on that point – but I think she's wrong. We all make mistakes once in a while: leave things unlocked that we could have sworn we locked up safe and sound. When Kristie visited Victor Soutar the day Melody disappeared, she left her car unlocked. Annette and Naldo Chapa, having murdered their daughter, drove to Soutar's place and planted that blood-stained sock in Kristie's car. Kristie was emotional that day, remember? She was facing up to the fact that Soutar's treatments were never going to help her conceive a child. Locking her car would have been the last thing on her mind.

KH: Well, with respect, Bonnie, that's your hypothesis: that she didn't lock her car and that the Chapa parents planted the bloody sock. No one saw them doing that, did they?

BJ: That's correct, no one saw them. The other part? Incorrect. It's not only my hypothesis. It's also the verdict of a jury, and therefore the hypothesis of the American judicial system, which I respect even if you and Ingrid Allwood don't. If Annette and Naldo Chapa murdered Melody – I'm saying 'if' to indulge you, Ken; we both know it's not an 'if' any more – then of course they planted the sock. How else did it get inside Kristie's car? Doesn't matter that no one saw them. We know it must have happened.

KH: But then the sock moved, didn't it? It didn't stay in the car. It ended up in Melody's school bag, which was later found in some long grass near a local gas station. You'd say Annette and Naldo Chapa must have moved it, I assume – and Dr Allwood asks, *Why would they do that?* Putting that sock in Kristie Reville's car – that's a successful piece of framing, isn't it? Nate Appleyard saw it, and if it had stayed in the car the police would have found it sooner than they did, on the property of Kristie Reville. So why move it? Dr Allwood's right, isn't she? There's no reason for the Chapas to want or need to do that.

153

BJ: You see, this is the danger with these questions that Allwood, and now you, leave hanging.

KH: What danger?

BJ: You only take the thought process so far – just far enough to cast doubt. It's sickeningly dishonest. Let's take it further: if the Chapas had no reason to move Melody's blood-soaked sock, that might mean they're innocent. Right? Okay, let's go with that. If they're innocent, that means someone else abducted and murdered poor little Melody. Either Kristie and Jeff Reville or somebody else must have done it – can we agree on that?

KH: I think so, yes.

BJ: Let's say Kristie and Jeff did it. So the sock's in their car because they're guilty as all hell, and they decide to move it to where? A bag that's covered in Kristie's DNA – okay, she often took Melody to school and must have held her bag a lot, but still, this bag's covered in Kristie's DNA and full of Melody's blood, her hair which shows evidence of arsenic poisoning, flies that must have come into contact with her dead body . . . I'm sorry, Ken, I can't help it. I don't know how anyone can talk about this horrific crime without getting emotional – you must have a heart of stone.

KH: It's a very upsetting case, Bonnie. Do you want to . . .?

BJ: I'm just fine, thanks, Ken. Let's get back to our hypothesizing. Why would Kristie move the sock *that she knows Nate Appleyard has already seen in her car* to Melody's school bag full of hair, blood and blowflies? Why link herself to the evidence of murder in that way? I can't see her doing that. Can't see anyone doing it.

KH: Then, according to you, the Chapas planted the sock in Kristie Reville's car, and also later moved it to Melody's school bag?

BJ: Absolutely.

KH: So they got lucky twice? Kristie Reville left her car unlocked twice, at two very opportune moments for Annette and Naldo Chapa?

BJ: I don't believe the locking of cars would have been at the forefront of Kristie Reville's mind on March 2, 2010. She was devastated to think that her infertility might be permanent, not temporary as she'd always tried to convince herself. That was what was going on for her that day. So yes, I have no trouble believing she might have forgotten to lock her car more than once.

KH: But Kristie herself says otherwise. She says no matter what state she was in, she always locked her car – on March 2, 2010 same as always.

BJ: I have a theory about that – one I can't prove. I don't believe Kristie wants to admit that her best friend, as she saw Annette – her only friend in the world, really – could do that to her. Kristie and Jeff still insist their good friends and neighbors the Chapas are innocent. It's heartbreaking, really. That's the problem with truly good people, though: they don't see evil. They just don't see it, don't recognize it.

KH: It was kind of like a mutual acquittal society, right? The Chapas saying the Revilles were innocent and the Revilles saying the same about the Chapas? Not what you'd expect.

BJ: Yeah. The Revilles naïvely believed the Chapas couldn't be guilty. The Chapas, meantime, *knew* the Revilles were innocent because they themselves were guilty as hell.

KH: In her article, Dr Allwood also raises the question of why there was so much blood in the school bag when the hair found to be Melody's indicated arsenic poisoning. Did the Chapas poison their daughter to death or did they kill her in a way that caused her to spill lots of blood?

BJ: Well, I can't believe I have to point this out, Ken, but the two are not mutually exclusive! You can poison someone *and* cause them to shed blood. For some reason Annette and Naldo Chapa changed their minds about the murder method. They started with poison, then made a new plan. I've no idea why. I don't understand the mentality of a parent who'd kill his or her own child, or any child, and I'm very glad I don't, frankly.

11 OCTOBER 2017

I jolt awake. It's light outside. The sun streams in through the windows. I'm on the sofa in my casita. My neck hurts, as if I've slept on it bent, and my mouth is painfully dry.

Shit. I must have fallen asleep halfway through the Bonnie Juno clip I was watching – that's the last thing I remember from last night: Bonnie arguing with a talk-show host. What was his name? Ken something.

I look for the iPad mini and find it on the floor. It must have slid out of my hands while I slept. I turn it on. The battery's down to 23 per cent. I'm going to have to go back to the resort shop at some point and ask Mason for a charger.

It's 9.20 a.m. I can't believe I slept so long and so heavily. I check for any further communications from Jess, Olly or Patrick. My heart leaps when I see I've got an Instagram comment from Olly. He's written, 'Jess says i have to write something so u know i am okay, i am okay, talk when ur back on 24/10 is that still when u r back?'

I post a reply: 'I'll definitely be back on

24 October, Ol. Can't wait to see you. Love you and Jess so much xxxx'.

Still no word from Patrick. He'll have to talk to me eventually, however angry he is.

I'll do some talking too. It didn't feel possible before. My brain wouldn't mould my feelings into a coherent form that could be expressed, apart from with a howl of anguish. My mouth wouldn't open. The opposite: I'd feel my lips press together tighter whenever Patrick appeared.

I couldn't speak, so I ran.

I'm not going to email him again. Any further attempt at communication would be a concession I can't afford to make. It's up to Patrick to make the next move.

I need water, lots of it, before I can do anything. I go to the kitchen and fill one of the glasses on the counter from the cold tap: drink, refill, drink, refill. Gradually I start to feel more human.

In the bathroom, I splash cold water on my face and enjoy the feeling of it running down my neck. Looking at my wet skin in the mirror, I think about the girl's green and black swimming costume I saw in another bathroom recently, hanging up to dry, and the rubber swimming cap . . .

Were they Melody Chapa's? Why would a girl who's supposed to be dead – who's presumably in hiding – go swimming at a busy holiday resort? Whatever number that room was, there was no private pool attached to it. If Melody swam, she must have done so in full view of other Swallowtail guests.

I'm reaching for a towel to dry my face when it occurs to me: something so obvious I can hardly believe I didn't realise sooner – immediately, as soon as it happened. How could I have missed it?

The bathroom. The door . . .

I go to the casita's nearest phone, pick it up and press '0' for reception. A woman answers, expresses the impassioned hope that I'm already having a truly great day, and asks how she can help to make it greater still. I ask for Riyonna.

'She's not in yet – for which I apologise – but I expect her to arrive at any moment. Can I ask her to call you right back? Would that be okay?'

'Yes. If she could call me back . . .'

'She sure can! No problem at all! She'll be delighted to do that.'

'That would be wonderful, thank you.' America: Land of Hyperbolic Overstatement.

I think of Bonnie Juno's description of Melody's parents: 'evil monsters'. Maybe she's right and that's what Annette and Naldo Chapa are, but the way she said the words, with such relish, made her sound like a monster too. Perhaps this is the unavoidable flip side of American overstatement. *Have an awesome day – unless you're an evil monster!*

Juno's excessive make-up in the clip – the smooth orange-beige mask where her skin should have been, her dark pink shiny lips, the bright blue glittery gunk above her eyes – made her look monstrous; so did her stiff, dyed-jet-black hair that never moved and her air of absolute confidence

160

that she was right about every single aspect of the Melody Chapa case. Even seated, she looked a foot taller than Ken, and she kept pulling herself up in her chair in order to glare down her nose at him more effectively. She'd worn heels that were at least six inches high for the interview. If I was built like her, I'd wear the flattest shoes I could find at all times. Most women would.

I wonder if Bonnie Juno made a decision early in her career to flaunt her height rather than be ashamed of it.

If the detectives come back today to interview me, if they believe me and take me seriously, how long will it be before Bonnie Juno finds out that some nobody of a tourist from England is putting forward a story that directly contradicts hers? What if she has her researchers try to dig up dirt on me, or attacks me on her show? She seems to be able to say whatever the hell she wants and get away with it.

Don't flatter yourself, Burrows. No big US TV show is going to be interested in you.

I consider going for a dip in my private pool, but if I do that and Riyonna rings I might miss the call. Also, I'm starving.

I ring room service and order breakfast: Eggs Florentine and English Breakfast tea with cold milk. While I wait for it to arrive, I look again at my list of search results from last night. Many of them are YouTube clips of Bonnie Juno that look similar to the one I fell asleep to last night. Those that aren't look to be different versions of the Melody Chapa story.

I spot, attached to one of the YouTube clips, the headline 'Where is Melody's Poggy? ask Bonnie Juno and Ingrid Allwood'. The video's dated 10 June 2010, three months after Melody disappeared.

I've no idea where Poggy is now, but two nights ago he was in room three hundred and twenty-something at the Swallowtail Resort and Spa, Arizona. At least I think he was.

No. I'm sure he was.

Sighing in frustration, I tap the white arrow to play the clip. Ingrid Allwood has a round pink face, large grey eyes, seashell earrings and a maroon scarf wrapped around her head; her piles of blonde curly hair spill over its edges. She's wearing sunglasses with chunky blue wooden frames, but on her forehead, over her scarf not her eyes. As Bonnie Juno – in red six-inch heels this time – holds forth, Allwood looks as if she's trying not to smile, as if Juno's nothing but a joke to her.

The clip begins with Juno in mid-flow.

BJ: . . . to speculate when it takes you in a direction you want to go in, but not when it might lead to a conclusion that supports my argument. And you have the nerve to deny you're a hypocrite? Ha! Don't make me laugh!

IA: That's simply not true, Bonnie. You seem determined to misunderstand me, so I'll explain again. I'm happy to speculate in all directions as long as we're clear that's all we're doing. You cannot claim to know where this Poggy toy is. It hasn't been found – anywhere.

BJ: No, and neither has poor little Melody's body. And yet that tragic little body – the dead body of a sweet, innocent girl murdered *by her own parents* – has gotta be somewhere, right? And mark my words, when it's found, Poggy will be found right there with it. No doubt at all.

IA: I'm afraid you can't say 'no doubt' about something that hasn't happened yet and may never happen.

BJ: In my heart, there's no doubt. Annette and Naldo Chapa took Poggy out of Melody's school bag and, wherever they've buried her, they buried him with her. In their twisted minds, putting her favorite soft toy next to her would have represented some kind of comfort. The message, one can only assume, is 'Sorry we killed you, but here, have your favorite snuggle toy as a consolation.' It's a horrific kind of warped sentimentality, just . . . beyond appalling to any normal human being, but it's typical of those two monsters. Let them sue me if I'm wrong about them.

IA: I'm sure they would if they weren't

devoting all their resources to trying to find their missing daughter.

BJ: Answer this: what genuinely distraught parents would fail to express any fears or worries about their kidnapped beautiful little daughter being interfered with? Being in the clutches of a sexual predator? That is every parent's worst nightmare. It's also one of the main motives for a stranger to abduct a child. Everyone knows this, we all know it. Yet not once – *not once* – has either Annette or Naldo Chapa expressed to the detectives searching for their daughter any fears along these lines. They haven't so much as mentioned the possibility of Melody being the victim of sexual violence.

IA: Not that you know of.

BJ: Ask Detective Larry Beadman if you don't believe me. He'll tell you. *Not once.* All of this is well documented. You know I'm not making it up. And let's not forget that the Chapas seemed to hold out no hope at all, from day one, that poor little Melody would be found alive and well. Nuh-uh. They publicly invited her killer to confess. Oh, they knew that sweet child was dead – no doubt about it.

IA: You keep insisting there's no doubt – and I believe you feel that way – but you're factually wrong. What you have is a strong hunch and nothing more. You don't, you *can't*, have certain knowledge of any of the things you claim to know. As a psychotherapist, I know that desperate, suffering families are capable of behavior that looks strange to those on the outside – yes, the Chapas' reactions seem a little off, but you're unwilling to believe just how normal that is.

BJ: And I suppose I haven't interacted with families that are beside themselves with grief and panic? All my years as a prosecutor in the DA's office in Philadelphia? Believe me, I know what's normal, and, what's more, I know what's normal for Philly – my home turf for so many years.

IA: Parental anguish is the same in Philadelphia as it is everywhere else in America.

BJ: And so is the lack of it. I know distraught parents when I see them. Annette and Naldo Chapa's reactions? Light years away from those of any innocent relative in pain that I've ever encountered.

IA: So they smell off to you. I hear that. But in relation to the toy, Poggy, your argument is weak.

BJ: No, it's not.

IA: All right, so Poggy wasn't in Melody's school bag when it was found, but it could have fallen out at any point. Kristie

165

Reville, crucially, did not see Melody zip up the side pocket she'd put the toy in. So, sure, someone might have taken it but it equally could have fallen out.

BJ: No, he couldn't. Incidentally, Poggy is a 'he', not an 'it'. He couldn't have fallen out. You oughta take a look at that bag. The pocket where Melody kept Poggy on school days was deep, and she pushed him right down inside it to make sure he wouldn't fall out. Kristie Reville watched her do it the day she disappeared, before they set off in the car to school. Poggy had never fallen out of that bag before and he didn't fall out of it the day Melody was taken and murdered. Satisfied? Annette and Naldo Chapa took Poggy out of that pocket, to bury alongside their murdered little girl, to make themselves feel like good people. It's truly sickening.

IA: You're being completely illogical. Let's say that's why Poggy was removed from the bag, so that he could be buried with Melody – and we should make clear here that Melody has not been declared dead, her body hasn't been found—

BJ: It hasn't been found *yet*.

IA: But, okay, let's say someone killed her and buried her with Poggy to keep her company . . . I don't see why you think it must have been her parents who did that, or in particular her mother, Annette. Kristie Reville, who's been described as like a second mother to Melody, could have had the same maternal impulse, couldn't she?

BJ: Kristie Reville had no motive to kill Melody. I don't buy this childless-woman-obsessive-jealousy line. That's yet another example of how women who aren't mothers are demonized in our society. Blame the barren witch! It's always been the way.

IA: As a childless woman yourself, don't you think you're more likely to want to blame Annette Chapa – the mother who was always too busy to look after her own child, and so sub-contracted out her care to a neighbor – than to blame Kristie Reville?

BJ: No, I don't think that. *You* think that. Thank you for suggesting that my child-lessness has impaired my judgment and made me want to condemn moms who also have careers. It hasn't. There's no evidence that Kristie Reville was ever jealous of Annette Chapa. She never tried to hang on to Melody for that little bit too long or anything like that. I've interviewed many of her friends and acquaintances who all report that her attitude to little Melody was healthy and normal as far as they could see. Kristie, according to all who knew her, was obsessed with having *a baby of her own*. She didn't want Melody. And she liked Annette Chapa – she wouldn't have harmed that family. She *didn't* – categorically did not. I'd stake my life on that. The truth will come out one day and then everyone who's vilified poor Kristie Reville will be sorry. And everyone will see Annette and Naldo Chapa the way I see them. I mean, for pity's sake, these are parents who have framed photos of the baby they lost all over their home. Their dead daughter – her dead body! I'm sorry but that is in no way normal behavior. Imagine how little Melody must have felt, seeing those pictures all the time. Oh, and what about the leaked email from Annette Chapa to another school parent in which she speculated that Jeff Reville might be gay, and that's why he and Kristie weren't making babies? Who do you think leaked that? Annette Chapa, of course. She wants to appear to be sticking up for the Revilles' innocence while secretly spreading a very different message: 'Look: possible sexual deviancy here!' We still live in a deeply homophobic world, and—

IA: Yes, sadly, we do, but wait . . . that makes no sense, what you just said. If

Melody were a boy and not a girl, maybe, but . . . are you saying Annette Chapa thinks people will be more likely to believe in the Revilles' guilt if she can persuade them that a gay Jeff Reville – who presumably desires men, or boys – would kidnap a little girl? How does that work?

BJ: It's simple. There's a lot of closed-minded people out there – disgusting bigots who equate homosexuality with pedophilia, and pedophilia with the snatching and harming of children. Plus, Jeff Reville is categorically *not* gay, so . . . you gotta wonder why Annette Chapa would choose that moment – with her daughter missing, and her and Naldo apparently distraught – to indulge in such malicious and groundless gossip. And going back to the many photos of Emory Chapa dead and all dressed up like a doll on the family mantelpiece where photos of Melody should have been . . . can you explain the *terrifying* false equivalence employed by Annette Chapa when talking about her two daughters? I've watched every interview she's given, at least twenty times. Have you?

IA: Well, I—

BJ: Answer: no, you have not. That's okay. Not everyone's as obsessive as me. Every single interview that woman has given, almost – since being told she needs to act like she thinks Melody might still be alive – she's talked about how Melody should be back at home where she belongs, how she should be with her mommy and daddy who love her so much. Staggeringly, she talks about Emory – Emory who never lived, who died *in utero* – in exactly the same terms! 'Emory should be here now with me and Naldo, to give us love and support.' For pity's sake, what mother would wish her tragically deceased baby back to life to comfort *her* after the loss of her other child? Who cares that poor Emory would then have to be in pieces over her missing younger sister, right? As long as she's there to make her mother feel better! Do you honestly not see how unwholesome and dysfunctional that is? In another interview Annette said, 'Emory should have been with Melody the day she disappeared. Kristie should have been dropping off two little girls at that school, not one. If Emory had been there like she should have, she'd have seen what happened to Melody.' Then she corrected herself and said, 'What I mean is, Emory would never have let anything happen to Melody.'

IA: What do you mean, 'she corrected herself'? To cover up what, exactly?

BJ: To give the impression that the fantasy that had just leaped into her mind was one where the focus was on saving Melody. But it wasn't. It was all about Emory — Emory being alive, going to school, as she should be doing. As she would be doing if she hadn't died. That she might have saved her sister was clearly an afterthought. This is what I mean by false equivalence. In Annette Chapa's twisted world, the loss of a child you've known and raised for seven years is on the same level as the loss of a baby in the late stages of pregnancy. I know I'll be called a monster for saying this, and I'm not in any way trying to minimize the agony of late-stage miscarriage or still-birth, but come on! What mother in Annette Chapa's situation — what *innocent* mother — would choose to talk on live television about the baby she lost eight years ago for even a second when she could spend all her airtime talking about Melody? She feels the two losses as comparable and on a par — that's my point.

IA: I see that. But I'm afraid that you and I, as women who have never lost a baby during the third trimester—

BJ: Oh, please. Ask a dozen women who *have* lost babies late in pregnancy and then gone on to have healthy children who get abducted, or harmed in some way. Ask them if Annette Chapa's reaction – constantly putting forward the loss of Emory, taking attention *away* from Melody – is normal. Or I can save you the trouble: it ain't. It's *light years* away from normal. And how about Naldo Chapa opening the door to Melody's bedroom and saying to Larry Beadman, 'This should have been Emory's room. We decorated it for Emory, before we lost her.' Word for word, first words out of his mouth. That, in my view, says it all. Annette and Naldo Chapa couldn't forgive Melody for not being Emory.

IA: Wow. I'm sorry, but you simply cannot say that.

BJ: And yet I just did, didn't I?

The doorbell of my casita rings, and it's like being pulled from one world to another. I push the iPad away from me, as if I've been caught breaking a resort rule.

As a friendly, freckle-faced young man talks to me about the weather and where I'd like him to put my breakfast tray, all I want to do is ask him about Melody. Did he follow the story on the news? Does he think Annette and Naldo Chapa are guilty?

I sign for my Eggs Florentine and let him go without interrogating him. He looks about twenty-two, and was probably busy in 2010 with the American equivalent of GCSE exams, not glued to TV news and talk shows.

Tarin: she's the one I should ask, if I want to indulge my new obsession. I try to persuade myself that I want to talk to her, and fail.

Eating my breakfast, which is delicious and not accompanied by guacamole, I stare at the phone and will it to ring. *Come on, Riyonna. Hurry up.*

I reach for the iPad, telling myself I can't keep doing this all day, I can't read everything.

Just one more.

This clip looks interesting: 'Mallory Tondini on *Justice With Bonnie*, September 2, 2010 – the interview that changed everything in the Melody Chapa case'. I'm also tempted by 'Dr Ingrid Allwood's Melody Chapa theory will blow your mind!'

Mallory Tondini: I've heard that name before. I think Tarin mentioned her. And what theory did the apparently cautious Dr Allwood eventually put forward?

I click on the Allwood link first and expect to see an article or blog, but I find myself looking at a chat room instead. Or chat forum – I'm not sure what to call it. There's a grid of boxes going down the page and in each box a different person has left a comment, many responding to comments higher up in the thread. There's a quote from Ingrid Allwood at the top: three paragraphs. This must be the mind-blowing theory. I'm about to start reading it when my eye is drawn to a name

I recognise lower down the grid: McNair. There's a comment from a Lilith McNair.

Is she Swallowtail's Mrs McNair, the old lady who turns up every year, selects a child at random and decides they're Melody Chapa?

And then . . . what? This year she happened to get lucky and find the real Melody at the very holiday resort where formerly she had only found fake Melodys? Crazy.

I can't decide if the Lilith McNair on the chat forum is bound to be the same woman or if it's too much of a coincidence . . . until I read her comment and all my doubts vanish.

It's her. She's written some long-winded nonsense about a 'spiritual seer', a close friend of hers who had a vision of Melody walking through a field full of flowers – red and yellow poppies. Melody was happy, she claims – beaming and joyful.

I laugh out loud. Mrs McNair's cousin Isaac also gets a mention here, as does his lymphoma. That must be what killed him. I wonder if he and Mrs McNair were close and if somehow that's what started off her obsession with Melody Chapa.

Hard to see why it would – a cousin dying of an illness is very different from a little girl murdered by her parents.

In her comment, Mrs McNair explains that in the seer's vision, Cousin Isaac was frolicking in the poppies too, with Melody. So this must be a special flowery field for dead people.

Then Mrs McNair puts forward her own theory: that Melody was killed by Mallory Tondini. Having made this claim, she ends her comment, 'Think about it. You'll see I'm right.'

That wouldn't explain why Melody's soul would be at peace in the vision. And I'm an idiot for thinking anything coming from Mrs McNair could ever make sense.

Who the hell is this Mallory Tondini? I can't wait any longer to find out. I close down the chat forum and click on the link to her interview on the Bonnie Juno show. So this is what the show's set looks like: a black and silver studio with two red chairs and 'Justice With Bonnie' emblazoned across a large screen behind them. Bonnie Juno's sitting in one of the chairs, wearing high-heeled black boots and a silver dress. I assume the woman in the other chair is Mallory Tondini. She looks about thirty and has a large forehead and an unusually high hairline. Her long dark hair is held back by some sort of clip on one side, and hanging loose on the other. She's wearing clothes that are so dark and undefined it's impossible to see what they are, but it's not only clothes that are covering her.

Captions in square and rectangular boxes and strips of all colours – blue, red, grey, yellow – take up most of the bottom half of the screen. All of the writing is white, and some of it's in capitals: 'Are Melody Chapa's parents facing imminent arrest?', 'BREAKING NEWS: STARTLING NEW EVIDENCE IN MELODY MURDER CASE', 'Help us to find Melody! Have you seen her? Call this number . . .'

How can they get away with calling it a murder case and at the same time asking viewers to help find Melody as if she's alive? The contradictions in this case are dizzying.

I came to Arizona to try and sort my head out. Thinking too much about Melody Chapa isn't helping. At all.

I make a decision: I'll watch this one last clip and then that's it – no more of this mind-bending true crime story for me. Dead or alive, Melody's nothing to do with me, and I can't afford to think about her any more. I've got a more important mystery to focus on: what's going to happen next in my own life? What's going to happen to my marriage and my family?

Only I know this mystery exists. Only I care about solving it.

> BJ: So, those of you who follow this show know that I promised you a special guest tonight. And here she is. Welcome, Mallory Tondini.
> MT: Thank you, Bonnie.
> BJ: Speak up if you wanna be heard, sweetheart. How d'you feel about being live on *Justice With Bonnie*?
> MT: A little overwhelmed.
> BJ: Well, please know you're very welcome here – in fact, I can't remember when I was last so delighted to welcome a guest to my show. Ladies and gentlemen, what you're

about to hear Ms Tondini say is going to change *everything* – and I bet I don't need to tell you this, but I'm referring of course to the tragic case of poor little Melody Chapa. Wait – did I say it would change everything? Correction: Ms Tondini's testimony *already has* changed everything. Why don't you tell us where you spent this morning, Ms Tondini – and with whom?

MT: Please, call me Mallory. I . . . uh . . . I spent the morning with Detective Lawrence Beadman—

BJ: That's Larry Beadman, lead detective in the Melody Chapa case.

MT: Yes.

BJ: And in a moment, we're going to hear what happened when Mallory spoke to Detective Beadman, but first I need to give you all a bit of background. As I'm sure the whole world knows – and I've never spoken about it publicly until now – I had a breakdown in June that caused me to be absent from this show for two months. There were many contributory factors: my obsessive, driven nature for one – *mea culpa* on that score. Then there was my despair at the refusal of detectives to take seriously my strong suspicion that Annette and Naldo Chapa were monsters, and wholly responsible for whatever had happened to sweet little Melody. There was my vile ex-husband, Raoul Juno, who chose a moment when he knew I was suffering extreme professional stress and public vilification to reveal to the world certain matters that were deeply embarrassing to me and that I would have preferred to remain private. The final straw that led to my breakdown was being arrested for disturbing the peace when all I was trying to do was extract an apology from my former spouse – an apology he *still* owes me for his despicable behavior. I'm sorry for crying, Mallory. I apologize to the viewers at home, also. The last thing I want is to make this about me and my personal heartaches.

MT: It's . . . Do you want to . . .

BJ: No, I'm fine to carry on. This is important. In my darkest hours after the breakdown, when I lay in bed unable to get up or speak to anyone or do anything productive . . . well, I had a lot of time to think. I went over every painful event of the previous few months, torturing myself with the memories. One of those memories was a discussion I'd had on live television with an unprincipled charlatan: Ingrid Allwood. That conversation sickened me at the time and continued to sicken me long after it was over. Lying in my bed, I kept replaying it – as if I could somehow make it come out differently, make Allwood see sense. In my head, I pleaded with her: 'Can you honestly claim that a mother who is innocent of murder and truly regrets the loss of her daughter – would that mother use interview after interview to say that, eight years ago, she had also lost another daughter? Would she talk about the two losses as if they were comparable? Wouldn't she be solely focused on Melody at that point?' Now, you all know what answer I'd give to that question, but that's not the point of what I'm trying to say. The point, ladies and gentlemen, is the number eight. Eight years ago. That's when Annette Chapa lost her first baby, Emory. *Eight years ago*. When I realized what that meant, I sat bolt upright in bed. Suddenly, I *saw* it. Hand on heart, I believe that the Lord granted me that insight to save me. Without it, I might have stayed in bed forever. Thank you, Lord. Now, you all at home, you don't know what I mean by any of this yet and you don't know how it relates to Mallory here, but you very soon will. Mallory, why don't you tell us where you live and work, and what your job is?

MT: I live in Philadelphia, and I work for the Perinatal Bereavement Program at the Hahnemann Hospital in Philadelphia.

BJ: So you work with women who suffer

late-stage pregnancy loss, correct? You offer a counseling program?

MT: I do.

BJ: And that's how you came to be acquainted with the Chapa family?

MT: Yes. Annette Chapa was due to have her first baby at Hahnemann Hospital—

BJ: That's Emory.

MT: Yes. But she lost the baby, quite late in the pregnancy. In those circumstances, the team I work for offers counseling—

BJ: And did the Chapas take you up on your offer?

MT: Yes, they did.

BJ: All right. Now, in a moment I'm going to share with the viewers at home the realization I had as I lay in bed in a state of emotional and psychological agony, but first, Mallory, I'd like to ask you to give us some concrete facts. Some dates. As someone who works at Hahnemann Hospital, you've been able to verify these dates. So tell us: when would Annette Chapa have had her first baby, little Emory, if that pregnancy had gone to term?

MT: If . . . if she hadn't died, Emory Chapa would have been born May 10, 2002. A C-section was scheduled for that day.

BJ: And Melody Chapa? She was born, by C-section, at your hospital. When?

MT: January 11, 2003.

BJ: And no one knows this better than you, Mallory, because . . .?

MT: In a situation like the one the Chapas were in, we offer them additional counseling in the event of a second pregnancy. We offer to be with them for the birth, because obviously it can be . . .

BJ: Of course – and did Annette Chapa want you at the birth of her second daughter?

MT: She did. She and Naldo – we'd grown quite close by this point – they both wanted me to be present for Melody's birth. And . . . I came on this show to say I don't think they would ever have harmed their own child. I know they didn't!

BJ: For the time being, please just answer the questions I ask you. So Melody was born alive and well at Hahnemann Hospital on January 11, 2003. Which means she was conceived when? When did Annette Chapa fall pregnant with her second child?

MT: Well . . . it would have been around April the year before.

BJ: April 2002. Nine months before January 2003. I'm not sure if everybody's figured out what this means, so let me spell it out: Melody Chapa was conceived in April 2002. *Emory* Chapa, had she not died tragically *in utero*, would have been born May 2002. This was the startling realization I had, folks – the one that told me to

181

get on up out of my stinking bed of despair, because I can *never* stop doing what I do, not now the Lord has shown me he needs me to do this vital work. What I realized was this: if Emory Chapa hadn't died, she'd have been still growing inside her mother's womb in April 2002, almost ready to pop out – which means Annette wouldn't have been able to conceive Melody. Now I'll put it more bluntly: if Emory Chapa had not died when she did, Melody Chapa would never have existed at all. Mallory – Mallory Tondini, from Hahnemann Hospital's perinatal bereavement team – everything I've just said is true, isn't it? Undeniable?

MT: Yes. It's true.

BJ: Thank you, Mallory. And you have my greatest respect for agreeing to come on *Justice With Bonnie* when we disagree about the likely guilt of Naldo and Annette Chapa.

MT: Bonnie, I only agreed to be on the show because Annette Chapa asked me to. She was afraid you'd distort the picture, and she wanted me, as someone who understands her and understands what she's been through, to try to put the facts in context.

BJ: What she wants is for you to defend her, in spite of the facts. I get it. But let's not lose our focus on those dates we've just heard, ladies and gentlemen at home. Those dates matter. Boy, do they matter! Let me tell you why: when I replayed in my mind the argument I'd had on live television with Ingrid Allwood . . . when I heard myself say that the Chapas had lost Emory *eight years ago*, it suddenly struck me: Melody was seven when she disappeared, when she died. If Emory would have been eight, I thought, that's not much of an age gap between them. Hardly any at all. 'Wait, Bonnie,' I said to myself. 'What if Melody couldn't and wouldn't have been conceived unless Emory had died?' Think about it, folks. Think about all the times you've seen Annette Chapa on your TV saying that Emory should still be here, should be comforting her parents in their hour of pain and need, should have been dropped off at school by Kristie Reville the day Melody disappeared. Think about Naldo Chapa showing Detective Larry Beadman the bedroom of his missing daughter Melody and the first words out of his mouth are, 'This should have been Emory's room.' That's an awful lot of 'should' from the Chapa parents. It's crystal clear, isn't it? They're *furious* that Emory isn't around any more because she *should* be. They desperately want her to be – that much is clear.

MT: But, Bonnie—

BJ: No buts, Mallory. I'm sorry, but any fool can see it! If Annette and Naldo Chapa think Emory should still be alive, that has to mean that they don't believe Melody should ever have been conceived. This is why I had my people find out where Melody was born, and it's how I came to meet Mallory here. I wanted to ask her a very specific question – not one about the Chapas this time. A question that would finally provide me with the proof I needed to make the police sit up and take notice. Now, Mallory, you and I first met ten days ago, didn't we? And what you told me put a great big smile on my face. Not only were you *in the room* when little Melody Chapa was born, but you'd known the Chapas for some time. You gave them counseling after they lost Emory, their first daughter. When I heard that, I cried out, 'Well, thank you, Lord!' Out loud. Right?

MT: Yes, you did.

BJ: And then I asked you a question. Do you remember what it was?

MT: You wanted to know when Emory would have been born if she hadn't—

BJ: Oh – sure, but that's not what I mean. For those viewers only just joining us, we've already established that if Emory Chapa had not tragically died in the womb, Melody couldn't have been conceived when she was and would therefore never have been born. But Mallory, what did I ask you next? I want our viewers to hear this from you, not me.

MT: You asked if it was common for a couple to lose a pregnancy, for a pregnancy to miscarry, and then for them to get pregnant again during the time when they would have been still pregnant with the baby they lost.

BJ: Okay. That's quite a mouthful, isn't it? Ha! But I hope everyone can follow what we're saying. *If Emory hadn't died, Melody wouldn't have lived.* That's simple, right? I figured: that must happen a lot. I haven't been blessed with children myself, but I wanted them oh so desperately for oh so many years – you have no idea! When I was married to my first husband – the vile and ruthless Raoul Juno; don't get me started on him! – I conceived twice. I lost both babies, one at ten weeks, one at thirteen weeks. Heartbroken doesn't begin to cover it. On both occasions, I said to Raoul, 'Let's try again. Please, let's not give up.' Both times, I could theoretically have gotten pregnant again – I didn't, but I could have – *before the baby I'd lost was due to be born.* So, I figured that had to be pretty common, for that to happen. Mallory, what answer did you give me?

MT: What you just said: it's common. Many women conceive soon after losing a baby – during what would have been their prior pregnancy, had that not failed.

BJ: Uh-huh. And you and your team, your colleagues – you support these women through these subsequent pregnancies, don't you? When they're nervous the same thing might happen again – that the pregnancy might not make it all the way?

MT: I do, yes.

BJ: So you're a real expert. Next I asked you if women in that position – in Annette Chapa's position after Melody was born, a healthy, live baby – do such women ever remark upon the fact that they wouldn't have this beautiful new living, breathing baby in their arms if they hadn't miscarried their previous pregnancy?

MT: Yes, they do.

BJ: What – sometimes, often? Rarely? Let's get some context here.

MT: Almost always.

BJ: I'm sorry, Mallory, I know this is difficult for you. It must feel as if you're helping me argue a case you don't agree with, but all I'm asking for is the facts. You think I'm hell bent on putting Annette and Naldo Chapa behind bars? Well, that may be so, but no fact has ever had an agenda. Facts are just facts. They're neutral, and they're all we have to go on, so . . . we need to hear them. Are you going to tell the viewers at home, or shall I?

MT: Women in Annette Chapa's position almost always say they feel conflicted: they're so happy to have their baby, obviously – that's a joyful thing, but at the same time, they know that baby wouldn't be there if they hadn't lost the baby that didn't make it. They feel guilty. They ask if it's okay to be happy about the new baby – whether celebrating its arrival is indirectly celebrating their deceased baby's death. I always tell them that of course that's not the case at all, that of course they must celebrate—

BJ: Did Annette Chapa say anything of this sort after Melody was born? You were there: a first-hand witness. Were Annette and Naldo overcome with joy when Melody made it into this world safe and sound?

MT: I'm sure they were, yes.

BJ: You're sure, huh? Did they express this joy that you're so positive was in their hearts? Verbally, I mean, or with their body language?

MT: No, but not everybody is the same.

BJ: What did Annette Chapa say to you when Melody was born, Mallory?

MT: She said it was a tragedy that Emory wasn't there with them. She felt

Emory should have been there to meet her little sister and she wished that she could have been.

BJ: She said those words: 'Emory *should be* here'?

MT: Yes.

BJ: She said that, knowing that if Emory *had* been there, Melody would not have been?

MT: That makes it sound . . . She didn't mean that! She just meant—

BJ: Did Annette ever say to you what, by your own admission, *almost every woman* in her position says – that she was over-joyed to have Melody, but also felt guilty? Did she ever ask you, as so many mothers have over the years, if it was wrong for her to be happy about Melody's arrival knowing it wouldn't have been possible if Emory hadn't died? Did Annette or Naldo ever say anything like that to you?

MT: No.

BJ: All the same, it came up in conversation, didn't it? Tell us how.

MT: I visited the Chapas at their home when Melody was three weeks old. Naldo seemed okay. Annette didn't. She was quiet and subdued. I was concerned. I thought maybe it was the kind of guilt we've been talking about.

BJ: So, although she'd never given you any reason to think she felt guilty, you wondered if Annette was punishing herself for being happy about Melody's arrival – in case that happiness could be construed, indirectly, as an acceptance of Emory's death?

MT: I wondered, yes. Like I said, that feeling is just so universal among women who've—

BJ: So did you ask Annette if this was the case?

MT: Yes.

BJ: And what did she say? How did she reply?

MT: Look, women who've just had babies say all kinds of strange and scary things. It's really common. And immediately afterward, as Annette did, they burst into tears and tell you they don't really mean it.

BJ: We should probably mention that this behavior is known among self-proclaimed experts as 'ugly coping', or 'coping ugly'. For those unfamiliar with the term, it means dealing with a traumatic incident in a way that's inconsistent with socially acceptable behavior. It was coined by Dr George Bonanno of Columbia University and it's now regularly used to defend murderers who are guilty as sin – so thank you for that, Dr Bonanno. It was used by Jose Baez to defend Casey Anthony, who went out partying and got herself a new tattoo saying 'La Bella Vita' when she was supposedly desperately worried about her

189

missing daughter, Caylee Marie. Mallory, I'll be honest: I don't have any more time for this 'ugly coping' theory now than I did back in 2009. And you haven't answered my question: what did Annette Chapa say when you asked her if she felt horribly guilty to be so thrilled to have her beautiful new baby Melody? I'm sure you're wishing now that you'd never told me what she said, but you did, and it's my duty to get this out there, so—

MT: She said it was the other way round. She said she felt as if, by allowing Melody to be born, she'd colluded in Emory's death. As if by having Melody, she'd somehow made Emory's death final and irreversible, and . . . sometimes this made her feel she hated Melody and wished she'd never been born. But—

BJ: And there we have it, ladies and gentlemen. Annette Chapa wished that her beautiful little daughter Melody had never been born. The woman is a monster. Mallory Tondini, thank you for joining us here on *Justice With Bonnie.* Next up, I'll be talking to the Chapas' lawyer, Lexi Waldman, and asking her: is there *anybody*, any monster out there, that she would not defend? Does she have no morals at all? See you after the break.

C an I really stop now, without knowing how the Melody Chapa story ends?

You promised yourself you would.

Yes, I did. But that was before I knew how much I'd want to know what happened after Bonnie Juno interviewed Mallory Tondini. Surely her theories alone weren't enough to make detectives arrest Annette and Naldo Chapa and charge them with the murder of their daughter?

There's still the last part of the overview to read. That's where the answers to my new questions will be. A quick glance shows me that part three is short. I have to read it. Then I'll stop. Then I'll concentrate on my own problems.

Melody Chapa – The Full Story

An Overview

The Murder of Melody Chapa: Part 3 – Bonnie Juno, Mallory Tondini and a Change of Direction

After Bonnie Juno's live interview with Mallory Tondini on *Justice With Bonnie* on September 2,

2010 – and in spite of Tondini's repeated insistence on that show that she did not believe Annette and Naldo Chapa had harmed Melody – the official investigation into the disappearance of Melody Chapa took a different direction. Annette and Naldo Chapa were cross-examined again and their home was searched more thoroughly than it had been previously. Once again, nothing was found. This time, however, Detective Larry Beadman decided to take it one step further and also search Melody's parents' workplaces. This, incredibly, had not been done before – no doubt because of the circumstantial evidence mounting against Kristie Reville.

At the back of a cupboard in Annette Chapa's office, Beadman and his colleagues found several garbage bags filled with books that were waiting to go to a charity auction. At the bottom of one they found some dead blowflies and larvae – the same species found in Melody's school bag. As stated earlier, these flies are commonly found on and near dead bodies, which led detectives to conclude that body parts belonging to a deceased person must have been inside the sack at some point. Laboratory analysis found that there was blood all over the inside of the sack. Forensic testing confirmed the blood was Melody's. In Naldo Chapa's office, a shirt belonging to Melody and covered with her blood was found in a hold-all that Naldo claimed he'd forgotten was there and hadn't touched for several years.

Melody's parents' protestations of their own innocence convinced nobody. They faced multiple charges, though both continue to protest their innocence to this day. In June 2013, after hiring and firing three different legal teams, they were finally found guilty of the murder of their daughter, Melody Chapa, and were later sentenced to life in prison without possibility of parole.

No charges were ever brought against Jeff and Kristie Reville. They turned down a lucrative book deal and never spoke publicly about the case. In 2014 they set up a children's charity that they still run: the Melody Chapa Foundation.

Many books have been written about this case and many questions asked. Most of these remain unanswered and perhaps always will. Who snatched Melody? Annette and Naldo Chapa were both provably elsewhere – so did they send someone else to abduct their daughter from the school parking lot, having set up solid alibis for themselves? Kristie Reville admitted shortly after the Chapas were charged with murder that she did not, as she first claimed, take Melody all the way to the school playground. Eager to get to the home of Victor Soutar, and running slightly late, she waved goodbye to Melody in the parking lot and then drove away. The walk from the parking lot to the playground is 75 yards, and there are parents and children walking there in large numbers at that time in the morning. Did someone grab Melody and bundle her into their car without anybody noticing? It seems unlikely, yet what other conclusion can we draw?

It has been suggested that if a third party acting for the Chapas murdered Melody and disposed of her body, it's unlikely that the garbage bag and the hold-all containing incriminating evidence would have found their way into the offices of Annette and Naldo Chapa. This is only one of the many contradictions the case has thrown up. Bonnie Juno has stated that she believes Annette and Naldo Chapa asked whomever they hired to do the hit-job on their daughter to bring them each a souvenir of the murder, and that this would explain the evidence found in their offices. 'Naldo got the bloodstained school shirt Melody was wearing on the day she died, and Annette got goodness knows what. I can't imagine she'd have been satisfied with five dead flies, so I'm guessing there was a garment in that sack when she first got it. I have no idea where that garment is now, but I suspect she moved it or disposed of it after seeing Mallory Tondini on my show. She knew the net was closing in and tried to ditch the evidence.'

Since the Chapas seem unlikely ever to admit their guilt, we will probably never find out for certain why they murdered their daughter, or had her murdered by a third party. Bonnie Juno has always maintained they did it because, ultimately, they could not forgive Melody for not being Emory – the daughter they lost.

On *Larry King Live*, Juno said, 'Let me tell you something about abusive parents, Larry. Most of them claim to love their children – and never more so than when those children are sitting quietly with neat hair and clothes, silently quaking with fear in case they put a foot wrong. Perfectly behaved children, sleeping children – they're not a challenge. They don't make an abusive parent want to hit out. Same goes for dead children. I firmly believe Annette and Naldo Chapa worshipped Emory *only* because she never lived, never caused them even one second of stress. She was their lost angel, a perfect memory. Melody on the other hand, she was a real flesh and blood person with needs and wants. Like all children, she must have had tantrums, broken things, cried, not been able to sleep some nights. Good, loving parents take all that in their stride but the Chapas, as we all now know, were not good and loving. They were monsters – monsters who killed their own beautiful daughter to punish her for the death of her sister. They're sick and wicked and I hope they rot.'

Neither Annette nor Naldo Chapa has yet revealed the whereabouts of Melody's body. So far it has not been found.

The sound of the doorbell reminds me that there's a world outside my head, beyond the story of Melody Chapa.

It must be room service, here to collect my breakfast tray.

By the time I get to the door, I've decided: I don't like Bonnie Juno, but I agree with her. Annette and Naldo Chapa are guilty.

Of what? Melody's alive, remember? You met her.

Also . . . if Kristie Reville's totally innocent, why did she have blood all over her arm? Nate Appleyard and the petrol-station man both saw it.

It's not the room-service waiter at the door. It's Tarin Fry, in white linen culottes, a navy blouse with a pattern of pink blotches, white sandals and a powder pink sun hat. Her eyes are hidden behind dark glasses. 'You get over your paranoid episode?' she asks me. Behind her there's a club car and driver waiting.

'Come on, we've got things to do. I'm tired of waiting and wondering. Let's find Riyonna, see if she's got those cops back here yet. Grab your room key. Let's go.' She claps her hands together.

I open my mouth to protest, but she's turned her back on me and is marching back to the club car. 'Wait!' I yell, and run back inside to get my handbag and casita key.

'Go, driver,' Tarin says once I'm in the club car. Then, to me, 'So – are we good, you and me?'

Is she asking if I'm still annoyed?

'Last night you asked why I didn't tell you sooner that Zel and me are on the third floor. It's because I have some pride. When you said the room Riyonna sent you to was on the third floor, I thought, "Hey, what a coincidence! We're on the third floor too!" I could have said it, but it's the kind of thing only a dick would say. Like, "Can you believe the weather we're having?" or "Haven't you grown since I last saw you?" So I didn't say it.'

'Fair enough. I'm sorry if I seemed freaked out. Listen, I've worked something out. Last night, when I was standing in the corridor talking to you, outside your room – you were in the doorway, and Zellie walked up behind you and went into the bathroom, didn't she? She went through a door on the right. The right from where I was standing, I mean.'

'So?'

'The room where I met the man and the girl was the opposite – the bathroom was through a door on the left after you walked in.'

'Nice!' Tarin sounds impressed. 'That's a useful way to narrow it down. I've made progress too. I've been asking around, and I've got the names of the guests in the other three rooms.'

'How did you manage that?'

'Charmed my breakfast waiter.' She grins. 'They have a typed list each morning of who they expect to turn up for breakfast. And right beside their name, there's their room number.' Tarin reaches into her shirt pocket and pulls out a small white envelope embossed with the Swallowtail logo. 'Wanna hear? Okay. Room 322: Carson Snyder and Yegor Lepczyk – both men. A gay couple. The waiter I spoke to, Oscar – he knows who they are, he's served them a few times. Says they seem young, fun, regular guests. So that's them ruled

197

out. Room 324: Robert and Hope Katz – drew a blank with Oscar. He can't recall ever meeting them and wouldn't know them by sight. Room 323: Suzanne Schellinger, a young businesswoman travelling alone, here for a conference in Scottsdale. Oscar knows who she is – says she's a little aloof and always on her laptop, obsessed with whatever dreary job she's wasting her life on.'

'He said that?'

'What? No, not the bitchy part. That's my take. So, anyway . . . I think it's pretty clear.'

'What's clear?'

'It's gotta be room 324. Robert and Hope Katz. That's your father and daughter. Those are the names Melody and her . . . minder, or whoever he is, are travelling under. Bet your bottom dollar. Open the door to their room and the bathroom'll be on the left.' Tarin shakes her head and chuckles. 'I can't wait for Bonnie Juno to get hold of this new chapter in the story. I *knew* she was wrong about the Chapas. Can't tell you how many times I said, "But there's still no body," to anyone who'd listen. Question is, will Juno ever admit it? Maybe her crimebusting sidekick, the Lord, will help her to solve this new phase of the mystery and do a better job this time. I'm sure he will. It seems to matter to the Lord that the ratings of *Justice With Bonnie* remain high.'

Our club car passes the tennis courts. They're all occupied – balls flying through the air and thwacking against rackets. How can people do it, in this heat? 'The gay couple, Carson Somebody and his partner . . .' I start to say, not sure what I want to ask. Why did my mind snag on them in particular?

Then my brain catches up. 'Yesterday, I overheard you say something to Zellie about the best choice always being a gay man. I wasn't deliberately eavesdropping—'

'Who cares if you were? Jeez, Cara, you're so *English*. It must be horrible. I must make sure never to visit your country. I wouldn't fit in.'

'What did you mean by that comment? What were you talking about?'

Tarin stares at me. 'Interesting question. You got some kind of conspiracy theory brewing?'

'According to Bonnie Juno, Annette Chapa said in an email that Jeff Reville was gay.'

'Did she?' Tarin shrugs. 'I was talking about hiring staff, for my shop. I interviewed a few people last week. Haven't made any offers yet because no one was quite right. No gay men applied. At *all*. That's what Zellie and I were talking about. I was saying: what I want is a gay man – not a straight man and not a straight woman.'

'Why not?'

'The women always wanna knock off early and come in late if they've got kids, and if they haven't got kids, they'll be trying to have kids, or if they're older they'll be wanting time off to babysit grandkids. I can do without all that. And straight men? They have wives who want them to

199

go home early, or get to work late after dropping the kids at school, or order a fondue set, or fix the screen door . . . and even though these guys don't wanna do any of that shit, they can't say no to their wives because they're a bunch of pussies.'

'What about gay women?'

'Two wombs instead of one? No thanks. Per couple, I mean,' Tarin clarifies. 'Oh – driver? Can we swing by the Studio Zone on the way? Might as well pick up Zellie from her art class. We're a bit early but the less time she spends with dying-of-cancer Hayley the better, far as I'm concerned.'

My shock must show on my face, because Tarin says, 'What? Oh, you think I'm cruel? You think it's nice for Hayley to have a friend? Look, I'm a mom. I don't want Zellie to get close to this girl and then be all cut up when she dies and start brooding about her own mortality. No one I cared about died till I was over forty – that's the way it should be. I mean, I lost my mother at twenty-two, but let's just say that was a death with some powerful upside.'

Who is this woman? What am I doing with her?

'This art class?' Tarin chatters on, oblivious. 'Other day they did portraits. They do a different art thing every day: spray paint, cubism, water-colours, you name it. Anyway, they needed models – and, what d'ya know, every art class parent loses a morning of their vacation, but that's fine. Guess what Zellie called the picture she painted of me? It was actually pretty good, apart from the title. *Irreversible Decline.*' Tarin laughs. She sounds more proud than annoyed. 'Nothing as simple as *Portrait of Mom* for my Zellie. And you know what they're doing today? Sculpture. Fucking sculpture! I am so *not okay* with art that takes away floor space. Same goes for shelf space, table space . . .'

She seems to have lost interest in what she's saying, which is lucky, since I can't think of a suitable response.

'Annette Chapa thinks Jeff Reville's gay?' she says suddenly. 'Are you sure? I never heard that.'

'I got it from the internet. Maybe it's not true.'

'Did you happen to come across Ingrid Allwood's ingenious theory during the course of your online investigations?'

I'm about to say yes when I realise that's wrong. I didn't. I was on the point of reading it, but I got distracted by seeing Lilith McNair's name, and then I clicked on another link and forgot all about it.

'Tell me,' I say.

'Allwood claimed – and I believe she's still standing by her hypothesis – that neither the Chapas nor the Revilles could have abducted and killed Melody without the help of the other couple. She thinks the four of them were all in on it, and their aim was to get away with it by planting evidence to incriminate *all* of them, all four. They knew it'd be impossible to destroy all the evidence, or leave none, but if each couple could make it look as if the other had tried to frame them, while also making sure there was other stuff to suggest each couple *couldn't* have done it, maybe they could all get acquitted. Or not even charged in the first place. Personally I don't buy it. I can't see an elaborate "Hey, guys, let's all frame ourselves!" plan ever attracting any support. Here we are.'

The club car stops outside a brown bungalow-style building, long and rectangular with a red door, along the bottom of which someone – a previous art class, no doubt – has painted a row of yellow and blue flowers with green stalks.

'Wait here,' says Tarin. 'I'll run in and grab Zellie, then we'll go find Riyonna. I'll be ten seconds.'

Normally when people say that, they mean they'll be at least twenty minutes, but Tarin is as good as her word. She and Zellie emerge from the building almost immediately.

They're arguing about Hayley. 'She's sick, Mother. I can do a painting for you any time.' Zellie doesn't say hello to me or acknowledge my presence. 'You're so selfish. Did you not hear me say she's getting worse?'

'But I'm a florist, and it's a painting of some flowers!' Tarin complains. 'I mean, do I need to spell it out?'

'Yeah, well, Hayley, despite not being a florist, loves it too, so just drop it.'

I try not to picture Tarin scrapping with a terminally ill child for a painting. Did the art tutor have to intervene? Apart from anything else, how was there time for it to happen? How much unpleasantness could Tarin pack into four seconds?

Probably quite a lot.

Tarin sighs, defeated. 'Hotel reception please, driver,' she says.

'Wait!' I say. I've seen something. Some*one*. In the distance.

It can't be. This is wrong. Wrong person, wrong place.

Oh, my God. It is. It's him.

I jump out of the club car and run, ignoring Tarin's cries of protest. I keep telling myself I must be wrong until there's no doubt any more, until I'm standing in front of him, out of breath and sweating.

'Hi.' He smiles as if there's nothing at all remarkable about us both being here and bumping into each other.

It's really him: my husband. Patrick.

11 OCTOBER 2017

I blink, inhale, exhale, repeat – *blink, breathe, blink, breathe* – but it makes no difference. Patrick is still here.

'You could try looking a bit pleased to see me,' he says with a wry smile. 'I ran to the airport like the romantic hero of a cheesy movie, determined to find my one true love.'

He's flown for ten hours to get here, and he doesn't seem angry that I disappeared without warning. I should be a little bit happy about all of this.

'No?' Patrick's sticking with the jokey tone, but I can see he's hurt. He must have expected me to burst into tears and throw my arms around him. 'All right then, how about some grudging admiration for my investigative skills? I successfully and single-handedly tracked you down.'

I can't bring myself to look at him.

'With great cunning and aplomb?' he tries again hopefully.

I need him to stop talking. The discomfort and shock I felt when I first saw him is turning into a swelling fury. If only I could yell at him my rage might dissolve, but I've never been able to let rip in that way. I'd rather make secret plans and disappear to another continent than tell anyone how I feel.

You're a joke, Cara. A mess.

'How did you find me?' I manage to say. Much easier than *I don't care what you want. I'm not getting rid of the baby.*

'Aha!' Patrick grins. 'You didn't leave many clues – hardly any, in fact – but you forgot one major thing. You forgot to delete your browsing history on the computer.'

'I wouldn't have known how to do that even if I'd thought of it.'

I never considered that he might ignore my clearly expressed need to be alone for a while.

What do you expect? You've got children. Responsibilities.

'Ah, well, you see . . . if you'd been a more tech-savvy fugitive, you might have got away with it. I could see you'd been looking at various resorts and hotels in America, and the one you'd looked at most often and most recently was this one. And then there was the location: *Camelback* Mountain. You don't usually run away from home, so there must have been some sort of catalyst – a straw that broke the camel's back. I wondered if Camelback Mountain might have appealed to you for that reason.'

'So you just ditched the kids, booked a flight and came?'

'Well, I checked you were here first. I rang up.

They wouldn't tell me at first – said they couldn't give out confidential blah blah. So I waited, rang back an hour later and asked to be put through to your room, as if I knew you were staying here. They fell for that. "I'm getting no reply from Mrs Burrows' casita, sir." I tricked the truth out of them, like an ingenious double agent.'

'The kids hate staying at your mum's. What about school?'

'What about it? Broadly speaking, I'm in favour of it.' Finally, Patrick drops the comedian act. 'You *ran away from home*, Cara. Without saying why, or talking to me, or anything. Would you have preferred me to shrug and say, "Ah, well, that was fun while it lasted, no point trying to get her back – better just accept it"?'

I didn't run away. I left. I'm not a child or a posses-sion that can be retrieved against my will.

'My note made it clear I was coming back. I told you exactly when: 24 October.'

'So I was meant to just sit at home and wait, with no clue what was going on in your mind or where you were? Come on! What was I supposed to tell Jess and Olly? Cara, what's wrong? What's the problem? Sorry, that sounds flippant. I don't mean it to. What I mean is: I want to make every-thing okay, but you're going to have to give me a clue. Is it about . . .' He stops.

'You can't bring yourself to say "the baby", can you?'

'Well, it's not a baby yet, is it?'

'Isn't it?'

'I don't know. It wasn't when you first told me. You said it was no bigger than an olive.' Patrick sighs. 'Do you desperately want to keep it? I mean . . . okay. Fine.'

'That's not what you said before. You, Jess and Olly all made your feelings clear: none of you want the inconvenience, you all think our family's exactly the right size—'

'We made our feelings clear because you asked us. You kept asking us. So we told you, and you nodded and listened and encouraged us to be honest, share all our reservations and anxieties. And then you punish us by leaving home? I mean . . . unless this is about something else altogether.'

'You've no idea, have you?'

'Right.' Patrick nods. I see the first stirrings of anger on his face. 'Because you haven't told me. Why don't you tell me?'

Breathe, Cara.

I could answer him – so easily, the words are almost bursting out of my mouth – but I won't. We shouldn't be having this conversation now, here. It was supposed to happen on Tuesday, 24 October at home. That's when I wanted it to happen. What I want ought to matter – and not only to me.

'I emailed you,' I say. 'You ignored my email. You could have replied and asked me anything you wanted to know. You didn't have to—'

'I didn't reply because I was already on my way here. I wanted to talk face to face. Is that so wrong?'

Maybe it isn't. All I know is that if I can't have these two weeks to myself – to think, to work out who I am and what I want – then I can't have any time, ever. This is my one chance.

'I told you when I'd be back. You should have respected that.'

'Sorry, but that's crap, Cara. You made a unilateral decision to disappear. All right, you had your reasons – ones you won't tell me – but having done that, you can't accuse me of imposing my terms against your will. At least I'm talking to you!'

'You never asked me – not once – if I wanted this baby!' I'm too angry and miserable to hold it in any more. 'You never asked me how I felt. Hours we spent talking about it, me asking you and the kids what you thought, how you felt, listening carefully to everything you said, all your reasons – the expense, and the stress, and where would the baby's bedroom be, and we can't move house, it's too much hassle, all of that – and *not one of you* asked me even once, even indirectly, in any way at all, what I wanted to do. You all treated me like someone who was chairing an important meeting, someone whose own opinions and feelings weren't relevant enough to be mentioned.'

'I assumed you were undecided. I'm sorry I didn't ask directly, but . . . for God's sake, Cara, we talked about it for hours. Jess, Olly and I all said what we thought and you could have done the same. Why didn't you? Wouldn't that have been the sensible thing to do, instead of waiting for us to ask you, so that you could go off in a huff when we didn't? Hang on – is that why you asked us over and over again, to remind us that we'd neglected to ask you? That's screwed up. Why not be more straightforward?'

'All right, I will. I'd like you to leave. I'd like you to go back to England, rescue our children from your mother's overheated house and take them back home, so that they can start going to school again. I'll be back on 24 October, as I said in my note, and we'll talk then.' Patrick tries to speak, but I raise a hand to stop him. 'If you do this one thing for me, it's very likely that I'll come back and admit you're at least partly right. I'll never think it's okay that you forgot to ask me how I felt about finding myself unexpectedly pregnant, but yes, I was weak and a coward, and I handled it all completely wrong. Then once I've apologised for being rubbish and you've apologised for being rubbish, we can talk about the baby and how we feel about it – and I *am* keeping it, whether you want it or not. I won't get rid of my own baby.'

'Cara, that's *fine* by me. And the kids. Look—'

'Wait. I haven't finished. I'm glad you think it's fine, but I don't want to, I *can't*, discuss it now. You need to go home without saying another word and leave me here, so that I won't always think you ruined something important I tried to do. I hope that makes sense.'

'Cara.' Patrick smiles as if I've said something sweet and amusing. 'I'm not going home without you. Please try to—'

'Then I'll go. I'll leave.' Without looking back, I run as fast as I can away from him.

'Cara!' he calls out. He's not following me – yet. He will, once he sees I'm not going to turn round like a well-trained boomerang and hurry obediently back to him.

I run and run. Where am I going? Back to my casita? No, to the car park. I've got my bag with me, with the hire car's keys inside it, my passport and wallet, my scan photo of the baby. That's all I need.

I have to get right away from Swallowtail if Patrick won't leave. I have to win.

'Cara.'

The voice – not my husband's – is quiet and comes from behind me. I turn to see who it is. A hand shoots out in front of my face, startling me. Something yellow moves fast, presses hard against my nose and mouth. I try to call out, but I can't make a sound.

I heard something on the radio the other day: a guest on a talk show was asked for her favorite word. She said 'holidays'. I thought that was cheating. I couldn't believe she liked the word for its own sake, for the sound of the vowels and consonants and the way they harmonize together. 'Holidays' is a nice-sounding word, but if it meant 'incredibly hard work', would she still have chosen it?

I don't have a favorite word, only two least favorites: 'parents' and 'family'. I can write them easily enough, but I hate saying them, and most of all I hate hearing them when I'm not prepared. But if 'holidays' meant 'parents' and 'parents' meant 'ice-cream' and 'ice-cream' meant 'family', I think I'd feel differently about all these words. So it turns out I had no right to think the woman on the radio was doing it wrong. It's too hard to separate the word from its meaning.

When I first made up the name 'Kind Smiles' for the only people who ever smiled at me, I was six years old. I'm fourteen now, but I can't stop thinking of them that way.

I must have been pretty naïve when I

was a little kid. I thought I could protect myself from my mother by not looking at her. It worked sometimes, but not always. One time I was sitting on the carpet surrounded by the toys and dolls I liked to play with. At the other end of the room, my parents were watching TV. On this particular day, one of my teddy bears, Rosa, had a secret she wouldn't tell anyone. The others were crowding around her begging to know, saying true friends don't keep secrets from one another. I was explaining, in Rosa's voice, that this was such an important secret that she couldn't possibly share it – not yet. I hadn't decided what the secret would turn out to be. I was looking forward to deciding later.

My mother turned the TV off suddenly. Having never shown any interest in my games before, she got up out of her chair, walked over to where I was sitting and picked up Poggy. Moving him around as she spoke for him, she said, 'You're not being fair, Rosa. Keeping secrets is wrong. You know that. We don't keep secrets in our family.'

I couldn't bear to see my mother's pale pink fingernails digging into Poggy's sides. The voice was all wrong too – nothing like the one I'd invented for him. I wanted to scream, 'Let him go!' but I couldn't. I was also worried about what would happen to Rosa, but Poggy was my main concern. If anything happened to him, I'd die.

My father did and said nothing, just watched.

'Tell Poggy your secret, Rosa,' said my mother.

'I don't know what it is,' I told her in my own voice. 'I haven't made up my mind.'

'Is that so?' she said. She dropped Poggy, snatched Rosa from my hand and took her out of the room, into the kitchen. I heard a drawer open. My father stared at the switched-off TV. A minute or so later my mother came back in, having cut Rosa into shiny brown pieces. She dropped them in my lap. 'That's better,' she said. 'No more secrets.'

PART II

OCTOBER 11, 2017

Tarin Fry drummed her bare feet against the floor, listening to the buzzing silence at the other end of the line.

Come on, pick up. Today, ideally. Lazy assholes.

Zellie would be back from her after-lunch nap-on-a-massage-table soon, to fill their hotel room with the smell of Alpine Arnica oil – her favorite scent of all the ones on offer in the spa, despite the vastly superior Ginger Root also being available – and this phone call was one Tarin didn't want her to overhear.

Though, come to think of it, maybe that was only delaying the problem, because there was no way Tarin could do what she planned to do without Zellie finding out eventually. No way at all.

'Ma'am?' A woman again, but a different one. Hopefully she'd be more helpful than the last one. 'Can I clarify: was it Detective Sanders or Detective Priddey you wanted to speak to?'

Tarin made a puzzled face at the phone. She'd never heard either name before.

'Tall and blond: Detective Bryce Sanders. Short

and dark: Detective Orwin Priddey.' The woman chuckled. 'We call 'em Starsky and Hutch.'

'How thrilling,' said Tarin flatly. 'Look, I don't know either of these two guys. Why are you asking me about them?'

'They're the two detectives who were at Swallowtail. I was told you wanted to speak to one of them.'

'Either of them. I don't care what color hair, just put one of them on the phone. Can you do that?'

'Oh, I see. Right. I'm with you. Putting you back on hold while I go track 'em down.'

'Great,' Tarin muttered, to nobody.

The hotel room door opened, then banged shut a few seconds later.

'I'm back,' Zellie called out. She appeared a few seconds later, in a waft of Alpine Arnica. 'That was the least-effort massage I've ever had. It was a *man*. He applied no pressure at all – basically just dripped oil over my back and smeared it around a bit.'

Tarin put the phone down. She wanted to tell Zellie about her plan if she was telling her, not have her overhear without knowing the score.

'Who were you calling?'

Tarin deflected her with a question. 'Did you see Cara Burrows on your way to or from the spa?'

'No. Why?'

'She's not by the pool or in her casita, or anywhere, far as I can tell.'

Zellie rolled her eyes. 'Right. So because you

don't know her exact whereabouts, you've decided she's *disappeared*. Please tell me you weren't just on the phone to the police. Seriously? Mom!'

'You could be right. Maybe she'll turn up.' Tarin decided to leave it until tomorrow to ring the police again. What were those detectives' names? She'd forgotten them already. Dark and blond, Starsky and Hutch.

They were more likely to listen after a whole night had passed. It was harder to claim someone was missing when you'd seen them that same morning. And if reporting Cara's absence from Swallowtail could wait until tomorrow, so could . . . her plan. The other thing.

Was Tarin really going to do it? Yes, she was. Why not? What harm could it do?

I open my eyes and I know: something's lost. Something important.

Did I lose it? Is it my fault?

The baby?

Please not the baby.

No, that's not what's gone. It's time. A whole chunk of it is missing. I don't know how much.

My hair has fallen in front of my eyes. I can't see properly – only flashes of yellow and green checked fabric and cheap dark wood. This isn't my casita. And I can't push my hair out of the way because . . .

My hands won't move.

I gasp, convulsed by a wave of shock that turns

the blood in my veins to ice. Someone's tied my wrists together. My ankles too.

A man's voice said my name. Just my first name, just 'Cara'.

Dread rises inside me until it's a lead weight on my tongue, stopping me from calling for help.

What do I know? What can I work out?

I've been unconscious. My head feels heavy and sore at the bottom, as if someone poured liquid metal into it that's now turning solid. I'm bathed in sweat, my clothes damp and twisted, my throat scratchy and dry. I need water. The thirst isn't full-on pain yet, but it soon will be.

The yellow cloth . . . that must be how he knocked me out, with chlorophyll. No, chloroform. Chlorophyll is something to do with trees.

Didn't anyone see anything? Patrick . . . but no, he couldn't have seen. I'd already run too far when it happened. I'd left him behind. If only I'd stayed with him, carried on talking . . .

Is anybody looking for me yet? Did the man carry me, unconscious, to his car, in his arms? Somehow he must have got me here without . . .

The thought dead-ends in my mind. *Here.* What does that mean? Where is here?

It's nowhere I recognise. I shake my head to shift my hair out of the way so I can see properly. I'm in a room, about fifteen by ten feet at a rough guess. There are dark wood kitchen cabinets of various sizes, some with windows showing glasses, mugs and plates. Others are solid with fake-wood veneered fronts, stained and chipped. No one has paid this place any decorative attention for a long time. It has an abandoned feel to it.

No. Don't think that. You haven't been abandoned.

Panicking is the worst, most stupid thing I could do. I'll get out of here. Soon someone – the man who brought me here – will come in, untie me and explain what's going on.

I need to keep thinking, keep trying to work things out. Arm myself with as much information as I can, so that when he comes back I'll be ready for him.

Whoever the hell he is.

His voice . . . was it one I recognised? The detective I saw at the spa? The man from the wrong hotel room Riyonna sent me to? Was it Mason, who gave me the iPad, or Dane Williamson, the resort manager?

Maybe it was someone I've never met but only read about: Jeff Reville, Victor Soutar . . . I try to remember other men from the Melody Chapa story, and can't think of any. Can't be Naldo Chapa – he's in prison.

It's got to be about her: Melody. Nothing in my life would cause this to happen to me – not even running away from home, abandoning my family without warning.

Why didn't I mind my own business, keep my mouth shut about what I saw in that hotel room?

Cara Burrows – is she safe?

She might have been, if only she'd said nothing.

If I'm not safe, my baby isn't either. Without a mother, Olly and Jess aren't safe. Patrick's not enough. My kids need me. They need me home. I have to get back to them, whatever it takes.

Think, Cara. Find a way out.

How far from Swallowtail am I? From the fullness of my bladder, I'm guessing I was unconscious at least an hour or two, maybe three or four. It's still light outside. Wait, the windows . . . They're wrong. Yellow and green checked curtains, but that's not the problem. It's the corners of the windows – they're curved, not sharp. Not right angles. They remind me of train windows.

This whole room is wrong. What is it? A kitchen? Then why is there a bed at the far end? A yellow bedspread with a pattern of small pink flowers, matching pillowcases. I'm lying on a caramel-coloured leather sofa that's more of a bench. It's hard as stone, its leather back embedded in the wall next to one of the two doors.

Kitchen, lounge and bedroom . . . everything's all stuffed in together. There's one chair, a dirty orange and brown monstrosity, and far too many cupboards, but the cooking area – hob, oven, work surface – is laughably small, like a miniature. Not quite doll's house size, but almost.

Wedged between the chair and the wall, there's a coffee table with books on it. The one on top of the pile, the only one I can see, is called *The Devil Dragon Pilot*, by someone called Lawrence A. Colby. The only thing on the walls is a television attached to a bracket and a calendar that's still on August's page. Above the grid for the days of the month, there's a cartoon drawing of a white kitten sitting in a pink and blue striped teacup, winking and waving.

I shuffle my body to the left so that I can see over the edge of the bench. The floor's linoleum – more grey than brown, and even more obviously fake than the kitchen cupboard doors. To cover it up – an understandable urge – someone's put down a bobbly navy blue rug that looks like an oversized bathmat.

All I can see through the windows is bright blue sky, wires, an electricity pylon. No trees or tall buildings. If I could stand up and see out of the windows . . . But with my hands and feet tied, that's impossible. Someone wanted to make absolutely certain I'd stay where they left me.

'Fuck,' I say out loud. 'Fuck!'

A tidal wave of fear seizes me, then sends me crashing down. All I want is my family. *Please.*

How could I have done this? I wanted so badly to get away from home, and now I might never get back there. All the problems I thought I had before, they were nothing – minor irritations. I was too blind to see it. Too lucky.

I have to try to get up on my feet. Swinging my legs, I propel my top half forward. I land badly – clumsy and unbalanced, with a twist of my right ankle – and fall to the floor.

Wincing, I rotate my foot to see if I've sprained

anything. I don't think I have. It hurts, but not enough.

I can't see a way to stand up now that I'm lying on the floor. It was easier from the leather bench – I could swing my legs over and downward. From this position, I can't see how I'd do it.

Unless I can somehow get onto my knees, and then . . .

The sound of scraping freezes the unfinished thought in my mind. What was that? A key in the door? There's a loud, clanking thud, like something banging against a metal sheet. The floor shakes beneath me.

Metal . . .

I know what this is.

I'm in a caravan, a trailer, whatever they're called. A mobile home. That's why all the different rooms are stuffed in together.

I hear the sound of a key again, and the door nearest to me opens. A man walks in wearing a checked shirt and denim shorts. Dusty brown lace-up boots.

'Cara Burrows,' he says. He looks terrible: grey-faced, tense, exhausted.

Of course it's him. I should have known.

'Please let me go,' I say in a firm, clear voice. 'Let me go and I promise I won't say anything. I won't tell anyone.'

'Cara, I'm sorry,' he says. 'I'm so sorry.' And he starts to cry.

OCTOBER 12, 2017

'Hey – isn't it your birthday next week?' said Detective Bryce Sanders as he pulled the car out of Paradise Valley police station's parking lot. 'Tuesday, isn't it?'

'Wednesday,' said Detective Orwin Priddey.

'Althea buying you dinner someplace special?'

'I don't know. We'll do something, I guess, but no plans yet.'

'You should celebrate your birthday, OP. Make plans, bud. You only live once.'

Three teenage boys were standing on the sidewalk up ahead. One was right on the edge with his back to the road. He looked as if he might fall into the moving traffic at any moment. Priddey thought about reaching over to beep the horn. On the other hand, he wasn't driving, so not his problem.

'Unless you're Melody Chapa,' Sanders added as an afterthought.

'What?'

'You only live once – unless you're Melody Chapa. If you're Melody Chapa you get murdered and then suddenly, seven years later, you're alive again and hanging out at a spa resort.' Sanders laughed. 'How much do you think a night in a place like that costs? More than I could afford, that's for sure. You'd be okay, married to a woman of means.'

'Waste of money.'

'We're lucky – we get to go there for free. Maybe today we can fit in a swim. I'm sure our resort manager friend Mr Dane Williamson wouldn't say no.'

'Today? We're going back there?'

Sanders nodded.

'Did that woman call again – Riyonna?'

'Nope.'

'Then why? I don't know why we bothered going the first time. That old lady's one blade shy of a sharp edge.'

'You sure about that, bud? Because I gotta tell you . . . there's been two more sightings.'

Priddey didn't react. It was all bullshit. He knew it and Sanders knew it. Still, he didn't care. Might as well spend the day at Swallowtail as anywhere else.

'And guess what?' Sanders tried again to arouse his interest. 'One of the women who saw Melody alive has disappeared. A Mrs Cara Burrows, from England. Then, after she vanished into thin air, there was a third sighting of Melody – this time by a Mrs Tarin Fry. She's the one who called me. Oh, and Riyonna Briggs? According to Tarin Fry, there's no sign of her either. I'm telling you, OP,

226

some shit's going down at that resort. I don't know what, but . . . some weird shit, that's for sure.'

'Some kind of group hysteria, most likely.' Priddey yawned. He didn't want to talk about Melody Chapa. If she was alive, great. If she was dead . . . well, that was hardly news. Either way, it didn't affect him.

He'd read everything there was to read about the case between 2010 and 2014, when the media coverage had finally started to dry up. He still remembered the names of everyone involved, even those with only a minor role – Shannon Pidd, Nate Appleyard, Victor Soutar – just like he remembered the car Kristie Reville had owned in 2010: a red Toyota Camry. He just didn't care about any of that stuff today, and he hadn't cared two days ago either, when Riyonna Briggs had first summoned Sanders and him to Swallowtail. If it was work, then he didn't care about it – that was the rule.

'How about if we find Melody alive?' said Sanders. 'Imagine that.'

'We won't find her. She's not there.'

'Yeah, you could be right. Still. *She* might not be there, but someone will be. You're in for a big surprise, bud.'

Priddey used to like surprises. He didn't any more. 'What do you mean?'

'Wait and see, OP. Wait and see.'

I wake with a gasp of shock. I try to open my eyes but it doesn't work.

Why not?

Crying. Endless crying, until the dark outside started to lift. Which means I'm looking at the new day through swollen narrow slits.

Bright light streams in through the trailer windows. *Sunny prison.*

I screamed myself hoarse last night. No one came, and I heard nothing. Either this trailer's in a secluded spot or else he knew no one who heard me would care. The first seems more likely. He'd have taped my mouth shut otherwise.

There's no way to tell what time it is. I'm starving, my bladder's so full it hurts, and the inside of my throat feels as if it's about to crack into hard pieces from thirst.

When will he come? I can't wait much longer.

It's not possible that he won't come back. Is it? He left me alone overnight, but he must know I need to use the bathroom. Yesterday he offered to take me to the bathroom and I said no, and now I feel as if I'm going to burst. If I weren't so dehydrated, the bursting would have happened a while ago. I also need food, water. Mainly water. If I could get to the tap, I'd never stop drinking. As it is, I can't bear to see it, even. Looking at it, imagining the water it could produce, is torture.

He wouldn't leave me to die.

No, he wouldn't. He said he was sorry. And he knows you're pregnant. He found the ultrasound photo when he searched your bag.

The man from the hotel room in the middle of the night, the one I should never have walked into.

I try to focus on this new fact. Yesterday I wondered who had done this to me. I listed names in my head. I couldn't add his to the list because I didn't know it. I still don't. But now I know it's him. I decide to count this as a step forward.

My eyes feel as if they'll fall out if I cry any more, so instead I try to think. It's not hard to work it out. If Riyonna hadn't sent me to that room by mistake, I wouldn't have seen Melody Chapa or heard her talk about Poggy. But I did. That's why this has happened to me. The man with Melody must have decided that the answer to the question 'Cara Burrows – is she safe?' was 'No'.

That has to mean there's hope. If I can convince him I won't say a word to anybody, or that I'll say a lot if he'd prefer me to, make sure the whole world knows I *didn't* see a girl who rubbed her head and mentioned by name the favourite cuddly toy of a murder victim. I'm just a poor, confused pregnant woman who doesn't know which way is up at the moment.

If I show I'm willing to cooperate, he might let me go. I can make him believe me, I know I can. He doesn't want to harm me. It was clear from his face, the way he spoke . . .

He seemed nice. In the hotel room, and yesterday in here, he seemed like a decent guy. So much so that I can hardly believe he's the one responsible for doing this to me.

No, Cara. You're the one to blame.

How could I have left the country and put an ocean between me and all the people I love? Space to think, time for myself . . . the idea of claiming now that I need these things makes me want to howl. All I need is my family. That's it. That's all I'll ever need – for the five of us to be together and safe.

I don't believe in God or karma or anything like that, but I know with absolute certainty that if I'm being punished, it's not for walking into an already-occupied hotel room. That was Riyonna's mistake, not mine. Mine was trying to pretend a two-week luxury holiday was some kind of amazing marriage-enhancing rescue plan.

How could I be so selfish? All the things Patrick, Jess and Olly said and did, or didn't say and didn't do, all the things I thought mattered so much and wounded me so deeply . . . I don't care about any of them any more. I just want to be at home with my family.

Somehow, this will happen. The man won't harm me.

But he might take the easy way out and leave you to die like this: tied up on a sofa in a trailer.

My stomach turns over at the idea, but I have to think through all the possibilities. That's the best strategy if I want to get out of here. I have to face it: if he can kidnap, he can kill.

I hear the scrape of the key in the lock and a big 'No' fills my mind. I so desperately wanted him to come back and now all I can think is that I'm not ready. I don't have a plan. I can't outmanoeuvre him. All I can do is beg, hope, pray.

Anything. Whatever I have to do to get out of here, to get free.

Heidi Casafina hated New York. Loathed the place. It wasn't the city's fault – she was aware of that – but, hard as she tried, she couldn't arrange for logic to affect the way she felt. Still, her time here was about to end and she ought to be grateful for that. It turned out that New York wasn't, after all, a trap she could never escape.

All her bags were packed. As soon as today's ordeal was over, she'd be straight to an airport and on her way back home to her parents in Indiana – not particularly exciting, but it would do for now.

Heidi had loved New York City from afar for most of her life, then made the move from Bloomington three years ago. Almost immediately upon arrival, she'd landed her dream job in television – or so she'd thought – working on a show that was as important as it was famous: *Justice With Bonnie*.

Heidi had started at the bottom – low-status, low-paid drudge work – and she hadn't minded a bit. Bonnie had made it all feel so worthwhile. She'd taken Heidi out for drinks after her first day at work, just the two of them, and said how thrilled she was to add Heidi to her loyal team. Heidi had been flattered by the attention. At the end of the evening, Bonnie had leaned over, looked her in the eye and said, 'You, Heidi Casafina, are destined for great things. You might look like a Disney princess, and you may be only twenty-three, but you're shrewd. And passionate. You remind me of the young Me. Stick around and you'll rise through the ranks *fast*.'

Soon enough, Bonnie made good on her promise. Heidi was an executive producer on the show within six months, and when a handful of her colleagues started to make their resentment apparent, Bonnie introduced a new rule: anyone who so much as looked at Heidi the wrong way was fired before they could open their mouths to defend themselves.

Almost from day one, it was clear that Bonnie's wish and expectation was that she and Heidi would have regular girls' nights out – drinks and dinner after work, always Bonnie's treat. 'Regular' meant three or four nights a week – whenever Bonnie's husband Will ('my second husband – the first was a monster' she would tag on to every mention of him) was out of town on business.

Bonnie was fascinating, and super smart. She came out with things no one else would dare say, or have the imagination to think in the first place. Like her very own theory: PSAS, also known as First Find Theory.

PSAS stood for 'Police-Suspect Attachment Syndrome'. Bonnie believed that when a serious crime was committed, instead of waiting however long it took for all the available evidence to be gathered before developing a theory, detectives tended to fixate on the first significant item of evidence, see who it pointed to, then form an obsessive attachment to the idea of that person as the perpetrator. It didn't matter if that was the only thing in the whole case pointing to that person, or if three weeks later there were seventeen pieces of hard evidence indicating that someone else was guilty; all that mattered to some detectives – 'too many, *way* too many,' said Bonnie – was the narrative they'd created around that first significant find, to which they then clung desperately, sometimes fabricating evidence or destroying evidence that contradicted their theory.

As a result, Bonnie argued, it was more common than anyone realized for the first suspect in a case to be charged and convicted, irrespective of their guilt or innocence. She'd said to Heidi at least twenty times in their years of working together, 'I'm a victims' rights advocate, Heidi. The accused innocent, in danger of losing their liberty forever, are as much victims of crime as the raped, the murdered, the defrauded. Don't forget that. All too often, detectives and attorneys unintentionally collude with criminals to ensure the safety and prosperity of the guilty. And that *has* to stop.' The wording varied slightly, but it was pretty much the same speech every time.

Then came part two of her spiel, also with only

minor alterations for each telling: 'Look at the Melody Chapa case – perfect example. Suspicion fell immediately on Kristie Reville and as a result, the red-flag psycho-alert behavior of Annette and Naldo Chapa around the disappearance of their daughter was determinedly ignored.'

Don't ever forget that, Heidi.

She'd forgotten nothing her boss had said to her since the day they'd met. Bonnie was fascinating even when spouting propaganda in praise of herself. When Heidi had realized that the regular after-work nights out meant she'd been officially appointed Best Friend as well as Favorite Colleague, she'd been thrilled. The problems had started when an attractive guy had moved into the apartment next door to Heidi's and they'd started dating. Heidi found herself wanting to spend more of her free time with Seth, but unable to contemplate saying so to Bonnie. Each time she tried to formulate the words in her mind ('We're going to have to change our routine. I can only see you two nights a week from now on.') she was aware of exactly how impossible it would always be to speak them aloud to the person who needed to hear them.

Bonnie, she had no doubt, would turn cold in a fraction of a second. Heidi had seen Cold Bonnie eviscerating those who crossed her, and had no wish to be on the receiving end of that. She'd lose her job for sure and no flattering recommendation letter for future employers would be forthcoming.

And so instead of taking any steps to cut down her Bonnie time, Heidi had found herself explaining to Seth that hanging out with Bonnie after the show had aired was part of her job.

He hadn't stuck around for long. After the break-up, Heidi didn't bother trying to date anyone else. She understood that she was trapped by the best job in the world and hated herself for not minding more. She couldn't bear to blame Bonnie for anything, but she allowed her grudge against New York City to grow and grow: the noise, the pollution, the rudeness, the snobbishness . . .

She told herself she ought to be feeling happier this morning. She was finally going to be able to leave the city behind and start a new life – hopefully a life with some room for life in it, not only work. She was about to be fired, and she ought to be ecstatic. Instead, she was full of self-loathing. Bonnie would never forgive her. That was all she could think about. She'd been told to wait in reception like an outsider.

'Ms Casafina?' The solemn-faced, not-much-older-than-teenage receptionist approached her cautiously as if she were a ticking bomb, not coming too close. 'Ms Juno's ready to see you now.'

Heidi said nothing as she was ostentatiously shown the way to walk by a girl who knew she knew the route as well as she knew her own name.

Bonnie was standing by her open office door, a broad smile on her face. 'C'mon in, Heidi. Sit down.'

So she hadn't turned cold. She was going to fire Heidi in the spirit of friendship, was she?

A strange, restful feeling came over Heidi. She wondered if she could get away with saying nothing at all, just letting Bonnie say whatever she had to say and nodding now and then. She picked the turquoise chair with a fat seat and tiny arms – Bonnie had five designer armchairs in her office for visitors, all in different colors – and sat down.

Bonnie sat opposite in her maroon leather captain's chair. 'So. A guy from Arizona – a detective, no less – calls *three times in an hour* to say there's a resort in Paradise Valley where *three separate guests* have claimed to have seen Melody Chapa alive, in the last few days – and you don't think that's worth mentioning to me? You dismiss him as a crank?'

'I'm sorry, Bonnie. I should have told you. I don't know what I was thinking.'

'Detective Bryce Sanders is no crank, Heidi. I've checked. His colleagues, his superior officers, they all *love* him. Wanna know the word I kept hearing? "Initiative". Like calling me. Luckily he called back a fourth time and got Steve instead of you, or I wouldn't know about any of this.'

'I don't blame you for being furious,' Heidi said.

'Not that, but a word that rhymes with it.'

'I'm sorry?'

'Curious. That's what I am. Why didn't you tell me about Sanders, Heidi?'

Oh, God. Couldn't Bonnie just fire her and get it over with?

'Okay, let me make this easy for you,' said Bonnie. 'It has to be one of two reasons. Either you thought Sanders was a timewasting nut-job, or . . . you thought he could be right, and maybe Melody's not dead after all, and you didn't want that news to get out.'

'I was trying to protect you.' Heidi fought back tears. 'Since your interview with Mallory Tondini, there's been a lot of respect out there for your judgment. Some of it grudging, sure, but still . . . respect. I was afraid that if Melody were to turn out to be still alive . . .' She shrugged. 'Her body wasn't found. It seemed unlikely but not impossible that she might not have been murdered after all. Naïvely, crazily, I hoped that if I blocked Bryce Sanders' attempts to contact you about it, he might give up and take the easiest course: tell himself these three spa resort guests were full of garbage, and move on.'

'So – let me get this straight – because you feared the damage to *my* reputation if Melody turned out to be alive, you hoped you could make it all go away?'

Heidi nodded.

'And, assuming you could make this little problem vanish, where would that leave Annette and Naldo Chapa?'

'Wrongfully convicted. Left to rot in jail thanks to me.'

'I see. And did you care about that at all?'

'A little bit, but I could have lived with it. Bonnie,

237

I thought you might fall apart if you were proved wrong over Melody – have a breakdown, or . . . I don't know. If I'm honest, I suppose, also, there was an element of fear for my own reputation. I work for the show too. Not for much longer maybe, but—'

'You think I've asked you in here to fire you?'

'Well, haven't you?'

'Okay, two things. First: I'm grateful for your loyalty. Truly. That you'd happily see two innocent people rot in jail to protect my good name . . .' Bonnie laughed. 'That's impressive, girl. I don't think there's anyone else on this earth who'd go that far for my sake.'

Heidi felt a new kind of fear: that Bonnie wasn't about to banish her. Her bags were packed and lined up by the door of her apartment, ready for that new life . . .

'But Heidi, if I was *wrong*, if I was part of an effort to put Annette and Naldo Chapa behind bars for a murder they didn't commit, that maybe *no one* committed . . . well, that can't be allowed to stand.'

'You're right, Bonnie. I . . . I don't know what came over me.'

'Lose no sleep, honey. We all make mistakes. I know that better than anyone. Remember, my monster of an ex-husband lined his filthy pockets selling the story of all the mistakes I'd ever made. It's okay – you don't have to pretend you haven't read it. Everyone's read it. Thanks to Raoul Juno, there's a whole lot of people out there who still think of me as a violent, incontinent, perverted drunk with an eating disorder. And – not that it matters – it wasn't twenty smores, it was six. Only six.' Bonnie tutted to herself. 'See, I'm getting all defensive again. Point is: I know all about making mistakes . . . but, Heidi, you don't ever need to protect me in that way. I'm not scared of being wrong. I've been wrong a hundred times, and no doubt I'll be wrong a hundred more. That's life. I can handle it.'

Heidi nodded.

'Now we've got that out of the way, let's move on to the interesting part: these alleged sightings of Melody. Three of them, in the space of less than a week.' Bonnie smiled. 'I've been waiting for something like this. Something big and noticeable. Something designed to cause a stir.'

'What do you mean?'

'Annette and Naldo Chapa are resourceful people – intellectually and economically. When all their appeals failed, I thought to myself, "They won't give up. They'll try something else, and whatever they decide on, no one'll see it coming. Well . . . here we are. This is it. Never underestimate the resilience of evil, Heidi.'

'You think Annette and Naldo Chapa are behind these sightings of Melody?'

'Alleged sightings. I'd bet my life on it.' Bonnie raised an eyebrow. 'Did I forget to mention I've been right a hundred and *one* times?'

239

'So, what, they found some other girl who . . . or someone acting on their behalf found . . .'

'We don't know there was another girl, do we? Not yet. All we know is what three people have said, and they've not even said it to us first-hand. They could all be lying.'

'Bonnie, can I just clarify . . . so I'm not fired?'

Bonnie looked impatient. 'Can you stop feeling sorry for yourself and book us and a film crew onto the next flight to Phoenix? If the answer's yes, then no, you're not fired. Now scoot. I've got calls to make.'

He walks in. Doesn't look at me. Jeans, blue and grey checked shirt, dark sweat patches under the arms. He's carrying something that looks like wrinkled plastic. As soon as he's closed the trailer door he starts to unwrap it. I smell food and my stomach growls in response.

'Got you lunch: a sausage and bacon sandwich,' he says, putting it down on the worktop in the little kitchen.

From where? I wonder. Are we near a café? Shops?

'And a can of Coke.' He's moved out of my line of sight, but I hear the thud as he puts it down. 'Not Diet, just normal. Hope that's okay.'

'Lunch?'

'Yeah, it's nearly two o'clock in the afternoon. You must be starved.'

'How long are you going to keep me here? If you let me go, I swear I won't say anything. I don't want to cause you any trouble, and I don't care what you've done, but you need to let me go. I'm pregnant. I have a family. You can't do this.' I'm talking too fast, going at it too heavy-handedly, but I can't stop myself. 'If you hurt me, people will find out. My husband'll be looking for me by now, the police—'

'Be quiet, Cara. You'll get your chance to talk, but for now I need you to listen.'

Get my chance? Because it's only fair that we take turns. His turn first. My turn to lie here tied up.

You fucking, fucking monster.

Staying silent is the hardest thing I've ever done in my life.

'Good. That's better,' he says. 'Okay, you need to eat and drink something. I'm guessing you also need to use the bathroom?'

'Yes.'

'So I'm going to untie your arms and legs, but in order to do that – in order to make sure it's safe for you to eat, drink, pee without risking anybody's security, I'm going to need to get out my gun from this drawer right here and keep it pointed at you the whole time. Do you understand?'

'Yes,' I say. The word 'gun' lands in my mind and keeps sinking, like a heavy stone moving through water. *He has a gun. In the drawer. He put it there beforehand, knowing he'd need it.*

'I don't want to scare you, okay? The gun is the only way for me to not need to keep you tied up the whole time. You understand, right?'

241

'No.'

'No?' He sounds surprised.

I hear the sound of a drawer opening and shutting. 'You can let me go and *nothing will happen to you*,' I sob. 'I won't tell anyone, ever. I won't say anyone took me anywhere. I'll say I was wrong about seeing Melody Chapa. I swear on my baby's life! All you need to do is—'

'Cara, I can't. Not today. Stop, okay?'

'Why can't you? Why? Why would I lie to you? You think I'd swear on my baby's life if I didn't mean it?'

'Cara, I—'

'If you won't trust me and let me go now, how will you ever? Are you going to kill me? Why, when you don't have to? Can't you see it's better for you if you just—'

'Shut up!'

I stare at the gun that's pointing at my face. Feel all my furious energy drain away. Was that me yelling a few seconds ago?

'You're going to kill me,' I whisper.

'No. I'm not. I'm going to take you to the bathroom, and give you some lunch. That's all I came in here to do today. As soon as you're calm, I'll untie you and—'

'That's all you came to do *today*, but what about tomorrow? Next week? Are you going to kill me then, or let me go? Because if you're going to let me go, it's better to do it now. You must be able to see that. And if you're going to kill me, why haven't you already?'

He sighs and runs his free hand over his face. 'Cara, believe me, if I could change our situation, I would.'

'Do you think I have some information you need or something? I don't! I don't know anything! I don't even know if the girl in the hotel room with you was her or not – Melody.'

'We're not going to talk about that today.'

'Stop saying "today"! How many more days are we going to spend in here? How long are you going to—'

'I don't know!' he bellows. His gun falls to the floor, shocked out of his hand by the explosion of his voice. 'I don't know, Cara. Stop asking me.'

It's a few seconds before my body stops shaking. Silently, I count to ten, then to twenty, watching the gun as I go through the numbers. If it was going to go off after falling so hard, it would have done it straight away. It's just lying there.

The man covers his face with his hands. He's shaking harder than I am. Can't wait to be gone and away from me. All I need to do is eat, drink, use the bathroom and then he can tie me up again and get out of here. Why won't I hurry up and make it easy for him? That's what he's thinking.

Once he's untied me, I need to find a way to keep him here, keep him talking to me. I can't bear the thought of being able to walk and move my arms freely for half an hour, only to then be bound by ropes again.

Maybe he would stay if I talked about something neutral: the Arizona weather or our favourite movies.

He's recovered a little and is pointing the gun at me again.

'I'm sorry,' I say. The words nearly choke me.

He nods. 'It's okay. I understand. This isn't easy for either of us.'

There are so many questions racing round my brain, but I'd be crazy to ask them. And I think I've worked out one answer at least.

'If I could change our situation, I would.'

I can see it all over his face: he doesn't know what's going to happen beyond today any more than I do. He's not in control of any of it.

This is someone else's operation. Someone else's plan.

OCTOBER 13, 2017

'Sir, with all due respect, you need to go *home*.'

Yeah, those were the words he'd heard. Detective Orwin Priddey couldn't believe it. Bonnie Juno – a woman he'd only seen on TV until today – was telling a distraught man whose wife was missing that he needed to get on a plane to London, England, and forget all about finding her.

Juno was running the show here, without a doubt – as surely as Priddey assumed she ran her own show. There were seven people present today – himself, Bryce Sanders, Juno, her Barbie-doll producer lady whose name Priddey forgot seconds after hearing it, the resort manager, Dane Williamson, a guest who claimed she'd seen Melody Chapa alive, and Patrick Burrows, husband of the missing British vacationer.

Swallowtail evidently prided itself on being well equipped for executive meetings. All present had a small tear-off pad, a pencil and two water glasses in front of them. At the center of the large table were twelve bottles of water: six still and six sparkling. So far, nobody had written or drunk anything.

In addition to the seven people, the strongest air conditioning Priddey had ever known was also present at the meeting. He kept telling himself he'd ask for it to be turned down if no one else did in the next five minutes.

'Go home?' Patrick Burrows looked as if he was struggling to keep himself together. 'I'm going nowhere till Cara's found. How can I? How can I go home and tell my kids their mum's missing? That I don't know where she is? First thing they'd ask is why I didn't stay and find her. So that's what I'm going to do. I found her once. I can do it again.'

'And was she pleased to see you when you confronted her?' Bonnie Juno asked. 'Was she hell! We all just heard it from your own mouth: she was mad that you'd disrespected her wishes. She set a boundary – October 24, her chosen return-home date – and you violated that boundary. The last words she spoke to you before running off were, "If you don't leave immediately, I will". Before I go on, let me check – am I *wrong* about any of that? Heidi?'

That was the Barbie producer's name: Heidi.

'It's what I heard too, Bonnie.'

'Dane? Detective Sanders?'

'Me too, Bonnie,' said Dane Williamson quickly. Priddey had the impression he wanted to get his agreement in before Sanders could. The two of them were sitting either side of Juno. At least Sanders had made it look like he'd just happened to pick the seat he was in and might as likely have chosen any other. Only Priddey knew different, from the goal-successfully-achieved look on Sanders' face that no one else would be able to interpret: wide, innocent eyes, cheeks slightly inflated.

Williamson wasn't such a smooth operator. He'd been visibly panting in his eagerness to get close to the famous TV personality. First thing he'd done after sitting down was shuffle his chair closer to Juno's – so much so that she'd felt crowded and moved hers nearer to Sanders, leading to more cheek-puffing.

'I heard that too, Bonnie, yes,' said Sanders.

'Oh, good,' said Juno. 'Well, then my ears *are* working. Mr Burrows, I'm going to speak frankly to you, and one day you'll thank me for it. I don't think Cara's gone far. Her car's still here, right? I think she's hiding out somewhere in this resort. But we've got a problem here. Your marital issues have gotten mixed up with this Melody Chapa business, and we need to act fast so we know what we're dealing with. *You* need to act fast. If, as seems overwhelmingly likely, no one's taken your wife and she's laying low by choice, avoiding *you* . . . well, we need to know that, super quick. Best thing you can do *by far* is get on a plane back to England. I'd bet my last thin dime Cara'll reappear the moment you're gone.'

'How will she know he's gone?' asked Tarin Fry, one of the three Swallowtail guests who had apparently seen Melody Chapa alive. 'Since we don't know where she is, we can't tell her, right? If she were sticking close enough to Patrick to observe his movements, I think we'd all have spotted her by now.'

'Oh, she'll know,' said Bonnie Juno. 'Trust me. He leaves—' she pointed over the tops of the water bottles at Burrows, arm fully extended – 'she'll pop back up.'

'Pop back up?' Tarin Fry muttered with a small shake of her head.

Juno turned to Dane Williamson. 'Dane, if you care about the Burrows family, tell Mr Burrows there's no room for him at Swallowtail. Mr Burrows, you wanna stay close by? Fine – go to Mesa or Glendale. I might sound harsh, but I'm trying to help you. You don't clear out of the way? Next time you'll see your wife'll be October 24, when she was always planning to go home, and you'll spend every second between now and then worrying that something terrible's happened to her. Dane?'

Williamson looked nervous. Perhaps he was imagining the headline: 'Resort manager forcibly expels distraught husband of missing tourist'.

Tarin Fry said to Juno, 'Leave Patrick alone. You're seriously going to drive him out of the resort where his wife was last seen?'

This was kind of fun. Priddey was enjoying his job more now that he officially didn't give a damn about anything but the paycheck.

Sanders was saying nothing. He was sitting right

back, looking at the wall, as if this part of the conversation didn't concern him.

'I have a question for Bonnie.' Tarin Fry again.

'Shoot,' said Juno.

'The way you said, "Oh, she'll know" a minute ago, meaning Cara will know as soon as Patrick leaves . . . have you seen Cara, or communicated with her since you got here? Are you helping her to hide?'

Juno smiled indulgently. 'What a peculiar question. No, categorically, I am not. Why would you think that?'

'Well, you were claiming certain knowledge of something you can't know unless you *know* – more than you're letting on.'

'Hah! Honey, that's my style.'

'Sure, I know that. But this is a matter of substance, not style. You made a claim: that Cara would know instantly if Patrick left. I'm asking you if you're able to substantiate that claim.'

Juno leaned forward and peered at her. 'You're the florist, right?'

'I'm *a* florist. For all I know there might be others around the table. Him, maybe?' Fry pointed at Sanders.

'No, ma'am,' said Sanders with an easy chuckle.

Priddey decided he liked Tarin Fry. She was entertaining.

'How come you're not an attorney, with all your talk of substantiating claims?' Juno asked her.

'I like being a florist.'

'Huh.' Juno looked puzzled by this. 'Well, all right, you made a fair point. I don't know *for sure* that Cara Burrows would reappear if her husband made himself scarce. It's a hunch, that's all.'

'Any chance we could get the air con turned down?' Sanders asked.

'Here's an idea,' said Tarin Fry. 'Patrick, you could leave temporarily, then come back in a few hours – put Bonnie's theory to the test. If Cara *pops up* while you're gone, great. If she doesn't, we'll know something's wrong and the police can start trying to find her like a real missing person.'

Juno gave a small shrug and nodded. 'Sounds like a good compromise to me.'

'While they're at it, they can find Riyonna too,' Fry added.

'Wait!' Bonnie held up a hand. 'Did I miss something? Dane, you told me Riyonna Briggs left of her own accord after you gave her a piece of your mind.'

'I talked to her, yes. She was . . . noticeably upset afterward. I maybe came down a little hard on her. Truth is, I couldn't believe she'd indulged Mrs McNair to the extent she had – going as far as calling the police, letting other guests hear what was going on so that everyone got scared and started imagining they'd seen Melody too. No offense to you two officers, but . . . Riyonna should have known she was wasting your time. Lilith McNair sees a different Melody Chapa every time she stays with us. Once it was a boy!'

Williamson looked around, clearly hoping for a favorable response to his punchline. No one reacted. Some of them had heard about Boy Melody before. Others didn't care.

'Riyonna said she'd wanted to be thorough,' the resort manager went on. 'It was Mrs McNair seeing Poggy that made her feel this time might be different and couldn't be ignored. Point is, however she felt about it, taking action without running it past me was unacceptable. Unprofessional. I told her straight out: she was lucky to still have a job after pulling a stunt like that. She left my office in tears.'

Bonnie Juno sighed. 'All right, so, chances are Riyonna's feeling like a fool, pride hurt, and she'll be back as soon as she gets over it. Heidi, get our people on to this. See if she can be tracked down, as a matter of urgency. Liaise with Dane when we're done here, get her number, address and the rest.'

'Will do, Bonnie.' Heidi made a note on her pad.

'Might be worth sending her a conciliatory text,' Sanders suggested to Williamson. 'In case she's too scared to show her face. You know: "Please come back, all is forgiven"?'

'Great idea, detective,' said Juno. 'Do it, Dane – now, if you wouldn't mind.' Williamson nodded and reached for his phone.

'This is ridiculous,' Tarin Fry blurted out. 'You're giving preferential treatment to a less likely hypothesis over a more likely one. Two women are missing. They should both be here at Swallowtail, and they're not. Both—'

'I think we all need to keep calm and not jump to the conclusion that anyone we can't see around this table has been snatched by a faceless abductor,' Sanders cut her off. 'This is how hysteria spreads, and believe me, once it takes hold, it's hard to make sense of anything.'

'I could not agree more, detective,' said Bonnie Juno.

'I'm glad the two of you agree, but I hadn't finished.' Tarin Fry's smile was cold. 'Okay, I won't say "missing" if you're squeamish. Two women, suddenly not here. One saw Melody Chapa alive and heard her mention Poggy by name, the other called the police after another resort guest saw the same thing: Melody with Poggy. Now, you're going to tell me this could all be a big coincidence – and yes, Cara and Riyonna both had reasons to run away that had nothing to do with Melody, I'm not disputing that. And before someone points out that Mrs McNair also saw Melody and I did too and no one's abducted either of us – obviously I'm aware of that. On balance, though, I still think Cara and Riyonna have been removed from Swallowtail and taken God knows where against their will. Here's why.'

Tarin Fry stood up and started to walk around the table, passing behind people's backs. Bonnie Juno adjusted her chair so that she could watch Fry head-on as she moved toward her. Priddey felt as if he was watching a drama in which everyone loved their own lines a bit too much. He wondered how long he'd have to sit here listening to them all.

'Cara first,' said Fry. 'She asks Patrick to leave, to allow her this much-needed time alone. He tries to persuade her to be happy about him staying, or he refuses to leave, or whatever. Cara wants to win this one, and the only way she can think to do that, if he won't go, is to disappear herself and leave him stranded. Right?'

Juno, Sanders, Heidi and Williamson all nodded. Patrick Burrows looked dazed, staring off into the distance as if he was alone in the room.

'Okay, good,' said Fry. 'So, what could be more stupid and self-defeating than for Cara to make her big point by *staying at Swallowtail*, the resort her husband refuses to leave? And he certainly won't be going anywhere once she's gone missing. She'd know that. This is a big resort but let's face it: if she's here, she'll be found by the end of the day – and there Patrick will be, waiting for her. Instead, she could have got into her hire car and been halfway to Santa Fe before Patrick had found his way to reception. I think that's what she'd have done.'

Priddey agreed. He said nothing.

'Moving on to Riyonna . . .' Tarin Fry had returned to her chair and was standing behind it. 'She'd been disciplined by her boss and she was upset. Mr Williamson, I have two questions for

253

you: is Riyonna a defiant, combative employee? And does she have another source of income aside from her job here? Rich husband or parents, anything like that?'

'No,' said Williamson. 'Riyonna's a very respectful employee. Friendly, courteous. And not in great shape financially since her divorce last year.'

'Deferential to your authority, would you say?'

'Absolutely. Apart from this one time.' He sighed. 'I should probably have been a little less harsh with her.'

'When she walked out of your office in tears, was it the end of her shift?'

'No. Nearer the beginning.'

Tarin Fry nodded and half smiled. 'Well, I don't know about you all, but if I were short of cash and I'd just had a warning from my boss after a major screw-up, the last thing I'd do is walk out before the end of my shift. Correct me if I'm wrong, but if you mess up at work and get called out on it, that doesn't entitle you to leave early.'

'No, it doesn't,' said Bonnie Juno thoughtfully. 'And if you needed every cent you could lay your hands on, post-divorce . . .'

'You'd apologize to your manager and get the hell on with doing your job,' Tarin Fry finished the sentence for her. 'The only way you *wouldn't* do that is if you have a problem with authority – and we've just heard that Riyonna doesn't. *I* might walk out and risk long-term unemployment and penury rather than eat humble pie served up by a jerk – no offense, Mr Williamson – but I don't believe Riyonna would.'

'Those are some very good points,' said Juno.

'I'm glad you liked them. Now I have something to say to you two.' Fry pointed at Priddey, then at Sanders. 'Instead of wasting your time combing every inch of this place for Cara, focus on room 324 and the elusive Robert and Hope Katz.'

'Whoa, whoa, whoa!' Bonnie Juno cut her off. 'Four rooms suddenly turns into one room? What about 322, 323 and 325?'

'*I'm* in 325, and I told you all already, Cara said the bathroom of the room she went into—'

'. . . was on the other side of the hallway,' said Juno. 'Yeah, you did. But we only have your word for that, don't we?'

'Yes, you do.' Fry didn't flinch. Turning to Priddey, she said, 'Trust me. 324's the one. Robert and Hope Katz. Who I'm betting don't exist. Another place you need to search? Cara's casita, where she was staying. Her kidnapper's DNA might be all over it. And she had an iPad with her, one she borrowed from the shop here, in the main building. See if you can find it. I don't think she'd have left it by choice. It was a way of contacting her kids. Oh – she used Instagram to do that, I think, so that's something else you should do: look and see if she and her kids have been Instagram-messaging each other or whatever the hell it's called. If one of the kids has sent her a message some time ago and she's not replied . . .

well, that's another sign she hasn't left here volun-
tarily, right?'

'I've a question for you, Ms Fry,' Bonnie Juno said.
'Mrs.'

'How come you and Lilith McNair are still here?
Is this master abductor not very thorough?'

Tarin Fry didn't miss a beat. 'Too thorough
would be too obvious. Even you guys, desperate
as you all are to pretend nothing's seriously wrong
here – even you couldn't reasonably explain away
four unexpected disappearances. No one needs to
remove Mrs McNair from the scene – the more
she talks, the more out-and-out crazy she sounds.
Better to leave her here to discredit, by extra-
polation, *all* sightings of Melody alive.'

Juno narrowed her eyes. 'And you?'

'I take good care of myself. I don't wander
around in a naïve haze like Cara and Riyonna,
thinking the world's a sweet and lovely place. You
don't believe me? Let's put it to the test. Hire
someone to try and bundle me into the trunk of
their car and drive me outta here. You'll see what
happens.'

'I wouldn't dare,' Bonnie Juno said wearily.

Tarin Fry turned on Priddey. 'Go to the spa and
find the bit of paper in the pot in the crystal grotto
that's got "Cara Burrows – is she safe?" written on
it. That's been there since before Cara disappeared.
She found it. It scared her, understandably.'

Having said her piece, Tarin Fry returned to her
chair and sat down.

Bonnie Juno closed her eyes for a few seconds. When she opened them, she said, 'Heidi, Dane – start the process of tracking down Riyonna Briggs. Try and find her quick so that we can disprove all of Ms Fry's clever theories. Uh . . . *now*?'

Dane Williamson and Heidi leaped out of their seats. Once they'd gone, Juno exhaled heavily and said, 'Good. Let's hope they get the right result soon: Riyonna safe, well, back at Swallowtail. Cara Burrows too. Goddamn it. I'll be honest with you guys: *no one* hates eating humble pie more than me.'

'How was it?' My kidnapper grins at me. A gun and a grin. I never thought I'd see the two together, both aimed at me. 'Better or worse than the first?'

'Better. The bacon was crispier.'

Today's lunch was another sausage and bacon sandwich. It turns out that getting food and drink brought to me in the trailer is as easy as asking questions is problematic. In the past hour, as well as the sandwich, I've had a decent cup of decaf coffee, a glass of orange juice and an apple. I've also had a shower: lemon and lime shower gel.

I guessed right: he's willing to stay and talk if I don't talk about Melody or our situation. That means more time with the gun pointed at my head, but it's worth it. Anything's better than the ropes digging into my wrists and ankles, cutting off my circulation.

'I don't much like bacon,' he says. 'People always say it's the thing they'd miss the most if they stopped eating meat, but not me. I wouldn't miss it.'

Miss most. Those words are nearly enough to set me off again. I manage to avoid crying or screaming.

'I need to ask you something,' I say in as casual a tone as I can manage. 'Not the same questions I've already asked, I promise.'

'Good.'

He looks grateful. He likes Well-Behaved Cara. I decide to take a risk. 'Look, I understand that you're not in charge of . . . whatever's going on here, and that you don't know the answers to a lot of the questions I asked before. But you can tell me one thing at least.' I force myself to smile.

'Okay. Shoot. Oh!' He waves the gun in the air. 'Sorry. Bad choice of word.'

'Yeah, let's change that to "*Don't* shoot".'

He laughs. My abductor finds me funny. That's nice.

He didn't protest at my suggestion that someone else is pulling his strings. It doesn't surprise me. He's a good guy and nothing is ever his fault – that's how he sees himself and how he needs others to see him.

'I'd be really grateful if I could send a message to my family. Obviously you're not going to hand me a laptop and leave me to it, but . . . if I told you what to say, do you think you could maybe—'

'No way. Sorry.'

'Please, hear me out. If you're worried about the message being traced to your computer, what about letting me write a letter? You could read it before I sent it. If I could just let my family know I'm safe, that I'm being looked after—'

'Cara, *please*.' From his voice, anyone would think I was torturing him – that I was the one with the gun and the ropes. 'Don't put us both through this. The answer's no.'

'But . . .' I can't stop the tears from spilling over. 'That's not fair. I'm sorry, I don't want to give you a hard time, but it's not. I don't know how long I'm going to be here, and—'

'You think I don't know that? It's not fair, no. Nothing about this whole goddamned mess is fair.'

Looking at his eyes, it's hard not to believe that he's thinking more of his predicament than mine. What is that, exactly? Having to feed and look after and talk to and deal with the fear and misery of a woman he might one day have to kill?

No. Stop.

If I let myself think that way, it'll only panic me. I can't risk goading him into killing me sooner than planned. And I have to believe that might not be the plan. If whoever's in charge definitely wanted me dead, I'd be dead by now. My only hope is to keep him talking, on subjects that don't get him agitated, until I can think of an idea that'll get me out of here.

'All right, if I can't send my family a message, maybe I can have something else I want.'

'Like what?'

I'm scared to say it. Scared of what it will mean if he says no.

'Folic acid.'

'What's that? You mean drugs?'

Does he think I'm asking for LSD? 'It's a health supplement. Pregnant women are advised to take it. I had some in my casita at the resort.' *And now I don't have it. I didn't get time to pack.*

'Sure, I'll get you some of that. No problem.' He looks happy. This is something he can easily agree to.

I feel worse than I did before I asked. His willingness doesn't mean he cares about my baby's life. It only means he wants to feel good about himself. If he's told to shoot me dead this time next week, he'll do it thinking, 'I did my best for her. I brought her that folic acid, didn't I?'

'Thank you,' I say. 'I'd also like some information.'

'You mean pregnancy-related?'

'No. About Melody Chapa, her parents—'

'No.'

'Why not?'

'Stop asking about Melody.' He's looking at the gun. A few seconds ago he was looking at me.

'Listen,' I say softly. 'If you want me to stop asking, I will, but can I tell you something first? Only because I think that if you understood why I was asking, you wouldn't mind as much.'

His eyes move around the room: up to the ceiling, over to the window. I'm wondering if he heard and understood me when he says suddenly, 'Go on.'

'Thank you.' *Here goes. Don't screw it up, Burrows.* 'I know I'm here because of something to do with Melody Chapa. Because I saw her and I told people. I understand all that. And I know a bit about the case. For example I know her body was never found. I read as much as I could online, once I knew I'd seen her. And now I'm here because of her, indirectly. I mean, I'm not saying it's her fault I'm here, but . . . I've got caught up in it all, and it's not my fault either. It's really not.' My voice cracks.

I stop and wipe my eyes. Feeling sorry for myself will get me nowhere.

He shuffles an inch or two closer to me. 'Cara, believe me, I know none of this is your fault.'

'What I'm trying to say is that knowing more about the situation – having more information – would make me feel so much better. Just being able to *understand*. Don't I deserve that? It'd be no threat to you or anyone else. I can't get out of here, I can't communicate with anyone. What harm would it do for me to know the story I've got mixed up in?'

'The less you know, the safer you are. Trust me on that.'

A burst of rage jolts me out of reasonable-negotiator mode. 'So it really is the old cliché, is it? You could tell me, but then you'd have to kill me?'

He scowls down at the gun. I will it to turn

round and shoot all its bullets into his face, one after another. If that happened, I could stand up and walk out of here. There'd be nothing stopping me. 'Don't joke about it, all right?'

'I'm sorry. That was inappropriate.'

He nods quickly, repetitively – as if he needs me to reassure him that I'm going to make everything okay. Whenever I thank him, apologise, cooperate, he shows signs straight away of being grateful.

'If you're not allowed to tell me the story, the true story, the secret part, how about bringing me a computer so that I can read and watch whatever's out there and in the public domain? Surely that can't do any harm. You can sit right next to me with the gun to make sure I don't try to send any messages.'

'No. Don't ask me again.'

'I don't understand.' A scream rises inside me. If he won't let me do anything apart from eat, drink and talk about things that don't matter, then I might as well be . . .

No. Don't even think it.

I can't give up yet.

'I'll stop asking when you give me an explanation that makes sense,' I say. 'Why can't I read articles about Melody Chapa on the internet?'

'It's better if you don't.'

'Better for who?'

'Please don't raise your voice to me, Cara.'

'Annetta and Naldo Chapa, Melody's parents?

See, I know their names. Is it better for them if the world believes they murdered their daughter? I can't see how.'

'I'll tie you up and leave if you carry on like this.'

'And if I don't you'll do what? Stay here pointing a gun at me and refusing to do anything that'd make my life bearable? What a choice.'

'If you drive me out of here with questions, I won't be back for a long time. Shit, Cara, the last thing I want to do is threaten you. Can't we just—'

'Is it Kristie Reville?' It can't be Annette and Naldo Chapa. They're in jail.

'Is she the one giving the orders? Or . . .'

No. It can't be.

Can it?

A girl I met once in the wrong hotel bathroom in the middle of the night. A scared fourteen-year-old child with a stained woollen toy in her hand.

Is it Melody? Is she the one who gets to decide if I live or die?

'Hey. Hey, wait.'

Tarin Fry turned to see Patrick Burrows heading toward her at speed. Good. She'd been meaning to seek him out after she'd checked on Zellie, but as he was here now . . .

'What are we going to do?' he said.

'We?'

'Yeah. Do you think they're going to take Cara's

disappearance seriously now? I mean, are we just going to leave them to it and hope for the best?'

'So suddenly we're a "we"?' said Tarin. 'After you let me make the case alone, and failed to say a single word in support?'

'What are you talking about? I agreed with everything you said. I thought you were brilliant.'

'Yet you didn't say so, in front of the detectives and the celebrity TV lady.'

Patrick looked confused. 'Well, there was no point both of us saying the same thing. Why, what did you think I—'

'Forget it.' Tarin cut him off abruptly. 'Shall we go inside? You'll burn if you stay in the sun – do you even have any sunscreen on? Of course you don't. So let's go to my room, so I can check on my daughter. And I'm not walking in this heat. I'll get us a club car.'

'From where?' Patrick looked around. 'I don't see any.'

'See the little white phone attached to the wall?' Tarin walked over and pressed a few buttons. 'A club car will now appear. Unless Bonnie Juno's crew's using them all. She takes precedence – with the police, with the hotel staff. Did you see that Williamson creep? He could barely restrain himself from licking her butt-crack.'

'I hate those club cars,' said Patrick savagely. 'I feel like an invalid, being taken everywhere in a wheelchair. Who decided it was a good idea to build a holiday resort too big to walk around?'

'It's American exceptionalism in action,' Tarin told him. 'I love it. Listen. Do you hear the distant sound of wheels coming closer?'

'That won't be coming for us. It's too soon.'

'Oh, that's ours. It's going to come round that corner any second now.' She smiled when she was proved right. 'Now, quit whining and get in. I have questions for you.'

Patrick waited until they were in the club car and on their way before saying, 'Questions?'

'Yeah. You told us all that Cara left home without telling you, leaving only a note, because she needed time alone. Why'd she do that?'

'She was pregnant.'

'Yeah, I know. And you know I know – we all just talked about it, did we not? So don't waste my time. Why'd she do it?'

Patrick looked trapped. He didn't want to tell her, evidently, but being English and no doubt more repressed than Tarin could possibly imagine, he even more didn't want to say it was none of her business. 'The pregnancy wasn't planned. We'd only ever wanted two children. Cara told me and our son and daughter that she was pregnant and she asked us what we wanted to do about it. We all answered honestly: none of us really wanted another baby. Me because, frankly, it's exhausting enough having two to worry about, and the kids . . . I think they were just scared. They like their lives as they are and didn't want anything to change. But . . .' He stopped.

'But what?'

'I don't know.'

'But *what*? Quit stalling.'

'When I found Cara here and we talked, it turned out she was angry that none of us had asked her how she felt about the pregnancy. She'd asked us but we hadn't asked her.'

'Seriously? None of you said, "How about you? What do you think about keeping this baby or getting rid of it?" Even though she's the one carrying it? Nice. I don't blame her for running away.'

'I didn't ask because I didn't need to.' Patrick looked upset. 'It couldn't have been more obvious that she wanted to keep it. And the more obvious it became, the less me and the kids tried to talk her out of it. We'd stopped voicing any objections long before she ran off. I think we'd all kind of accepted it. I thought she knew that.'

Tarin groaned. 'You thought she knew? But, like, you didn't discuss it? None of you said, "You know what? If you want to keep this baby, then so do we. Let's do it, and all will be well." Instead, you all just quietly stopped voicing objections, and expected Cara to be happy with that. And meanwhile, from start to finish, none of you directly asked her how she felt?'

Patrick sighed. 'If you put it like that, it sounds terrible. Maybe it is. If I had the time over, I'd do it differently.'

'I doubt it,' Tarin muttered. 'Anyway, we agree

about one thing: Cara hasn't disappeared by choice. We need to do something. If the local cops won't notify the FBI, then I will.'

'The . . . the FBI?'

'Absolutely. Missing British tourist, murder case from Philadelphia spilling over to Arizona? Damn right the FBI. And here's what you're going to do to help me. You said before that you and Cara share an email account. That's a little pathetic, given you're two full-grown adults, but at this point I'm hardly surprised if it's true. Is it true?'

'Well, I have a different one for work, but—'

'Okay, here's the plan. You're going to send an email to yourself from that account, as if from Cara. Say, "Can't write much. Need help. Me and Riyonna have been kidnapped. Tell police." Keep it really basic and short.'

Patrick flinched. 'Have you lost your mind? You're asking me to lie to the police? No. Not a chance.'

'You want the feds here double quick? So do I. This is the way to do it.'

'They'd trace it to my phone in a matter of minutes.'

'No, they wouldn't. That happens in movies, not in real life. Yeah, they can trace it but it'll take them a while. In the meantime, they'll have been searching for Cara and Riyonna more effectively than anything we can expect from our two local cops, Smarmy Sanders and Passive Priddey. *Pointless* Priddey.'

The club car pulled up in front of the main hotel doors. Patrick followed Tarin as she marched through the lobby toward the elevators. 'Come on, I can't do that and you know it,' he said.

She rounded on him. 'Do you want to find your wife while she's still alive?'

'Don't say that.'

'For Christ's sake, Patrick. You need . . . Get in the elevator. You want to find Cara safe, you need to do this. I'd do it if I could but I don't share an email address with your wife. You do.'

'I've told the police the password. I can tell you too. It's bungalow, all lower case, then the number 77 – bungalow77.'

'Great. So now I'll do it – fine – and the police'll tell you about it and you'll do what? Say it's me? Because that's pointless, isn't it?'

'No, I wouldn't. I wouldn't say anything.'

'Can you even hear yourself?' Tarin asked, incredulous. 'You're really that much of a pussy? You won't do it in case you get in trouble, but you'll let me do it and say nothing?'

Patrick groaned. 'All right, fair point. I'll do it.'

'Thank you.' Tarin couldn't help making a dismissive noise. 'You're a real pushover, huh?'

The elevator doors opened. She stepped out and stood with one foot in the corridor to stop them from closing. 'What was that sound?'

Patrick moved to follow but she pushed him back. 'Wait. I can hear a maid's cart. Wait there. Keep the doors open.'

She tiptoed forward and peered round the corner, then came back shaking her head. 'Unbelievable. Fucking unbelievable.'

'What did you see?'

'Don't ask questions. Follow me and back me up. Don't contradict anything I say.'

'Back you up doing what?'

Tarin walked purposefully out of the elevator and turned the corner. A short, rotund maid, a Latina, was half in and half out of 324, the room belonging to 'Robert and Hope Katz'. Her cart was in the doorway. There was a clear plastic bag full of trash in her hand.

'Excuse me, ma'am,' said Tarin. 'I'm Detective Tarin Specter, Paradise Valley police. This is my assistant, Detective Patrick . . . Ross. Who authorized you to clean this room?'

'It is on list they give me.' The maid looked confused. 'No one say I not to do?'

Tarin hardened her face and exhaled, as if in disbelief. Actually, there was no 'as if' about it. The disbelief was as genuine as her detective status was fake. Even if they all suspected Cara had vanished by choice, anyone with a brain would have given the order for all four rooms – 322, 323, 324 and even 325, Tarin and Zellie's room – to be left untouched for now. If there was even a chance that a not-dead Melody Chapa had been inside one of those rooms . . .

Dane Williamson should have thought of it. Detectives Sanders and Priddey should have thought of it. Bonnie Juno should certainly have thought of it. Tarin hated to think how much DNA might just have been vacuumed up.

'Have you done 322 and 323 yet?' she asked the maid.

'No, ma'am.'

'Good. Okay. I'm gonna need that vacuum cleaner and the bag of trash in your hand. Then get the hell out of here. No more cleaning any rooms on this floor until I personally tell you otherwise, you hear me?'

The maid nodded frantically.

'Apart from 325, which you can clean as usual,' Tarin added, thinking of the toothpaste she'd accidentally squirted all over the basin this morning.

'I do 325 already.'

'Fantastic. In that case . . . thank you and goodbye.'

Once the maid was gone, Tarin handed the vacuum cleaner to Patrick and said, 'Get the bag out. Hide it somewhere. And if you tell me you don't know how to remove a vacuum-cleaner bag, I'll knock your head off.' She started to rummage in the trash bag.

'I know how to do it. Tarin, I don't like this. I really, really don't like it. We just impersonated police officers.'

'Yeah. I noticed you giving your all to the role. Ever considered a stage career?' She looked up at him. 'I know you don't like it, Patrick. I hoped I'd made it clear that I give zero fucks for what you like and dislike right now. I need you to send that message to yourself from Cara. Soon. Like, *now*. And once you've—' She broke off suddenly.

'What is it?' Patrick asked. 'Have you found something in the rubbish?'

'No. Goodbye, Patrick.' Tarin's hand shook, as if the piece of paper she'd just pulled out of the bag was too heavy to hold.

'Is that dried blood on the edge of that page? What have you found? Tell me!'

Tarin folded the paper and put it in her pocket. 'If you want me to trust you, do what I've asked you to do.'

'Tarin, you and I are on the same side here.'

'You might say that, but how do I know it's true?' she said matter-of-factly. 'How, for instance, do I know that the person who abducted Cara and maybe hurt her – maybe *killed* her – isn't you?'

I can't decide what I want more: to be safe forever, or to be me forever. The Kind Smiles say I have to choose, and that having both together is impossible. I know they're right. As long as I have this face, there's a chance I'll be recognized. Some people change a lot between the ages of seven and fourteen, but I haven't. I'm still recognizably me. And, as if my face wasn't dangerous enough, there's also the chocolate button on my head – that's what the Kind Smiles call it. Not many girls look exactly like Melody Chapa and also have a brown circle of skin at the top of their foreheads, sticking out of their hair.

The Kind Smiles say that, in the end, it's up to me. It has to be my choice and decision. In spite of all they've done for me, the lengths they've gone to for my safety, they wouldn't force me. I'm going to have to force myself, because I can't let them down now. We all know what the sensible choice is, and they've risked everything for my sake. If that means I have to let a doctor cut my face with a knife, I'll have to do it. I will do it. If there's one thing I'm better at than anyone else in the world, it's switching off my feelings and doing what-ever I have to do to make others feel better.

I'm not scared of ending up uglier than I am now. Poggy is ugly, but that doesn't stop me loving him. And I know that in most people's eyes my mother is beautiful and my father is handsome, and I don't want to be anything like them.

JUSTICE WITH BONNIE (October 13, 2017)

THREE POSSIBLE SIGHTINGS OF MELODY CHAPA, ALIVE, AT ARIZONA HOLIDAY RESORT – WAS SHE MURDERED IN 2010 OR NOT?

DO YOU KNOW ROBERT AND HOPE KATZ? CALL OUR HOTLINE!

BJ: Good evening, and welcome to tonight's episode of *Justice With Bonnie*. Now, as a result of some simply *extraordinary* events that are unfolding in Arizona in relation to the Melody Chapa case, we're broadcasting live tonight from the five-star Swallowtail Resort and Spa in Paradise Valley. Behind me is the resort's multi-million-dollar spa building, and I'm joined by Detective Bryce Sanders. Detective Sanders, what in heaven's name has been happening here?

BS: Well, Bonnie, it seems that three guests claim to have seen Melody Chapa alive, here at Swallowtail, since Tuesday October 10. One of those guests, a British tourist from Hertford in England, has since *disappeared*.

BJ: This is surprising news to say the least! As far as the American legal system knows, poor little Melody Chapa was murdered in March 2010. Her parents, Annette and Naldo Chapa, are serving life sentences for her murder. Which means on the face of it . . . these three guests must be crazy, right? I mean, what other explanation could there be? Dane Williamson, you're the resort manager, so tell me – are you putting something in the food that's affecting your guests' eyesight?

DW: Haha. No, Bonnie, I can assure you we're doing no such thing. We're continuing to serve delicious food here at Swallowtail, created by one of America's—

BJ: Tell us about these three guests and what they say they saw.

DW: Well, the first was Mrs Lilith McNair, a regular guest here. She claims to have seen Melody Chapa leaving the resort in the middle of the night. The second guest to see Melody was Mrs Cara Burrows.

BJ: The British woman who's currently missing, right? Wife and mom, expecting her third baby?

DW: Yes, indeed. Mrs Burrows hasn't checked out, and she was supposed to be staying a while longer, but at present her whereabouts are unknown. The third

Swallowtail guest to see Melody was Mrs Tarin Fry from Lawrence, Kansas.

BJ: Right, and we'll be joined by Mrs Fry in a moment, but first let's go now to our very own Heidi Casafina, who's inside the hotel. And for those of you who think that means she's close to where I'm standing now, let me tell you, this resort is *enormous.* Heidi, you're on the third floor of the main hotel building, standing in the corridor by the elevators – tell us why.

HC: Well, Bonnie, this is where a really quite bizarre story began for Cara Burrows from Hertford, England – and we can only hope and pray that it ends with her being found very soon, safe and well. Mrs Burrows arrived at the resort late at night on October 9, and was sent by a possibly over-tired receptionist *to a room that was already occupied.* She walked in and, in doing so, woke the room's inhabitants who, according to Mrs Burrows, were a man of around forty, forty-five, and a teenage girl. She later told people at the resort that she was sure the girl was Melody Chapa.

BJ: So, Heidi, which room was this? Can you show us?

HC: *Great* question, Bonnie – and one with a confusing answer. So, I *am* near the room Cara Burrows was sent to in error, but I can't tell you which one it is, because Cara didn't remember the room number. According to those who spoke to her last, she remembers clearly that she took the elevator up to the third floor, and that she came out of the elevator, turned sharp left . . . and there was the door to the room she went into. Bonnie, if you watch me now, you'll see why this is a problem – because look, there are two sets of elevators, directly opposite each other.

BJ: Which means two ways to turn sharp left, depending on whether you step out of *those* elevators or *those* ones. What we're now seeing – you all can see it as clearly as I can – is Heidi's demonstration of the possible directions Cara Burrows might have taken. So Heidi, you've just taken one of the two sharp left turns – oh, my, look what's in front of you!

HC: Exactly, Bonnie. *Two* doors. Rooms 322 and 323. And now, look, if I scoot over here and do *this* sharp left turn instead . . .

BJ: The same thing: two doors. 324 and 325. So, Heidi, it seems that the room Cara Burrows was sent to by mistake could have been any one of four, correct?

HC: That's true, Bonnie. Although I believe room 325 is occupied by one of the other two women claiming to have seen Melody: Tarin Fry.

BJ: Thank you, Heidi. We'll rejoin you shortly, but just let's go back to Detective Bryce Sanders for a second. Detective Sanders, what have you found out so far about these four rooms?

BS: As Heidi just told you, 325 is Tarin Fry and her daughter. Long story short, Bonnie, three of the four rooms are assigned to guests we've located and spoken to – that includes Tarin Fry. The fourth room appears to be assigned to a 'Robert and Hope Katz' but we've been unable to find them at this point.

BJ: And I believe there's a number on the screen for our viewers to ring if they know of a Robert and Hope Katz. But I'm keeping an open mind about that, because it's all too easy to assume Robert and Hope Katz and room 324 are where we ought to be focusing our suspicions. So let's talk about the guests in 322 and 323 for a second. In 322 we have a young couple. I won't say their names and compromise their privacy. Oh – and Robert and Hope Katz, if you're real, innocent, law-abiding citizens, I apologize for compromising yours, but finding you is more important right now. So, Detective Sanders, this young couple in 322. They are, I believe, a veterinary surgeon and a construction worker respectively, both from Tennessee. Then in 323 there's a businesswoman, in telecoms marketing. Detective, have these three people been interviewed yet?

BS: I've spoken to them all personally, yes. I'm satisfied they're on the level and have nothing to hide.

BJ: That makes me wonder how easily satisfied you are, detective. Maybe I'll talk to them myself later. Back to Heidi on the third floor. Heidi, what happened when Cara Burrows let herself in to whichever room it was? She woke the man and the girl and . . . then what?

HC: I'm told she went straight into the bathroom, Bonnie, and saw that it was full of another guest's possessions: bathing suits, razors, rubber swim cap, hair accessories. Then she heard voices that let her know she wasn't alone. She heard a girl's voice say, 'I spilled Coke on Poggy,' and then a man and a girl appeared in the doorway of the bathroom. The girl was around thirteen or fourteen, Mrs Burrows estimated, and she was *rubbing her head* – right here – and continued to do so for as long as Mrs Burrows had her in her sights.

279

BJ: So, the very spot where poor little Melody had a distinguishing mark?

HC: The exact spot, yes. The girl was holding a stuffed animal in her hand, according to what Cara Burrows told people later, and she described that animal as being not quite a pig and not quite a dog, but a little like both. And looking stained with Coke or some other dark liquid. But, as Cara Burrows is missing, we've only got this second-hand.

BJ: Sounds like Poggy to me, Heidi – but then, anyone could do some research and then describe the most famous stuffed animal in America. So, I take it Mrs Burrows was embarrassed, made her excuses and left the room immediately?

HC: Apparently so. And now, as we know, she's missing. Bonnie, it's also worth mentioning that Cara Burrows had apparently never heard of Melody Chapa and knew nothing about the case until she heard Lilith McNair talking about having seen Melody. Later Mrs Burrows decided she'd seen the same person, and she found out only then who Melody was.

BJ: Thank you, Heidi. Mrs Lilith McNair, who also claimed she saw Melody, has sadly declared herself unwilling to speak to us. Dane Williamson, resort manager: I guess not everyone cares all that much about a murdered little girl and a missing British mom?

DW: Don't be too hard on Mrs McNair, Bonnie. She—

BJ: Spends a lot of money at your resort?

DW: I was going to say that she can get a little confused sometimes. She's claimed in the past that several other children were Melody Chapa – including one who was a boy.

BJ: Oh, Lord! So one of the three guests who allegedly saw Melody has an excess of imagination. Another is Lord alone knows where, and so can't tell us a damn thing, and the third is in room 325 – one of the rooms under suspicion. I hate to sound like a conspiracy theorist, but this smells *way* off to me. I should say at this point that I still believe Melody Chapa was murdered by her parents. My view hasn't changed – yet. But if I'm wrong and Melody's alive, we need to find out. So I'm going to make a direct appeal. Cara, sweetheart, you don't know me but believe me, I care about your safety and the safety of your precious baby. Come back, please, if you can. Get in contact – with this show, with the police, with your husband. Detective Sanders, what's your theory about Cara's present whereabouts?

BS: Bonnie, we know that Mrs Burrows didn't take her rental car. At this stage, we believe she's probably still somewhere at Swallowtail.

BJ: Then get out there and find her, detective. Let's talk now to the third guest at Swallowtail who claims she saw Melody: Tarin Fry from Lawrence, Kansas. Mrs Fry—

TF: Call me Tarin.

BJ: All right, Tarin. Tell us what you saw. And when.

TF: I saw a teenage girl with long, dark hair. I didn't notice if she had a brown mark near her hairline, I'm afraid. She was walking past the tennis courts. I was in a club car going in the opposite direction. She was holding in her hand a knitted toy that, yeah, looked like a cross of a pig with a dog. I knew what Mrs McNair had said she saw, and also what Cara had told me – we'd spent some time together by then – so what I mainly thought when I saw the girl was, 'She could well be the same girl Cara saw and Mrs McNair saw.' Then later I Googled some of the more fanatical Melody Chapa conspiracy sites, and I found sketches of what Melody would look like at various ages. You know, they take a photo of Melody at seven and use some kind of software . . . Anyway, that's when my

282

blood ran a little cold and I thought to myself, 'That's her face. That's the girl I saw.'

BJ: Fascinating. And when did you see this girl?

TF: Yesterday. Eight thirty, eight forty in the morning, approximately.

BJ: So after Cara Burrows had disappeared. Let me ask you something: is it possible you saw a dark-haired teen holding *something* and you convinced yourself it was Melody with Poggy?

TF: Why would I want to convince myself? I don't stand to gain or lose either way.

BJ: I'm not saying you'd *want* to – only that if you believed Cara Burrows and Lilith McNair—

TF: I did believe them. Long before they saw her, or I saw her, I believed she was very likely still alive. Her body was never found. Now we know why. We also know that strands of Melody's hair were found in 2010 that showed evidence of arsenic poisoning, and blood was found, and blowflies . . . Sounds like someone went to a lot of trouble to fake her murder. If I were you, Bonnie, I'd be asking: who'd want to pretend a little girl was dead if she wasn't? And why?

BJ: I feel like I ought to be offering you a job on our show, Tarin.

TF: No, thank you. Why isn't the FBI here yet? Has anyone called them?

BJ: Thank you for your insights, Tarin. Now, we've found that online picture of Melody aged—

TF: Wait a second. I'm not done yet.

BJ: Hey, Tarin? This is my show. When you have a legal show of your own—

TF: Cara's not the only one who's disappeared. Riyonna Briggs, the receptionist who sent her to the wrong room her first night here – she's missing too. I'm certain someone's taken them both. Cara found a piece of paper in the spa with 'Cara Burrows – is she safe?' written on it. Why aren't you mentioning that? Also, what about the credit card Robert and Hope Katz used to reserve their room – has that been traced? If not, why not?

BJ: Whoa – slow down, lady. I've heard nothing yet about the Katz credit card – but that's a very good question, and I'll ask Detective Sanders in a moment. Now, before you get too carried away, Tarin . . . Riyonna Briggs is not missing. She left work suddenly after her boss criticized her. She left his office in tears and at speed, and she's probably at home licking her wounds.

TF: I don't think she—

BJ: Thank you, Tarin Fry. What a character, ladies and gentlemen! Didn't you love her? We'll be back with you after a short break so stay tuned.

14 OCTOBER 2017

The sound of jangling keys wakes me with a start. For a fraction of a second, I'm in my bed at home with Patrick snoring next to me and the ceiling shaking as the kids stomp around on the floor above, getting ready for school. *Another ordinary day . . .*

Then it hits me: where I am, where I'm not, where I might never be again.

Another day in this nightmare. Another morning in hell.

By the time the trailer door opens, my mind has plunged through every feeling I wouldn't wish on my worst enemy.

Except my abductor. I'd wish all bad things on him. He's the first worst enemy I've ever had.

I don't blame him less because none of this was his idea. I blame him more.

This morning he has a tray in his hand.

'I got you another sausage and bacon sandwich. Made sure the bacon was crispy. And coffee, and juice. Pink grapefruit this time, for a change. You like grapefruit? Cara? You okay?'

I don't answer. What's the point?

He puts the tray down on the kitchen counter. I wait for him to start his usual routine: take the gun out of the drawer, then come over and untie me. Instead he turns and starts walking back to the door.

Is he leaving? How can I eat or drink if he doesn't untie me? 'Wait!' I say.

'Don't worry, I'm not going anywhere. I'm getting something else. Can't carry everything in all at once.'

I close my eyes and swallow hard as I try to imagine what something else might be. Another weapon? A knife?

When he returns, he's holding a thick pile of papers and a smaller, flat object with a pattern of hexagons on it, like patchwork – green with white dots on one patch, solid pink on another . . .

As he comes closer, I see that the papers aren't loose but bound. Though not properly, not with a spine like a book. See-through plastic covers . . .

'You need to read this,' he says, putting it down beside me.

'What is it?' There's nothing where I'd expect the author and title to be, only a blank white front page beneath the plastic.

'A book. Read it.'

Something about his expression makes me brave enough to ask, 'Are there . . . answers in it?'

'Yes. There are.' He allows the smile that was playing around his mouth to show itself.

I try to copy it, reflect it back to him. He thinks he's brought me a treat.

'What you said yesterday . . . you were right. I figured you deserved to know some stuff, and it wouldn't do any harm. Like you said.'

And Melody agreed?

A thought I had before I fell asleep last night comes back to me. She's fourteen now, but when her murder was faked she was only seven. There's no way a seven-year-old could formulate and carry out a plan like that. Was Gun Guy in charge at first and then, gradually, as she got older, Melody took over? Did she figure out a way to manipulate him over the years, so that he finally ceded all power to her? Could a twelve-, thirteen-, fourteen-year-old do that?

If she can do it, maybe I can too.

'I want this . . . time you spend here to be as bearable for you as possible, Cara. Look what else I've got.'

He holds up the flat thing. It's a laptop computer in a patterned case – that's what the patchwork thing is.

No way he'd choose that pattern. A fourteen-year-old girl would choose it, though.

My throat tightens. The computer's a step too far. Why is he giving me so much of what I want all of a sudden? It makes me feel uneasy.

'Are you going to let me send a message to my family?' I ask. Hearing myself say the words makes me feel faint with hope, dizzy with terror. If he says no . . .

'Breakfast and bathroom first. Then we'll talk.'

It seems to take forever, but finally it's over and Gun Guy sits beside me on the sofa. Puts the gun down on his other side. There's no way I could lunge and reach around him to get it. It's too far. 'Which first?' he asks. 'Do you want to read a bit of the book first, or watch something you might find interesting on the laptop?'

Both. Both now.

I shrug helplessly.

'Okay, let's start with this, then.' He opens the laptop and types in a password. I can't see what it is. He typed it too fast. 'I've got a video to show you, but first I want you to read something – a public statement Jeff and Kristie Reville made after Melody's parents were charged with her murder. Take your time to read it. There's no hurry.'

Because I'm going to be locked in here till I die?

He says, 'Kristie and Jeff remained loyal to Annette and Naldo Chapa till the end. As you'll see.'

There's a reference number at the top of the screen that's something to do with Philadelphia police; a date, a title – 'Statement made by Kristie and Jeff Reville' – and their address. I skim over all this and start to read the statement itself.

We have been informed today by our lawyers that Annette and Naldo Chapa have been charged with the murder of their daughter Melody, and that we will face no charges relating to this matter.

It is impossible to put into words the immense relief and gratitude we feel to have been finally exonerated. We both adored Melody, and would never have dreamed of doing any harm to her. We loved her as if she were our own daughter.

These past few months have been distressing and gruelling for us as our good names have been dragged through the dirt that is the court of uninformed public opinion. We have discovered that knowing yourself to be innocent of a crime is of scant consolation when the whole world believes you are guilty. There is a very real, life-ruining sense in which guilt truly dwells in the eye of the beholder and is not merely the objective fact our justice system believes it to be.

We are deeply grateful for the support of all those people who spoke up for us, and even those who did no more than point out that nothing had so far been proven against us. And to everybody out there who believed we were guilty of murder and continues to believe it, we say this: we do not hold it against you. If we had not known for certain that we were innocent, we too might have been convinced by the media and the online mob that we must be murderers. We understand that the harsh and widespread condemnation we received was a reflection of how much people cared about Melody — and for that love and care shown for her, we will always be grateful, even if we suffered as a result.

We are and always will be grateful, also, for the support of Bonnie Juno and the *Justice With Bonnie* team. They argued for our innocence from day one and we appreciate their efforts on our behalf. However, we cannot endorse or condone the punitive and accusatory approach that the same team has taken with regard to our neighbors and friends Annette and Naldo Chapa.

Annette and Naldo are now in the position that we were in not long ago: the whole country, it seems, believes they murdered Melody. There is much talk of evidence against them, as there was when we were suspected. We would ask that people reserve judgment and keep an open mind. In our opinion, Annette and Naldo cannot have harmed Melody. Knowing them as we do, we cannot bring ourselves to believe they are guilty. We also know from our own experience that the same piece of solid evidence can be used as the basis for any number of made-up stories, and often the story that sounds the most likely on a superficial level, the one that's easiest to tell, is the only one that is heard, irrespective of the facts.

Evidence, in this case as well as in a more general sense, only goes so far. We have no proof but we believe in our hearts that Melody is still alive and out there somewhere. Her body has not been found, and so we cling to our hope that she is safe and well.

Until she is found — until the person who stole her away from her life is caught and punished — we intend to stand by Annette and Naldo Chapa. We know that, for taking this position, we will be accused of disloyalty to and betrayal of Melody, and all we can do is restate our firm belief that her parents are innocent. The real betrayal of Melody would be to accept as the truth what feels to us like a lie, and allow the truly guilty party in this matter to escape the consequences of his or her heinous actions.

'Did Kristie and Jeff Reville change their minds after Annette and Naldo were convicted of Melody's murder?' I ask.

'Nope.'

'So are the four of them still . . . friends?'

Is that a stupid question? Do convicted murderers who've been imprisoned for life have friends? I suppose some of them must: friendships conducted by letter, occasional meetings across a table in a room full of other murderers and their loved ones . . .

'No.' My kidnapper's voice hardens. 'That's Annette and Naldo's doing, not Jeff and Kristie's. Won't let them visit – nothing.'

One thing seems clear: he's pro-Revilles, anti-Chapas.

'Can I see the book now?' I ask him.

He nods and hands it to me.

I open it and turn to the first page with writing on it. It starts without a chapter heading or number or anything:

> For the longest time, I thought my sister Emory was the lucky one. Sometimes I still feel that way. She died before they could kill her. No life at all is better than a life spent waiting to die . . .

Priddey was glad to be out of Swallowtail's spa complex. He'd known such places existed, dropped Althea off at one once for a friend's birthday celebrations, but seeing it from the inside was something else. It made him think of a religious cult: blissed-out people walking around in identical white robes – walking too slowly, all with the same blank eyes and bland smiles.

He had seen only one interesting facial expression the whole time he'd been in there: a young woman had looked at him almost aggressively. Perhaps he'd broken a spa rule.

The staff didn't wear the white robes. They had a different uniform – baggy pants, tunic, name badge. As far as Priddey could tell, they'd all told him the truth: none of them had seen Cara Burrows in the spa more recently than her husband Patrick had last seen her.

Priddey had been allowed to look at the contents of the silver pot in the crystal grotto. He'd found many dubious expressions of angst and also the bit of paper Tarin Fry had talked about, with 'Cara Burrows – is she safe?' written on it. Beneath those words, someone – maybe Cara herself, but Priddey knew better than to assume – had written a reply to the effect that she did not feel safe, having read the above.

That piece of paper was now in Priddey's pocket. As he'd slipped it into an evidence bag, he'd caught himself wondering: could it be true? Could Melody be alive?

Just take the note to Sanders. He can do the wondering.

Priddey was about to climb aboard his club car when he heard a raised voice. Female. 'Hey, cop!'

He turned. The girl with the aggressive expression was marching toward him, barefoot, still in her white robe. Out here, she looked a lot younger – not much more than sixteen or seventeen. 'Are you here to find Melody Chapa?' she asked.

'Melody Chapa was murdered seven years ago,' Priddey said.

'You don't sound sure about that.'

'Don't I?'

'No. You don't. Don't sound like you care either. Have you found Cara yet?'

'You know Cara Burrows?'

The girl nodded. 'Kind of.'

'What's your name?'

'Giselia Fry. Zellie, colloquially.'

Colloquially? *Hold on – Fry?*

'Are you the daughter of Tarin Fry?'

'Yeah. Shoot me. It'd be the kindest thing.'

Priddey couldn't help smiling. 'Your mother's been helping us.'

'No, she hasn't. That's why I'm out here in a bathrobe. She's lying to you.'

'What lie?'

'She told you that she saw Melody, after Cara Burrows disappeared. She did *not* see Melody.'

'How do you know?'

'She told me. Boasted about it – how the two jackass cops had totally fallen for it.'

'Your mother boasted about lying to the police to you, her daughter?'

'Yep. And much as I don't want to be, like, an

informer, Cara and Riyonna Briggs are missing, so I thought I'd better say something, in case it matters.'

Priddey wondered if this was some sort of joke.

'So when your mom told us she'd seen Melody Chapa alive, here at the resort yesterday, that wasn't true?'

'No.'

The girl seemed genuine enough.

'Why'd she lie?'

'According to her, or according to me? Because, personally, I think she can't bear for there to be a drama unless she's got a main part. But that's not what *she'd* say. She'd say she did it to make sure you'd take the story seriously, about Melody being alive. With Cara gone and that crazy old lady as the only other witness, she feared you might not, so she decided to step up.'

'Lying's not going to help us find Cara Burrows,' said Priddey.

'I know that. She disagrees. Why do you think I'm telling you? Assuming you think at *all*.'

Priddey let the insult pass.

'Also, just before I came over to the spa, I walked into the bathroom of our hotel room and she was sitting fully dressed on the side of the bath. She saw me and stuffed something up her shirt sleeve, then completely denied it. Even though I'd seen her, and she knew it.'

'What sort of something?'

'Paper. That's all I could see,' said Zellie.

Priddey nodded. 'Well, thanks for telling me.'

'Are you going to speak to her?'

'I s'pose so. I'll keep your name out of it.'

'Don't bother. It's pointless. Who else would have told you?' Zellie shook her head in disgust. 'You *suppose* so? Are you just pretending to be a cop? You don't seem much like a real one to me.'

Priddey cursed under his breath as she walked away.

'Why've you stopped reading?' asks my kidnapper.

'Did you expect me to read it all in one go, immediately?'

'You don't find it interesting?'

No, it's just that I have such a busy schedule: first staring down the barrel of the gun you're pointing at me, then praying I'll think of a way to get out of here, then wishing you dead . . .

'I'd like to hear your thoughts, when you're ready to share them,' he says.

'Well, it's clearly supposed to be written by Melody Chapa.'

He tenses. He didn't like me saying that. Was I not meant to work it out? It's so obvious.

'Supposed to be?' I can hear in his voice that he's scared of the answer I'm going to give him.

'There's no way this was written by a fourteen-year-old.'

'Why do you say that?'

'It's too polished. Sentence by sentence, it's too neat and flowing. I have a very intelligent, well-read thirteen-year-old daughter, but she doesn't write like . . . like a published book by an adult. Neither did anyone I worked with when I was education officer for a charity and working with teenagers and reading their stuff every day.'

'Fourteen's plenty old enough to write well. Mozart did some of his best work when he was under five, didn't he?'

'No.'

'He didn't?' My captor frowns. 'I heard he did.'

'I think he wrote "Twinkle Twinkle Little Star" when he was a child, but I'm not sure you can call that his best work. I'm not actually sure he wrote it. It might be one of those things everyone thinks is true but isn't. Like Melody being dead.'

'Are you going to start being unpleasant? Is that what you think I deserve?'

He's serious. It makes me want to fight for my version of reality – the true version. 'You mean because you haven't beaten me or starved me, or killed me yet? You've brought me bacon sandwiches, so I should be grateful? Here's a tip to help you with the rest of your life: no one you knock out with chloroform, tie up with ropes and lock in a trailer against their will is ever going to be grateful to you. There: I've just saved you a lifetime of disappointment.'

He sucks in his lips. The skin around his mouth turns white.

I shouldn't have said it. I need a strategy, not to flip back and forth between placating him one minute and attacking him the next.

'What charity?' he asks quietly.

'What?'

'You said you used to work for a charity.'

'Why does that matter?'

'Doesn't.' He shrugs. 'Just making conversation.'

'Please don't feel you have to.' I don't mean to sound sarcastic and I hope I don't. There's no point in antagonising him. I just don't want to have to talk to him.

'I'm not doing it out of a sense of obligation,' he says. 'If things were different, you and I might be friends. Don't you feel that? Cara?'

'We could still be friends,' I say expressionlessly. 'On one condition: you let me go. Right now. If you do that, I can forgive everything that's happened so far.'

Hearing my cold, rigid voice, I want to cry. I know I'm handling this all wrong. Not that there's a right way to react when kidnapped, but . . . I ought to have a carefully thought out plan. I should decide how to act around him, how to talk to him, and then stick to it, but my fear and anger make it almost impossible to pretend, to stop myself from blurting out what's inside my head at any given time.

A mix of disappointment and disgust contorts his face. 'Cara—'

'It's not hard,' I talk over him. 'You care about Melody, clearly. All you need to do is care as much about me. I have a husband and children. She doesn't. You want to get to know me better? All right: I was education officer for a charity called

Heartlight. My husband's name is Patrick. He runs a company that frames sports memorabilia. My kids are Jess and Olly. I gave up my job when I had Jess and suddenly my family was all that mattered to me. But then I got pregnant again by accident and I discovered that I was the only one who cared about our family. The rest of them said, "New baby? No thanks." That's when I wondered, for the first time, if I'd been wrong to give up my career for a family that, it turns out, no one gives a shit about apart from me.' Why am I saying this? I sound as if I hate Patrick and the kids, when all I want is to get back to them.

Still, I can't stop. I take a ragged breath and say, 'I mean, they care about *themselves*, sure, but not about the family as a whole – or else they wouldn't be so keen for me to get rid of the newest member of it, this new baby. That's how I ended up in Arizona alone. I couldn't look at them, couldn't risk opening my mouth in their presence in case I started screaming things at them that I could never take back. So, I upped and left, treated myself to a holiday in Arizona. Do you feel you know me better now? Are we friends? Do I sound to you like someone who deserves to have a life, as much as Melody Chapa does?'

He turns his head away at the mention of her name, as if I've said something offensive.

For minutes, he doesn't speak. Then he reaches for the computer, saying, 'I want you to see this video.'

He mentioned a video before. And he brought the book . . .

For some reason, there are things he wants me to know, or to believe. So that I'll think well of him when he finally releases me, or so that I'll think well of him before I die? If I withhold my good opinion and make it clear I'm still unconvinced, will I live longer?

I concentrate all my energy on not punching him in the head while he taps on the keyboard.

'Here we go,' he says.

It's on YouTube: a woman and a man on a stage with dusty wooden floorboards. Black shiny material behind them on all sides. The man's sitting on a high-backed wooden chair, facing the camera, wearing a checked shirt and brown corduroy trousers. Bald on top, metal-rimmed square glasses, tufts of brown hair on the sides of his head. A beard that's brown at the sides, auburn in the middle. He looks about fifty. Olly would say he looks like a nerd.

The woman's short – not much taller than the chair the man's sitting on – with wavy, golden-brown hair in a ponytail. She also looks to be in her late forties, early fifties. Her face, particularly her mouth, makes me think of a duck. She's walking slowly around the man. In her hand is a paintbrush with green paint on its tip. After circling him twice, she stops, stares at the camera and says, 'The great image has no form.'

The man, also straight to camera, repeats the line: 'The great image has no form.'

'Everything is a continuum,' says the woman.

'There are no objects, only non-objects,' says the man.

Her: 'Art cannot be separated from reality.'

Him: 'Art is not a representation of reality.'

Both of them together: 'Art is reality and reality is art.'

The woman uses her brush to paint the word 'The' on the man's forehead, then passes it to him. He gets up out of his chair, revealing himself to be considerably taller than her. Then he bends down and paints something on the stage. When he straightens up and stands back, the camera angle shifts to show what he's painted on the floorboards: 'great image has no'.

The woman steps forward, and the man paints the word 'form' on her forehead. They hold hands and bow.

That's it: clip over.

'Kristie and Jeff Reville?' I ask. 'I read online that he's an art teacher and she's an artist.'

'Yeah, that was Jeff and Kristie. I wanted you to see that. So you'd know.'

'Know what?'

'That they could never hurt anyone. They're good people. Some of the best.'

Did he watch a different clip from the one I saw? To me the Revilles seemed deranged. Anyone who makes a video of themselves painting green words on each other's foreheads . . . that doesn't say normal to me.

Also, when the person vouching for you is a man who kidnaps women and holds them at gunpoint . . .

'Was it one of them who wrote the book, the Melody book? Jeff or Kristie?'

'Why do you think that?'

'I notice you're not saying, "Of course not. Melody wrote the book." I can't think who else it could be apart from Kristie or Jeff Reville. I doubt it was you, and it's hardly going to be Annette and Naldo Chapa. The bit I've read so far doesn't show them in a good light.'

'Cara, Cara.' He exhales slowly. 'When it comes to those two, there is no good light. If you doubt they deserve to be where they are, then I've got something else you need to see.'

'However terrible they were as parents, if Melody's alive, they shouldn't be serving life sentences for her murder.'

He's reaching for the laptop again. 'See what you think once you've watched this. You'll see Annette and Naldo didn't lose any sleep over their missing daughter. Not a wink.'

JUSTICE WITH BONNIE (August 27, 2012)

BJ: Welcome back to the show. We have with us in the studio computer forensics analyst Dr Lucie Story. Welcome, Lucie.

LS: Thanks so much, Bonnie. It's great to be here. I'm the biggest fan of the show.

BJ: That's so sweet of you. Well, we do our best here on *Justice With Bonnie* to help deliver justice to victims and their families. Although, in this case, as you probably know, this show believes that the family of little Melody – her parents Annette and Naldo Chapa – are the guilty parties.

LS: Bonnie, after what I've seen first-hand, I can't disagree with you, though obviously that's for a jury to decide at some point in the future.

BJ: I only wish I had the faith in juries that I once had. But, Lucie, you're here today to tell us what you found when you did a forensic analysis of Annette Chapa's online activity during the period between when Melody went missing and when Annette and Naldo Chapa were charged with her murder. You performed this analysis yourself, didn't you?

LS: Yes, I did, at the request of the Philadelphia police.

BJ: And what did you find?

LS: Melody disappeared and was reported missing on March 2, 2010. At first, as I'm sure most people are aware, the suspicions of the investigating detectives were focused on the next-door neighbors, Jeff and Kristie Reville. The first time there was any indication of suspicion in the direction of Annette and Naldo was March 22, when *you* said unambiguously on this show that you suspected them, Bonnie.

BJ: That's right. I'm proud to say that I wasn't afraid to speak up when everybody else was either too stupid or too scared to put their necks on the line. I could see it straight away: those parents knew where their daughter was because they'd put her there. But tell our viewers at home, Lucie – how is that date, March 22, relevant to what you found when you examined Annette Chapa's laptop?

LS: Okay, here's the thing: between March 2 when Melody disappeared and March 22, when you said live on this show that you believed Annette and Naldo Chapa were responsible for their daughter's disappearance, there was a pattern to Annette Chapa's internet use.

BJ: And the relevant issue here is the times

at which she used the internet, not so much what sites she visited, correct?

LS: Yes. Though later, the sites she visited become relevant – but I'll come to that in due course. So during that period – March 2 to March 22 – Annette Chapa didn't work. She was at home, focused only on finding Melody, according to her. Finding—

BJ: Finding her dead, not alive. She seemed convinced little Melody was dead.

LS: Exactly what I was about to say. Finding her body, and her killer – and we have that from Annette's own mouth. So, during this period – March 2 to March 22 – Annette was online not constantly but regularly. With reasonable frequency all day and evening. Then, at around eleven, eleven thirty at night, that'd be it – no more online activity. And then she'd be offline until around eight, eight thirty the next morning.

BJ: And so a reasonable person would assume . . .?

LS: That she was asleep.

BJ: Sure. I mean, who wouldn't get an unbroken nine hours' sleep a night immediately after their daughter got abducted, right?

LS: I suppose Annette Chapa might not have been asleep throughout those nights.

I mean, she might have been lying awake sobbing for all we know. And I can't comment on the psychology of it, Bonnie – that's not my area of expertise. I know Ingrid Allwood has said that misery, anxiety, depression – these things can lead a person to take refuge in sleep, and even, in some cases, bring on a sort of narcolepsy – that's assuming Annette Chapa *was* asleep . . .

BJ: At this point, I'm not willing to dignify any more of Allwood's nonsense with a response. But let me ask you this: did you check the pattern of Annette Chapa's online activity *before* March 2, 2010?

LS: Yes, I did. Pretty much the same, though obviously Annette was working right up until the day Melody disappeared, and her online activity reflected that. But the pattern in the evenings was the same. Eleven, eleven thirty, it looks as if she logged off and went to sleep.

BJ: And then no more online activity at all until eight, eight thirty the next morning?

LS: No, when she was working she woke up earlier. Her first log-on was typically six thirty, seven.

BJ: Which makes sense if she had to go into the office. But, Lucie, you agree with me that 11.30 p.m. to 7 a.m., changing to 11.30 p.m. to 8 a.m. after Melody

307

disappeared – we're not seeing a radical upheaval to her routine here, are we?

LS: No. It's more or less the same.

BJ: Which is why a certain celebrity psycho-therapist is talking out of her rear end. Whatever misery or depression Annette Chapa suffered after Melody disappeared, it didn't cause her to sleep all that much more than usual – only an extra hour or so in the morning, and that was clearly down to not needing to get to the office. She sure had herself some great lie-ins after murdering her daughter! I'd love to ask Ms Allwood – I refuse to call her 'Doctor' – if she's ever before come across a mother whose beloved child goes missing and it barely affects her sleep patterns at all.

LS: Bonnie, I'm not pretending to claim that I know the hours Annette Chapa slept or stayed awake in March 2010. The evidence I've gathered shows only when she was on and offline.

BJ: I understand that, and people will draw the only conclusion that's plausible: that Annette Chapa did not lose any sleep over her missing daughter. On the contrary, she got an extra hour of sleep every day thereafter. Now, tell us what changes after March 22, in regard to Annette's internet use?

LS: From March 22, the pattern completely changes, Bonnie. I assume Annette must have grabbed a half-hour of sleep here and there, but from March 22 onwards, there are no long eight- or nine-hour stretches when she was offline. And when I say none, I mean it: none.

BJ: That is truly fascinating, isn't it?

LS: It really is. There's not much of a pattern at all after March 22. Some nights internet activity would stop at around 2 or 3 a.m., other nights it'd stop at 4 or 5. Once stopped, it might start again an hour and a half or three hours later. But what can be said with certainty is that, after March 22, Annette Chapa did not get another proper night's sleep. And it's particularly noteworthy that, March 22 through March 25, she seems to have got no sleep at all.

BJ: She was on the internet, all night?

LS: It appears so, yes.

BJ: All right, so let me get this straight: Melody's disappearance didn't keep her mom awake nights, but it seems me saying live on air that I thought she was guilty as sin . . . did? Is that a reasonable conclusion to draw?

LS: Well . . . certainly when I looked at Annette Chapa's internet activity between March 22 and March 25, I found that a lot of it was focused around you. In layman's terms, she thoroughly checked you out.

BJ: And I guess that's not surprising. If someone went on America's favorite legal show and accused *me* of first-degree murder, I'd do a whole lot more than check them out. What's more surprising is what happened between March 22 and September 28, 2010, when Annette and Naldo Chapa were finally – thank the Lord in his mercy! – charged with little Melody's murder. Tell us about that.

LS: As I've said already, Annette Chapa did not get a solid night's sleep after March 22.

BJ: So that's *six months* of no proper sleep. That's incredible! And also horribly telling, in my opinion. Look, I spoke up on March 22, sure, but no one listened. No one wanted to listen. The whole world was convinced Kristie and Jeff Reville had abducted and killed poor Melody, and that I was wrong and dumb and vindictive to insist otherwise. The evidence, back then, seemed to point to the Revilles, and that didn't change until September 2, when I had Mallory Tondini on the show. So why on earth didn't Annette Chapa calm down, around early April, say, and think to herself, 'Looks like no one's paying attention to that horrible Juno woman – I don't need to worry about her'? Why didn't she start sleeping again round about then?

LS: Obviously I can't answer that, Bonnie. I don't know what was going through her mind. I can tell you, though, that in her shoes, I'd have been petrified if I thought you suspected me of murder, and I don't think that fear'd be easy to lose. Everyone knows you're tenacious, that you care passionately about justice and you're unlikely to give up. Also, that your specialty – and this show's specialty – is cases where the wrong person falls under suspicion while the right one's ignored.

BJ: It's true that I can't abide detectives and DAs who take one look at a case and decide to play Pin-the-Guilt-on-the-Patsy . . . Well, there we have it, ladies and gentlemen: when it was only an insignificant little irritation like a missing daughter who might be dead, Annette Chapa still managed to get her regular eight or nine hours' sleep every night. The moment she perceived her own well-being was at stake – that I suspected her and would do whatever I could to bring her to justice – suddenly she doesn't sleep so good any more, poor little lamb.

LS: I suppose it's possible to be a selfish, unloving mother and still not be a murderer, but—

BJ: Oh, please!

LS: You know, Bonnie, I hope I'm not speaking out of turn, but I feel a little uncomfortable about the forthcoming trial and the charge of murder specifically, when no body has been found. I wanted to ask you—

BJ: No body, but plenty of blood, Lucie, and strands of little Melody's hair showing clearly that she was poisoned with arsenic while alive, and what's known as coffin flies in two locations where Melody's blood was also found – the kind of flies you only get where there's a dead body. That's why, even without a body or a crime scene or eye-witnesses, a grand jury made the decision it did: to put Annette and Naldo Chapa on trial for murder. It's only a shame the death penalty was taken off the table. Thank you, computer forensics analyst Dr Lucie Story, for joining us. And we're back after the break, when we'll be joined by Naldo Chapa's former assistant, Julie Smithfield. We'll hear what it was like to work closely with Melody's father, and I'll be asking Miss Smithfield how she feels about

Chapa's imminent trial for the murder of his daughter, and whether she can shed any light on the character of his wife and the nature of their marriage and family life.

OCTOBER 14, 2017

So Swallowtail, in addition to all its other assets, had a maze. Only a small one, Priddey had been told by Dane Williamson, but popular with guests nonetheless. It was known as the Meditation Maze on account of the guided meditation walks that took place within it on Tuesday and Thursday evenings and Sunday mornings.

'Don't worry about reaching the butterfly,' Williamson had said with a grin as he'd waved off Priddey's club car. 'It's not the destination that counts. It's all about the journey.'

Priddey had been on that journey, on foot, for nearly forty minutes, looking for Tarin Fry. No chauffeur-driven club cars in the maze, sadly. The green passageways were too narrow. Each one looked identical to the others. Every corner seemed to whisper, 'Try me, try me. You haven't before. I might be the one.' Priddey had discovered that the more a corner looked like a rock-solid option, the more likely it was to lead to a dead end. None of the bristly slabs of hedge had any distinguishing features. Wherever he was in the grid of green, the sun beat down on him. If he'd known he was going to be stuck in here this long, he'd have brought a hat.

What the fuck was the point of a maze? And what did people do who never chanced upon the right route? Statistically it stood to reason that that would occasionally happen. How did they get back? Once you'd found the center of the maze, was that it: ordeal over? Was there a quick way out? Priddey wished he'd asked Dane Williamson some or all of these questions before setting out.

As he walked, he called out Tarin Fry's name and Cara Burrows' also. A maze would be the perfect place to hide out, as long as you had weather-proof clothing and supplies of food and water. If you heard footsteps getting nearer, you could easily move off in a different direction.

Priddey hadn't told Williamson why he wanted to check out the maze. He wasn't normally secretive, but with Bonnie Juno and her crew hanging around, he felt inclined to keep things to himself for as long he could. Truth be told, he didn't want anyone to know what he was doing until he himself knew. Did he care that Zellie Fry thought he was a jerk? Or was it that this wanting to know – about Melody, about Cara Burrows, about Riyonna Briggs – was contagious? If so, where did that leave the resolution he'd made eight months ago? If it was work, he wasn't supposed to care.

He sure as hell didn't care for being lost in a maze with only the word of a Swallowtail maid to go on. She said she'd seen Tarin Fry at the entrance to the maze an hour ago. The rest of her story was verging on the incredible.

After another ten minutes, Priddey decided to stop telling himself that any left or right turn in the distance looked promising.

'Mrs Fry!' he called out wearily. 'Tarin Fry? Can you hear me?' Hearing a scrambling sound, he stopped and called her name again.

'Who is that?' a woman's voice answered. Near-by. American. Wherever she was, she was close. *Hallelujah.*

'This is Detective Orwin Priddey. Is that Tarin Fry?'

No answer.

'Is that Riyonna Briggs?'

'Oh, please. You think Riyonna's hanging out in a maze? Is that your best theory? Why? Just for kicks?'

'Ma'am, what's your name? Who am I speaking to?'

'It's me – Tarin. Hate to disappoint, but there's no girly get-together in full swing here. I'm alone.'

'I need to talk to you.'

'You are talking to me. If you want to see me while we talk, come find me at the center. You're almost there.'

'Any idea how I get to you?'

An incredulous laugh from Tarin. 'Come on, you're right here. If I stick my finger through here I can touch you.'

Priddey scanned the foliage around him, but saw no protruding fingers.

'Can't you see the butterfly? Large, hideous sculpture, wings poking up over the hedge?'

'No. Going by the experience I've had so far, if I walk in what I think is the right direction, I'm going to end up further away. Do you think you could come find me?'

She said something in response but he couldn't hear it. From the tone, it sounded like a grumble. Then, 'Sure. Don't move.'

Half a minute later, Tarin Fry appeared in front of him. 'Come on,' she said, beckoning.

'Where are we going?'

'Back to the butterfly. There are benches there, and shade.'

Priddey wanted to get out of the maze, but he said nothing. A little while longer wouldn't kill him. Same as with the job. He'd get out soon enough – out of this grid of green and out of the police.

The butterfly turned out to be a stone sculpture at the center of a large, round water feature that dribbled and spouted in several directions at once. Around this, in a small hexagonal courtyard paved with hexagonal stone slabs, were five benches with curved backs. Priddey and Tarin sat side by side on the only bench that wasn't in direct sunlight, under another sculpture: a shiny silver tree with a curved-mirror trunk and wide, flat leaves providing much-needed shade.

'The Two-tailed Swallowtail, state butterfly of Arizona.' Tarin gestured toward the sculpture. 'I'm from Kansas. We don't have a state butterfly. We do have a state insect: the western honeybee. But

317

I mean, who wants some asshole insect that stings? I'd rather have a butterfly.'

Priddey came straight to the point. 'Mrs Fry, have you been impersonating a detective?'

'No.'

'No? Are you sure?'

'You're using the wrong tense: past continuous or pluperfect or whatever, instead of perfect. I haven't *been* impersonating a detective, no – not for a prolonged period or on a regular basis. Now, if you were to ask me if I have ever, in the recent past—'

'Did you impersonate an Arizona detective? Yes or no?'

'Once, briefly, yes. And it's damned lucky for you that I did.'

Understanding that no contrition would be forthcoming, nor any fear of consequences displayed, Priddey moved on. 'You used deception to gain access to room 324, by impersonating a police officer?'

'Yeah.'

'And . . . now you're hiding in a maze?'

'Hiding? If I'd wanted to hide, you'd never have found me. I came here to *think*, not to hide.' Tarin giggled suddenly. 'Wanna know what's funny? The maid who let me in, she should have known I wasn't a cop. She'd seen me before. I could see her thinking, "Isn't that the lady from the room over there?" A few days ago she came in and tried to start cleaning too early and I had to shoo her out. But, when push came to shove, she nodded and let me in because I seemed *so certain* I was a detective. Just goes to show, huh? Lie with supreme confidence and idiots will believe you, even when the evidence of their own eyes contradicts what you're telling them.'

Priddey sensed she was watching him out of the corner of her eye. 'I guess that's true,' he said eventually.

'You really don't care, do you? Smarmy Sanders only cares about getting onto the Bonnie Juno slander show, and you're either some kind of weird Buddhist or lacking a brain lobe. I might not have the badge, but I'm more of a detective than either of you. Who was it stopped a maid who'd just vacuumed up a truckload of potential evidence in room 324, and took the bag off of her? Not you or Sanders, and not Bonnie Juno either. You all think Cara's fine, she just ran away when her husband showed up and it's nothing to do with the Melody Chapa mess. You're wrong. She's in danger. If you don't want to do anything about it, can you put me in touch with someone who might?'

Priddey thought about Lynn Kirschmeier. She'd be perfect. She was FBI Phoenix, and nothing would take the shine off Bryce Sanders' sunny temperament like her unexpected arrival on the scene. Trouble was, the last thing Priddey wanted was to be in touch with Lynn again, and that was Sanders' fault, like so much else.

Lynn could easily have heard about Cara Burrows' disappearance on *Justice With Bonnie*.

That could be the official line, if Priddey brought her in without okaying it with Sanders first. Priddey knew Lynn would never tell Sanders she'd got the tip-off from him.

'What did you find in room 324?' he asked Tarin Fry.

'Apart from the vacuum-cleaner bag I took into evidence? Nothing. Strong chance you'll find Melody's DNA in there if you can be bothered looking.'

'You didn't find a piece of paper, then? One that your daughter later caught you looking at, in the bathroom – prompting you to stuff it up your sleeve?'

Tarin Fry looked thrilled at the mention of her daughter. 'Zellie's spoken to you?'

'According to her, you were lying when you said you saw Melody Chapa yourself. You only said it because you believe Cara Burrows and Mrs McNair saw Melody, and you wanted to . . . lend support to the idea that she's alive.'

Tarin laughed and clapped her hands together. 'Well, good for Zellie! I raised that girl right. She has a mind of her own.'

'Is what she told me true?'

Tarin squinted at him. Then she made an irritated tutting noise and said, 'You know what? I'm going to trust you, and if you let me down, I'm going to make sure you regret it for the rest of your life. But as for Sanders and Bonnie Juno? I'll never trust them, so anything I say to you is confidential. You don't pass it on. Deal?'

'I'm not supposed to withhold information from Detective Sanders. He has seniority.'

'And yet you hate him so profoundly,' said Tarin.

Priddey felt the muscles in his face tighten. How did this woman know so much?

'I'm a florist,' she answered his unasked question. 'Think about when people buy flowers. Weddings. Funerals. Anniversaries. Buyers of flowers are emotional, and I see *all* the emotions, believe me. So now I recognize them, and when people try to hide them, too. It's not hard. The look on your face when you say Sanders' name and talk about how you have to defer to his authority? You're the guy buying an expensive wreath for the funeral of the man who married the only woman you ever loved, hoping that if you spend more than you can afford, no one'll guess how much you're looking forward to dancing all over your rival's grave.'

Tarin opened her bag, pulled out a folded sheet of paper and handed it to Priddey. 'Here.'

He opened it up. It was a scruffy but, at the same time, impressively detailed line drawing of a man, in pencil. Above the image, someone had scrawled in childish handwriting, 'Doodle Da . . .' The rest of the second word was blurred; someone had spilled a dark substance on the paper or dropped it into something.

'What's this?'

'From room 324. The piece of paper Zellie saw me stuffing up my sleeve. Stupid maid left it in the room – forgot to take out the trash, clearly.

That's Coke all over it, and the word you can't read is "Dandy".'

'How do you know that?'

'When Cara walked into that room on her first night here, with the man and the girl in it, she heard the girl say, "I spilled Coke on Poggy. *And Doodle Dandy*."'

Priddey allowed his disbelief to show on his face. 'You've said nothing until now about Doodle Dandy.'

'I know. I didn't mention it because I thought it was an unnecessary distraction. Poggy was the important part, and I didn't want to muddy the waters. It doesn't matter. The point is: here's Doodle Dandy. And I found him in the trash from room 324 – which proves that's the room Cara was in, where she met Melody Chapa, alias Hope Katz. I'd bet good money that Dandy's the name of the guy – Melody's chaperone, AKA Robert Katz.'

'Based on what?' Priddey asked.

'My Zellie's been doing an art class since we got here. They've done drawing, painting, mosaic-making . . . Guess what they did first of all?'

'I can't.'

'Doodling. Which means this comes from art class, right? Kids have no imagination any more. Their titles are all *Watercolor Mom*, *Spray-paint Dad*. They're plastered all over the art studio walls. Except Zellie – she called her painting of me *Irreversible Decline*. Ha!'

'And you think Doodle Dandy's meant literally

– a doodle of Dandy?' Priddey was sceptical. 'How many guys are called Dandy?'

'There only needs to be one,' said Tarin impatiently. 'Look for anyone associated with Melody with Dandy as a first name, last name or nickname.'

Was that an order? To Priddey, Dandy sounded like a small child's mispronunciation of 'Daddy'. But that was impossible if the girl who'd done the drawing was Melody Chapa. Her daddy was in jail.

'Also, this means Melody was in that art class, at least for the doodling part,' Tarin went on. 'Zellie says lots of kids dropped out early, once they saw how demanding it was going to be. Ask the teacher. I bet you'll find the name 'Hope Katz' on that list. Also . . . I've been thinking about Riyonna Briggs.'

'What about her?'

'Try to find her and talk to her. If you can't find her, investigate her – without telling Sanders, Bonnie Juno, Dane Williamson or anybody who might try and send you off in a different direction. I think that's how you'll find Cara, via Riyonna.' Tarin Fry laid her hand over her stomach. 'Gut feeling.'

Priddey said, 'I'm not clear if you think Riyonna Briggs is in danger or if you're implying she's responsible for the disappearance of Cara Burrows.'

'I'm not clear either. Luckily there's a way to get clear when you're not – it's called investigation. It's called detective work. I suggest you give it a try.' Tarin Fry stood up and walked purposefully across the courtyard, like a woman who knew exactly where she was going.

15 OCTOBER 2017

The sound of the key turning, the door opening: *scrape, click, creak*. I've taught myself to keep still when I hear these familiar noises. They don't mean I'm going anywhere, or that anything will change. It seems odd that I used to say to myself, 'Stay calm. Don't get your hopes up.' This morning, after my fourth night in this godawful place, there's no adrenaline rush, no pounding heart. Nothing.

'Cara?'

I don't look up. What's the point of asking more questions, starting yet another conversation? He's never going to let me go.

I've tried everything I can think of – everything apart from making him believe I've given up hope.

I haven't. But one day I might have to, and if I do, this pretence – my practice run – will have gone some way towards preparing me for the worst.

'Cara? You okay? I brought you some breakfast. Delicious and nutritious. Seriously, this stuff's good for you – the baby too. I was given strict orders: no more fry-ups.'

This sets my heart going faster. Then I feel like

a fool. Whoever wants me alive and healthy today might change their mind by tomorrow. Or maybe they only want to reassure me so that I'll be off my guard.

This morning my kidnapper is bare-chested, wearing only jeans and Nikes. My throat closes up when I see those familiar swirls of dark chest hair. This is the second time I've seen him half naked. Last time it wasn't his fault, but this time it is.

Last time I was sure it would never happen again.

How dare he come in here like this, as if we're a happily cohabiting couple? It's no big deal to him. He won't even have thought about it. In his mind, he is dressed enough.

Not in mine.

He's holding a tray in his hands. There's a glass of orange juice, and a plate with a white shapeless blob and a green shapeless blob on it. 'What is *that*?' I say.

'Egg white omelette and wilted spinach.'

It looks disgusting. Like a grotesque parody of the Eggs Florentine I had in my casita the other day. Before this happened.

I can't bear to think about before. This is my life now: this trailer and a man I hate and wish dead.

'Can I have a bacon sandwich instead? I don't think I can eat that.'

'Cara, this is really good for you. And the baby.'

'I'd be sick if I tried to swallow it.'

'Listen, you're not the only item on anybody's

agenda,' he snaps. 'Know what I mean? This is today's breakfast – take it or leave it.'

'I'm sorry, do you have other women tied up in trailers all over Arizona? That would be a pretty extensive catering operation, I can see that.'

'Funny,' he says, tight-lipped. I imagine that, silently, he's congratulating himself on his restraint.

What's funny is that it turns out I can be viciously sarcastic and not care at all. Tears fill my eyes as it occurs to me that if I could have laid into Patrick in the same way, even just once, I might not have felt the need to flee the country. And then none of this would be happening to me or to my family.

No point wishing. You can't undo the past.

'Let's try to get along, shall we?' says the man in a sulky voice. 'We have until now, however difficult the circumstances.'

'I agree. Let's not spoil an enjoyable incarceration.'

He puts the tray down on the table. 'Why're you being like this all of a sudden?'

'I'm being like this because, given the options available to me, it's the only way I have to exercise my freedom. And if you couldn't work that out without my help, you can't be all that bright.' If he's stupid and unimaginative, there has to be something I can do, some way I can outwit him.

He takes the gun out of his back pocket, puts it down next to the tray and helps me to sit up. I flinch as he unties my wrists and his skin touches mine.

'Go ahead, exercise your freedom,' he says. 'I won't take it personally.'

'My body needs exercise too,' I say. 'After breakfast, can we go for a walk? With the gun if that's the only way, just . . . anything. I need to move. Properly, not just walking little circles around this room.'

'Sorry.' He picks up the gun and points it at me. 'You can't go outside. Too risky. Eat your food.'

'When can't I go out? Today? Ever? You can't do that! I have to be allowed to go outside. Even prisoners are.'

'I'm sorry, Cara.'

'There's no knife or fork.'

'What? Oh. Sorry.' He pulls a white plastic fork out of his pocket, the same one the gun came from, and throws it across to me. It lands on the tray.

The omelette is still warm, though barely. And yet he carried it into the trailer uncovered; no plastic wrapping, no solid silver dome-lid like at Swallowtail, to keep hot food hot. That has to mean . . .

How did I not work this out sooner? He's got two trailers. I'm in one, and he sleeps in the other. With Melody probably – like in the hotel room. I never hear the sound of a car before he comes in, so his trailer must be within walking distance. That's where he cooks my food, or maybe Melody cooks it. Maybe it's not a trailer but an isolated house, and I'm somewhere on its land.

I'm not sure if it helps me to know this, assuming I'm right. Still, it feels good to have even the tiniest bit more information.

After a few mouthfuls of flavourless egg white and a few sips of orange juice, I have the energy for more conversation. 'Freshly squeezed,' I say, nodding at the glass. 'Nice touch. If I ever get to rate this kidnapping on TripAdvisor, I'll give it four stars instead of three.'

He stares into the distance as if I haven't spoken.

'We have to work something out,' I tell him. 'I need exercise. I need to get out of this small, enclosed space. So how about this: we wait till it's dark – middle of the night – and then you come and get me and we drive out to somewhere really isolated and just walk around for an hour or so? Then we come back. You can keep me tied up while you drive and have the gun on me the whole rest of the time, while we're walking. I don't see any risk to that. Do you?'

'Let me think about it.'

I want to scream.

Keep calm, Cara.

I close my eyes so as not to have to see the gun pointed at me, rising and dipping in his unsteady hand. I try to imagine myself somewhere else. Not home – that's too painful. I mustn't think about how it would feel to be home.

Swallowtail: that big beautiful blue swimming pool . . . Smooth, long strokes, one side to the other. Or maybe I'll yell, 'Marco! Polo!' at the top of my lungs like the girl with the thick sausage-plaits.

Wait.

What was that? Something passed through my

mind so quickly, I missed it – like a ghost glimpsed in a mirror that's gone before you've turned round.

Something to do with the girl with the plaits . . .

'Cara, eat. You won't have the strength to walk anywhere if you don't get some food inside you.'

Walking, running . . .

I think of Lilith McNair, what I heard her say. *'I saw her* running. *Melody, running . . . How come she can run all of a sudden? Can my cousin Isaac* run? *Let me tell ya, he can't even* walk!*'* Mrs McNair's cousin Isaac who died of lymphoma . . .

Unless he didn't die. Nothing she said or wrote online made it clear he was dead. I just assumed it. It's equally possible he's still alive, but very sick. Yes, that would work.

Putting that together with the girl in the swimming pool . . .

Oh God. Am I right? I so desperately want to be right. I could do something with this, but how can I know if it's true?

'Cara?' I hear the click of the gun's safety catch. Whatever's showing on my face, it's worried my jailer. Good. Let him be scared. Let him be terrified, in the way that only those who know they're doing something terribly wrong can be.

The Marco Polo girl's sausage-plaits were flying around like two thick ropes, all over the pool that day. No member of resort staff batted an eyelid. *Everyone* I saw in the Swallowtail pools had their hair uncovered.

Which means there's no rule saying bathing caps

must be worn. Yet in the room Riyonna sent me to by mistake, Melody's room, I saw one of those horrible rubber swimming caps. At least that's what I thought it was.

Not exactly pink, not quite beige. Skin-coloured.

'Cara, what's the matter? Is something wrong?'

No one would wear one of those things by choice. Only someone incredibly precious about the condition of their hair, and I can't believe Melody Chapa would have worried about chlorine damage. What she cared about was covering up the brown mark near her hairline that might have given away her identity, the mark she hid by rubbing her forehead the whole time I was looking at her. That rubber cap would have hidden it very effectively when she was out and about at the resort.

It would also have drawn attention to her as The One Doing Things Differently. In a pool full of uncovered hair, one girl wearing a bathing cap would stand out. Melody, who was officially dead, couldn't be allowed to attract attention in that way, so somebody came up with an ingenious idea: reinvent her as Hayley the terminal cancer victim. Hope Katz might have been her fake name for room-booking purposes, but around the resort, in the Art for Beginners class with Zellie Fry, Melody played the part of poor tragic Hayley who always made sure to wear her flesh-coloured rubber cap, the one that made everyone believe she'd lost all her hair to chemotherapy. Wrap a scarf around her head so no one could see the join – easy.

The more I think about it, the more likely it seems.

Hayley the cancer sufferer . . . it makes perfect sense. Mrs McNair saw her around the resort and recognised her from the picture she'd seen online of Melody as she would look at fourteen. She knew Hayley was Melody, but no one would listen to her because she'd previously said the same about lots of other children who weren't.

When she saw Melody running at night, holding Poggy, she became even more convinced she was right. The words I overheard – 'How come she can run all of a sudden? Can my cousin Isaac *run*? Let me tell ya, he can't even *walk!*' – were both confused and, at the same time, entirely logical. Mrs McNair recognised not only Melody but also the girl with cancer that she'd seen around the resort. And she knew enough from her cousin Isaac's lymphoma to know that terminally ill people generally aren't too good at running fast. She was trying to tell Riyonna she finally had proof that the girl she thought was Melody couldn't be who she claimed to be – because true terminal cancer sufferers don't sprint like healthy people.

Long dark hair flying out behind her, Mrs McNair told Riyonna. Why would she mention that unless she saw it as further proof: that the girl calling herself Hayley hadn't lost her hair, that it was all an act?

The only problem with my theory is Tarin. I was with her in the club car when she went to pick up Zellie after art class. She was annoyed because she'd wanted a painting of Zellie's and Zellie had insisted on giving it to Sick Hayley instead. If Hayley – Melody – escaped from Swallowtail in the small hours of my first night there, how can she still have been in the art class afterwards to argue with Tarin over a painting? No way she'd have gone back. Too risky.

Unless . . .

'Cara, what the *fuck* is going on with you?'

I've made him angry by keeping my thoughts to myself.

This is like Cousin Isaac all over again. Cousin Isaac only needed to be sick, but I assumed he was dead. Same with Hayley and art class. Tarin never said Hayley was there that day. She said, on the contrary, that Hayley had taken a turn for the worse. That's why Zellie had been so intent on giving her the painting as a gift: because she was sicker than usual. That means she might have been absent from the class, and the fight I assumed was between her and Tarin was actually between Zellie and Tarin.

There's no reason to assume Hayley was there that day. None at all.

I look up at my jailer and smile. 'Your plan is doomed,' I say, nowhere near as confident as I sound. It could work, though. I've been silent and visibly preoccupied for only a minute or two and he's looking more panicky with every second that passes.

His Adam's apple is going wild in his throat. The

gun waves up and down. 'What do you mean? Tell me what you mean.'

He's consumed by his need to know what's in my mind, in case it could harm him. I can use this.

Don't look at the gun. Don't let it scare you off course.

'Put the gun's safety catch on and put it down by your feet. Then I'll tell you.'

'No. No way.'

'My ankles are tied. You're not at risk if you put it down. It'd take you five seconds to pick it up and release the safety thing – and I can hardly run over to you, can I?'

He shakes his head. A droplet of sweat runs down his forehead.

'Put it down or I'm telling you nothing,' I say.

His mouth sets: a hard line. I start to count. Eight seconds later, he does it: lays the gun down on the floor.

'Thank you.'

Can I do what I need to do next: control him using nothing but a mixture of withholding and suggestion?

'The rules have changed, as of now,' I tell him. 'I've worked it all out – everything. You want to keep Melody safe. I get that. But you're going to fail unless I help you. First thing: I want to know who you are. What's your name?'

This is never going to work. It's impossible. I'm not that lucky.

'Leon,' he says. 'I'm Leon.'

⋆　⋆　⋆

'What in the Lord's sacred name are you doing over there?'

Bonnie Juno's voice – Tarin would have known it anywhere. She didn't rush to answer. She wouldn't have thought it needed saying: she was swimming with her daughter. Anyone familiar with breaststroke and water wouldn't need to ask. 'Oh, God, it's Non-Bon-Jovi,' Zellie murmured.

'Ugh. Doesn't she make you wanna not wave but drown?' Tarin whispered. *Fun's over, time to get out*, she told herself, but her body disobeyed the order. She inhaled slowly, wishing she could store the cool, wet, green smell inside her to draw upon whenever her reserves of inner peace were running low. She loved this pool so much, and would have liked to figure out a way to prevent everyone but her and Zellie from using it. She wanted it to be theirs alone.

Not much chance of that – it was part of the resort, the only part that club cars couldn't reach on account of there being no paths. Thankfully most of Swallowtail's clientele saw no reason to venture out to this farthest outpost.

A person shouldn't need to get away from it all when 'it all' was a five-star spa resort, but Tarin did at least once a day, and this was where she came. Between thirty and forty lengths and the urge to strangle all those who had displeased her usually subsided. But now here was reality in the shape of Bonnie fucking Juno, lumbering over in her electric blue dress and leopard-skin stilettos to spoil everything, and thoughts of strangulation once again filled Tarin's mind.

She dipped her head under the water and held her breath until Zellie prodded her. Emerging, she said breathlessly, 'Why Non-Bon-Jovi? It sounds funny, but it isn't when you think about it. Makes no sense.'

Zellie flipped over to float on her back. 'As in Jon Bon Jovi, Mother – star of your appalling CD collection.'

'Yeah, I got that part. But apart from the "Bon"—'

'Non-Bon because unattractive – like, *so* unattractive. Non-Jovi because far from jovial. Put it all together and you get Non-Bon-Jovi.'

'Huh.' Tarin frowned. 'I can't decide if that's brilliant or terrible.'

Undeterred by receiving no answer to her question, Bonnie Juno was moving closer, teetering on her high heels. She stopped when she reached the edge of the reeds and said, 'What even *is* that? Is it a pond?'

'Hello, Bonnie.' Tarin hauled herself out of the water and pulled on her robe. 'No. Though, confusingly, it's called The Pond. It's a natural swimming pool, designed to look like a pond. No chemicals.'

'Natural?' Bonnie wrinkled her nose. 'Is it full of frogs and slimy creatures?'

'I don't know. I've never met a frog in here, but maybe.'

'I don't get it. This resort's full of beautiful

swimming pools with waiter service at your lounger and you choose to swim here? It must be filthy.'

'Nope,' said Tarin. 'See the water garden on the other side of the little wall? That's the regeneration zone. Somehow – don't ask me how – that part cleans the part you swim in. All those aquatic plants over there are . . . doing something. Eating invasive algae, or something like that.'

'It looks horrific to me.' Bonnie leaned over to peer in.

'From your appearance, I'd guess you're not a fan of natural,' said Zellie, who was still in the water.

'Hah.' Bonnie seemed to appreciate that. 'No, I am not. That's for sure.' She turned to Tarin. 'Have you seen Detective Priddey in the last hour?'

'No. He missing too?'

Bonnie pursed her lips. 'I had my people look into room 324, the Robert and Hope Katz angle. You talked about tracing the credit card they used to reserve the room?'

'Yeah. And?'

'Turns out you were right. The card used to secure the booking didn't belong to any Robert and Hope Katz.'

'So those are fake names. I knew it.'

'Yeah, but that's only one side of the story. The other side is who the card did belong to.'

'Who?' asked Zellie.

'Your daughter's eager to find out, Mrs Fry. Are you? Or do you know already, and is that why you're not asking? I wonder, are the two of you in cahoots?'

'Who? Me and Zellie?' asked Tarin.

'No, not you and Zellie. Tell me, did you deliberately point us in the direction of your co-conspirator because you've decided it's all getting too risky for you now, so it's time to cut her loose? Is that why you told us to find out whose card was used?'

'My co-conspirator?' Tarin laughed. 'I promise you, the last time I met anyone I wanted to be in a cahoot with was more than a decade ago. I had fewer wrinkles, fewer chins . . . shit, those were the days.'

Bonnie half smiled. 'I guess the state of Non-Bon comes to us all in the fullness of time.'

'There is *no way* you could have heard that,' Zellie protested.

'And yet I did. So go figure.'

'I apologize for my daughter's rudeness,' said Tarin. 'She gets it from her father. What name was on the credit card?'

'Riyonna Briggs.'

'I thought you were going to say Detective Priddey.' Zellie sounded disappointed.

'Riyonna?' said Tarin. 'Wow.'

'Yeah,' said Bonnie. 'She wasn't taken by force, nor did she leave in floods of tears because the boss-man yelled at her.'

'She ran before the cops could find out she was part of it.' Did this mean what Tarin thought it meant? She needed to get away from Bonnie so that she could think; away from Zellie too.

'So now we leave no stone unturned in our hunt for that lying, good-for-nothing schemer,' said Bonnie, in the righteous tone that Tarin knew so well from her TV show. 'Because wherever she is, that's where we'll find Cara Burrows – hopefully not too late to save her.'

Tarin and Zellie exchanged a look. 'You think Riyonna took Cara?' Tarin asked.

'Yes. I do,' said Bonnie Juno.

'Leon?'

He nods.

'Surname?'

'Why do you need to know that? If I tell you that—' He breaks off with a grimace. 'Look, how about if I tell you my nickname instead of my last name? Since childhood. It's Dandy. The people I'm close to call me Dandy.'

I hear the girl's voice in my head. *I spilled Coke on Poggy. And Doodle Dandy.* Melody's voice.

'Dandy?'

'Yeah, 'cos of Leon being like lion. When I was little my mom used to say I was her dandy lion, dandelion . . . you know.' He looks embarrassed. 'It got shortened to Dandy and it stuck.'

'And your surname, please?'

'Cara, come on. I'm trying to cooperate with you, but—'

'No. You're trying to compromise with me

338

– different thing. I don't want to compromise. I want you to answer my questions. All of them. And you're not thinking straight. You've decided I'll be able to trace you by your surname but not by Dandy. That's silly. You think if there's an appeal for information about a man called Leon, known as Dandy, people won't ring in and name you? Of course they will: surname and all. So you might as well tell me.'

'Cara, I can't.'

'Then I won't tell you what I've realised, and how it's going to trip you up and land you in prison for a long time.'

His eyes dart to and fro. 'I'd like to tell you but I can't.' He looks incredulous suddenly, as if something impossible to believe has been suggested by a voice only he can hear. 'You think I *want* to keep a pregnant woman locked up here? Away from her family? Jesus, Cara! I *like* you. You seem like a great person.'

'"Cara Burrows – is she safe?" Did you write that?'

'What?'

'Did you write it on a piece of paper and put it in the pot in the crystal grotto?'

'No.'

For some reason, I believe him.

'Something I don't understand,' I say. 'You got Melody out of Swallowtail double quick once you knew I'd heard her mention Poggy. But why take the risk of having her there in the first place? It's a holiday resort, full of people. She's supposed to be dead. Why not hide her somewhere where she can scream "Poggy" at the top of her voice from now till Christmas? Why not keep her here, for instance?'

'We did.' Leon slides down the wall into a seated position. 'Right here, in this trailer. And others. For years.'

I inhale sharply. I knew, but it's still a shock to hear him confirm it. 'So the girl I saw was Melody Chapa. She's alive.'

'Yes.'

'Her parents didn't murder her.'

'No, they didn't. But they would have done if we hadn't gotten her out.'

'Who's "we"?'

He shakes his head. 'Sorry. You'll get no names from me. Believe it or not, all the people involved in the rescue plan are good people. We did what we did to save Melody's life. It was necessary.'

'You didn't answer my question: why take her to a spa resort and risk exposure?'

'How would you feel if you'd been shut up in trailers for seven years, never allowed outside, never going on holiday?'

'Ask me in seven years' time. By then I'm bound to know the answer. Unless I'm dead.'

Saying these things aloud makes me feel as if they can't happen in real life.

'We didn't think it was a risk.' Leon sighs. 'Melody's face has changed so much – she wasn't a podgy little kid any more, she was a willowy, beautiful teenage girl. I didn't think there was a snowball-in-hell chance of anyone recognising her.'

And you made her call herself Hayley and wear a fake scalp that covered her one distinguishing mark, just to be sure. You made her pretend to have terminal cancer. Some holiday that must have been for her.

'She knew not to take Poggy out of our room, or to mention him. She only did because you walking into the room woke her from a deep sleep.'

'And spoiled everything. I know. But I'm interested: what was the plan you all made after I was inconsiderate enough to cross your path? Kidnap me, get me locked up quick – that was the first step. That makes sense. But what then? The way I see it, there aren't many options. Either you kill me . . . but no, that won't work. Tarin Fry knows everything I saw and heard, and I doubt she'll let it drop – especially not with me missing. Unless you're going to kill her too.'

'I don't want to kill anyone. I never have, and I hope I never will.'

Then what? They must have thought beyond the very first stage of getting me safely locked away. What would I be thinking, in Dandy Leon's position? What plan would I make?

'If Melody's not dead, that means her parents shouldn't be in jail. But if they get out, then she has to go and live with them again. She's still a minor. I'm not sure how a judge would deal with a minor who said, "I loathe my parents. Please can I live in a shabby trailer with gun-toting Leon instead?" He might say, "Sorry – off you go with Mum and Dad." You can't let that happen,' I say slowly. 'Not when you've gone to such lengths to fake her murder in order to get her away from them.'

Oh, God. I can think of only one possibility.

'Is the plan to keep me here until Melody's an adult?'

Leon says nothing. Stares down at the floor.

'Then you let me go and I go home to my family, who are just starting to get over my death – they've assumed I'm dead by this point – and move on with their lives. And you and your fellow plotters are safe: I know Melody's alive but how can I prove it, any of it, when I don't know who you are? Was that the idea?'

Leon shakes his head. He looks tired – as if he can't be bothered with our battle of wills any more.

'The idea was – *is* – to get plastic surgery for Melody,' he says. 'It's going to happen soon. A month or so, we think. Six at the most. It's taken this long to find someone whose discretion we can rely on.'

'To get rid of the tell-tale brown patch of skin,' I say.

He nods. 'Also to make a few other changes to her face, so it's further from the one online that all the obsessive freaks have learned by heart. Once the surgery was done, we could have let you go. You wouldn't have recognised Melody if you'd seen her again, and you wouldn't have known who I was – no way in hell you could have found out.'

'But now, because I've made you tell me that you're Leon the Dandy Lion, you're going to have to kill me? And I've brought it all on myself. Correct?'

No response. I want him to deny it, even if I wouldn't believe him.

I swallow down the fear that burns my throat, and say, 'Kill me if you want – but then you don't get my help with avoiding that long spell behind bars. Your choice.'

He lunges for the gun, grabs it and points it at me. I lurch backwards, banging my shoulder against something.

'Tell me what you know, or think you know! Right now, or I shoot!'

You can do this, Cara. Don't let him distract you.

'No. I told you: we're following my rules now. Not yours.'

He moves to touch the side of his head and knocks the gun against it. As if he forgot it was in his hand. 'Jesus Christ!' he bellows.

He has no idea, any more, what he's doing.

'Let's start again,' I say. 'What's your name? Leon what?'

'Reville. Leon Reville, okay? Are you satisfied now?'

Detective Orwin Priddey was hearing, in great detail, about a dog. It was interesting, but not in the way the speaker intended.

The dog's name was Stoppit – 'Because he was

so boisterous as a puppy, and I kept having to yell, "Stop it! Stop it!", and after a while he started to react as if that was his name, so I thought, might as well change it!' – and its owner was Janelle Davis, Riyonna Briggs' best friend. She looked around fifty: tall, white, athletic, with laughter lines around her eyes, chin-length dark brown hair and a fringe that was dyed orangey-red, as if someone had set fire to it at the front. Her clothes were stylish but dirty, with muddy paw-prints visible on her white linen pants.

She and Priddey were sitting out on the verandah of her small house in Scottsdale, drinking home-made lemonade that was so good, it almost made up for the endless dog talk. Stoppit, who looked a lot like an overgrown hairy rat, was asleep on Davis's lap. Each time she moved, he woke up and growled, then fell instantly back to sleep. It was beyond Priddey why anyone would want a thing like that in their life.

He tried again to steer the conversation in a useful direction. 'So you said Riyonna was Stoppit's . . . godmother?' It wasn't what Davis had said, but Priddey was too embarrassed to repeat her exact words.

'No, no. Haha! I'm not crazy. Oh, darn it! Sorry, darling.' She stroked the dog, who had snarled in response to her laughing, and continued in a whisper. 'He's such a friendly boy when he's not tired, but if he's trying to sleep and I disturb him, he makes his displeasure known.'

'You were saying, about Riyonna?'

'So I was.' Her voice was back at normal volume. 'Well, I'm sure even a non-dog-owner like you would know that dogs don't have godmothers. I mean, there's no official religious ceremony or anything. That's why I thought it'd be kinda neat to invent a new word: *dog*mother. Ri's his dogmother. We made up our own little ceremony. It was so cool, really – you shoulda seen it. See, Stoppit absolutely adores tennis balls, but only when they're brand new and bright lemon-yellow . . .'

'Excuse me, ma'am . . . Like I said, I really don't have too much time, so if I could ask you again . . . You're sure you haven't seen or heard from Riyonna at all these past few days?'

Before setting off from Swallowtail, Priddey had searched the internet for anyone connected to the Melody Chapa case who went by the name of 'Dandy'. He'd found nothing. Then, still following Tarin Fry's instructions, he'd started on Riyonna Briggs. Thanks to her lax Facebook privacy settings, he'd discovered Janelle Davis and was able to glean from comments and photos that she and Riyonna were close friends who went back years. Finding Davis had been easy enough. If only talking to her were the same.

'I'm sure,' she said. 'But I'll tell you when I *will* hear from her: Wednesday. That's Stoppit's birthday, and Ri never misses a year. Last year she got him a water bowl with his name painted on it: Stoppit Nicodemus Davis.'

Nicodemus? Unbelievable.

'Wednesday's my birthday too,' said Priddey, holding back a sigh. Typical. The inflated furry rat was his spirit animal.

'Really?' Davis emitted a squeal of delight. 'Stoppit-poppet! Our visitor here has a birthday same day as you! Isn't that an incredible coincidence?' The dog opened one eye and growled. 'Oh, Janelle, you are such a terrible mother,' Davis admonished herself. 'Each time the poor boy falls asleep, you wake him up. What kind of mama does that?'

'So Riyonna's due to come here Wednesday?' Priddey asked.

'Oh, yeah. She wouldn't miss *a certain little boy's* birthday, not for the world. I'm not saying his name cuz he wakes up when I do. As to where Ri is right now . . .' Davis shrugged. 'Maybe that pig-headed boss of hers went too far and pushed her over the limit. She could be off hunting for a new job, and not a minute too soon. I've been telling her for years she should get out. I've never met Dane Williamson, but he sounds like an asshole: nice as pie to anyone he needs to impress, awful to those lower down in the pecking order. I hate that type.'

'I'm surprised you're not more worried about Riyonna,' Priddey told her. I've looked at your Facebook interactions. The two of you normally communicate several times a day, but there's been nothing since October 11. That doesn't strike you as strange?'

'Well, I guess.' Davis looked momentarily confused. Then she narrowed her eyes and grinned. 'Y'know what? Maybe Ri's met a nice guy and she's busy banging his brains out. That would be *great*. She's had no action at all since breaking up with Deray – or, I should say, since *he* broke up with *her*. Cast her aside like she was garbage. That man well and truly broke her heart. Stoppit adored him too, and missed him so much after he left – pined for months. But thinking about it, when Ri first met Deray, I couldn't get hold of her for about a week and a half. She was drifting above it all in a haze of loved-up bliss. I'll bet that's what's going on now.'

Stoppit, Nicodemus, Deray. Three unusual names . . .

On a whim, Priddey said, 'Miss Davis, do you know of anybody called Dandy, or with Dandy as a nickname?'

'Dandy.' She frowned and chewed her lip. 'Yeah.'

'You do?'

'Hold on, it'll come to me. I've heard that name not too long ago. *Dandy* . . . Oh, I've got it!' She gave Priddey a knowing look. 'Is that him?'

'Who?'

'Ri's new man? Come on, spill!'

'I have no idea who Dandy is. That's why I asked you.'

'I'm not sure I believe you, detective. You have an inscrutable face. People must tell you that a lot.'

'No. Never.'

'Huh. Well, a few weeks ago, Ri and I and *a certain little boy* . . .' – she nodded down at the dog – '. . . were at a barbecue, and Ri took a call and acted kind of private about it, which was unusual for her. She doesn't normally hide anything from me. But this time she said, "Hey, Dandy," and then hurried off to stand by a tree quite a way from where I was, like she didn't want me to overhear the conversation. When she reappeared looking all fake-innocent, I said, "So who's this Dandy, then?" and she *lied* about it.' Davis laughed. 'Ri never lies, but I swear she did that day. She said, "Not Dandy. Andy – from work," and I said, "Oh, yeah? So how come I've never heard you mention an Andy-at-work?" and she sorta dodged the question. I didn't push it. Figured she'd tell me in her own time. But now it's all falling into place. She's got a new man in her life – Dandy – and she's gone off somewhere with him. Like I said: she'll be back by next Wednesday. No way she'd miss a *very important* birthday party.'

'And you know nothing about Dandy?'

'Nothing at all. I just heard her say the name. That's literally all I can tell you.'

'How long have you and Riyonna been friends?'

'*Long* time. Since childhood. We lived on the same street in Philadelphia, went to the same—'

Stoppit raised his head and snarled loudly.

'Ssht!' Davis tapped his head gently with the flat of her hand.

Philadelphia. The word rolled around Priddey's

348

mind. Melody Chapa had been born in Philadelphia, lived in Philadelphia, been murdered in Philadelphia. 'So how come you and Riyonna both ended up in Arizona?'

'My ex got a job here. I followed him and then, couple of years later, Ri followed me. She'd been to visit a few times and loved it, loved the climate, and then—' Abruptly, Davis broke off.

'What?' said Priddey. 'You were going to say something else.'

'I told you already: she moved out here a few years ago.'

'How many years?'

'When she moved? Let's see, it was after Chad and I broke up, and around the same time I thought of getting a dog, and Ri and Deray got married fall 2014, so . . . it must have been fall of 2013. October, I think.'

'Miss Davis, I'd appreciate it if you could tell me whatever it was you decided not to say before. If Riyonna's in any kind of trouble, it might help us to find her.'

'Well, she doesn't like to talk about it, but I guess that doesn't mean you and I can't. It's not like it's a secret. Ri did jury service in Philadelphia – *years* ago, this was. Like, fifteen years or something, I don't remember precisely. It was a murder case: man who'd strangled his wife – and before you ask, that's all I know. Ri told me no other identifying details. Really did *not* want to talk about it. But I know she found it traumatic. She was 100 per cent certain the guy was guilty, but the defense team charmed the other jurors and he got acquitted. It was unbearable to watch, she said, unbearable to be part of, though obviously it wasn't her fault. She and only one other woman had said "guilty" from the start and stood their ground. Others had been all for convicting him at first, but then allowed themselves to be talked round.'

'And Riyonna found this experience upsetting?'

'Oh, boy! She kept going over and over it, blaming herself, saying she didn't do enough to persuade the other jurors – though it was clear to me she'd done all she could. She's too sensitive for her own good, really.'

'And this was around fifteen years ago?'

'That's right,' said Davis.

'Then I don't understand,' Priddey said. 'If it was part of why she wanted to leave Philadelphia, why'd she only move to Arizona four years ago? Why wait ten years?'

'Oh, I see. No, she was okay at first. Then she got called for jury service a second time. You can imagine the effect that had on her.'

Jury service in 2013. The trial of Annette and Naldo Chapa? Priddey wondered.

'She rang me in tears, asked if she could move in with me for a while. I said sure, why not? That enabled her to excuse herself from jury service on the grounds that she had an arrangement to move to Arizona, like, the following week. She didn't tell them when she'd made that arrangement or why – asked me to pretend we'd agreed it months earlier.'

'So she didn't actually do a second stint of jury service?' Priddey abandoned his promising theory.

'No. She couldn't have handled that *at all*. She handed in her notice that very day and came out here. Boy, all these serious questions.' Janelle Davis shuddered. 'I'm getting a little concerned. Ri's okay, right? I mean, she's not in danger from some psycho guy who should have been locked up years ago, is she? I've gotta tell you, her romantic judgment has never been the best.'

'We've no reason to think she's come to harm,' said Priddey. 'We just need to find her.'

'Soon as you do, will you have her call me?'

'I'll pass on the message.'

'I guess you'd better remind her about a certain little boy's birthday too, if you do find her.' Davis pointed at Stoppit. 'Like I say, she wouldn't normally forget, but if something freaky's going on in her life, who knows?'

'Right.' Time to finish off that lemonade and leave.

'He'll know if she's not there for his party,' Davis muttered, more to herself than to Priddey. 'He knows all our special occasion traditions and he knows Ri's always there. What will I do if she's not shown up by Wednesday?'

'Leon Reville,' I repeat. 'So . . . what, you're Jeff Reville's brother? Kristie's brother-in-law?'

'Jeff's cousin.' He puts the gun down and covers his face with his hands. He might be crying.

Things are starting to make sense. I think it through out loud. 'Kristie and Jeff lived next door to the Chapas who were psychologically abusive parents. They could see that if they didn't take action, Annette and Naldo would end up killing Melody. They couldn't go to the authorities because the kind of mental torture I've been reading about in Melody's book is very hard to prove . . . and seven-year-old Melody would probably have been too scared to speak out against her parents. So Kristie and Jeff roped you in and made a plan: make Melody disappear, fake her murder. Allow suspicion to fall first on Kristie – that was clever. But then have proof emerge that it was Annette and Naldo Chapa and, as if by magic, they get carted off to prison for the rest of their natural lives.'

Nothing from Leon. He's still got his face covered up.

'Well? Am I right?' I'm not sure I need an answer. How can I be wrong? There's nothing else that could explain everything.

Finally, he moves his hands and looks at me. 'You're right,' he says, almost inaudibly.

Time to fake some kindness.

'Leon, listen. You wish I hadn't walked into your hotel room? I wish the same thing. It's not my fault I did and it's not your fault either. We've ended up where we are by accident, but it can still be okay. Nobody needs to know about any of this.

I swear to you: I'll tell nobody about you or these last few days. I'll say I don't remember where I've been, that I was wrong about seeing Melody. All I want in return is to send a message to my kids on Instagram saying I'm safe and well. You can type it for me. I won't touch the computer.'

His eyes flit around the trailer. I don't think he's been listening.

'If you do that for me, I'll be grateful, won't I? Leon, *look* at me. Think about the kind of person you know I am. I'm just a mum who loves her kids and wants to get back to them. I don't want any trouble. Why would I? I don't want anything bad to happen to Melody.'

He's looking at me more steadily now.

'Do I think that what you, Kristie and Jeff did was the right thing to do? No. I have to be honest and admit that I don't.'

'If we hadn't done it, they'd have killed her. Haven't you read enough of Kr—' He stops, but it's too late.

'Kristie's book? So Kristie Reville wrote it?'

We wait.

'The story belongs to Melody,' Leon says eventually. 'It's hers. Kristie only wrote it down. She converted it into what it is now.'

I knew it. Not only from the too-polished writing style, but also the choice of words. The paper I found in the crystal grotto pot said 'Do Mom and Dad love me?' In the book, it's always 'My parents' or 'My mother and father'.

'If it was that bad for Melody at home, you could have made the police or social services take it seriously. I can't believe that was impossible. Did any of you even try?'

'You're naïve if you believe that, Cara. Seriously.'

'Look, I might not agree with what you did, but I agree that Melody's better off if she never has to see her parents again.'

'Yes, she is.'

'Which is why I won't breathe a word about this to anyone once you let me go.'

'Let you go?' He looks confused. 'Shit, Cara, I can't . . . I thought you just wanted to send a message to your kids?'

'That first. Then you're going to let me walk out of here. You're going to set me free. And you'll tell Jeff and Kristie, and Melody, that none of you has anything to fear from me. Because that's the truth. If you're worried about admitting you let me go, you can say I escaped. Maybe you could say I threatened you – if you didn't let me go, I wouldn't tell you the thing you need to know to keep all three of you out of prison – you, Jeff and Kristie.'

'You did threaten me,' Leon says in a dull voice.

'Leon, if you do this for me – help me tell my kids I'm okay and then let me go – I swear I'll tell you what you need to know. You have to trust me. Please?'

He stands. Picks up the gun, doesn't point it at me. 'The message . . . yeah, I can do that, I guess. But I can't let you go, Cara.'

Shit. Shit shit shit. 'Thank you,' I say. For now, the message is enough. It's progress – significant progress. *Be patient, Cara.*

'No messages can be sent from this computer, though, 'cos it's registered in my name. I've got an iPad that can't be traced back to me. I'll fetch it.'

'Thank you. I really appreciate this, Leon.'

A few seconds later I'm alone in the trailer. Locked in. My ankles are bound but my wrists are untied. He forgot to take the precaution of tying them before he left.

Nothing I can do but sit tight. Even if I could somehow use my hands to get out of here, I wouldn't be able to do it in time. Not before he's back with the iPad.

Think. Work it out. There has to be a way.

I thought he'd agree to let me go, but maybe this is better. I have nothing to tell him that will help him. If he'd agreed to set me free in exchange for useful information, he would soon have discovered my lie. That was a stupid, crazy plan, born out of desperation.

Now, on the other hand . . .

I hear the key again. The door opens. Dandy the lion is back with the iPad. I was expecting one the same size as the one I had at Swallowtail, but this is twice the size. Not a mini. Where did he get it from? His car, outside?

'Okay, so what do I do?' He's holding the iPad in his left hand. The gun's sticking out of his pocket. 'Instagram, right?'

He walks over and sits down next to me.

'Thank you. Thank you so much.' I start to cry. It's partly relief and partly horror at my own reaction. My gratitude is real.

'Look away while I type in my code.'

I avert my eyes. The gun's still in his pocket, but the wrong one. I'd have to reach around him to grab it.

'Okay, you can look now. Here's Instagram. I'll need your ID and password.'

'Docendo79's my username. Password's my name then 79 – all letters lower case.'

'Here we are,' says Leon.

Now. Now is my chance. If I don't take it, I might not get another.

I stiffen my body and gasp.

'What?' he says. 'What is it?'

'Did you hear that? Outside?'

'What? Tell me.'

'A voice. It sounded so close.'

'I didn't hear it.'

'How could you not hear it? It must have come from right outside. Are they here?' I try to sound as frightened as I can. 'They're here, aren't they? Jeff and Kristie – they're here to kill me. You called them! You're too much of a coward to do it yourself.'

'Cara, calm down.'

'I heard a voice, Leon. I didn't imagine it. I heard someone say, "Helen".'

'Helen?'

Oh, shit. Shit, shit. I said the wrong name. Not

Helen. Something similar . . . Fear and adrenaline are messing with my memory.

'No . . .' I can still save this. I have to. My heart feels as if it's swollen to twice its usual size and is pushing to burst out of my throat.

What's the right name? You had it a few minutes ago. Hayley. That's it.

'Not Helen,' I say. 'Hayley – that was the name.'

'Are you sure?' His eyes widen, suddenly full of fear. 'I think so.'

Why did I say that? I should have said, *Yes, I'm positive*, but I don't trust my memory now, after such a serious slip-up. I need buttons, like my hire car. M1, M2 – one for Hayley, one for Helen.

No. None for Helen. There is no Helen.

What's wrong with me? Am I going crazy?

Memory button one. Memory button two.

I frown as something occurs to me: a strange detail. Does it change anything? I'm not sure, but it strikes me as odd. It's such a tiny, niggly detail. And yet . . .

Leon's put down the iPad. He's holding me by my arms, shaking me. 'Cara, are you sure they said Hayley?'

'Yes,' I whisper, and then, 'Shh.' As if I'm still trying to listen to something outside the trailer.

He believes me. Releasing my arms, he heads for the trailer door, treading slowly and gently so that no one outside can hear him.

As if he hasn't got a prisoner to guard. As if we're an ordinary married couple and our burglar alarm has gone off in the middle of the night. He's the brave husband, creeping downstairs to check we're safe . . .

I calculated right. He never saw me talking to Tarin and Zellie at Swallowtail – he and Melody left too soon after I got there. As far as he's aware, there's no way I could know about Hayley.

At the door, he pulls his gun out of his pocket. Armed against the outside world, off in search of the imaginary target I created for him.

He's gone. I'm alone. The door's closed, but he didn't lock it.

He didn't lock the door.

I hear running footsteps.

The iPad, unlocked. The door, unlocked. What should I do? I have so little time. Maybe no more than seconds.

iPad first. I grab it and start to type a comment beneath Jess's latest photo: 'I'm in trailer don't know where. 2 hours (guess) from Swallowtail. Tell police: interview Jeff Reville colleague again re M bloody sock in car. Car seat move forward – did Kristie mo'

I hear footsteps again. Closer. Walking around the trailer, crunching on something.

This is crazy. I'm typing when I should be getting the hell out of here.

I drop the iPad and start work on the ropes around my ankles. It's easier than I expected: a simple series of knots. I don't need ingenuity or strength, only patience. Hard, when he could re-appear any second.

By the time I've undone all the knots, the noise outside has stopped. No footsteps, nothing.

I stand up. My legs are agony from being tied together for so long and I fall after my first three steps.

Get up. Get out.

Ignoring the pain, I force myself back onto my feet, take a step, then another.

I'm nearly at the door when I think about Jess and Olly. Are they lying awake at night wondering if I'm dead?

Moving as quick as I can, I go back to the iPad, praying the screen won't have locked itself. If I need the access code, I'm in trouble.

The screen's darker, but not black. I tap it and it lights up again. There's my unfinished comment still sitting in the box. What should I add? That I'm fine? Safe? What if I'm not? What if Leon shoots me as I try to run away?

His name: Leon, or Dandy – that's the most important thing to add. And Hayley, fake Hayley with her fake cancer . . .

I'm about to start typing again when I hear footsteps in the distance . . .

Think, Cara. Move.

My heart thumping like a wild thing, I post my comment as it is: incomplete. It's the best I can do. Then I run: to the door, out of the trailer, in a random direction. Past an electricity pylon, into a cluster of trees. There are no other trailers, no houses that I can see.

I stop suddenly, frozen by the enormity of what I've just done. My breath feels dangerously audible and visible, as if it's announcing my presence to everyone for miles around.

Move. Can't stand still – he'll run after me and catch me. When I start to run again, my brain screams at me to stop; that it's a trap – I'm not running away from him, but somehow towards him. Not knowing where he is, I won't be able to avoid running smack-bang into him at any second. The idea is so terrifying, it's almost enough to make me want to turn back. At least when I was locked up and held at gunpoint in the trailer, I knew I would see him. Now, when I might not, a surprise glimpse of him in the distance would be enough to stop my heart.

Ignoring all threats from the panicked voice in my head – that he will step out from behind the next tall cactus and the next rock, and the next, and the next – I run and run. I have to believe I'll get back safely.

If I could only know where he is . . . That he's behind me, not ahead . . .

Think about something else.

I think about Jess. What if she reads my message and thinks I didn't finish it because something stopped me: a knife in the gut, or a bullet through the brain? That's what I'd think. The idea makes me want to howl, but I can't risk Leon hearing me.

I'm not dead, Jess. I'm going to live. I'm on my way home.

★   ★   ★

360

Priddey was deleting messages from Sanders, when his phone buzzed with a new call. No caller ID. He was in the back of a cab, nearly at Swallowtail. He expected it to be Sanders, but the voice was a woman's. 'Orwin, it's Lynn. I got your message.'

'Lynn?'

'You want the full title? Assistant Special Agent Lynn Kirschmeier, FBI.'

'I know. I didn't think you'd call back so soon.'

'Yeah. This Melody Chapa story was on our radar before I got your message. Bonnie Juno's in town, huh?'

'Yeah. Lucky us.'

'We need to talk,' Lynn said. 'Where are you? At the Swallowtail Resort and Spa?'

'That's where I'm supposed to be.'

'And where Bryce Sanders is, yes?'

'Yeah. My *superior* officer.'

A sharp drawing-in of breath from Lynn. 'Life doesn't always go the way we want it to,' she said.

Priddey, Lynn Kirschmeier and Sanders had all started in the police at the same time. It wasn't long before it became obvious to Priddey that Sanders had no principles. He was a moral vacuum, a predator without conscience who did whatever he felt like doing at any given time. He violently assaulted those he arrested if they looked at him 'the wrong way', took bribes, some of them sexual, and made it clear – to Priddey at least – that he had a lot of fun doing all these things. He seemed, from the start, proud of his bad behavior, and told Priddey there was nothing he could do about it – it would be Sanders' word against his if he were to say anything, and it was obvious who'd be believed. That Priddey knew Sanders would present a more compelling version of events than his own more truthful one only made him hate the man more.

Then one day Lynn Kirschmeier had confided in Priddey: thanks to a private investigator, she had proof that Sanders had been making a pile of money on the side, selling drugs he'd seized from a suspect's apartment. She'd asked Priddey if he knew anything about Sanders' antics – anything he'd be willing to share. Priddey told her – all the detail he'd been bottling up for nearly a year. The knowledge that there existed concrete evidence against Sanders changed everything for him. But Lynn, it turned out, wanted to offer Sanders a less humiliating way out. With an unhappy Priddey by her side, she told Sanders that if he left the police and left Arizona and never came back, she'd bury the incriminating evidence and make sure it never surfaced.

Priddey didn't agree with her way of handling it, but he could see the logic. Handsome, blond, charming Bryce Sanders, in spite of his cruel streak and nonexistent morals, was popular with his colleagues – more so than either Lynn or Priddey. 'They'll never forget we did it, Orwin,' she'd said. 'Even those who think we did the right thing, they'll feel differently about us. It'll be a black mark against us forever.'

Priddey had convinced himself that he didn't mind doing it Lynn's way. Sanders would be gone, never to return; that was all that mattered.

Except he did return. Lynn Kirschmeier joined the FBI, and, once she'd been out of the way for a few years, back Sanders came with the same detestable charming smile all over his perfect boy-next-door face. The Paradise Valley police force could hardly contain its excitement, especially the women.

Sanders must have known Lynn would say nothing now – no way she'd risk her stellar career as an FBI agent. If she told the truth, Sanders would too: he'd go public with her failure to report his crimes all those years ago. Priddey, if asked, would have to reveal that, yes, Lynn Kirschmeier had known Sanders had stolen drugs and then profited from their sale, and that he'd known too. Priddey would willingly have trashed his own career for the sake of ruining Sanders, but he couldn't bring himself to do that to Lynn, who, he thought, must have known for some time now that Sanders was back and had conspicuously failed to contact Priddey to discuss what they ought to do about it – about as conspicuously as he'd failed to contact her.

'Don't worry, OP – I'm a changed man,' Sanders had said to Priddey with a wink, soon after reappearing. 'This time, I'm gonna be good as gold.' When he'd heard those words, Priddey had known not only that Sanders didn't mean them, but also that his intended meaning was the precise opposite. What he was trying to say, knowing Priddey would understand the true message, was, 'You'll see nothing, you'll be able to prove nothing, but I'll be doing whatever the fuck I want, as I always do.'

On the surface, Sanders had indeed been good as gold since his return – so good, he recently got the promotion Priddey had earned. 'You'll be next, bud,' he'd consoled Priddey with fake magnanimity. Or at least Priddey assumed it was fake; after what he and Lynn had done, he couldn't believe Sanders' friendliness to him was genuine. He wasn't the forgiving sort; no, he'd worked out that he could wound Priddey more effectively by pretending to be his best pal, appearing to play by the rules, and forcing Priddey to fake his side of an apparently great working relationship.

Priddey's response to Sanders being promoted above him was to stop caring about anything and everything that related to work. From now on, he'd take his paycheck and put no heart or initiative at all into his job, until he thought of something else he could do. He'd found that easy until this Swallowtail thing cropped up. Most of what his working days threw at him was pretty unoriginal; this Melody Chapa business was different. He couldn't think of a single scenario to explain and reconcile all that seemed to be happening here. That frustrated him, and made him want to try and find the answer.

'Meet me at Cartel Coffee Lab, 7124 East 5th

Ave, soon as you can.' Lynn was gone before Priddey could answer. He understood: together, they'd attempted a heroic act that had failed, and now she didn't want to talk to him any more than he wanted to talk to her.

He told the cab driver the new destination, then keyed 'Chapa murder trial' into the search box on his phone's screen. He'd been right: Annette and Naldo Chapa had stood trial in 2013 – June of that year – but not in Philadelphia as Priddey had assumed. Instead their trial had taken place in Lehigh County, Pennsylvania, after it had been decided they were unlikely to get a fair hearing in their home city. Bonnie Juno's belief in their guilt had proved contagious all over the country but nowhere more than in Philadelphia, where some people had started wearing T-shirts emblazoned with Juno's motto of the moment, 'Guilty as hell!', with 'Melody RIP' in smaller letters underneath.

Was it crazy that he now believed it might be true – that Lilith McNair and Cara Burrows might have seen fourteen-year-old Melody – purely because an FBI agent was taking an interest? Probably. Chances were, Kirschmeier was only interested in the missing British tourist angle.

If the Chapas were tried in Lehigh County, then Riyonna Briggs, who lived in Philadelphia at the time, wouldn't have been in the running for that particular jury even if she hadn't opted out by moving to Arizona. No connection there, then. So why did it feel as if there had to be one?

Priddey typed, 'Riyonna Briggs, murder trial, Philadelphia' into the search box.

Here we go . . .

Riyonna Briggs was one of several jurors who had given interviews to the press after a man named Benjamin Chalfont had walked free from a Philadelphia court, acquitted of the murder by manual strangulation of his wife, Elyssa.

Reading small print in a moving vehicle was making Priddey feel nauseous. He pressed the button to open the window a little.

There had to be a link, via Riyonna Briggs, between this Chalfont case and the Chapas. Or maybe there didn't. Either way, Priddey wasn't ready to give up.

He keyed 'Benjamin Chalfont Melody Chapa' into the search box and pressed return. No joy. He tried every combination of names he could think of: Elyssa and Annette, Naldo and Riyonna. Nothing.

'Excuse me?' said the cab driver.

'Are we here?' Priddey looked up.

'Not yet. The road's blocked up ahead, see? So you can either get out and walk one block that way . . .' – he stuck his arm out of the window and pointed – '. . . or I can drive you to the door, but it's gonna take a while longer.'

'Longer's okay,' said Priddey, who wasn't done searching yet. Besides, weren't cabs supposed to take you right to where you wanted to go?

What about Jeff and Kristie Reville? They never

stood trial for anything, but still, it was worth a shot. You never knew where you might find a connection. He put 'Jeff Reville Benjamin Chalfont' into the search box and pressed return. Next he'd try, in conjunction with Chalfont's name, Victor Soutar, then Larry Beadman or maybe Nate Appleyard – all the names he'd read while refreshing his memory of the Melody Chapa case last night.

Deep in his bones, Priddey couldn't believe Riyonna Briggs' experience as a juror in Philadelphia – so traumatic it ultimately made her relocate to Arizona – wasn't connected to Melody somehow.

Benjamin Chalfont. Annette and Naldo Chapa. Two murder trials, both in Pennsylvania, both with a connection to Riyonna Briggs . . .

The search results appeared on the screen. Priddey did a double take. 'Holy freaking hell,' he breathed.

He blinked and looked again. *Still there*. He clicked on the top result and started to read, his heart pounding.

The driver had to tell him twice that they'd arrived at Cartel Coffee Lab. Priddey got out of the cab. He rotated his right shoulder, which had stiffened up during the ride – too much jabbing at his phone with his thumb.

There was only one question he wanted answered now: did Assistant Special Agent Lynn Kirschmeier already know, or was he about to give her the shock of her life?

Sometimes I think I'd like to see my parents again. Not in the real world, but in a safe, fantasy way, where I'd know they couldn't harm me. There are questions I'd like to ask them. By 'them', I guess I mean my mother. She's the one with the answers. I'm not sure my father ever understood any of it – not even his own part in it.

I'd ask about the time my mother was waiting for me after school when she was supposed to be working in a place named Oakmont. I was surprised to see her, and for once she looked happy to see me. She told me to sit in the front seat, and as we drove home she said, 'So, then. I hear you have a boyfriend.' She said it in a confiding, best-pal tone I'd never heard her use before.

I was six years old. Of course I didn't have a boyfriend. The whole idea scared me. Sharona in my class had told everybody that Woody Finnigan was her boyfriend, and they'd walked around the playground holding hands a few times and looking pleased with themselves, as if they knew a secret the rest of us didn't.

We all knew it was only pretend, but it still made me feel horrible to think about it. What if he tried to kiss her and she couldn't make him stop? What if he had stinky breath? This was what my friends and I had been discussing all that day, fascinated and horrified at the same time. I wondered if my mother had heard something from someone and misunderstood, thinking it was me instead of Sharona. All the same, I couldn't see who would have told her.

'No,' I said. 'I don't have a boyfriend.'

'C'mon,' she said with a little laugh. 'You can tell me. I'm your mom. If you can't tell me, who can you tell?'

'But I haven't got a boyfriend.'

'Don't lie, Melody.'

'It's not a lie. Boys are disgusting.'

'So how come Kristie told me different? She says you have a boyfriend named Woody Something.' Her voice had lost its pally warmth.

'No! Woody Finnigan, but he's Sharona's boyfriend, not mine.'

How could Kristie have said that to my mother? She always listened to me properly and remembered things I said. That was why I loved her more than I loved my own parents, though I felt guilty for that. And whatever I told her, she knew not to tell my mother. She understood what life was like for me at home.

'I told Kristie about *Sharona* and Woody, not me and Woody,' I explained.

My mother pulled the car over to the side of the road, switched off the engine and turned to face me. 'Melody, you are going to tell me the truth. You have one last chance to do so. Is that clear? Only one chance.'

Frozen in my seat, I nodded. As so often when I was with her, the only part of me that could move was the tears. It didn't occur to me to wonder what would happen if I failed at my last chance. I took for granted that my fate would be so unimaginably horrible – so much worse than my day-to-day life, which was plenty bad enough – that it wasn't worth risking.

'Do you have a boyfriend by the name of Woody Finnigan?'

'Yes,' I whispered.

'You do?'

'Yes.'

'Uh-huh. Since when?'

'Last week.'

'I see.' She started driving again. We didn't exchange another word all the way home. I cried, and she pretended not to notice.

When we pulled up outside our house, she said cheerfully, 'Don't think I don't know you lied to me, Melody. You can't fool me. Woody's not your boyfriend. You told the truth the first time: he's Sharona's boyfriend. I got chatting to her mom while I was waiting for you at the gates. She told me all about it.'

With that, my mother went inside, leaving me alone in the car, glued by terror to my seat. She had to come out and get me a half-hour later. She pretended not to be able to imagine why I wouldn't have just followed her into the house like I usually did.

I couldn't allow myself to think about it while I was with her, so I did my best to act normal. Later, in bed, I tried to figure it out, but the more I thought about it, the less it made sense. Nothing like this had ever happened before. I wondered if trying to get me to lie was going to be her new game, but she never did it again.

If I met her today, or in twenty years' time, and asked her what the Woody Finnigan incident was all about, would she tell me? Would she even remember?

OCTOBER 15, 2017

Lynn Kirschmeier's hair was shorter. She'd had it cut into what Priddey thought of as a 'serious woman' style. It was a haircut that female politicians seemed to favor – Hillary Clinton, and Angela whatever-her-name-was, the German chancellor. In her pale gray suit, Lynn could have been a president or a prime minister. In other ways, she hadn't changed at all. She still drank orange juice straight from the bottle, still wore no make-up and too much perfume.

She had a colleague with her – a young black man in a blue suit, which he wore with a shirt that was the exact same shade of blue. His tie, at least, was a different color: dark red. Lynn introduced him as Agent Jomo Turriff. It was he who asked Priddey for the full story and told him to omit no detail. If Turriff had ever heard of small talk, he showed no sign of it – not even a one-line ice-breaker.

Three black coffees later, the two agents were up to speed. Lynn had smiled at Priddey's description of Janelle Davis and Stoppit; Turriff had not.

'Let me get this right,' he said. 'Tarin Fry admitted she lied about being a detective to get the trash from room 324 off of the maid, and she also admitted she never saw Melody Chapa alive – she only said so to make sure you took the other sightings seriously?'

'Yes, and yes,' Priddey confirmed.

In response, Turriff's face moved not an inch.

'Do you have the drawing she gave you – the Doodle Dandy one?'

Priddey produced two evidence bags from his pocket and handed them over. 'The doodle and the notes from the crystal grotto,' he said. Turriff took them without a thank you. The guy was no charmer, that was for sure. After her experience with Sanders, maybe Lynn deliberately avoided working with that type of man.

'What's your impression of Fry?' she asked Priddey.

'She's smart. Single-minded. A little ruthless, but not necessarily in a bad way. I think she's worried about Cara Burrows and didn't think anyone was taking her disappearance seriously enough.'

'A liar's a liar,' said Turriff flatly.

Lynn made a face at him that he couldn't see, but Priddey saw it. It was a 'For Christ's sake, get the stick out of your ass' face.

'Liar or no, I agree with her,' she said. 'You should have called us in as soon as Cara Burrows went missing, Orwin.'

We don't always do what we should, Lynn. As you know.

'Not that I'm blaming you,' she added. 'Detective Sanders should have brought us in if he's the one calling the shots.'

She said his name without missing a beat.

'There's something you need to know.' Priddey addressed his words to Turriff. 'The jury service Riyonna Briggs wanted to avoid . . .'

'What about it?' said Turriff.

'At first I thought that might somehow link to the Chapas' trial, which was the same year, but I was way off the mark there. Riyonna wouldn't have known in advance which case she'd get as a juror, and anyway Melody's parents were tried in Lehigh County, Pennsylvania, not Philadelphia. But I couldn't let it go that easy. I thought, there has to be something, some connection.'

'And you found one?' Lynn asked.

'I did. It goes back to Riyonna Briggs' first jury experience – the trial of Benjamin Chalfont. Far as Riyonna was concerned, Chalfont was undeniably guilty. Others thought so too at first, but got persuaded by a few of his defenders on the jury. In the end, only two jurors stuck with guilty and wouldn't be talked out of it. I know this because Riyonna gave an interview shortly after the trial. She talked about her distress at the injustice of Chalfont's acquittal – her own, and the distress of the only other juror to stick with a guilty vote. When I saw the name of that other hold-out juror, the one who wasn't Riyonna Briggs, my eyes damn near popped out of my head.'

'Who?' asked Turriff.

'Kristie Reville.'

Lynn whistled.

At last, a facial expression from Turriff: a frown. 'So Melody Chapa's neighbor and babysitter sat on a jury alongside Riyonna Briggs. Who works at the resort where guests are claiming to have seen Melody Chapa alive.'

'Yep,' said Priddey. 'And that's not all.'

'It sure isn't.' Lynn pulled her phone out of her pocket, pressed a few keys, then passed it across the table to Priddey.

'What's this?' he asked.

'We're pretty sure Cara Burrows wrote it. She left it as a comment beneath a photo her daughter posted on Instagram. Daughter told father, who told Sanders, who – eventually, way later than he should have and not exactly willingly or graciously – handed it over to us.'

She looked at Priddey to see if he'd understood: in all ways that counted, she was now more powerful than Sanders.

It didn't matter. That didn't make anything okay.

Priddey read the message twice: 'I'm in trailer don't know where. 2 hours (guess) from Swallowtail. Tell police: interview Jeff Reville colleague again re M bloody sock in car. Car seat move forward – did Kristie mo'

'"Did Kristie move the sock?" we think,' said Lynn. 'Cut short, obviously.'

Why hadn't Cara Burrows been able to finish typing that sentence?

Priddey agreed 'mo' was probably the beginning of 'move'. And the last full use of 'move' was in relation to the car seat, not the sock.

'Orwin? What are you thinking?'

He was thinking that he wanted to carry on thinking a while longer.

Kristie Reville was in the driver's seat when Nate Appleyard noticed Melody Chapa's bloodstained sock on the floor of her car. She moved her car seat forward to cover up the sock, but it was too late – Appleyard had seen it and told police.

Wait. Wait.

'I think I know what this means,' Priddey murmured. He half stood up, then sat down again. 'If I'm right . . .' But why had nobody spotted it at the time? It was so obvious once you thought about it. Or maybe it wasn't. Maybe it was only blindingly obvious if you knew what Priddey knew. Which, currently, Lynn and Turriff did not.

'I need to tell you something. Something big.'

'Is this the "That's not all" you mentioned a minute ago?' Lynn asked. 'Go ahead, tell us.'

So Priddey told them.

At last, a road. Tall cacti and jagged rocks on the other side and, in the distance, the mountain.

Camelback Mountain or a different one? I can't tell.

No cars on the road. Not a single one.

The road is red sand, like the floor of the crystal grotto.

I have to stop here. I can't go any further. I've been running for more than an hour, maybe two. Stumbling, really, more than running. All the bones in my body feel broken and every part of my insides aches. My bare feet are covered with blood, my ankles swollen.

I sink down to my knees when I hear a noise, in case it's a gun being fired, but it's okay. It's nothing. I'm safe. *For now.*

The silence builds around me, making me nervous, and I begin to wonder what the noise was if it wasn't a gun. A car engine starting?

Please let a car come. Or a van, or a person. Anything. Anyone but him.

Please. I have to get back home, back to safety. Have to make sure my baby's okay.

No, not a car, please, on second thoughts. If a car comes, he might be driving it. He's bound to be. I picture myself at the centre of a circle that he's drawn a red line around. He can still get to me, wherever I am in the circle. I have to get out of it – but how can I, when I don't know where the boundary is?

I should stand up, in case I need to run again, but my legs won't move. The thought of putting my weight on my feet makes me cry.

I fall onto my side and lie there for a while on the edge of the grass, where it meets the road. There's a cactus near me with leaf-tips sharp enough to be lethal weapons.

Hearing a rumble, I pull myself into a seated position.

It's a car. An engine. That's what I heard, and now it's getting nearer. I can see it coming towards me along the road.

My mouth fills with bile.

Oh, my God. It's him. It must be. He can't have got me to the trailer without a car, and who else is this likely to be, really, if not him looking for me?

I look again at the sharp-leafed cactus. There's no way I could tear off one of those thick rubbery tentacles and pierce his heart with it; if I could, I would.

All I can do is try to drag myself off the road, away from him. I sob as I half roll, half crawl, trying to hide in the dirt and gravel and rubble by the roadside.

I hear a door slam.

'Excuse me, lady? You okay? You need help?'

Is this a dream? Because that voice didn't sound like him.

I don't want to allow myself to hope. Maybe it is a dream. I don't care if it is. I like it so far. 'Yes, help, I need help.'

'We need to get you to a hospital. Or maybe the police. No, hospital first.'

'No. Swallow.'

'I beg your pardon?'

'Swallowtail.' Part of me still can't believe that

something good has happened. A voice in my brain whispers, 'This might be him in disguise. Or a friend of his, sent by him.'

'The spa place?'

I force myself to look at the man's face. He does not look too kind, or suspiciously helpful. He looks a little bored, and irritated, and innocent. Unconnected to Leon Dandy Reville.

He's my best bet.

'Yes,' I say.

'Lady, I don't think you're going to be allowed in there in your condition.'

'I'm staying there.' I lift my right arm and look at it before sliding my hand slowly into the pocket of my shorts, wondering if I can trust my memory from what seems like so long ago.

Yes. It's there.

I pull out the key card for my casita. It has the Swallowtail logo on it. I try to hold it up to show it to the helpful man, but my fingers won't work properly and I drop it.

'Swallowtail,' I say again. 'Please take me to Swallowtail.'

I figured something out today, something that links back to a conversation I had with my mother years ago.

'Would you like a little brother or sister?' she asked me one day at the breakfast table. My father was there too. He looked surprised. I think I must have been about four years old at the time.

'Not a sister,' I said quickly. Emory was my sister. Having a sister, to me, meant having a dead sister, and I already had one of those. A brother was different. I could imagine having a not-dead brother, but that would be unbearable in a different way. I would love him, and I would have to watch him suffer. Or, if my parents planned to be much kinder to him than they were to me, then he would have to watch me suffer, and, if he was anything like me, that would make him sad and scared.

'And not a brother,' I added once I'd thought it through.

'Neither?' said my mother. 'Why not? I know you don't love Emory, but you might love a new sibling.'

This was designed to make me feel guilty. I *did* love Emory, or at least the idea of her. At the same time, I wondered: how can you love someone who died before you were born?

'I suppose some people are too selfish to love anyone but themselves,' said my mother in a matter-of-fact tone.

My father ate his toast and drank his coffee, looking out of the window as if nothing important was being said, nothing he needed to pay attention to.

'Actually, I *would* love a baby brother,' I said. I must have felt braver than usual that morning. 'But I'd be afraid he'd die.'

'Is that so?' said my mother. 'Well, they say you always kill the thing you love.' She glanced at my father, who ignored her.

I didn't know what she meant. Was she saying she thought I would deliberately kill my own little brother?

At that moment, she seemed cut off from my father and me in a way I couldn't quite fathom. When she next spoke, her voice had a faraway sound, as if she'd drifted off into a private world. 'You know, I don't think that's right,' she said. 'I think it's the other way round: you love the thing you've killed. But only once it's too late.'

'Annette,' said my father in a warning tone. 'No more.'

My mother responded instantly, snapping back to her normal conversational mode. 'Yes,' she said. 'What a horrible, macabre subject.'

Wait, wait. Those words ran through my mind so often when I lived with my parents. *Wait, wait, that's wrong. Something's not right. I just need a chance to work out what it is.*

While my mother and my father talked about plans for the day ahead, I silently replayed what I'd heard:

> Her: *You love the thing you've killed.*
> *But only once it's too late.*
> Him: *Annette. No more.*

I'd only ever known my mother to show love for one person: Emory. After she was dead. While she was alive, I wasn't around to witness anything, so I can't speak for how my mother felt about her then.

I wondered if my mother had deliberately killed Emory. She'd told me Emory had died in her tummy. My father had said so too, but maybe it wasn't true.

As soon as I was old enough to understand, the Kind Smiles told me about Mallory Tondini and showed me the famous interview she did on TV. After that, I had no choice but to believe that Emory had died in my mother's womb. In one way it was a relief to know this, but it also confused me. I'd thought I understood and clearly I was wrong. Mallory Tondini worked at the hospital and had been there when my parents had lost Emory, so if she thought it was a natural death then it must have been.

I asked the Kind Smiles what they thought about all of this, but they didn't seem to want to talk about it. I asked if there was a way my mother could have eaten or drunk something that made Emory die inside her, without Mallory or anyone at the hospital noticing. They said they didn't think so. I couldn't work out why they looked so sad if that was true. It was obviously better if my parents hadn't killed my sister.

I don't know how it took me until today to see it: I was only with the Kind Smiles in the first place because of what they feared my parents would do to me. My mother was talking about me, not Emory, at the breakfast table that day. She was unhappy about her inability to love me, and she knew that the only way she *could* love me was if she killed me first. I think that's what she was trying to communicate to my father: 'You want me to love Melody? Fine, but the only way it's going to happen is if I kill her first. Loving Emory's easy – she's dead.'

No wonder the Kind Smiles felt they had no choice but to get me out of my parents' house.

OCTOBER 16, 2017

Orwin Priddey steeled himself as he got out of his car, seeing Bonnie Juno striding toward him across the resort parking lot. As someone who spent much of his life trying to prevent any honest expression of his thoughts or feelings from making its way into the outside world, he'd never felt comfortable around people who spoke their minds no matter what the consequences. And when that quality was coupled with a ferocious determination to get your own way at all costs, as it was in Juno . . .

'Hey, detective!' she yelled at him over the tops of the assembled cars. 'There you are! Where the hell have you been? Now, you'd better tell me right this second and not feed me some bullshit line: where's Cara Burrows?'

Determination was one of Priddey's qualities too, though he was less demonstrative about it. As a result, people rarely expected him to stand his ground. Often they didn't realize that was what he was doing until a gradual awareness started to creep up on them: *I asked him to do X, and he didn't say he wouldn't, so why's he still not done it?*

384

It was a feature of human interaction that had interested Priddey for some time: that unless you told the world explicitly who and what you were – 'I'm a kickass blowhard who takes no prisoners and you'd better believe it'; 'I'm a home-loving soccer mom who's all about her kids' – there was a strong chance that even those closest to you would perceive you incorrectly, or, perhaps more depressingly, not have any ideas about you at all.

'Quit stalling!' Juno tantrummed, her red face now nearly touching Priddey's. 'Where is she?'

'I'm sorry if you haven't been kept in the loop.' It never did any harm to start with an apology. 'Cara's safe. She's been found. Or rather, she found her way back without any help from us.' He wasn't about to claim credit for someone else's achievement.

'Are you for real? You think I don't know that? Lord in heaven, please don't tell me I know more about what's going on than you do.'

'I don't know about that, ma'am.'

'I know Cara got back here yesterday – hitched a lift, got looked over by doctors, all of that.'

'She sustained a few minor injuries in the process of escaping, but she'll be fine. So will her baby.'

'What I don't know is where she is now,' Juno steamrollered on. 'I can't find Detective Sanders or Dane Williamson. Agents Kirschmeier and Turriff are treating me like I don't exist! Clearly they never switch on their televisions!'

'I don't think media liaison is their priority at

the moment,' said Priddey. 'Having said that, I know that no one's deliberately trying to exclude you. I'm on my way to the Rutherford B. Hayes room now, a little late. I'm surprised you're not there already.'

'The Rutherford Behave room?' Juno flinched as if he'd said something obscene. 'What is that?'

'Rutherford B. Hayes. Former President of the United States.'

'What the hell does he have to do with anything?'

'Nothing. Just, there's a meeting room here named after him and that's where I'm headed now.'

'I see,' Juno said through gritted teeth. 'So you're on your way to a cosy heads-up that no one's told me about. The feds arrive and all of a sudden I'm out in the cold!'

'Not at all.' As long as Juno wasn't angling in on Cara Burrows, Priddey was happy to reassure and placate. 'Agent Kirschmeier wants and expects you to be there. No cameras obviously.'

'Why obviously? And if Kirschmeier wants me so much, how come no one said anything to me about any meeting? I know when folk are avoiding me! And I know why: you're all terrified of hearing how wrong you are. You think Annette and Naldo Chapa can't be behind all this? You really believe that?'

So she was still pushing that angle. The woman was incredible. Annette and Naldo Chapa: faking their daughter's death for seven years in order to make sure their convictions for her murder stick. It made zero sense.

Don't take the bait. She wants you to ask why they'd ever do that, so she can spout more crap.

'No one's avoiding you, ma'am. Come with me now and you'll see.' Priddey tried to lead the way and failed. Leaders need at least one person following them.

Juno stood firm. 'Wait a second. It's Cara I'm most interested in. Where is she right now?'

She was with her husband in a casita that the resort reserved for important visitors. Her children were on their way over from England with their grandmother. Priddey had no intention of telling Bonnie Juno any of this. Cara Burrows needed time alone with her family more than she needed to help boost the ratings of, as Lynn had called it last night, *Distorting Justice With Bonnie.*

'Something funny, detective?'

'No ma'am.'

'I need an interview with Cara on tonight's show. Which means Heidi needs to prep her for it, and—'

'No. Sorry. No interviews with Cara Burrows.'

'*What?* Are you insane? Without her, there's a gaping hole in the story!'

'It'll have to be filled some other way.'

'Detective, you are trying. My. Patience.'

Althea, Priddey's wife, described it as his super-power: the ability to say nothing and look neutral for as long as it took for his opponent to run out of steam.

'I was so wrong about you!' Juno exploded. 'I never had you down as a bully, but listen to you now! Without letting Cara decide for herself if she wants to talk to me, you're taking all autonomy away from her and making that choice on her behalf. How're you any better than her abductor, I'd like to know?'

'Mrs Burrows has made it clear to Agents Kirschmeier and Turriff that she wishes to be left alone with her family.'

As if the mention of his name had summoned him, Turriff appeared at that moment. He was walking purposefully toward them. 'Come on,' said Priddey. This time Juno followed.

'We're waiting for you both,' Turriff called over as they approached.

'See?' said Priddey. 'Like I said: you're invited. No one's avoiding you.'

'Cara Burrows is,' said Juno sulkily. 'She has a *duty* here. I don't think she realizes—'

'There's been a development,' Turriff cut her off. He looked only at Priddey as he said, 'We've got them: Leon Reville and Melody. They've been found.'

Melody Chapa was drinking warm milk in the living room of a house somewhere in Phoenix. Near Phoenix, anyway. She didn't know precisely where she was, and it was making her feel funny. In the past seven years she'd been moved around a lot, but Dandy had always shown her each new place on a map first. She'd liked that. Maps were amazing. When she grew up, she wanted to be a cartographer. She didn't know exactly what the job involved, but it sounded serious and important, and if it meant looking at maps, she knew she'd enjoy it.

The house had a white-painted front, a pillared porch and a fat garage that stuck out awkwardly at the side. Melody thought it was ugly. From what she'd managed to work out, it belonged to the FBI. Or they were allowed to use it. There was a woman in the house named Jennifer who was nice, but nobody seemed to think she was important, or at least the two agents didn't – Lynn and Jomo.

Maybe this house was Jennifer's home. She hadn't asked any difficult questions yet, and it didn't seem as if she was going to. She was something to do with the FBI too, but she was also a kind of babysitter. She looked like a grandma. She had brought a blanket, even though it was hot. Who would want a blanket?

Melody hadn't wanted to be rude and say, 'No thanks,' so she'd laid Poggy down on the tiled floor and covered him with it. Jennifer seemed to think that was an okay thing to do. She hadn't objected.

The milk tasted disgusting. Melody regretted choosing it over orange juice. She'd thought she liked milk but this was the first time she'd had it warm. What would Jennifer think if she left most of it?

Melody was scared about lots of things, but the

thing that frightened her most was not knowing what people were going to think about her from now on. By 'people' she meant strangers, and that was everyone in the world apart from a handful of people. She'd always known what Dandy thought of her, since the first day she met him. 'You're a brave girl, Melody,' he said to her. 'Nothing that's happened is your fault.' He had repeated those lines many times since their first meeting when she was seven years old.

Melody also knew what Kristie and Jeff thought of her: that she was perfect and brilliant in every way. This was obviously not true, though it was sometimes nice to hear.

What Melody thought and felt about all of them was harder to work out, but she'd never cared about that. Her own emotions and opinions weren't a threat to anybody, whereas those of others could definitely harm her. Like Zellie from the art group who'd said one of Melody's paintings was 'cloying', whatever that meant. And like Kristie, who said, 'I love you so much, Favorite Child, and much more.'

Melody had grown to hate the nickname over the years. It was silly, when Kristie didn't seem to know any other children. And the idea of being a favorite was alarming. It was pressure, like an arm pressing down on your throat. And now there was the new pressure of knowing that the whole world was thinking things about her. Melody didn't like it at all.

It had been okay when everyone believed she'd been stolen away from her parents and murdered. Everyone knew what opinion to have about that. And when it was decided that her parents had killed her, Melody had known that, still, she wasn't the only one, and that was a comforting thought. Dandy had said that of all the children who are murdered, most times their own parents are guilty of the crime.

Now it was all different and frightening. Soon everyone would know that Melody had pretended to be a murder victim when she wasn't. People would think she was a liar. They wouldn't understand that it wasn't like that. And, worst of all, Dandy wasn't here to tell her not to worry, that it was okay because lots of other girls had also pretended to be murdered and kept up the pretense for years and years – which Melody knew they hadn't.

She'd done a lot of pretending. Not only to be dead, but also, as Hayley, to have cancer. Would the world blame her? Or would people say she was only a child and couldn't be held responsible?

Dandy would know. He was also the only person likely to give her a truthful answer. But Melody had no idea if she would ever see Dandy again.

'So you've got Leon "Dandy" Reville, but not Jeff or Kristie or Riyonna Briggs,' said Bonnie Juno.

Lynn Kirschmeier nodded. 'Those three are still in the wind, but the very best agents are on it, here and in Philly.'

'The very best, huh?' Juno sounded unimpressed. Priddey wasn't surprised. She was the sort of person who recognized no one's achievements but her own.

Also present were Jomo Turriff, Bryce Sanders, Heidi Casafina, Dane Williamson and Tarin Fry.

Sanders took a sip of water from his glass. 'Has Melody been asked about the book?' He directed the question to Turriff, not Lynn. He hadn't looked at her once; Priddey was watching.

Turriff nodded. 'Says she told the story to the Kind Smiles, who wrote it down. That's all she'll say – Kind Smiles. She won't name names, just clams up.'

'Leon Reville told Cara Burrows that Kristie Reville did all the actual writing,' Lynn says.

'I'm uncomfortable with the way you're all leaping to conclusions,' said Heidi Casafina. 'We don't know for sure that this girl's Melody.'

'DNA results'll be a while, but it's her,' said Lynn. 'If you're not convinced now, Ms Casafina, you soon will be.'

'What's that supposed to mean?'

'It means shut up and listen,' said Tarin Fry.

'Bonnie, do you think it's her?' Heidi asked. 'Do you think this girl is Melody?'

Juno looked at Lynn Kirschmeier. 'She says she's Melody Chapa, right?'

'Yes, she does.'

Juno shrugged. She looked dazed. 'Then I believe her, I guess.'

'So what's the theory?' Tarin Fry asked. 'Or to put it more bluntly . . . what the hell happened here?'

'I'd rather not speculate,' said Turriff.

'Allow me, then,' said Tarin. 'Kristie Reville and Riyonna Briggs sat on the Benjamin Chalfont jury together in 2003. We know they were both convinced he killed his wife, but no one else was, so he got off. It's not hard to imagine what happened next: righteous discussions about how the law's an ass, how too often it allows the guilty to walk free, meaning there's no real protection or justice for anyone. You want justice, you're gonna need to get it for yourself – no one else cares. Then, years later, Kristie Reville figures out she's living next door to a couple she's certain are a danger to their daughter—'

'Excuse me.' Heidi Casafina turned to Turriff. 'How long are you going to let her carry on like this, making it up as she goes along? I mean, who *is* she? Some florist from Kansas? Why's she here?'

'I have a question too,' said Bonnie Juno. 'What are we all doing here around this table? Is there new information? Because if there isn't—'

'My time's as valuable as yours, Ms Juno,' Lynn told her. 'Yes, Agent Turriff and I have new information to share with you.'

'Then let's hear it. The way I see it, there's a whole lot that doesn't add up – like the idea that Riyonna Briggs, if she's involved in this fraudulent plot, would send Cara Burrows to the very hotel room she reserved with her own credit card, with her name on it, to hide Melody in. Why would she self-sabotage like that?'

'You never heard of someone under pressure making a mistake?' said Sanders.

'A lot of mistakes seem to have been made here, detective. Why did Leon Reville snatch Cara Burrows, can somebody tell me? What was the point? She'd already told her friend Tarin about seeing Melody – the whole story.'

'Leon Reville didn't know that, maybe,' said Priddey.

'As the only person here who knows Riyonna well, I can't believe she's involved in anything illegal,' said Dane Williamson.

'Because she respects the law?' Tarin Fry rolled her eyes. 'Trouble is, after seeing wife-murderer Chalfont walk free, she thinks no one else does – no one but her and Kristie Reville. It's clear they felt they had no choice.'

'How is that clear?' Heidi Casafina threw up her hands. 'You're just making things up! Nothing is clear.'

'What's Leon Reville saying so far?' Priddey asked Lynn.

'Read the book,' she said.

'I don't have it.'

'No, that's what he's saying. It's *all* he's saying. Just keeps repeating it: "Read the book, it's all in the book."'

'Is this your brilliant new intel?' Bonnie Juno sneered. 'Leon "Dandy" Reville telling us all to read a book?'

'He's not telling *you* anything.' Lynn took the sting out of her words with a broad smile. Juno still looked stung. 'And no, that is not the information we want to share with you. Agent Turriff?'

Turriff took his cue and stood up. 'Before she left the trailer, Cara Burrows sent a message to her daughter using Instagram,' he said. 'As follows: "I'm in trailer don't know where. 2 hours, open parentheses, guess, close parentheses, from Swallowtail. Tell police: interview Jeff Reville colleague again re M bloody sock in car. Car seat move forward – did Kristie" . . . and then the letters "m, o".'

'M, o?' said Tarin Fry. 'As in modus operandi?'

'No, as in the first two letters of the word "move". If Mrs Burrows hadn't feared that Leon Reville might come back any second and deprive her of her escape opportunity, she'd have completed that sentence. Having spoken to her, I can confirm what it would have been: "Did Kristie move the car seat back again before she drove away?"'

'I'm totally lost.' Heidi Casafina sighed heavily. 'Could not be more so.'

'How about you, Bonnie?' Lynn asked her.

'I'm following,' said Juno with a nod. 'I think I know where you're going.'

'Let me explain,' said Turriff. 'When Mrs Burrows arrived in Phoenix, she rented a car – a Range Rover. It had a feature she'd never encountered before: memory buttons numbered one to four, so that four different driving positions can be stored. You want to drive the car after your spouse has driven it? Just press button M2, the seat automatically adjusts to your most comfortable driving position. Next time spouse gets in, she presses M1, seat goes back to her ideal setting.'

'Is your wife's first name Spouse, Agent Turriff?' Sanders chuckled to himself. Everybody ignored him.

'The day Melody Chapa went missing, Jeff Reville's colleague, Nate Appleyard, saw her blood-stained sock in Kristie Reville's car,' Turriff went on. 'Jeff and Kristie Reville were in the car, talking. Appleyard approached them. Kristie was visibly shocked, and looked like she'd been crying. Appleyard saw the stained sock on the floor of the car. He stated very clearly: the sock was positioned about three inches in front of Kristie Reville's foot. That means, obviously, that Kristie's foot was easily visible. That means nowhere near the gas pedal. When you've got your foot on the gas, someone standing outside the car couldn't see three inches in front of it.'

'True,' said Heidi Casafina, 'but I still don't see—'

'Kristie Reville is only five feet two inches tall,' said Turriff. 'She's a short lady. Nate Appleyard said that, shocked by his sudden appearance and knowing he'd seen the sock, Kristie moved her car seat forward to cover it up. And then, he told police, she drove away.'

'So what?' Sanders shrugged. 'I don't see the significance.'

'I'll explain, Detective Sanders,' Lynn said

smoothly. 'Leon Reville showed Cara Burrows a YouTube video while she was in the trailer. In it, Kristie Reville was standing on a stage. Cara saw how short she was. That's when she remembered what she'd read online about Nate Appleyard and the sock. She thought about driving positions – how different people set the driver's seat differently. Thanks to the four memory buttons on her hire car, this was fresh in her mind. She started to wonder. Kristie Reville moved her seat forward to hide the sock from Appleyard, and then she drove off – that's what Appleyard told police. That means, doesn't it, that after moving her seat forward, her feet reached the pedals. She wasn't too far forward to drive comfortably. Appleyard didn't see her move the seat back again before she drove off.'

'Which means,' Turriff took over, 'that *before* Appleyard crept up on her, Kristie Reville must have pushed her seat right back to where she couldn't reach the gas pedal or the brake – back to three inches behind where the bloodstained sock lay. Only, why would she do that? Who does that? Who parks up and then pushes their seat right back?'

'You've gotta be kidding me,' said Heidi. 'Anyone who wants to stretch their legs after a long drive, that's who. I've done it myself, I'm sure.'

'I'm with Heidi,' said Sanders.

'Maybe,' Turriff conceded. 'Another hypothesis is that someone who wasn't Kristie drove the car last, parked it in the parking lot of the school where Jeff Reville worked, then got out, retrieved their own car and drove away. This someone would have been a much taller person than Kristie.'

Taller than Riyonna Briggs, too, thought Priddey. Jeff Reville was pretty tall, but he'd never learned to drive. His cousin Leon was, like Priddey, on the small side for a man.

From Heidi's face, it was clear she hadn't figured out yet who this possible tall driver might be. But then, why would she? She still didn't know about the Chalfont trial.

'This is insane,' she said.

'No, it's logical,' Lynn corrected her. 'Cara Burrows thought of it and so did Detective Priddey here when he read Cara's Instagram message to her daughter. You see, he'd just made his own exciting discovery.' She stopped to take a sip from her bottle of orange juice. 'He'd found out that the trial that had brought Kristie Reville and Riyonna Briggs together, Benjamin Chalfont's murder trial, had also brought them into contact with someone else. Someone with much longer legs than Kristie Reville's.'

'Kristie Reville and Riyonna Briggs thought it was an outrage that Chalfont walked out of that courtroom a free man, but they were only jurors,' said Turriff. 'Imagine how the lead prosecutor must have felt.'

That was the moment when Heidi's expression changed.

The brief silence in the room was the heaviest Priddey had ever known.

'I think you know who we're talking about now, Heidi,' Lynn said with quiet authority. 'A former prosecutor from Philadelphia? Who gave it up to become a TV show host?'

Heidi's face had lost all its color. She turned to her boss. 'Bonnie, what's going on?'

'Bonnie Juno,' said Turriff. 'Correct. That's who prosecuted Benjamin Chalfont. That's who decided – years later, along with Kristie Reville and Riyonna Briggs – that sometimes, if you want to save an innocent life, you have to take the law, and justice, into your own hands. Isn't that right, Ms Juno?'

'And we get there at last,' said Juno with a smile.

'Anything else you want to say, Bonnie?' Lynn asked her. 'Or shall we save it and do it live on tonight's edition of your show?'

'Bonnie, tell them it's not true!' Heidi had started to cry. 'What are they accusing you of? I don't understand.'

Turriff said, 'Ms Juno, before you decide how you want to respond, bear in mind we still have the DNA samples from Kristie Reville's car back in 2010.'

'Don't worry.' Juno waved her hand in the air. 'I'm no fool. When it's over, it's over, right? I gave it my best shot, and I failed. It happens. But you still need something from me – something more than an admission. You want to know where Jeff and Kristie are. Where Riyonna is. There's only one way you're ever going to find out, and that's

399

if I tell you. So.' She raised her eyebrows: a challenge to Turriff and Lynn.

'The live-on-your-show-tonight offer wasn't serious,' Lynn told her.

'Oh, that's not what I want. It's hardly my show from now, is it? Not any more. Heidi, you take it over. Change your name, distance yourself from me. Make the show your own. I'll give you exclusive access to the story: the *true* story of what happened to Melody Chapa.'

For a second, Heidi looked happy. Dazed, startled . . . but also kind of ecstatic. Then she shook her head violently and scrunched up her face, as if she'd just realized that this great offer from her boss was some kind of punishment in disguise. 'I can't do it,' she said. 'I have to . . . no, I can't. After what you've done, I *can't.*'

'Yes, you can, Heidi,' said Bonnie Juno firmly. 'Agent Kirschmeier, what I want isn't something for myself.'

'Let me guess,' said Lynn. 'The starving orphans in Africa? The refugee children from Syria? We all know philanthropy's what you're all about, Bonnie – philanthropic child abduction in particular.'

'I'm going to need a cast-iron guarantee that Melody won't be sent to live with her parents once they're out of jail,' said Juno. 'A fully binding guarantee, checked out by my legal team, so I know you're not trying to cheat me. Give me that, and then I'll tell you what you want to know.'

23 OCTOBER 2017

'**M**um, did Tarin Fry say you should divorce Dad?' Jess asks as we drive along a road that looks as if it's made of hard-baked pink sand. We're on our way to the Clearwater Resort and Spa in Sedona, two hours from Paradise Valley.

'Did she?' Olly asks his sister, sounding confused as he often does when he's been absorbed in a game on his phone and missed a whole chunk of conversation. 'Don't divorce Dad, Mum. It's none of Tarin Fry's business. But if you do, I'm living with Dad – he plays football with me. You always make excuses.'

'Yeah, but in Mum's favour, she actually listens when you speak to her?' says Jess. 'Dad does that old-person thing where he can't listen and do something on his phone or computer at the same time. So you ask him, like, "Shouldn't we be setting off to school now?" and he doesn't answer for ten seconds, and then he's like, "I think it's in the fridge."'

'Yeah.' Olly laughs. 'Hashtag Senile 2k17.'

'Tarin didn't tell me to divorce Dad,' I say. 'And

she's the last person I'd take life advice from. She's married to someone she can't bear to go on holiday with.'

I know Jess won't leave it there. A few minutes later she says, 'But you said Tarin was glad you left Dad once. So why wouldn't she try to make you do it again?'

'Tarin can't *make* me do anything, love. She's not the Wicked Witch of the West.'

'Are we sure about that?' Patrick mutters. 'Trying to make me send an email to myself saying, "Help, I've been kidnapped, love, Cara."' He makes a noise of disgust.

'She wanted me to tell you she'll never forgive you for not sending it.' I smile.

'She'd have landed me in an Arizona jail if I'd listened to her!'

'Who's the Wicked Witch of the West?' Olly asks.

'Never mind, Ol.' Mentally I add to an ever-growing list: must make sure new baby watches *The Wizard of Oz* and *Annie* and *E.T.* and all the classics I love, all the movies Jess and Olly refuse to watch because they look 'old and lame'. Maybe I'll build a wall between the part of the house where the baby hangs out and the part where Jess and Olly live. If I don't, the baby will be mocking Patrick and me by the time he or she is six months old.

I feel guilty as soon as the thought has passed through my mind: it's the sort of joke I used to make without thinking, the kind I'll never now be able to make without a hollow feeling plunging through my stomach.

I take it back. No walls, no oceans, no barriers, no unspoken conflicts separating any of us, ever again. I'm nervous about letting Patrick or the kids out of my sight. My biggest anxiety about this trip we're setting off on now is that, for a period of time, I will have to be in a room that doesn't contain my husband and children. I've made Patrick promise to keep a keen eye on Olly and Jess every second I'm not there to do it myself.

'Tarin's amazing,' I say, wanting to stick up for her despite her low opinion of my husband. Does that make me disloyal? I don't think so. Yes, Patrick is flawed, and can be inconsiderate, but so am I; so can I. As much as it hurts my pride to admit it, I have to face the fact that finding out about the new baby caused both me and Patrick to behave badly. Not just badly; appallingly. His failure to ask me how I felt was matched by my inability to say, 'You've really hurt me and pissed me off, and we need to talk about that.' To take a chunk of our savings and disappear instead, scaring my children out of their wits, undermining the certainty they've always had that our family's a safe place – that was unforgivable, unless . . .

Unless we all decide to forgive each other. That, I'm starting to think, is what loyalty means: not pretending those close to us are perfect, but ceaselessly loving and devoting your life to people you know are severely flawed, because you don't expect them not to be; you adore them anyway. From now on, I'll think about what's wrong with my own character every time I find myself dwelling on one of Patrick's faults, or Jess's or Olly's.

Whenever my guilt about what I did gets too intense, I'll remember the wise words of another deeply flawed person, Tarin, and they'll make me feel better. Three days after I escaped from the trailer, she took me for lunch at a hotel called the Biltmore and gave me a pep talk: 'Cara, I cannot tell you how pissed at you I'm going to be if you take away the wrong moral from this story. I mean it. None of the bad stuff that's happened to anybody happened because you needed a break and treated yourself to a stay at Guacamole HQ. You blew Bonnie Juno's plot wide open by sheer chance, and it's *great* that you did. It does not *in any way* mean no woman should ever leave her irritating husband at home and head for a five-star hotel, and if I ever hear you try to spin it that way, I will freak out, I swear. I do it at least once a year – irritating husband, left at home – and I've never stumbled across a murder victim who's not dead. So that proves it – in my favour.'

'Why is Tarin so amazing?' asks Olly.

'She suspected Bonnie Juno's involvement from the start,' I tell him. 'She heard her quite blatantly tell the police that *she* and *her* team would look into Riyonna Briggs' disappearance – in a way that sounded to Tarin as if she wanted to make sure no one else looked.'

It's funny the things that stick in your mind and become the most powerful memories. I'd struggle, now, to visualise the inside of Dandy's trailer, but I can still vividly picture Riyonna's distraught face when I told her she'd sent me to room 324 and there were people already in it, a man and a girl. She nearly started crying. I thought she was unusually solicitous and conscientious. Now I know the truth, it seems so obvious: her distress was too extreme. It was the horror of someone who's afraid they're going to land themselves and their friends in prison for a very long time, all because of a stupid, careless mistake.

Even so, I can't bring myself to think of Riyonna as a bad person. When she wrote 'Cara Burrows – is she safe?' on that piece of paper, I don't think she meant to ask if I was a risk; I think she was worried about me and wondering if I would be safe, given what I'd seen. She feared Bonnie Juno would order Dandy to kill me, and the thought terrified her – or maybe that's just what I'd like to think. I can't prove it.

'Mum?' says Olly.

'Yes, darling?'

'If you hadn't gone to the Swallowtail resort and seen Melody Chapa, would Bonnie Juno have got away with it? Would Melody's parents have stayed in prison forever?'

'I don't know,' I say, at the same time that Patrick says, 'Probably.'

'What will happen to Melody now?' asks Jess.

'Where will she live? Will she have to go back to her horrible family?'

'Lynn Kirschmeier thinks almost certainly not. After everything Melody's been through, the courts are unlikely to send her back to abusive parents. Detective Priddey told me Melody has an aunt in Portland, Oregon. Everyone seems to think she'll probably end up living with her.

'How long will Bonnie Juno and all the people who helped her go to prison for?' Olly asks.

'I don't know, Ol. No idea.'

'Are you nervous about meeting Melody for the first time?'

'Olly, don't bombard Mum with questions,' says Patrick.

'It's not the first time, stupid,' Jess says wearily. 'She met her in the hotel room, remember?'

'Yeah, and their second meeting's going to be at a different five-star resort,' says Patrick. 'The biggest mystery in all of this, one no law enforcement official has yet explained to me, is how Melody keeps ending up in all these plush resorts. Swallowtail would have been on Bonnie Juno's tab, but who's funding this latest jaunt?'

'Shut up, Dad, you noob,' says Jess. 'Trust you to think about all the boring things.'

'Lynn Kirschmeier said they'd decided to move her well out of Phoenix,' I say. 'I don't know why, but there must be a reason. Hiding her from the media, possibly.'

'I think she's a secret oligarch,' says Patrick.

'Only willing to come back from the dead if she can get champagne and caviar delivered to her sun-lounger on a silver tray.'

'I'm not stupid,' Olly says quietly to Jess in the back seat. 'The first time Mum met Melody, she didn't know who she was, and Melody was pretending to be someone else. This is the proper first time, today.'

'I suppose so.' Then, as if realising she's slipped up, Jess adds, 'But I'm still right. *Are* you nervous, Mum? About meeting her? I wonder what you'll talk about. I wouldn't know what to say.'

I wouldn't either. I don't.

'I'm not particularly nervous, no,' I lie. 'I'm sure it'll be fine.'

STATEMENT FROM BONNIE JUNO —
OCTOBER 23, 2017

Dear Fellow Americans,

The first thing I'd like to say is that I love my country and my fellow countrymen and women. I also love the law, which has been my vocation my entire life. But there's something I love even more, and that's Justice. And by that I do not mean my show, *Justice With Bonnie,* though I have loved that too with all my heart. No, I mean Justice, that shining light that all civilized people should prize higher than any other virtue. Justice that means every citizen getting what he or she deserves, and, equally importantly, not getting what they don't deserve.

Sometimes the law cannot, or will not, deliver true justice. I passionately believed that to be the case with regard to Melody Chapa and her parents, Annette and Naldo Chapa. When my friend Kristie Reville told me about the horrors that were going on in that family—when she told me she was frightened that if we couldn't get little Melody out of that house, her parents would find a way to bring about her death — I knew I had to take action. That's why I did what I did: figured out, along with Jeff, Kristie and Leon Reville, and with help from Riyonna Briggs, a way to save Melody. Trust me when I say that the authorities, had we taken our concerns about little Melody to them, would ultimately have proved unable to perform an effective rescue operation. After listening at length to Kristie's description of the behavior of her sinister next-door neighbors, I understood what subtle and brilliant monsters Annette and Naldo Chapa were. They were expert at ensuring that nothing could be proven against them. Their torture methods were ambiguous enough to guarantee they'd have gotten away with it forever if I hadn't stepped in.

Kristie, Riyonna and I first met in a court of law. Together, we witnessed a terrible miscarriage of justice that we were unable, in spite of our best efforts, to prevent. We witnessed a mockery of justice that no one seemed able to recognize apart from the three of us. We weren't willing to stand by and let another equally heinous crime take place under our noses, not if we could help it.

I am prepared to face the law's punishment for what we did. I would never have disclosed the whereabouts of my associates, but I am prouder than I can express of them all for willingly coming forward almost immediately. We now stand strong together. Kristie, Jeff, Leon and Riyonna are happy, as am I, to pay the price for what we did. We judge it to be worth it, whatever time we end up serving behind bars.

It will be worth it, because — quite simply — we succeeded in saving Melody Chapa's life. Her parents, far from being delighted to discover their daughter is alive after all these years, have disowned her for a book she wrote while she was in hiding and what that book reveals about their true characters. I think that fact alone speaks volumes.

I might not be able to present my show any more, but I am still the legal geek I've always been, and I hate loose ends as much as I ever have, so I'd like to share with you a few answers to the questions I would ask if I were the American public. Were we planning to kill Cara Burrows? Absolutely not. As soon as it was safe to release her, after Melody's plastic surgery, she'd have been free to go. She might have been able to lead the police and the FBI to Leon Reville, but never to Melody — I'd have made very sure of that — and that was all any of us cared about: Melody's safety, Melody's future.

What exactly was the plan made by myself and my fellow justice-seekers? This question has been fairly thoroughly answered by Jeff Reville already, but I want to give my version. On March 2, 2010, Kristie took Melody to her school. I had arranged to be in Philadelphia at the agreed time, and I also drove to the school parking lot that day in a car I'd rented under a false name. When the school parking lot was empty, Kristie and I swapped cars. She drove mine to Victor Soutar's home. I drove hers, with Melody in it, to where I'd agreed to meet Leon Reville. He took over Melody's care at that point.

We hadn't told Melody the plan. That was hard — explaining it all to her later on. Little children usually love their parents, however terrible those parents may be. Rest assured, we did everything we could to reassure and comfort Melody. Indeed, the only reason I drove Kristie's car that day and she drove mine was because we knew Melody felt so perfectly at home in Kristie's battered old Toyota.

Kristie and I had arranged to meet later that day in the parking lot of a different school, the one where Jeff Reville worked. At that point we swapped our cars back around. I left the driver's seat in the tall-person driving position that has been much commented on in the media, and I left the bloody sock on the floor of the car as planned. Nate Appleyard wasn't supposed to see it. It was there for the police to find, as soon as they got around to searching Kristie's car.

To add a layer of security, we arranged it so that, at first, suspicion would fall on Kristie and Jeff. For that, we needed to make them look pretty guilty — hence the bloodstained sock. Otherwise, if we'd had everything pointing to Annette and Naldo Chapa's guilt right from the start, they might have been taken much more seriously when they pointed out that they were being framed, as they inevitably would have. As it was, by the time Melody's parents were charged, nobody in America suspected Jeff and Kristie, and everyone suspected Annette and Naldo not only of murder but also of trying to frame Jeff and Kristie.

It's much harder to claim you're being framed when the whole country is convinced you've just been caught trying to frame someone else.

Ours was a risky strategy, but it worked, and that makes me proud. I even had Jeff and Kristie issue a public statement protesting the Chapas' innocence—because who would do that for a couple they themselves had framed for murder?

There were other things we did that I had to fight for, against the disagreement of all of my four helpers — risky things. The blood on Kristie's hand and arm, for example (which, incidentally, was Kristie's own and not Melody's). And the bloodstained sock moving, as if by magic, from Kristie's car to Melody's school bag, where it would eventually be found by police. Everyone but me felt that these parts of the plan were inadvisable because they made Kristie look not so much framed as actually guilty. Why was there blood on her arm? Did she really leave her car unlocked twice, so that Annette and Naldo Chapa could first place Melody's sock in her car and then, later, take it out? That seems highly implausible! Surely it's more likely that Kristie moved and hid the sock after Nate

Appleyard saw it in her car? Why, asked my worried team of helpers, would I want to include anything in our plan that implicated Kristie so blatantly?

The answer — as I told them all at the time, and I'm happy to say that they eventually bowed to my greater knowledge, as a former prosecutor, of crime scenes — is that, in reality, the only people who look wholly and purely innocent once all the evidence is in are the most cunning of the guilty. You who are reading this statement might not know this but please trust me: in the vicinity of a murder, the truly innocent always, without exception, have details attaching to them that cannot easily be explained away. I don't know why this should be the case; I only know that it is. I wanted Kristie and Jeff to have their 'Yeah, but hold on, what about . . .?' questions that would always make people wonder. Every once-suspected innocent person I'd ever encountered in both of my professional lives — as prosecutor and as legal commentator — had such questions hanging in the air around them, even after someone else had gone to jail for the crime.

And, let's face it, Kristie might have cut her arm that day by coincidence, and she *might* have left her car unlocked twice, and Annette Chapa *might* have decided moving the sock from the car to the bag was a more effective way to frame her friend and neighbor. . .All these things are possible. The fact is, the biggest danger to us all, as well as to little Melody, was that it should look as if there was no muddle, no irreconcilable details, no discrepancies, because someone had a foolproof plan.

Mallory Tondini's testimony was entirely, one hundred per cent genuine. Annette Chapa really did say all those terrible things in Mallory's hearing, and that's another fact that ought to speak for itself in explaining and justifying (in my opinion) what I and my fellow justice-seekers did.

We had to do some terrible, soul-destroying things along the way. We needed Melody's blood in substantial quantities. We needed her hair to show that she'd ingested arsenic. I won't dwell on the details. Suffice to say that we had sound medical advice at every stage (I can't and won't reveal the source, naturally), and we did everything we could to make these various ordeals as painless and tolerable for Melody as we could.

And now to the plastic surgery side of things. Several commentators have asked why we waited so long. Why not do it straight away and let Melody try and lead a normal life, instead of keeping her hidden away in one trailer after another? The answer is a combination of reasons. We didn't want to do it too soon after the arsenic and the blood-letting, but the main thing was that we needed Melody to be old enough to understand the implications of the surgery, and for her consent to it to be meaningful and valid. Was fourteen still too young? Maybe. As a side note, I should also say that, even when you're the great Bonnie Juno, it's not easy to find a skilled cosmetic surgeon who'll agree to take your money and keep quiet about something like this. Getting blowfly corpses and larvae from cops who owe you favors is a walk in the park by comparison. We eventually found a suitable cosmetic surgeon (again, no names), but of course we won't now be making use of that person's services.

Why were we reckless enough to allow Melody to be out and about at a busy holiday resort? First, the poor kid needed a vacation. But we probably wouldn't have risked it if it weren't for an extraordinary coincidence. Riyonna Briggs had moved to

Arizona to be closer to her best friend, and she'd happened to land a job at a resort that had Mrs Lilith McNair as a regular guest. When Riyonna told me that Mrs McNair picked a different child every year and insisted that child was Melody Chapa, I saw a chance. Where better to hide Melody? If anyone said, 'Wait, isn't that Melody Chapa?' surely the resort staff would all groan and say, 'Oh, Lord, not another one! Mrs McNair's craziness must be contagious!' Everyone knows by now how we dealt with what we saw as the only possible risk — the brown mark near Melody's hairline — so I won't comment further on that, apart from to say that I deeply regret any hurt this part of our story has caused to cancer sufferers and their families. I am of course aware that cancer is a devastating illness and not merely an accessory to be used when it suits a particular agenda; I did, however, feel I had no choice in the circumstances; hence 'Hayley' came into existence.

Melody loved her holiday at the Swallowtail resort. She swam a little, and took an art class, and generally had a ball. She's a lovely girl and she's strong. She'll be okay now, whatever happens. One wonderful result of the truth coming to light is that now Melody will be able to be properly reunited with Kristie and Jeff Reville once they've served their sentences. The three of them can then live openly as a family if they wish to. Finally, Kristie and Jeff will be able to provide Melody with the loving parenting she never got from her own parents.

If our plan had succeeded, this would never have been possible. For many years, we had to limit the number of times per year that Kristie and Jeff could see Melody to one or two. Those years were agony, particularly for Kristie, who wrote hundreds of letters to Melody to make up for the lack of face-to-face contact. Then, more recently, we settled into a routine of once a month, but in order for these reunions to pass undetected, we had to spend large amounts of money and jump through many practical hoops. For Kristie and Jeff, knowing that they will now be able, one day, to conduct their relationship with their beloved Melody quite openly is a dream come true.

Given this, how can I have any regrets? I have none. Actually, that's not true. I can't help wishing that Mrs Cara Burrows from Hertford, England, had stayed at home with her family instead of coming to Arizona when she did — for her sake, not mine. I regret that she became entangled in this. I also regret that I had to try to convince her husband that her aversion to him was so strong, she'd vanished by choice and solely in order to avoid him. It didn't make me feel good about myself to say those things to a distraught man who had flown all the way from England. I console myself with the knowledge that Mrs Burrows is happily reunited with her family now, and that's all that matters. I bear her no grudge and wish her and her loved ones all the best.

I've wondered, often, if it might have been Fate that caused Riyonna Briggs to make the stupid mistake with the hotel room number. She claims it was her guilt on account of what we'd done, and the way it was messing with her mind, but I thought to myself as soon as she told me, 'Maybe we're not meant to get away with this. And maybe that's okay.' I told her, 'Dial 911. You've had a report of a supposedly dead girl, a murdered girl, seen alive at your resort, so that's what you do—you call the police.' Riyonna protested, but I said, 'It's what an innocent person would do.' At the same time as I was telling Leon Reville to get

419

Melody the hell out of there before detectives started nosing around the place, I was thinking to myself, 'This might be it. If the Lord wants us to be stopped, calling in the cops ought to take care of it.'

When it became clear to me that the FBI knew the full truth, I didn't deny it and I didn't complain. Ultimately, I care little for myself. I have tried to be the humble servant of Justice and of our dear Lord, and I hope I've succeeded. My love for both remains as proud and strong as ever.

Love, ultimately, is all that matters: spreading and sharing love, while banishing hate. Kristie and Jeff Reville love Melody with all their hearts. So much of the love in our plan came from them. The Machiavellian plotting, the plan to ride roughshod over the law of the land? That was where I came in — me, and, at the risk of sounding vulgar, my money, because let me tell you, you can't pull off something like this without extensive resources at your disposal.

If you want to blame anyone for what we all did, blame me. Kristie, Jeff and Leon Reville and Riyonna Briggs have nothing but good inside them.

23 OCTOBER 2017

The Clearwater Resort in Sedona is surrounded by beautiful red rocks on all sides. Boynton Canyon, it's called, and it's stunning. In many ways, apart from the vivid redness of the landscape, it's similar here to Swallowtail. There's a main building, a network of little roads, many casitas, gleaming turquoise swimming pools, club car chauffeur service.

And now me. And Melody Chapa.

I'm sitting on the sofa of the casita where she's staying with her new chaperone – a grey-haired bespectacled woman called Jennifer. Melody's sitting in an armchair opposite me. 'This must be strange for you,' I say, hoping it will start a conversation. It's my second attempt. I expected when I got here that Jennifer might help with the awkward introductions phase, but she's said virtually nothing. She's arranging things in the kitchen area less than two metres from where Melody and I are sitting, but it's as if she's in a separate universe. I suppose the FBI must train these people to appear invisible. 'It's certainly strange for me.'

Melody nods. 'Detective Priddey told me you have children,' she says.

'I do, yes. Jess and Olly. Jess is about your age. They're here. I mean, not *here* here, but . . . at the resort. They're with their dad, probably ordering smoothies somewhere.'

She's watching me. It's as if she's waiting for me to say more.

'I'm expecting a third child, who *is* here.' I pat my stomach.

'What will you call it?'

'I don't know.'

'My favourite girl's name is Georgia.'

'That's a lovely name.'

'Agent Kirschmeier says my parents don't want to see me. They say I've lied about them – that I lied in my book – so they don't want to talk to me. They refuse. Do you think that's true?'

Oh, God. I was hoping the small talk might last a bit longer.

Don't be a coward, Cara. She asked you a question. This is all so much worse for her than it is for you.

'I think you can probably trust what Agent Kirschmeier tells you,' I say.

Melody nods. 'I guess I don't blame them. My parents, I mean. I wrote some . . .' She hesitates. 'I wrote some *things* about them.'

'You mean you told Kristie, and Kristie wrote them?'

I've been thinking a lot about Kristie and her ghost-writing of Melody's book. The parts I read were full of doubts about Kristie herself, and Jeff, presumably. The Kind Smiles. 'Melody' had written in several places and in various different ways that she didn't know if she could trust them or not. In places they came across as gauche and insensitive. Did Kristie include those sections because Melody had expressed those sentiments to her and it would have felt wrong to omit them, however unflattering they were, or was it more complex than that? Was it the guilt in Kristie's unconscious mind making itself known, using Melody as a mouthpiece? Or – worst, most cynical possibility of all – did Kristie, or Bonnie Juno, calculate that the best way to make it look as if Melody wrote the book herself was to have her express doubts about the person who actually wrote it?

A look of confusion passes across Melody's face. 'Yes, Kristie wrote it all down. It's still my book, though. It's my story.'

'Of course.' How will anyone ever be able to talk to this girl in a normal way? All I can think is that she was hidden away for seven years, forced to collude in the most horrific lie.

'If one of your children wrote bad things about you in a book, would you ever forgive them? Would you ever talk to them again?'

'I'd forgive my children whatever they did, and I'd always want to talk to them and have them in my life.' *But I'm not Annette or Naldo Chapa.* 'And if your parents don't feel that way, they're to blame for that, Melody. Not you.'

She nods. 'Because they're bad parents. Not like you. You're a good parent. I could tell the first time I saw you. I thought you were nice.'

Bad parents, good parents, bad things, nice . . . Unsurprisingly, her vocabulary is basic. I wonder what her story, written entirely and only by her and not edited by Kristie Reville, would look like.

'Kristie says her and Jeff have always been my parents if that word means the people who look out for you,' says Melody. 'Do you think that's true?'

'Well, I suppose—'

A loud hissing noise starts up, swallowing the rest of my sentence and making me jump. It's Jennifer in the kitchen; she's turned on a tap.

Melody leans forward, wide-eyed. 'I don't remember,' she whispers.

'What do you mean? What don't you remember?'

'The things Kristie wrote in the book that happened to me. I don't remember them.'

My breath stops in my throat. I feel dizzy. The eyes I'm looking at are ones I've not seen before: two dark tunnels of terror. The girl who was here five seconds ago is gone. This Melody is a different person.

'You don't remember any of them?' I ask her.

She shakes her head, then glances over at Jennifer. Is she waiting for her to turn, or for the tap to go off? I think so. I think she's worked out that, for as long as the water's running, we won't be overheard.

'Kristie said I told her about the things when I was little, but I just don't remember. Do you think that's bad? And I pretended I did, because Jeff said I did too. And then *I* said I did, to the other Kind Smiles. To Bonnie. She believed it because I helped to . . . to make it seem true. That's bad, that I did that.' She's speaking quickly. To say as much as she can while the tap's still gushing?

'So . . . when your mother cut up Rosa the bear, and when she talked you into pretending Woody was your boyfriend – you don't remember those two things happening?'

The tap goes off. Jennifer turns round. 'Okay, I've finished in the kitchen,' she says brightly. 'Cara, would you like a drink. Coffee?'

'No thanks. Melody? Do you . . .' I can't ask the question, not now we've got an audience. I've said too much already. *Stupid.*

'What's the matter?' Jennifer asks in a different, more alert voice. 'Melody? Is something wrong?'

'No, thanks, Jennifer. I'm fine.' She's a better actor than I am. A lot better.

But this is crazy. Jennifer's on our side. She's on Melody's side. There's no reason to hide this from her.

'Listen . . .' I start to say.

'Yes.' Melody looks straight at me, but it's not the same girl who spoke so urgently a moment ago. This is Official Melody. Public Melody. 'I remember all the things you just said: Rosa, and Woody.'

'But you told me you didn't.' Panic rises inside me, all the way up to my throat. It's my word against hers. Hers, and Kristie and Jeff Reville's.

The only loving parents she's ever likely to have.

'You can tell Jennifer, Melody. Everyone's on your side – me, Jennifer, the police . . .'

'Okay, I'm going to need to know what this is about.' Jennifer's moving briskly towards us, as if we're a fight in a bar that needs breaking up.

'It's nothing,' says Melody calmly. 'I do remember, Cara. Really.' She doesn't seem scared any more. 'I remember all of it.'